G000023737

Sweet Bergamasque

QUENTIN SMITH

Copyright © 2019 Quentin Smith

The moral right of the author has been asserted.

Apart from any fair dealing for the purposes of research or private study,
or criticism or review, as permitted under the Copyright, Designs and Patents
Act 1988, this publication may only be reproduced, stored or transmitted, in
any form or by any means, with the prior permission in writing of the
publishers, or in the case of reprographic reproduction in accordance with
the terms of licences issued by the Copyright Licensing Agency. Enquiries
concerning reproduction outside those terms should be sent to the publishers.

This is a work of fiction. Names, characters, businesses, places, events
and incidents are either the products of the author's imagination
or used in a fictitious manner. Any resemblance to actual persons,
living or dead, or actual events is purely coincidental.

Matador
9 Priory Business Park,
Wistow Road, Kibworth Beauchamp,
Leicestershire. LE8 0RX
Tel: 0116 279 2299
Email: books@troubador.co.uk
Web: www.troubador.co.uk/matador
Twitter: @matadorbooks

ISBN 978 1838591 304

British Library Cataloguing in Publication Data.
A catalogue record for this book is available from the British Library.

Matador is an imprint of Troubador Publishing Ltd

In a soldier's eyes, the wine ration has a place almost equal to that of ammunition. Wine is a stimulant that improves morale and physical well-being. To secure his ration a soldier will brave perils and challenge artillery shells.

Marshal Philippe Pétain

The same stormy, wet weather that delayed Hitler from attacking Western Europe immediately after his successful invasion of Poland resulted in very poor wines right across Bordeaux. The 1939 vintage went down in history as the worst of a very poor decade. The summer was late and interrupted constantly by stormy, wet and cold weather. The harvest was very late indeed and the wines were inferior, slightly perfumed but unremarkable.

Chapter One

Monpazier, August 1948

Jean-Marc did not realise that he had been followed as he pressed Patrice roughly against the cool stone of Monpazier's vaulted arcade. He could smell the crisp minerality of the ancient limestone despite Patrice's sweaty gasps, heavy with garlic and alcohol.

"What the hell are you doing?" Patrice cried out. The baguette he was holding fell and rolled on the paving, leaving a spray of crumbs.

Jean-Marc thrust the pistol harder into his victim's back, feeling the silencer slide off a rib as Patrice flinched and inhaled sharply. "I have been looking for you for years, you traitor," Jean-Marc hissed into the unwashed locks of Patrice's black hair, reeking of Gauloises smoke.

Behind them, projected onto a large makeshift screen, flickering images of Bogart and Bergman captivated the audience gathered in the market square around picnic baskets stocked with bread, cheese and wine as they watched *Casablanca* under a moonless sky. Having not long before started the second reel on the GBN projector beneath the central market stalls, Jean-Marc knew he had just ten minutes to conclude his business before the next reel change would be

1

due. It was not good form to keep an audience waiting, as he had learnt to his cost when the film had broken during *Le Colonel Chabert* in Issigeac the previous summer. Enjoying the spectacle was all well and good, but the paying audience demanded a hefty measure of professional attentiveness from his travelling Fauvette Cinema *plein air*.

"What do you want?" Patrice said.

Jean-Marc tensed his body and leaned into his victim. "Revenge, you bastard. This is for Monique."

Patrice tried to look around nervously, the deep creases in his brow briefly evident, illuminated by Rick Blaine's white suit glowing brightly from the screen as Humphrey Bogart's voice vibrated across the medieval bastide town.

At the sound of a click from the pistol Patrice's eyes widened suddenly and his mouth fell open slackly. "I didn't do anything to Monique," he protested, raising his hands helplessly against the limestone wall, dirty fingernails splayed.

"The hell you didn't, you killed her – all of you – killed her!" Jean-Marc felt himself grimace, baring his teeth like a predator preparing to strike.

Patrice seemed frozen against the stone, unsure what to say, swallowing, blinking rapidly. Jean-Marc glanced around at the screen to see Bogart talking to Claude Rains. There wasn't much time before he would need to make the next reel change.

"I didn't kill her, I swear!"

"No, you got the Germans to do it for you, didn't you?" hissed Jean-Marc.

"No!"

"Goodbye, Patrice," Jean-Marc whispered icily.

"No, wait!"

As Jean-Marc's finger tightened against the scored surface of the trigger he felt something hard press against his spine.

"You are under arrest, Monsieur Valadie. Give me your weapon," said an assured, husky female voice.

2

Jean-Marc froze and turned his head, pressing his pistol ever more firmly into Patrice to discourage any attempts at escape. "You?" Jean-Marc gasped, surprise rippling through his body as he recognised the intruder. "Who the hell are you?"

Patrice breathed in rapid, shallow gasps, sweat beading on his skin, his eyes wide and frightened.

"I am Inspecteur Balletty from the Sûreté in Paris. I have been on your trail for months, *monsieur*, and I am placing you under arrest, Jean-Marc Valadie, on suspicion of the murders of Anton Caumont, Nicolas Renard, Gregoire Sabron and Louis Lafargue, not to mention the attempted murder of this gentleman, whose name I do not know."

Patrice emitted an anguished wheeze. "It was you who killed all of them?" he said. "In God's name, why, Jean-Marc?"

Jean-Marc laughed derisively. "You know perfectly well. Revenge, my old comrade, for what you all did to Monique."

"No! You have got it wrong," Patrice said, his voice rising in desperation.

"Monique was executed, that's what I know, and it was you and all of them, my so-called friends, who were responsible. You betrayed her to *les Boches*."

"Jean-Marc, listen…"

"How could you?" Jean-Marc hissed, grinding his teeth. "Was it because she loved me and not you?"

"Monsieur Valadie!" Balletty said firmly. "This is your last warning."

"Enough!" Jean-Marc shouted. "It ends, now."

He felt Balletty's pistol press into his back even harder. "*Monsieur*, give me your gun and I will not have to shoot you," she said in a calm but firm voice, leaving Jean-Marc in absolutely no doubt about her conviction. "The *epuration legale* is a matter for the police, not vigilantes."

3

Behind them the screen blazed brilliant white as the film reel ended abruptly. People stood up and began to whistle, turning their heads left and right as they called out.

"The reel has ended, I have to change it," Jean-Marc urged, craning his neck to meet Balletty's eyes.

"Give me your gun, *monsieur*."

Jean-Marc breathed hard and swallowed ineffectually, his mouth dry and sticky. "This is absurd," he protested, briefly lifting his left arm off Patrice in a frustrated gesture.

"Not from where I am standing, *monsieur*. Now, very slowly, give me your—"

A loud explosion burst in Jean-Marc's ears, echoing around the Place des Cornières.

Chapter Two

June 1940

Gathered around the wooden kitchen table on which the black Bakelite *Radiophone Français* took centre stage, Jean-Marc, his wife Isabelle and their son Claude listened intently. The unhurried flicker of an amber candle flame reflected on their taut faces was the only suggestion of animation. Crumbs were scattered across the table, vestiges of a meal long forgotten, eaten during a time of peace and normality, well before the impossible news had shattered their lives.

Jean-Marc listened to the tense voice on the radio, distorted by static interference, relaying news of the German Wehrmacht having crossed the Maginot Line, the French army in disarray, tens of thousands dead, hundreds of thousands more taken prisoner. The *drôle de guerre* was finally over. It was all over. Jean-Marc's hands were clasped together tightly, digging dirty fingernails into his knuckles. Isabelle held one hand up to her pale face most of the time, except when she occasionally touched her forehead with a trembling finger and swept back tousled locks of auburn hair. Claude nursed a thirteen-year-old's glum stare, biting the inside of his cheek, a pimple on his nose glistening like a volcano in the candlelight.

"Mon Dieu," Jean-Marc said every few minutes, his lips barely moving.

Claude's eyes flicked apprehensively to his father, whose calloused hands covered his unshaven face, and then flicked back to the radio. The Germans were advancing on Paris and it was estimated that millions of ordinary French people were already on the move in a mass exodus heading south.

Isabelle made a strange little whimpering sound and Jean-Marc looked up at her sharply, conscious of the boy's bewildered eyes beside them. The broadcast ended and the strained sounds of *La Marseillaise* filled the tense silence. Jean-Marc lit a Gauloises and dropped the extinguished match onto the table as blueish smoke curled around his face. He leaned back in his wooden chair, which creaked like the remnants of the free French republic.

"What will happen, Papa?" Claude asked. The boy looked ashen.

Jean-Marc leaned forward and turned the radio off. He shrugged as he blew smoke out through his nose and mouth. "I don't know, my boy. But you must not worry, we will be safe down here in Bordeaux. They are not interested in us." Jean-Marc tried to sound reassuring.

"How can you say that?" Isabelle said, her face twisted as though in pain, her head angled to one side, glaring at Jean-Marc accusingly.

Jean-Marc glanced at his son, whose concern boiled over in his eyes, and shook his head just a fraction, as if to say, *Not in front of the boy.*

"Look at what they are doing to the Jews in Germany, look at what happened in Berlin. Now that they have invaded we are not safe anywhere in France!" Isabelle was becoming hysterical, her eyes widening like a cow with bloat.

"Do you want to go up to bed, Claude?" Jean-Marc said quietly, placing a hand on the boy's shoulder.

"No, Papa. I want to know what is going to happen," he said, his chin trembling. "We will be alright, won't we?"

"We have to leave," Isabelle said, panic in her eyes as she looked from Jean-Marc to Claude and back again.

Jean-Marc exhaled in disbelief, his hands grasping at the air around him. "And go where, Isabelle? Take Claude and little Odette out of their home, onto the road. Where to, huh?"

Isabelle stared back, wide-eyed. "I don't know – Spain? I have a cousin…"

Jean-Marc leaned back and made a guttural sound, drawing on his Gauloises. He stared at his wife and shook his head.

"And what of the vineyards, mmmh?" He swept an arm around, leaving a circular trail of cigarette smoke hanging in the air. "This was my father's land, my father's father's, and his father before him. It is our home, Isabelle, it is our livelihood."

Jean-Marc and Isabelle glowered at each other, he with a smoking Gauloises clasped in front of his face, she with her chest heaving and her moist, bulging eyes seemingly at bursting point.

"Will the Germans kill us?" Claude asked.

"No," Jean-Marc said quickly, turning to the boy. "They will not."

Isabelle bit her knuckles and wailed. "These are your children, Jean-Marc. Would you risk their lives so glibly?"

He leaned forward. "We have nothing, Isabelle – the last nine summers have been so poor nobody is buying our wine. We need this vintage to turn it around. The spring has been good, the vines are healthy and full of promise. What would you have me do? Abandon the grapes on the vines now? Flee with nothing but the clothes on our backs?"

Isabelle glared back at him.

"Please don't fight," Claude whimpered, on the verge of tears.

"I am not going to wait until the Germans are here in the streets and we have to hide like animals. I am leaving with our children, going somewhere safe," Isabelle declared, pushing her chair back to stand up.

"No, Mama, please," Claude wailed, tears streaming down his face, looking to his father for intervention.

Jean-Marc pressed a balled fist against his mouth, staring at the flickering candle. *Merde.* What a mess this was. Unbelievable. He had been Claude's age when war had broken out last time – the war to end all wars – and yet now, just twenty-six years on, it was happening all over again.

"Can we just sleep on this and see what happens tomorrow?" Jean-Marc pleaded in a subdued voice. "Maybe the English—"

"Maybe the English!" Isabelle scoffed. "Open your eyes, Jean-Marc. You are a Jew in a Europe now controlled by the Germans. First it was Czechoslovakia, then Poland, then Denmark, then Norway, and now it is France." She paused, her chest heaving with vented emotion. "We must leave, for the children's sake, can you not see that?"

Jean-Marc stared at his wife and son. Did they know what they were asking of him? The Valadie family had made wine on this sacred land outside Saint-Émilion for two hundred years. One did not scamper away from this like a frightened dog. The Valadies had stayed on through the Great War and he would do the same again now.

"They are not even in Paris yet, Isabelle. They may never come this far south." Jean-Marc spoke softly, as though trying to convince himself as much as her.

"What will they do to Jews?" Claude asked, strings of mucous now hanging beneath each nostril.

Isabelle moved over to embrace her son, encouraging him from his chair, glowering at Jean-Marc. "Nothing, my boy, you will be safe in Spain – far away from the Germans," she said.

8

Jean-Marc lowered his head and sighed.

"We leave in the morning," Isabelle announced before marching out of the room with Claude under her protective wing.

Claude turned to look at Jean-Marc, tears in his puffy eyes. *How does one explain war and hate to a boy?* Jean-Marc thought. *How does one explain love and devotion to one's land and vineyards, the heritage that runs in a family like blood in one's veins, only thicker, sweeter?*

As though sensing his master's torment, the brown Basset Hound that had been lying in front of the crackling hearth clipped its way over to Jean-Marc and began to lick his hand where it hung limply off the end of the armrest.

He stroked the dog's head for several minutes, staring expressionlessly at the quivering candle flame, then picked up the pewter candleholder and walked through to the *salon* where he placed it on top of the grand piano. Jean-Marc stood beside it without moving, reaching out to trace a finger along the copper inlay set into plum pudding mahogany. The inconsistent candlelight revealed its boxy outline atop intricately turned and carved legs, standing like ballerinas on brass castors.

Sitting down at the keys he stared at the faded gold leaf *Pleyel* lettering and then began to play Debussy's *Clair de Lune*, sorrowfully, slowly, pausing often; his thick, dirty fingers producing surprisingly delicate and melancholic cadences. His dog sat beside him quietly, his tail swishing on the oak flooring. How could he leave all this behind? This piano was nearly as old as Château Cardinale itself, bought by his great-grandfather Ignace when Cardinale's wines were the toast of high society and money flowed decadently.

Isabelle's words echoed in his ears: *We leave in the morning.* He stopped playing. How could this be happening? Yesterday life was idyllically normal; tomorrow... He shut his eyes.

Chapter Three

One week later

Jean-Marc paused as he gently fondled the fragile new vine shoots between calloused fingers. The air was perfumed with the optimism of new growth, of strawberries at the end of each row, of a new season's harvest in its infancy, fuelled by warm days and mild nights. Pulling out a pair of secateurs from the depths of earth-stained, capacious trousers, he began to clip off the excess growth at the tips, cutting back twenty, thirty, sometimes even forty millimetres, as his experience suggested. He worked mechanically, willing his thoughts away from his family: where were they, were they safe?

The dog was lying at his feet, facing the sunshine, panting as though he had been chasing a rabbit. Suddenly his ears pricked up and he closed his mouth, turned his head and appeared to focus his eyes.

Jean-Marc glanced down at his dog. "What is it, Pascal? Do you smell something?"

The dog looked at him and sat up, emitting a rumbling sound from his throat. Jean-Marc cast a perfunctory look across the expanse of his vineyards and continued to prune. Then, moments later, he heard the sound of horses' hooves. He recognised the horse long before the rider, who waved from a distance. It was someone from his neighbour's property, Château Millandes. Jean-Marc's distance vision was poor. It ran in his family but he never bothered with glasses because all his work was at arm's length.

"Jean-Marc!" called the rider.

Dropping the secateurs into his baggy trousers, Jean-Marc petted Pascal and rubbed his ears. The dog licked him enthusiastically. As the rider neared Jean-Marc finally saw who it was. "*Bonjour*, Gregoire. What brings you over here?"

Gregoire dismounted and pulled the reins down over the horse's head. He was young, puce-faced, the heir to Château Millandes, ink-black hair as wiry as a Quercy sheep. "Your vines look good," Gregoire said, fingering the foliage as he approached. "We have been lucky, eh? No frosts, no pests."

"Yet," Jean-Marc retorted.

Gregoire chuckled. "God surely will not serve us with a summer like last year – again. Even He likes good wine, don't you think?"

"Your father lets you ride his horse?" Jean-Marc remarked, gesticulating towards the chestnut stallion.

Gregoire planted his hands on his hips and contemplated Jean-Marc. Both men wore soiled dark trousers held aloft by braces over loose-fitting linen shirts, heavy leather boots on their feet. But Gregoire wore something else: the superiority of the heir apparent.

"Something has happened, Jean-Marc. My father wants to speak to you."

"What is it?" Jean-Marc said quickly, placing both hands on the taut wire used to train the shooting vines, Guyot-style.

"He will tell you. Come over when you have cleaned up." Gregoire paused, casting an eye across Jean-Marc's vineyards. "Have lunch with us," he said, turning back to Jean-Marc and then studying the vines beside him. "Are you not trimming back too much so early?"

Jean-Marc bristled. Gregoire might well come from Château Millandes, but *he* had been pruning vines on his property since the boy was in nappies. "Tell your father I will be there at one o'clock," he said irritably, returning his attention to the vines.

"Doesn't Isabelle usually help you with the pruning?" Gregoire said once he had mounted the horse.

Jean-Marc looked up cautiously and stroked his bushy moustache. "She is not here today."

Jean-Marc walked over to Château Millandes with Pascal following him eagerly. Millandes adjoined his land and it was quicker and more pleasant to walk through his vineyards to access it than to take the Renault out onto the road. Château Millandes was grand by Bordeaux standards: a double-storeyed stone house with gabling, wrought iron balconies and clusters of chimneys, quaintly wrapped in a tangle of colourful ivy. Around the cobbled courtyard numerous outbuildings complimented the main house's imposing character. Much to Jean-Marc's chagrin, Château Millandes had been widely tipped for impending *Grand Cru* status by the Syndicat Viticole in 1930, enabling his neighbour to capitalise on the publicity and demand a higher price for his wines. As he cast his eyes about enviously the benefit of money was evident wherever he looked.

"Jean-Marc!" A portly man with meaty forearms and warm brown eyes, full around the midriff, tousled grey hair and matching moustache, walked towards Jean-Marc, his cream linen shirt unbuttoned enough to reveal a chest of silver hair.

"Alphonse," Jean-Marc returned with restrained warmth.

The two men embraced and kissed on each cheek. Alphonse smiled and pointed to Pascal. "Do you go anywhere without that dog?"

"What has happened?" Jean-Marc asked.

Alphonse wrapped an arm around Jean-Marc's shoulders and guided him into the château. Pascal followed, his claws clipping the cobbles, tail wagging contentedly.

"As if enough has not happened," Alphonse said, twirling his free arm in the air. "It is enough to make a grown man weep."

"Twice in one lifetime is too much," Jean-Marc said, glancing around at Alphonse's fine mahogany furnishings and painted cream walls.

"We are sounding like our grandparents, aren't we?" Alphonse said, attempting levity. "Do you remember Federico and Angelica Masi?"

Jean-Marc detected the seductive aromas of freshly prepared food within the château: onion and lemon and coriander. His stomach rumbled. He had not eaten a square meal in days and Alphonse was always a good host. "Winemakers from Tuscany?" Jean-Marc ventured.

Alphonse nodded, but sombrely. He sighed. "They are here with me."

"Why?"

Alphonse stopped, just paces away from the stone patio that nestled beyond French doors where Jean-Marc could see the elderly Italian couple talking to Marthe, Alphonse's wife, and his two sons, Gregoire and Olivier. He looked into Jean-Marc's eyes intensely for a moment, long enough to unsettle Jean-Marc.

"You will want to hear what Federico has to say, my friend," Alphonse said before making a grand entrance onto the patio, pleasantly shaded beneath a venerably gnarled mauve wisteria.

After formalities Alphonse lavished them with goblets of his blood-red Grand Vin as conversation covered the promising spring bloom, the fruiting of the vines and hopes for a good summer. Inevitably talk drifted towards the humiliation of defeat at the hands of the Germans. They bemoaned the politicians who would not take responsibility. Alphonse showed them an editorial in Le Figaro ridiculing the French response to attack.

"Listen to this," Alphonse said, folding the broadsheet into a square on the table. "*The soldiers blamed their officers; the officers pointed the finger at politicians; the Left blamed the Right and the Right blamed the Left.*" He shook his head. "*Marshal Pétain blamed the Popular Front, who blamed the military. Many blamed the Communists and they all blamed the Fascists – and the Fascists blamed the Jews.*"

Federico sighed heavily when he heard this. "Just like Mussolini in Italy."

They ate freshly baked *fougasse*, duck liver, and wild mushroom omelettes, all washed down with quantities of Alphonse's delicious Grand Vin 1928. One thing they all agreed about: Bordeaux badly needed another vintage to match that one.

"These are the last of my '28s," Alphonse announced to murmurs of dismay. "I still have more, but I have hidden the rest behind false walls in the caves."

Jean-Marc stared at Alphonse. "Why?"

"Have you not heard the stories of looting and theft by the Wehrmacht?" Alphonse said bitterly.

Jean-Marc felt his mouth dry up and quickly gulped at his wine.

"In Champagne they behaved like hooligans, plundering cellars and feasting like drunken teenagers. In Paris they have emptied entire wine stocks from the top restaurants, all those not quick enough to hide their best wines. The same down through the Loire and Burgundy. We have everything to fear, Jean-Marc, and I am calling a meeting of all local vignerons to warn them."

Jean-Marc felt nauseous, Isabelle's prophetic warning now ringing in his ears. "I will brick in my '28s as well." He wiped his hand across his moustache. "Even my '34s, they are probably worth protecting."

"I have done the same," Alphonse concurred. "Nothing else worth hiding from the '30s. If you have anything older, the '26 or '24, hide them too."

"No," Jean-Marc said, unable to stop himself from looking down. His wines did not keep quite as well as Alphonse's.

"But leave a few bottles from the good vintages out, so as not to arouse too much suspicion." Alphonse shrugged and made a face. "And don't forget, you must cover the new wall with spiders to make cobwebs. Gregoire and Olivier collected dozens of spiders and they have already spun webs all over the fresh brickwork." Alphonse chuckled. "It looks so old now, as if it's always been there."

Jean-Marc stared open-mouthed at Alphonse as his two boys sniggered like adolescents. Olivier was barely out of school, still lanky and undeveloped, always to Jean-Marc's mind copying his older brother.

"We also piled firewood against the new wall, don't forget that – anything to make it seem old and permanent."

"Is this really necessary?" Jean-Marc said sceptically, thinking of all the work that lay ahead of him.

Alphonse leaned forward and placed an elbow on the starched white tablecloth. "Do you want *les Boches* to walk in and take your best wines, to loot your hard-earned cellars as they have the great Champagne houses?" Alphonse paused and raised an index finger. "And another thing, Jean-Marc: you need to think about Isabelle and the children."

Jean-Marc clenched his teeth. Was Alphonse now to tell him what to do with his family as well? Was it not enough that he already basked in the promise of *Grand Cru* status? Beneath the table Jean-Marc passed pieces of liver to Pascal, who licked them out of his hand with a warm, wet tongue. "What of them?" he said, irritably.

"Listen to what Federico has to say," Alphonse replied, leaning back in his creaking chair as he folded his arms.

Federico, wearing a straw Panama hat over grey hair, bushy eyebrows and a pressed black suit, his olive skin lined and worn by the Tuscan sun, told them how Mussolini was persecuting the Jews in Italy. Ever since *Kristallnacht*, Jews in vulnerable countries were fleeing for their lives. With tears pooling in his veined eyes he described his heartbreaking decision to abandon their vineyards around the medieval hilltop town of San Gimignano, with berries already formed on the vines, as the Fascist and anti-Semitic grip tightened on Italy. After a bracing gulp of wine he faced Jean-Marc and told him that he feared the German occupation would visit the same persecution on France.

"You abandoned your vineyards?" Jean-Marc said in disbelief.

Federico nodded, his face melancholy and drawn. "I have loved and tended those vines since I was a boy beside my father. To leave them was the hardest thing... I have ever done."

Angelica placed a gnarled hand on top of his and squeezed until her knuckles blanched. She began to weep into her starched napkin and Jean-Marc, regretting his choice of the word 'abandoned', feared that Federico might cry too.

"You should take your family away from here," Alphonse said, "to safety."

Jean-Marc hesitated, fearing judgement from his friends, unsure now whether he had made the right decision with regard to his family. Vivid reminders of that final emotive exchange with Isabelle surfaced suddenly, like rising vomit.

"I do not know where she is," Jean-Marc mumbled, searching blindly beneath the table for the warmth and comfort of Pascal's muzzle. "She has gone."

Alphonse's face slackened. "And Claude, Odette?" he asked, leaning forward, frowning.

"She has taken them with her," Jean-Marc said without looking up.

Gregoire and Olivier straightened and Jean-Marc did not miss the exchanged glance, as if to say, *I knew it*, as though they had placed a wager on it.

Alphonse creased his face. "Where has she gone?"

"I don't know," Jean-Marc sighed. "She spoke of Spain."

"When?"

"The day after the Germans invaded."

"You should have gone with them, my friend," Federico said. "She was right to fear."

"But *les Boches* are not even in Bordeaux," Jean-Marc protested.

Alphonse blew air through his lips. "They will be by the end of the week from what I hear. I have spoken to Rothschild."

Jean-Marc unfurled his hands briefly, suppressing the urge to say, 'So what?'

"He knows Marshal Pétain," Alphonse said.

Jean-Marc bristled at the glib mention of Bordeaux's elite circles that Alphonse now frequented while he himself merely looked in from the outside, from a humbler social circle.

"We are not going to be spared any of the occupation's miseries," Alphonse continued. "It's all about collaboration now."

Jean-Marc felt his blood pounding in his ears, and both hated Isabelle for being so right, and regretted not believing her sooner. "What did Rothschild say?" he asked.

"He asked Pétain to intervene in the persecution and detention of French Jews in Paris, to negotiate a settlement for them as French citizens," Alphonse began, pausing as the silence around the table lengthened. In the background a clock chimed pointlessly.

"And?" Federico prompted.

"Pétain said he could not."

"*Che palle!*" Federico said in dismay, rubbing his worn face roughly, stretching the skin away from his bleary eyes. "Now that France has fallen Hitler controls all of Europe. He will hunt down the Jews here too."

Angelica's eyes brimmed with tears again and Federico placed a consoling hand over hers. Jean-Marc replayed Isabelle's words over and over in his mind. He had not wanted to believe her; for that matter he still did not want to believe Federico. It was surely just the usual rumours and rhetoric. After all, nothing had happened yet.

Alphonse looked up with heavy eyes, directing his gaze towards Jean-Marc. "You should get out, my friend."

"I cannot go now," Jean-Marc said. "I will not abandon our family vineyards to *les Boches*. This vintage will be good, I feel it, and I need it to save the farm. If I go now I will have nothing. Cardinale will be ruined."

"You will have your life, and your family," Alphonse said. "You can always start again."

Jean-Marc put his glass down on the table. His appetite, even for the delicious 1928 Château Millandes Grand Vin, had expired. Looking down, he was met by Pascal's liquid eyes and nuzzling wet nose.

"I will hide if necessary. I have a cellar under the house." Jean-Marc paused. "Isabelle will be safe with the children, I'm sure, and return when the war is over." Jean-Marc was aware of Alphonse exchanging looks of disapproval with Marthe and Federico. "What about you, Federico?" Jean-Marc challenged, meeting the old man's judgmental gaze. "Where will you go?"

18

Alphonse got up to refill glasses and Marthe offered an olive-wood platter of cheeses, aromatically perfect at room temperature.

"I am going to shelter Federico and Angelica in my caves. I have miles of tunnels with wine, barrels, equipment and so on stored in them," Alphonse said. "There is plenty of room for you too, Jean-Marc, and Pascal." He glanced down at the dog pressed against Jean-Marc's thigh.

Downing the last of his wine, Jean-Marc stood up suddenly. He felt disorientated for a moment, conscious of all eyes staring at him.

"Thank you for a delightful lunch, Marthe, *très bien,* but I have much work to do in my vineyard." He called the dog. "Come, Pascal, we must go now."

"Wednesday night, Jean-Marc, 6pm," Alphonse called after him. "Rothschild asked me to call a meeting in the *Mairie* in Saint-Émilion. Tell everyone you see."

Chapter Four

Jean-Marc rubbed his arms briskly and shuddered involuntarily from the damp, cold air that seemed to ooze out of the moist limestone walls of the underground Romanesque cathedral. Immersed in white noise from the discordant murmurs of scores of local wine farmers wearing heavy linen shirts and berets and grasping glowing Gauloises beneath bushy moustaches, Jean-Marc surveyed the company assembled around the towering stone columns of Saint-Émilion's ancient Benedictine sanctuary.

The atmosphere was tense, the talk all about the uncertainty of invasion. What would happen next? How unfair it was that after so many poor harvests war might deny them celebrating the anticipation of a good vintage again.

"Gentlemen!" It was Alphonse, trying to bring some order to the gathering. "Gentlemen, please."

Alphonse was wearing a black jacket over his shirt, buttoned to the top, straining over his full belly. He stood in front of the altar, candlelight dancing on his face like mischievous goblins.

"Why are we not in the *Mairie* as planned?" someone shouted from the back.

"Yes, this is no place to meet, beside the catacombs," another voice added.

"Gentlemen, be quiet please and let me speak," Alphonse said again, arms outstretched like a preacher.

"Why is it you, Alphonse?" a voice heckled. "Where is Rothschild? Why is he not speaking to us?"

"Yes, where is he?" shouted someone else.

Jean-Marc could see the growing impatience on Alphonse's face.

"He has left Saint-Émilion," Alphonse said. Suddenly the voices of dissent quietened until all that could be heard was the scrape of an occasional boot on the damp saltpetre of the floor. "No one expected the Germans to reach Bordeaux so quickly. They are everywhere."

"Where is he?" a man right in front of Alphonse asked.

"He has fled to America," Alphonse replied, and hesitated. "But his wife has been arrested."

Suddenly a shiver of murmurings spread around the room.

"What for?" a lone voice shouted out.

Alphonse's determined gaze found Jean-Marc, who knew exactly what Alphonse was thinking: *You should leave too, my friend, this is no place for you now.* "Because they are Jews."

The burble of chatter rose in intensity amidst excitable glances between people.

"Gentlemen! Listen to me. We decided to meet here in the secrecy of this underground chamber because we do not know where the German eyes are, how far they penetrate. The *Mairie* is too public," Alphonse continued.

"Did you call us here just to tell us Rothschild has gone?" a man said contemptuously. "After all, if he is a Jew…"

"Will you just listen to Alphonse," Jean-Marc shouted irritably, his voice rising above the dissenting rumble. Everyone quietened down.

"We need to stick together, all of us vignerons, for the Germans will try and take from us what they can. They have done this already in Champagne and in Burgundy, looting and

21

pillaging. We must work together to protect our greatest treasures," Alphonse said.

Jean-Marc looked up towards the ceiling, roughly hewn out of a solid block of limestone. Two carved angels touched halos. They were going to need the protection of every available angel in Saint-Émilion.

"I urge you to work quickly. Hide your best wines: the '28s, the '29s, the '34s, even '24s if you have them..."

"We do not all have underground caves, you know," someone said snidely.

Alphonse ignored this remark. "Build false walls in your cellars, hide the wines behind piles of firewood, barrels, rubble – anything. Make the plasterwork look older using cobwebs, beat old carpets and use the dust."

"What will *les Boches* want from us?" a voice shouted out.

"I don't know," Alphonse said. "All we can be is prepared – prepared for the worst." He held up a newspaper and waved it above his head. "Hitler is quoted in *Le Figaro* as saying that the real profiteers of this war will be the Germans, and that they will emerge bursting with fat." He continued to wave the newspaper. "*Our* fat, gentlemen, our produce, our wine."

A murmur of dissatisfaction reverberated around the room.

"We are fortunate in a way. We have seen what the Germans have done in Champagne, in Paris, so we are prepared for them. I will not let them take away my precious '28s and '29s without a fight!" Alphonse raised his voice, like a true orator.

This evoked a cheer from the audience. Jean-Marc shuffled uncomfortably. He had been too young during the Great War but this time he felt the butterflies of deep-seated nervousness unsettle his belly.

"We will have to be careful. No speculation. No loose talk. Gossip could cost lives. Despite our petty differences we must stick together. We have the glorious treasure of Saint-Émilion to safeguard." Alphonse raised a balled fist. "For France!"

"For Pétain, for France!" echoed the dissonant response from the assembled vignerons. "Fuck *les Boches*!"

Jean-Marc swallowed bile.

Chapter Five

"Papa!" Olivier shouted, running into the house.

Alphonse was hunched over a ledger, grasping a fountain pen, the nib of which was stained with blue ink that had discoloured several of his fingertips. He squinted through a twisted pair of round reading glasses perched on the end of his bulbous nose. He looked up, peering over the glasses.

"What are you doing?" Olivier asked, stopping at the desk and leaning on his knuckles, a little out of breath.

"I am studying my wine stocks for each vintage, deciding what to hide, what to leave out," Alphonse explained. "What is it?"

Olivier, his face still burdened by a youthful rash of acne beneath a quiff of dark hair, stared at his father through widened eyes. "The German soldiers have occupied Château Cardinale."

"What?!" Alphonse stood up, dropping the pen onto the ledger, such that it left an ink splatter on the paper where it fell.

"I saw their trucks arrive an hour ago and perhaps a dozen or more soldiers get out and force their way into the house," Olivier said with a mixture of horror and bemusement on his face.

"*Sacré bleu!*" Alphonse muttered, rubbing his moustache and leaving a smudge of blue ink on the end of his nose. "What of Jean-Marc?"

Olivier shrugged. "Haven't seen him."

Alphonse walked to the window and stared across in the direction of Château Cardinale, partially obscured by his timber barn and a copse of sweet chestnut and silver birch trees beyond that.

"Without warning, you know – they may have caught him. Once inside his house they will quickly realise that he is a Jew," Alphonse said with his back to his son, as though thinking aloud. "*Merde!*"

"What should we do, Papa?" Olivier said.

"What can we do?" Alphonse said animatedly, turning sharply to face Olivier with his arms outstretched helplessly. "We cannot just show up there with a houseful of soldiers – who knows what they might think?"

Olivier's eyes suddenly widened, as though he had registered something. "What if they find Federico here?"

"We must be very careful. Federico and Angelica will have to stay in the cellars from now on – no wandering around, not with soldiers right next door."

Alphonse swallowed, but his throat was dry. He never expected the war to come to him so quickly, nor quite so close to his front door.

The luminous light of a full moon bestowed on the young vine leaves a powder-blue hue – like cerulean velvet – that swam in Pascal's eager eyes as he looked up at Jean-Marc, his tongue lolling out of his mouth as he panted. It was still, not a breath of air, not even the hoot of an owl, just the occasional pumping sound of Jean-Marc pressurising the sprayer slung over his shoulder. He moved furtively down the rows of vines, inspecting leaves for spidery cobweb growths, the sign of

25

Oidium infecting the plants. When he saw something suspicious in the soft moonlight he would inspect the underside of the leaf for small spots, telltale signs of powdery mildew.

He was troubled by the presence of mildew in his vineyards so early in the season, especially after such a good start to summer. Could God not cut them some slack, he wondered? After several poor seasons one after the other, He finally sent a promising spring only to follow it up with the damned Germans and now mildew. It was as though He was toying with them.

The fine spray of pesticide misting out of the angled nozzle began to sputter. Jean-Marc pumped the handle on the cylinder vigorously but to no avail. He sighed.

"I am out of copper sulphate, Pascal, and I still have half the vineyard to spray," Jean-Marc muttered to the dog, who lifted his ears as he listened attentively. "*Merde!*"

Slowly they picked their way back along the neat rows of vines towards a looming shadow, a vacuum in the night sky, the darkened expanse that was Jean-Marc's house. He gently opened the barn door, doing his utmost to minimise the creaking, and very carefully placed the sprayer inside, with Pascal pausing loyally beside his leg. Moving to the side of the building, Jean-Marc looked up mournfully at his house, its windows shrouded in darkness, before sweeping aside a thick curtain of dangling ivy and descending a few steps into brooding shadows, hidden from the generous moon's light. A twig snapped and Jean-Marc's heart leapt in his chest. Pascal growled, but Jean-Marc quickly patted his head and muzzle to quieten him.

"Jean-Marc, it is me, Gregoire," whispered a voice.

"*Mon dieu*, you scared the life out of me."

"Papa saw someone moving in your vineyard in the dark. He asked me to have a look," Gregoire whispered, his face

26

illuminated as he stepped into the moonlight. He carried with him a leather saddlebag slung over one shoulder and a shotgun over the other.

"You shouldn't come out here during the curfew, Gregoire. It is too risky," Jean-Marc hissed.

"And what about you, working amongst the vines?" Gregoire retorted sharply. "Are you crazy?"

"I cannot work during the day – when else must I spray the mildew?"

Gregoire shrugged indifferently, very much as if to say, *It is not my problem and I am only here because Papa asked me to come over*. "Papa has sent you some food: *saucisson*, *fougasse* and Brie." Gregoire held out the saddlebag.

Jean-Marc grunted and nodded, gratefully taking the bag. Pascal emitted excitable whining sounds as he smelled the meat. "Tell Alphonse I said thank you."

"There is another thing," Gregoire began, inching closer and bending lower, casting a distorted shadow on the gravel. "Rumours are that the Germans are arresting Jews and deporting them. Papa says you should leave here. It is too dangerous to be in your vineyards, even at night."

Jean-Marc spat on the gravel. "I am safe in the cellar, no one knows I am here."

"Papa says you should come and join us, hide with Federico in the caves."

"And who will tend my vines?" Jean-Marc retorted.

Gregoire blew through his lips, his facial expression indeterminable in the muted light. "It is dangerous, Jean-Marc."

"This is my home, Gregoire. Thank you for the food, and the warning."

Gregoire turned to walk away.

"There is one more thing," Jean-Marc said. "Could you please ask your papa if he has any spare copper sulphate to sell me?"

Gregoire turned. "We have mildew too, you know – it is very difficult to buy pesticide this year."

Jean-Marc knew he would never get copper sulphate over the lofty needs of his important neighbour, and continued his way down the steps towards a dark oak door leading into his vast underground cellar. Once locked inside he lit a candle and walked in between oak wine barrels piled six high beneath the vaulted stone ceilings. The smell of damp, the sourness of fermentation and the vanillins of oak filled his nostrils as he and Pascal made their way deeper into the labyrinth, flanked on each side by wine bottles stacked to chest height on the cold flagstone floor.

Jean-Marc fingered the bottles as he walked, tracing a fine line in the dust, recalling the challenges of each vintage, the last time he had tasted the wine, how it was developing; the rising anticipation of what the next sampling might herald. Many of the wines were made by his father, some by his grandfather, and a few by his great-grandfather. How could he abandon them?

"Tonight we will eat well, Pascal. What should we drink though, eh – 1929 or 1933?"

Pascal wagged his tail and licked Jean-Marc's hand in response.

"Good taste, my friend, '29 it is. One less for *les Boches*."

Chapter Six

Jean-Marc was jolted awake in the darkness by the sound of heavy footsteps reverberating on floorboards overhead. He did not know what time it was, nor even whether it was night or day as the cellar was devoid of natural light. Lying on his back with the coarse woollen blanket pulled up to his chest, Jean-Marc stared up into the darkness, trying to fathom the muted noises.

He could definitely discern boot-steps, and heavy objects – presumably weapons – being placed roughly on his polished furniture, the occasional splintering sound of glass breaking, then something heavy being moved, scraped across the floor in short bursts, and underlying it all, muffled voices populated with emphatic Germanic consonants. He imagined them discovering the plethora of Jewish ornaments present in his house: a menorah, the Star of David, mezuzahs on the doorways. Was it these that they were destroying, or was it merely their presence that evoked in the Germans a destructive spirit?

A loud, determined hammering sound made the walls and floor above him vibrate – perhaps someone knocking nails into his wood panelling. Jean-Marc winced. Throughout every new, shattering sound of uninvited intrusion in his abandoned home the white noise of boots stomping in every direction

29

echoed in Jean-Marc's ears, like soldiers being drilled on a parade ground.

Pascal emitted a throaty gurgle, the preamble to a growl born of his protective instinct. Jean-Marc quickly patted his muzzle, hushed him and drew him closer in the dark. If Pascal were to bark the invaders might well be alerted to their presence. Jean-Marc's little game of evading the occupiers would be up, and as he had not even registered as a Jew with the authorities in Saint-Émilion, his situation would not be favourable. He felt nervous perspiration erupt on his lip as he hoped Pascal would remain silent.

The sounds above continued for hours, quietening for a period, during which he could hear the clink of his wine bottles, the odd one being dropped and rolling, empty, on the oak-plank flooring. The voices became garrulous, playful, and occasionally very loud. Later more glass shattered and something heavy was moved, crashing onto the floor with ominous creaks. Jean-Marc tried to close his mind to the destruction happening beyond his control, but within his consciousness.

And then eventually the sound he had been dreading. Someone was at his beautiful grand piano, butchering his way through some Teutonic piece, Beethoven, perhaps. Laughter and then a crash of notes before someone else began to play with more delicacy and prowess. *Für Elise* – he recognised it, almost enjoying it for a few moments. But before long he imagined drunken soldiers leaning on the piano, food and wine bottles being placed carelessly on the polished mahogany, perhaps even smouldering cigarettes, leaving stains and possibly worse. He prayed that they would lose interest in the music and leave his family heirloom alone.

Jean-Marc bit his lip, for there was nothing he could do, and wished that he could not hear the torturing sounds. He and Pascal had eaten all the *saucisson* and *fougasse* from Alphonse

30

and despite his nervousness his stomach rumbled rebelliously. Thirst was easy to quench, and in the gloom of darkness that his eyes had partially acclimatised to, he selected a bottle randomly from a stash nearby, fumbling with the corkscrew and drinking straight from the neck of the bottle.

He offered a little to Pascal, but feared allowing the dog to become inebriated lest he should make excessive noises. The voices moved outside and he was gripped with fear that they might discover the secret opening to his underground cellar. Soon the penetrating staccato of gunfire followed by breaking glass and laughter stirred Pascal into a near frenzy. Jean-Marc was terrified that the dog would bark and reveal their position, to such an extent that he momentarily pondered what he might have to do to keep the dog quiet. Could he silently suffocate his beloved companion? He did have a knife for cutting the bread and *saucisson*, but… no, that was unthinkable. Pascal was all he had. He was family.

When the soldiers tired of shooting at bottles in Jean-Marc's vineyard they retreated indoors again and it became mercifully quiet. Perhaps they were asleep. Deeming it safe after not hearing so much as a footstep, Jean-Marc very carefully opened the cellar door an inch. It was dark outside, but for the glow of the moon. He shut the door and returned to his makeshift bed of straw and matting.

Opening another bottle of wine in the dark, he took a gulp, recoiling sharply. It was weak and astringent, and it could have been from any of a number of 1930s vintages. If only he had left these upstairs for the soldiers to guzzle like drunkards.

He lay back and tried to sleep, constantly concerned about where Pascal was and whether he might make a sound. His mind wandered to Isabelle and the children, wondering where they might be sleeping, whether they were safer than he was. Isabelle's words echoed in his head: *I am not going to hide like an animal.* Thank God she could not see him now. Thoughts of his little Odette, always upset by separation from her papa, suddenly brought a tear to his eye. He prayed to God that she was safe and sleeping soundly.

Aside from worrying about the wellbeing of his family, he worried about the integrity of his property, his house in which the billeted soldiers had settled themselves and audibly made unsolicited alterations, and his vineyard, brimful of slowly ripening fruit. What would become of it all at the hands of the callous invaders? Would there even be a Château Cardinale 1940? He shook his head silently; what a catastrophe that would be. Château Cardinale had never missed a vintage in two hundred years, not even during the coalition conflicts and the Napoleonic Wars, and the Great War after that. There had been a bottle of wine for each and every passing year.

Chapter Seven

A black Mercedes 260D saloon stopped outside the *Mairie* in Saint-Émilion, a red ensign bearing a black and white swastika fluttering on each side of the windscreen. The motorcade included several armed motorcyclists bringing up the rear on BMW R75s with sidecars and a PKW in which a clutch of armed Wehrmacht soldiers sat. The sun shone, the swastika fluttered regally from the *Mairie* flagpole, silhouetted against a faultless blue sky: winemakers' weather.

The driver alighted and opened the rear door of the Mercedes, standing stiffly to attention and raising his right arm in the Führer's salute. A man of medium build unwound, seemingly reluctantly, into the warmth of a Bordeaux summer's day and coughed as he became engulfed in a cloud of blue diesel fumes. He wore a black Schutzstaffel uniform, black leather jackboots and an officer's Luger. Nodding feebly at the driver he walked through the rusted fleur-de-lys adorned iron gates towards the *Mairie* entrance, which was flanked by Wehrmacht guards.

"Hauptsturmführer Bömers, welcome to Saint-Émilion. How was your journey?" said one of the assembled officials at the entrance of the *Mairie,* bending at the waist in a show of effusive subservience.

Bömers stopped and stared at the man, removing his SS cap and smoothing a slick of moist brown hair against his sweaty forehead. "Long, and hot. But it is always a pleasure to be back in Bordeaux."

The official smiled thinly, angled his head like a maître d'hôtel and clicked his heels in a show of military etiquette.

"Is Hauptsturmführer Kühnemann here?" Bömers fired back.

"No, sir, he is overseeing matters at the port in Bordeaux."

"And what about Generalleutnant von Faber?"

The official exchanged edgy glances with his comrades in arms to either side of him. He licked his lips and appeared unable to hold Bömers' gaze.

"Well? He is the senior officer in charge of Bordeaux, is he not? Is he also not here?" Bömers persisted, straightening up and straining his face into a sneer.

"*Mein Hauptsturmführer*, I believe the general is lunching with his wife at Château Pichon-Longueville today," the official said, shrugging his shoulders apologetically.

Bömers studied the sweaty official's face and adjusted his grip on his brown leather satchel. "Very well."

"Your office is this way, sir, please follow me," the official said quickly, breaking the uncomfortable and intrusive personal confrontation by walking briskly down the creaking wooden hallway.

"I want you to arrange a meeting with Philippe de Rothschild immediately," Bömers said as they walked down the long corridor, the walls adorned with photographs of the local vineyards, famous châteaux and portraits of eminent vignerons.

"Er…" The official hesitated, opening a door to his left to reveal a large wood-panelled office. "We cannot find Baron de Rothschild."

"What do you mean, you can't find him?"

"He appears to have... fled, sir."

Bömers straightened his back, angling his head to face the man. "What about the rest of his family?"

"His wife has been arrested."

"Then who is at Château Mouton Rothschild?" Bömers said sharply.

The official cleared his throat. "Nobody, sir, just soldiers and the farm manager."

Bömers pursed his lips and raised his eyebrows before marching into his new office, spinning on his heel to face the official once more. "In that case get Alphonse Sabron in here... first thing tomorrow morning."

The official stared at Bömers for a moment too long without response.

"Château Millandes, that is where you'll find Sabron," Bömers said and moved away to his desk, dumping his satchel unceremoniously on the polished surface, taking in his new office with a studious expression.

"Can I get you anything, Hauptsturmführer?" the official said, shrinking back slowly towards the doorway.

"Yes, I am very thirsty. Can I have a glass of iced water please, with a slice of lemon?"

Chapter Eight

"What do you want?" the Wehrmacht soldier asked in a challenging voice, raising his Mauser.

Gregoire and Olivier stopped in their tracks, staring at the rifle. Alphonse took a few friendly steps forward and engaged the soldier with a broad smile that pushed his grey moustache upwards.

"We have come to tend the vineyard for our neighbour," Alphonse said in German.

The soldier could not hide his surprise. He turned his head around and looked back at the main house where half a dozen soldiers languished on the stone steps, grey tunics open to the warming sun. "Where is your neighbour?" he asked, taking one hand off the Mauser to place a glowing cigarette between his lips.

"He has fled with his family," Alphonse said.

"*Jüden, ja?*"

Alphonse nodded.

"Why bother?" the soldier said, blowing smoke out of his nose.

"Don't you want to drink good wine this year? Do you want all of this to go to waste?" Alphonse replied, sweeping his arm across the panorama of rows of vines.

The soldier narrowed his eyes and plucked the cigarette from his mouth, smoke curling out of his nose and mouth. He had not shaved and his tunic bore the evidence of revelry in the form of splashes of red wine.

"Oberjäger?" the soldier called out over his left shoulder.

Gregoire and Olivier exchanged an apprehensive look that was quickly settled by Alphonse, who turned to them with a Gallic shrug and a warm smile. He began to speak to them in French about the vines, how good the fruit was looking and that perhaps all that would be needed was to clear the ground beneath the vines of weeds.

Gregoire examined a vine leaf, turning it over. "Mildew," he said.

Alphonse nodded and sighed.

"*Ja*, what is it?" said a young, clean-shaven man who had drawn up to the soldier's left shoulder, his tunic open to reveal a chest turning pink beneath the summer sunshine.

"Good day, sir. I am Alphonse Sabron, a neighbour, and my sons and I wish to tend this vineyard, prune, clear, check for diseases…"

The soldier spoke quickly to his senior officer, explaining that the owner was a Jew who had fled. The *Oberjäger* rubbed his chin and stared in turn at Alphonse, Olivier and Gregoire.

"What is in your baskets?" the *Oberjäger* asked sharply, stepping forward.

Alphonse held his basket out for inspection, revealing a few hand tools and a baguette. The soldier picked up and examined a pair of secateurs, dropped them in the basket and moved on to Gregoire and Olivier's baskets, sniffing loudly.

"How long will you be?"

Alphonse shrugged and turned to his sons, emitting a low sound. "It will take a while, it is only the three of us… that is why we brought food," Alphonse said.

The *Oberjäger* seemed lost for an objection and after drawing a deep breath, he nodded and started walking back to the main house, turning suddenly. "We will watch you," he said, pointing to his eyes.

Alphonse sighed with relief and he and his sons disappeared into the vineyard, starting at the furthest end and walking the rows, pulling out weeds, tying up shoots and occasionally pruning back excess growth, conscious of the German stares following their movements. It was hot, the sun prickling on their backs, and Alphonse adjusted his beret.

Gradually they edged closer to the main house, then drifted along another row and moved down the slight incline away from the soldiers. Lunchtime came and the Germans disappeared inside, bored and hungry. Alphonse's eyes met Gregoire's. They were alone in the vineyard.

"I will go," Alphonse said. "Give me the *saucisson* and *comte* from your baskets."

"Be careful, Papa," Olivier said, touching his father's hairy forearm. Olivier's peachy, youthful complexion was glowing crimson from the warm sunshine.

Slowly, pausing often to prune and tie vines, Alphonse made his way towards the house while Gregoire and Olivier moved off in different directions. There were no soldiers outside now and Alphonse could hear the sound of cutlery scraping on crockery and the banter of male voices sharing alcohol. Quickly, he slipped towards the side of the house and disappeared beneath the canopy of ivy.

Tapping cautiously on the cellar door, he hissed into the crack of the doorjamb, "Jean-Marc! It is Alphonse, let me in."

It felt like an eternity before Alphonse became aware of activity behind the door. He realised that Jean-Marc would be very cautious, but it was in fact Pascal that he could hear: the unmistakeable clipping of his claws on the stone floor and his panting.

"It is me, Alphonse. I have food for you."

Nothing happened.

"Gregoire and Olivier are pruning your vines to distract the soldiers."

Suddenly the door opened wide enough for a pair of eyes to peer out, squinting against the blinding light.

"Come on, you crazy fool!" Jean-Marc whispered.

Pascal licked Alphonse's hands and rubbed against him, dizzy with excitement, his tail wagging furiously.

"Shhh!" Alphonse whispered to the dog, pressing his finger against his lips as if the dog would understand. "Pascal could give your position away, you know. It is unnatural for dogs not to bark."

Jean-Marc, covered in days' worth of untended facial hair, shrugged and gratefully accepted the baguette, tearing off a piece and chewing hungrily. Breaking off sausage, he held out a piece for Pascal.

"Are you mad, coming here like this, in the middle of the day?" Jean-Marc said.

"I cannot come at night, it is too suspicious. At least I have a reason to be here now," Alphonse said. Above his head he could hear the sounds of heavy footsteps and muffled voices, occasional raucous laughter and a few German swear words that he recognised.

"What are they doing to my house?" Jean-Marc asked.

"I have not been in."

"They have been hammering, and smashing, and moving things. They have no right," Jean-Marc said.

"You cannot stay here, my friend, it is far too dangerous. If they find you..."

"I cannot leave my house," Jean-Marc replied obstinately. "Nor my vineyards," he added, gesticulating towards the door.

Alphonse stared at him. "You cannot do much for your vineyards hiding in here anyway."

39

QUENTIN SMITH

"I owe it to my papa, to my *grand-père*, and to all my ancestors who made wine here. Surely you understand?" Jean-Marc said.

Alphonse nodded. Of course he could understand. "What if they hear Pascal?"

Jean-Marc looked down at the dog, whose liquid eyes met his, tail wagging. He held out more sausage.

"This is war, Jean-Marc, it is not a game," Alphonse continued.

Jean-Marc nodded feebly, reluctantly. "OK, the dog has made me nervous, I will admit it. Perhaps you can take him. But I want to stay."

"But—"

"For now. Once I leave, Alphonse, that is it – I cannot come back."

Alphonse shook his head. "Don't eat all the food at once. We cannot risk coming every day."

Jean-Marc's eyes held Alphonse's gaze, his unshaven features and tousled black hair resembling that of a homeless hermit, and his body odour already ripe enough to sting Alphonse's nostrils.

"Any news about Isabelle?" Jean-Marc said.

Alphonse shook his head and Jean-Marc's gaze fell to the floor.

"How do my vines look?" Jean-Marc asked.

"Good. Some mildew, yes, we all have it. There is not enough copper sulphate this year."

Jean-Marc moved away into the gloom and sat down on an upturned barrique, biting into the *comte*.

"We could sneak you out tonight, you know," Alphonse persisted.

Jean-Marc chewed silently. "Thank you for the food, Alphonse. Look after Pascal for me."

40

Once outside in the blinding glare of afternoon sunshine, Alphonse ensured that Pascal stayed by his side and looked across the rows of vines to catch his sons' attention. They saw him, straightening in the vineyard. There was no sign of any soldiers and Alphonse indicated that he was returning to their farm. Gregoire nodded and lowered his head again, continuing to work between the vines.

"Hey, you!" called a soldier.

Alphonse froze.

"Where did that dog come from?"

Alphonse turned to see a Wehrmacht soldier brandishing a bottle of wine by the neck, Mauser slung over his shoulder. His grey tunic must have been buttoned hastily, drunkenly or perhaps both, for the collar on one side rose higher than the other.

"It is my dog, it followed me here. I am taking it back to my farm."

The soldier made no response, his dissipated eyes lingering on Alphonse as he drank from the bottle. "Keep it away from here." He leered.

Alphonse nodded, not wishing to antagonise a drunken soldier greedily swilling Jean-Marc's wines like beer.

"If it comes back I may have to shoot it," the soldier said, and then laughed coarsely.

Alphonse silently cursed Jean-Marc's stubbornness and hoped his sons would not linger too long in his vineyard.

Chapter Nine

The olive-green Stabswagen skidded to an abrupt halt on the gravel outside Château Millandes, liberating dust that floated away ethereally. An armed Wehrmacht soldier alighted from the passenger side and nodded to the two soldiers on motorcycles who had escorted them. Chickens crossed the courtyard in a frenzy, while the watery brown eyes of a chestnut horse watched the intruders calmly over a panelled stable door as it chewed a mouthful of straw. The only sound to challenge the soldier knocking on the heavy oaken château door was the discordant spluttering of the two motorcycle engines spewing oily smoke into the clean air.

Alphonse opened the door wearing only a stretched vest and baggy brown trousers held up by a pair of worn black braces. The sight of four armed soldiers outside his front door unnerved him and he instinctively glanced across to the cellars to check that the doors were shut. Then he thought about Jean-Marc, and his own (perhaps foolish) foray onto Château Cardinale's vineyards the previous afternoon. What if the soldiers stationed there had not been quite as drunk and inattentive as he had thought?

"Monsieur Sabron?" the soldier asked, stiffening to attention formally, heels snapped together.

"Yes?" Alphonse smoothed his bushy moustache and peered out into the courtyard. "Is there a problem?"

"Come with us, please. Hauptsturmführer Bömers wants to see you." The soldier turned slightly and gesticulated towards the Stabswagen.

Bömers – that name was awfully familiar, Alphonse thought. Surely it could not be the same man? "What is it about?"

"I'll be honest, *monsieur*, I do not know."

"Let me get my coat and tell my wife," Alphonse said, retreating into the house without shutting the door.

He emerged minutes later wearing a brown woollen jacket and blue beret, a smoking Gauloises hanging from the corner of his mouth. He turned to see Gregoire and Olivier watching them anxiously through a narrow upstairs window.

Arriving at the *Mairie* in Saint-Émilion a short while later, Alphonse was helped out of the cramped back seat of the Stabswagen and escorted up the pathway. Red geraniums and lilac lavender sprouted healthily from open wine barrels now used as planters on either side of the neatly gravelled path. They marched up the wooden stairs of the building he knew so well to an office at the end of the first-floor corridor, overlooking the town square and the imposing bell tower of the underground cathedral. From behind the desk, the compact figure of a man dressed in a black SS tunic stood up and walked around the furniture, extending his hand to Alphonse.

"Alphonse! Good to see you, my friend," Bömers said with a grin splitting his face in two.

Alphonse could not hide his surprise as he shook Bömers' hand. "Heinz, what the hell are you doing in that uniform?" Alphonse said.

"Sit, sit," Bömers said, motioning towards the empty chairs around the desk. He waved the soldier out of the office and walked across the creaking floor to a tall glass cabinet and extracted two glasses and a bottle of wine. "Château Ausone, 1924," he said, kissing his fingertips in a flamboyant gesture. "What could be better?" Bömers extracted the cork with a practised flourish, sniffed it longingly and finally poured a generous glassful for each of them, spilling red wine onto the desk in his haste.

"I don't understand," Alphonse said.

Bömers lifted his glass and passed the other to Alphonse.

"A toast, to many years of productive collaboration," Bömers said before burying his nose in the glass and sniffing the bouquet, his eyes closing in apparent ecstasy. "With everything going on I quite forgot to open this wine earlier. Forgive me, old friend."

Alphonse swirled his wine absently as he studied Bömers. He had known the man for ten years or so, a wine merchant in Bremen to whom he had sold thousands of cases of wine over the years.

"I have been sent here to buy wine for the Reich," Bömers said.

"You are in the SS?" Alphonse asked cautiously.

Bömers fingered the uniform. "Nominally a *Hauptsturmführer* in the eyes of the military, but a wine merchant at heart." He smiled and pressed the flattened palm of one hand against his chest.

"You are the *weinführer*?" Alphonse said.

Bömers smiled unevenly, pulling his pencil moustache further up one shaven cheek than the other. His carob-brown hair was oiled and combed back immaculately with a centre parting, revealing a high forehead. "Is that what they call me?"

Alphonse had no appetite for wine and placed the glass down on the desk, untouched. Bömers did not fail to notice.

"The '24 is drinking beautifully. Try it." Bömers took a mouthful and swirled it noisily around his mouth.

"Are you here to clean out our cellars?" Alphonse said, ignoring the invitation.

Bömers emitted a disparaging sound and moved across to sit on the corner of his desk in front of Alphonse. The leather of Bömers' Luger holster creaked as it strained on his waist belt. Alphonse studied the man carefully, a man he had entertained in his house, who had eaten at his table beside Marthe, a man who had walked his children through the vineyards. Inevitably, he found himself staring at the gleaming Luger, imagining his erstwhile friend pointing it menacingly at someone. Bömers put a finger to his lips thoughtfully, his eyes gazing towards the far corner of the room.

"So vulgar," he said.

"You've done it in Paris, in Champagne..." Alphonse began.

"*I* have not done it," Bömers said, pressing his index finger into his chest. "The Führer believes that we are entitled to profit from all the bounties of occupied France, that is true, but I believe more in a fair and mutually beneficial business arrangement." Bömers spoke his words carefully.

"Mutually beneficial?" Alphonse said.

"It would do us no good to disrupt the very machinery that turns out the world's finest wines, now, would it?"

"Your soldiers are doing a pretty good job of looting and pillaging right now," Alphonse spat. "They are like drunken students at a summer party."

Bömers' face hardened. "Yes, I've heard about this. It will stop, I assure you. There will be discipline and order. I have von Faber's word."

"Von Faber?"

"Generalleutnant von Faber, senior officer of occupied Bordeaux."

Alphonse took a deep breath and leaned back in his chair, taking in the sumptuous surroundings of the office, once the seat of the town's mayor. The portraits on the wall were unchanged, mostly familiar to him by name, but for the addition of Adolf Hitler; the *Tricolores* was gone and replaced by the *Krummkreuz* of the swastika.

"What do you want from me?" Alphonse said quietly.

Bömers stood up and walked to the window overlooking the town square, placing one hand against his lower back. Down below German soldiers dominated, though locals in berets were seated at several café tables. Despite being July it was very quiet: not a single tourist in sight where Americans and British would normally be milling about everywhere, buying wine and eating at the restaurants.

"I need someone to negotiate with, someone to act as a spokesperson between me and the vignerons."

Alphonse's heart sank. This would be a thankless and impossible task, attracting nothing but scorn and derision from his winemaking peers, and almost certainly falling short of his German masters' expectations. "Why me?"

Bömers turned sharply. "I'll be honest, I would have chosen Philippe de Rothschild but..."

"He is Jewish, can you blame him?" Alphonse said.

Bömers pulled a face. "The racial politics of Europe is not my business, Alphonse. Wine is my business."

Alphonse studied his old friend, his former friend – for he was unsure how to regard Bömers in this current context – under no naive illusion that this new relationship would be anything other than challenging.

"Surely you mean wine *was* your business?" Alphonse mocked, pointing casually at Bömers' SS tunic and Luger.

"I will still be buying wine from you."

"You will be *buying* wine from us?" Alphonse said, unable to hide his surprise.

Bömers nodded and lit another cigarette. "Does that seem so unnatural? We are not uncivilised, you know," Bömers said, drawing on his cigarette.

Alphonse shrugged and looked down. He knew he was a pawn in a much bigger game, and he felt it too. Who was Bömers, though? Was he the bishop, the queen? Certainly not the king. How many people did Bömers answer to?

"The Reich is demanding a great deal of wine. There will certainly be quotas to meet." Bömers rubbed his chin thoughtfully as smoke curled around his head. "Reichsmarschall Göring has a considerable penchant for the wines of Bordeaux and he would make the entire area his personal wine cellar if the arrogant pig had his way."

Alphonse eyed the glass of wine in front of him. The brick-red velvet liquid was beginning to talk to him as his personal fears subsided. The 1924 Ausone would be very good, too good to waste only on German palates. He remembered 1924 as though it was yesterday: what a September, what ripeness and intensity of flavour.

"What sort of quotas?" Alphonse said, succumbing and lifting the wine to his lips, savouring the complex aromas of tobacco and leather and oak.

"One, two million bottles a month."

Alphonse almost spat the wine out, sitting forward abruptly. "That will ruin our international markets!"

Bömers scratched his head, then smoothed the ruffled hair back into place, meticulously. "There are no more international markets, my friend. Do you think the Führer will let you sell to the Americans, or the British?"

Alphonse instantly began to realise the impossibility of his new position. He imagined returning to the winegrowers and passing such news on to them, their outrage and fury. "What if we refuse to sell to you?" he asked without looking up.

"You can sell to the Reich, or you can pour your wine into the Gironde. You Bordelais cannot drink it all."

Alphonse bristled. "And who agrees the price?"

"I do," Bömers said.

47

"At twenty Francs to the Deutschmark? It will still be daylight robbery. How do you expect us to sustain ourselves?"

"That was Göring's doing, and he is not a man to upset," Bömers replied icily, savouring a mouthful of wine with a smack of his lips.

Alphonse looked into Bömers' eyes, aware that his body was shaking with growing anger and frustration. "This is not fair, Heinz," he said.

Bömers sat down behind his desk and refilled his glass. "This is war, Alphonse, and there is nothing fair about it. But it will not last forever. Let us make the most of our predicament because when hostilities are over I hope that we will still be friends."

Alphonse stared at his hands in his lap, the dirty fingernails and cracked skin from tending his vineyards and mending barrels, labours that now seemed inevitably to be solely for the benefit of their occupiers. "How do you expect me to go back and tell the farmers what we have to do?"

Bömers leaned forward and poured a little more wine into Alphonse's virtually untouched glass. "How do you expect me to go back and tell Göring and the Führer that you will not?" Bömers cocked his head to one side and raised his glass. "Whether we like it or not we are in this together, my friend. I get to be in Bordeaux for the war and you have a market for your wine – while all around us Europe burns. Mmmh? Are we not in perhaps the most enviable positions compared to so many?"

For an instant Alphonse almost found himself agreeing with Bömers as he stared open-mouthed at him. Then he thought of Federico and Angelica, and Isabelle, Claude and little Odette. "Are you crazy?"

Bömers chuckled, his mouth open and his head flung backwards, revealing his dangling uvula. "Drink, Alphonse, toast our new venture. If we work together at this you might

48

even emerge from the war as a rich man. What could possibly go wrong?"

Alphonse emitted a disapproving and strained guttural sound.

"Imagine if you had Klaebisch here instead of me?" Bömers said with some amusement etched on his face.

"Who is he?"

"He is the heartless military shit destroying Champagne."

Chapter Ten

Jean-Marc lay on the coarse straw mattress, his nostrils filled with the dank smells of the cellar, now unpleasantly tainted by the ammonia odours of his own urine. In the distant corner flies buzzed around his faeces, warmed by the midsummer temperatures to the ripe and pungent extent that it repelled him. He chewed on a wine cork and contemplated his predicament. Tired of hearing the destructive sounds of callous and careless young German soldiers swaggering about his house, constantly inebriated on his carefully crafted wines; tortured by the fears that the hammering sounds might signify nails been driven into the magnificent wood panelling or the century-old oak flooring, or perhaps family heirlooms being smashed for firewood. He was at breaking point.

Saturated by his impotence and inability to protect his property, present in ghostly form only to witness through the fog of questioning doubt what deeds were being perpetrated upon his beloved family home. He despised the invading Germans, uninvited, uncouth and intolerable. He had even found his palate recoiling from the taste of some of his wines, so lovingly and carefully constructed over the years, but now being consumed as a staple liquid, a life-sustaining fluid, the delicate flavours and complexities merely a distraction from the helplessness of his situation.

There he was again, the loudmouth Hans bellowing at his fellow soldiers from the kitchen, banging pans and crockery together until something broke. What in God's name was he doing? What would be left of Jean-Marc's cherished home when they finally left? What would Isabelle say when she returned?

Isabelle. His mind wandered. Here he was, living like a rat in the cellars beneath his house, unable to show his face and look upon the developing vines in his vineyard, stretched out before the humble château. Where were his wife and children? Were they safe? He felt instantly foolish, thinking what she might say if she could see him now. The proud man who had refused to abandon his beloved vineyards in the face of a marching German invasion was now cowering in the dark, smelly shadows beneath his house, unshaven, unwashed and entirely dependent on the beneficence of his neighbour.

Jean-Marc spat the cork out, watching it spin across the stone floor in the gloom. He felt his stomach rumble. Eating had become something he only contemplated when Alphonse or Gregoire knocked on his door surreptitiously. He ate about every second day. What if they didn't come back? He would be forced to leave the cellar in the dead of night when silence finally descended upon the floors above him, the mob of degenerates, sated on his wines, descending into a sonorous slumber.

Suddenly, he heard a sound from the cellar door and sat up sharply, his heart speeding up. A scratching sound. They'd found him. Where could he hide? Leaping up, he looked left and right, seeking the best dark tunnel to follow and hoping that his attempt to hide behind piles of maturing bottles would be successful. The scratching continued and was accompanied by sniffing. Jean-Marc frowned. He had not heard any human voices. What time of day was it? Light seeped lazily through the cracks around the solid doorframe, but was it midday, afternoon, or later?

Carefully, he tiptoed over to the door, listening. Scratching, pawing and sniffing. In a heartbeat he felt both elation and suffocating fear. Was it Pascal, come in search of his beloved master and unknowingly about to betray his hiding place? He was afraid that if he called out to Pascal he might whine or bark with excitement. Perhaps Pascal could smell him, for at that moment the dog began to emit the yowling sounds of a beast pining for its owner as the scratching intensified.

Jean-Marc felt beads of sweat forming on his forehead as he fled deeper into the cellar. If *les Boches* came in, he thought, they would smell his urine and shit and when they found it they would surely know that someone was hiding in there.

Then came the sound he'd been dreading. German voices, alerted to the presence of the dog. "*Es ist schon wieder dieser Hund!*"

Jean-Marc heard the clamouring sounds of heavily booted feet and the clatter of equipment, perhaps rifles, being handled. He closed his eyes, realising that his discovery could only be minutes away.

"*Ich werde ihn erschiessen!*" shouted another voice, more shrill, less considered, followed by the sounds of weapons being cocked. A loud explosion, like the crack of a whip, made him jump, followed by another and another. Pascal yelped and Jean-Marc heard a frantic scraping of claws at the door as the dog perhaps tried to make his escape.

German voices bellowed and yelled, the cries that emboldened red-blooded hunters. More loud bangs. Then silence. The voices murmured for a while, milling about, and then slowly returned to the house. Jean-Marc almost wept with relief. They were not coming to look for him. But what had they done to Pascal? Was he still alive?

Leaning against the cold stone wall and rhythmically slamming his balled fist against it, Jean-Marc wanted to scream from the frustration of his helplessness as the acrid smell of cordite filtered through the cracks and stung his nostrils. He was unable even to protect his own dog. Perhaps it was time to admit defeat and leave Château Cardinale, to try and do what he could from the safety of Alphonse's property.

He wanted to fight back against the Germans, not cower in his cellar like a frightened animal. Having chosen to safeguard his vineyards over his family, he knew he had to do something extraordinary to justify that decision, which was beginning to look foolhardy. The realisation that he was unable to tend the new vintage fell heavily upon him. This was all he had known since boyhood: the machinations of making wine. How could he fulfil his chosen destiny now? He badly needed a raison d'être.

Chapter Eleven

"We must go and tell Jean-Marc," Alphonse said, his elbows on the dinner table, a piece of torn baguette in each hand.

The aroma of simmering *coq au vin* evaporated into the air and seemed to calm Marthe and the two boys, who ate in silence, heads bowed. Marthe seemed on the verge of tears but fought them back with each mouthful of her signature dish.

"I hate what they are doing to us," Olivier said bitterly, his eyes not straying far from his hot food. "I want to fight back. I want to do something."

Marthe emitted a sound, half a hiss of air and half a gasp, the sound of a mother fearing for the continued safety of her child. She covered her mouth gently with an open hand, her fingers trembling barely noticeably.

"We cannot afford to attract any attention to ourselves," Alphonse said, looking at Olivier sternly. "We have a responsibility to Federico and Angelica, and I hope soon to Jean-Marc too."

"He should have left with his wife months ago. Why should his stubbornness now endanger us?" Gregoire said.

"If he had, he would be in even more danger than he is now," Alphonse said.

Gregoire shrugged. "But *we* wouldn't."

54

"Don't talk like that, Gregoire. He is our neighbour and our friend."

Gregoire laughed derisively.

Alphonse stared impassively at his son and pulled a face. "What is it?"

"You don't even know?"

"Know what?"

"He despises you, Papa, because Château Millandes is almost certain to become *Grand Cru* and Cardinale is not. He is jealous and small-minded." Gregoire made a dismissive gesture with his hand.

"Nonsense," Alphonse said, glaring at his son, rubbing his bushy eyebrows that were knitted together like a hawkmoth above his proud nose. "Don't be so disrespectful."

"Poor Isabelle," Marthe said, wiping her mouth with a napkin and stirring the chicken on her plate aimlessly. "It is unbelievable… quite inconceivable." Her lip quivered as she stared into her food. "Those poor children."

Alphonse took a mouthful of food but did not enjoy it. The flavour was there but he could not bring himself to savour it. "Tonight we must go and fetch Jean-Marc. It is becoming too dangerous for him to stay in his cellar," he said.

"Papa…" Gregoire protested. "It is dangerous for us too. Look what happened to the dog."

Alphonse ignored him. "Tonight. There will be no moon."

Gregoire and Olivier exchanged a furtive glance that did not elude Alphonse. But he bit his tongue and continued to eat. Afraid that the Germans might surprise him with another impromptu visit they now ate alone, leaving Federico and Angelica in the cave cellars, hidden from the light of day. Jean-Marc would at least be company for his Italian refugees.

"We could do with Jean-Marc's help with the upcoming winemaking anyway," Alphonse said, "especially as we will have all his grapes to vinify as well."

55

"What if his grapes are shit?" Olivier said with a smirk and a rebellious giggle exchanged with Gregoire.

"Gregoire, watch your tongue," Marthe said sharply.

Alphonse stared down his youngest son's insolence. "No matter. The Germans want so much wine they cannot be fussy."

Marthe raised her eyebrows as she turned to Alphonse. "You can be so sure of that? Heinz knows his wines. You taught him, after all."

Alphonse dismissed this. "He won't bother us."

"Alphonse, you yourself told me he was wearing an SS uniform when you met him," Marthe said.

"So?" Alphonse said.

"He is a German officer now, with responsibilities to his superiors. He will not be the same Heinz Bömers that dined with us at this very table three years ago. We are at war with them now. Like it or not, he is the enemy." Marthe pushed her chair back and stood slowly, pressing a hand into the small of her back as she straightened. She gathered the half-eaten plates of food. Nobody, it seemed, had had much appetite. "Cheese?" she asked.

They all shook their heads. "No, my dear," Alphonse said.

Marthe lingered with the pile of plates balanced on her arm. "You be careful tonight."

Chapter Twelve

Alphonse walked with trepidation, aware of his heart beating, pulsing, his mouth dry. Gregoire followed sullenly behind him, wordless and evidently tense. They entered Jean-Marc's vineyards and slowly made their way towards the main house. Looking left and right Alphonse picked random bunches of grapes, cut them with secateurs and tossed them into his basket. The fruit looked good, Alphonse thought, but not as ripe as his own. Château Millandes was certainly blessed with topography that seemed to trap the sun, and a considerable proportion of very old vines. But to be fair he had also been able to prune leaves back, exposing bunches to the sun, something Jean-Marc had not been able to do at Château Cardinale that year.

"There is a lot of mildew, Papa," Gregoire said.

"I see it."

It did not take long for them to be challenged. "Halt!" shouted one of the German soldiers, brandishing a Mauser menacingly. "What do you want?"

Alphonse held one hand up and faced the approaching soldier with a brave smile, squinting into the sunlight behind the soldier.

"I am Alphonse Sabron from next door. I have come to check on my neighbour's vines."

The soldier swaggered to a halt five yards away from Alphonse, rifle clutched under one arm at hip height. His eyes narrowed as he studied the baskets that Alphonse and Gregoire held. Lifting his rifle cautiously, he approached them.

"What have you got in there?"

Alphonse tilted his basket to reveal its contents: secateurs, three bunches of red grapes, a baguette, and a glass beaker with hydrometer.

"What is that?" the soldier asked brusquely, pointing at the glass apparatus.

"It is a hydrometer, for measuring the ripeness of the grapes. It indicates when they are ready to be harvested," Alphonse said.

Beside him Gregoire puffed on a Gauloises, unable to disguise his discomfort. The soldier stared at them and examined the items in the basket, as if touching them would help him determine subversive activities.

"Who is the bread for?" he asked, licking his lips.

"For us, of course. We might be here a while, taking samples," Alphonse said, maintaining a smile.

The soldier glanced over his shoulder towards the house where a few colleagues sat about on the stone steps. "No. We cannot be watching you all the time you come here. Go back to your property."

"And who will harvest these grapes when the time is right?" Alphonse said.

The soldier shrugged indifferently. "We could eat them." He laughed.

"Do you know how many bottles of wine this vineyard will produce, bottles your *weinführer* is expecting to ship back to Germany?" Alphonse said with surprising insolence in his voice.

The soldier glared at him and bared his teeth. "I said no."

58

Alphonse submitted with a little nod and quickly picked a bunch of grapes right in front of the soldier.

"Come, Gregoire, let's go back. I'll speak to Hauptsturmführer Bömers about this."

"You speak to him," the soldier sneered as they walked away. "Wait!"

Alphonse froze. The soldier approached and fixed him with a cold stare before gazing down into the basket. With deliberate and shameless leisure he grabbed the baguette and waved them on. Alphonse sighed and walked, nodding at Gregoire to follow him quickly. This was not good news and would make reaching Jean-Marc even more difficult as their presence on his property was now forbidden. Once out of sight of the soldier he picked a few more bunches of grapes for sampling.

"Forget about the damned grapes, Papa, they are not your concern," Gregoire said.

"They are, my son, we are all in this together. Jean-Marc is not my enemy, the Germans are."

That night, after midnight, Alphonse returned to Château Cardinale under cover of a cloudy and moonless sky. He covered his shiny silver hair with a black beret and wore his darkest clothing. He forbade Gregoire or Olivier from accompanying him and refused to take a weapon, saying that such a find on him would only worsen his predicament. What would be his excuse if accosted, he wondered? How could he explain his presence on his neighbour's farm just hours after being banished from it? What reasonable excuse could anyone offer for sneaking around so late at night, well beyond the curfew?

No, he simply could not be caught, and he had to proceed as there was no time to lose. They had been unable to get food to Jean-Marc for three days. *Stubborn fool*, Alphonse thought. Still, one's desire to protect one's property could not be underestimated. Perhaps he would have done the same in Jean-Marc's shoes.

Alphonse crept along in the shadows, keeping low, moving slowly, pausing often to listen for the sounds of any human presence. How he craved a cigarette, but the pungent smell of tobacco smoke would certainly alert others to his presence.

Once he reached the walls of Jean-Marc's house he began to tremble slightly. Now he was within spitting distance of the lions' den and all it would take was one soldier to walk casually around a corner and he would be apprehended with no chance of escape. He slithered down under cover of the ivy and began to scrape and knock softly on the door, calling Jean-Marc's name in whispered tones.

It took an eternity for Jean-Marc to respond. He too must have been frightened and wanting to be sure it was not the Germans at his cellar door. As the door opened barely an inch Alphonse was overcome by the stale smell of human habitation; the nasal sharpness of ammonia and fetid overtones of faeces. Jean-Marc stared back at him, unshaven and unkempt, his face betraying the realisation that Alphonse's empty arms did not bear food.

"You must come with me, it has become too dangerous," Alphonse urged in hushed tones.

Jean-Marc hesitated, turning and studying his shelter.

"I have news about Isabelle. You must come, my friend," Alphonse said.

At the mention of his wife's name Jean-Marc stiffened and then moved quickly to retrieve his shotgun, pausing to snuff out a candle beside his makeshift bed. He locked the door on the way out as Alphonse kept a wary lookout.

The night was still and not a sound emanated from within the house. Moving furtively and keeping to the shadows, they covered the ground quickly and soon Alphonse began to feel a wave of relief wash over him as his boundary neared.

Once safely inside the manor house at Château Millandes, Jean-Marc's true state of dishevelment was revealed. He stank.

"Marthe, please run a hot bath for Jean-Marc and then we will eat," Alphonse said.

"Please, can I eat something first? I am starving." Jean-Marc said, still shielding his eyes from the brightness of electric lights he had not seen for some time.

Once he had eaten and bathed, and changed into fresh clothing from the wardrobe of a begrudging Gregoire – his closest fit – Jean-Marc sat down with Alphonse. The boys were asleep. A clock ticked in the background.

"Where is Pascal?" Jean-Marc asked.

Alphonse looked down and scratched his ear with a bent little finger. He sneaked a glance towards Marthe, who was tidying up. "They shot him."

"What?!" Jean-Marc shouted.

"I am sorry. He wandered over, looking for you, no doubt. The bastards shot him."

Jean-Marc twisted his face in anguish and clenched a fist.

"It is lucky that he did not reveal your hiding place, Jean-Marc."

"I am going to kill those *Boches* bastards. *Merde!*" Jean-Marc hissed through clenched teeth, tightening his fist until the knuckles turned white.

Alphonse studied his friend, a good twenty years his junior, impulsive and passionate much like his own boys, yet also stubborn and loyal to things that mattered. He breathed heavily in anticipation of what he had to tell Jean-Marc. "As I said, I also have news about Isabelle," Alphonse said quietly, meeting Jean-Marc's watery eyes.

Jean-Marc's face fell into dispassionate neutrality as he waited. "Are they safe?"

Alphonse took a deep breath and opened his mouth, trying to select the right words. "We got word that Isabelle has been detained by the Germans. I am so sorry, Jean—"

"Detained?" Jean-Marc said, his face twisted. "You mean arrested?"

Alphonse nodded. "The Germans have set up an internment camp for Jews at Merignac, just outside Bordeaux."

"A camp... in France?"

"It's just a holding facility. They move them out – after a while – to Drancy."

"But how, I thought she was in Spain?" Jean-Marc protested, pushing his chair back and walking around the table.

Alphonse shrugged. He did not know where she had been apprehended. In truth, he did not even know if the information was entirely accurate, but it was all they had.

"What about Claude and Odette?" Jean-Marc said quickly.

Alphonse looked up at his friend. "Sit down, Jean-Marc."

Jean-Marc's face drained of colour as he sat down without protest.

"They have been deported to a temporary camp outside Paris."

"No, no, no! This cannot be happening!" Jean-Marc wailed, banging his fist down on the table so forcefully that the cutlery rattled. But his voice was merely a stringy protest, a half-hearted objection to a deed already done, a deed monstrously irreversible. His head dropped onto his arms.

"What camp?" Jean-Marc said, lifting his head suddenly.

"They have rounded up thousands of Jewish children and taken them to the Velodrome," Alphonse said ruefully.

"But... but... what about our Prime Minister? Surely..."

"Laval has said... nothing," Alphonse said quietly, his voice trailing off with shame towards the end.

"Where are they taking the children... *my* children?" Jean-Marc said, his face screwed up with tormented anguish.

Alphonse lowered his eyes and his head. He could not bring himself to tell Jean-Marc what people were saying.

"This is my fault. I should have listened to Isabelle. I should have gone with them months ago. Damn my foolish pride," Jean-Marc sobbed, his shoulders moving like pistons beneath the woven jacket. Then suddenly, he looked up with pink, swollen eyes.

"We must fight back, Alphonse. I want to fight back. We have to show these damn *Boches* how unwelcome they are, how much we hate them. Damn it! Damn it! My children..."

Chapter Thirteen

Jean-Marc could not sleep that night in the cool cellars of Alphonse's expansive cave system. He was unaccustomed to the sounds of other people: Federico snored and Angelica coughed right through the night. Their sleeping areas were separated only by a few stacked wine crates and a suspended tarpaulin, though it was far more spacious and comfortable than the tiny cellar in which he had been hiding. Looking around at the vast cavern and the numerous tunnels leading off into the limestone cliff beside Château Millandes' *grand maison*, Jean-Marc was powerless to suppress a wave of envy of the facilities available to his illustrious neighbour. What a perfect environment in which Alphonse could age his noteworthy and opulent Merlot-rich wines, he thought.

The next day he was distracted by the intensifying business of the approaching harvest. He helped Alphonse to complete the tests on grape samples using the Baume's hydrometer. A beaker full of pressed grape juice from each quadrant of Alphonse's extensive vineyards – the vast south-facing areas, the undulating western field and the one basking in the reflected heat of an old medieval abbey wall – were each tested with the floating hydrometer to reveal sugar content and therefore predicted alcohol concentration after fermentation. The men stood around an upended oak barrel in the cellars with the glass instrumentation scattered across its convex surface.

"Your grapes are good this year, Alphonse," Jean-Marc said with a slight tug of jealousy in the back of his throat. He had crushed a grape between his fingers, testing for softness as a sign of slight dehydration, and in so doing revealed brown seeds.

They had also tested his own grape samples, taken by Alphonse on his last visit to the vineyard, which were definitely better than 1939 and 1938, but not as ripe as Alphonse's. Was it just that he had been unable to tend his vineyard as he usually would, Jean-Marc wondered, or was this the subtle difference between his wines and those of his more highly regarded neighbour?

"We must harvest," Alphonse said.

"I agree," Federico said, nodding enthusiastically as he studied the Baume hydrometer floating in the grape must. "Twenty degrees Brix is not bad."

"How will we do it? There are only seven of us," Jean-Marc said, "and three of us are not supposed to be seen during the day." He hesitated. "I have no Jewish papers, if they catch me..." He drew a finger across his throat.

"Neither do I," added Federico.

Alphonse pursed his lips. "I have spoken to Bömers about the labour problems. I told him most of our workers had been called up to the French army and they are now in POW camps following the German invasion. He knows the harvest will be a disaster if we do not have manpower to bring in the grapes. Everyone is facing the same problems."

"What did he say?" Jean-Marc asked.

Alphonse shrugged and emitted a wheezing sound. "What can he do? He cannot release prisoners of war from Germany – they are in all probability being used as labour over there, making cannons for the Germans."

"But they want us to continue to produce and supply them with wine as if nothing has changed?" Jean-Marc said.

"In a nutshell."

"*Merde! Boches* bastards," Jean-Marc hissed. "It is impossible."

"We should harvest your grapes first, they are ripe and the better quality," Federico suggested to Alphonse in a calm and measured voice. "Then, while Jean-Marc and I crush the grapes and commence fermentation you and the boys can bring in his grapes."

"But what if it rains while we wait?" Jean-Marc protested. "My crop could be ruined."

Alphonse placed a hand on Jean-Marc's shoulder. "I know it is not a perfect plan, but it is probably the best we can manage with so few of us. If you are caught out there in the vineyards you will end up in Drancy, my friend, and no good can come of that."

Jean-Marc looked sharply at Alphonse who seemed to recoil slightly, perhaps regretting the implication of his words. Jean-Marc felt as much a prisoner here as he had been beneath his own house: helpless and still dependent on others. Was this freedom? "OK," he said. "I'm sorry."

"Bömers wants a million bottles a month, Jean-Marc. The Germans will buy your wine, even if..." Alphonse faltered.

"Even if it is not as good as yours, is that what you mean?"

An awkward silence enveloped them for a moment.

"In any event, I still have to obtain permission from Bömers to enter your vineyard to harvest. Last time we were there the soldiers told us not to return."

Jean-Marc held his head in his hands, thinking about the state of his beloved Château Cardinale and the lovingly tended vines, now neglected and choked by weeds, subject to the whimsical destructions of indifferent Germans.

"We must help each other, Jean-Marc. I will help you get your grapes harvested and sell your wines to Bömers. You and Federico can help me do the vinification and bottling."

Jean-Marc gripped the edges of the wine barrel with both hands and nodded in reluctant acceptance. He was not the master of his own vineyard this year; he was certainly not even the master of his own life. But it was not Alphonse's doing, it was *les Boches*.

They began to harvest the next morning, before sunrise, with cool dew droplets still clinging hopefully to the vine leaves. Jean-Marc and Federico stayed in the cellars and washed down the tanks and vats with hoses, cleaned and prepared barrels for the fermentation, and checked on stocks of empty wine bottles. Bömers and his entourage arrived unannounced at Château Millandes just after noon to see Alphonse. Accompanying him, as usual, were several armed soldiers.

Jean-Marc listened to the muted conversation from behind the safety of the cellar doors, ready to make a run for the cave depths if they should venture any closer. The conversation seemed convivial from their expressions, even if the words were muffled. Jean-Marc realised then that he could not be seen outside during daylight hours. It was simply too risky. Such a surprise visit could have seen him caught and dragged away at gunpoint.

He watched as Bömers retired into the house with Alphonse, presumably for a glass of wine and perhaps a little *fougasse* and cheese. His armed entourage remained outside, examining the farm courtyard with disinterest. Jean-Marc shrank back from the doors as he and Federico hastily took refuge behind barrels to avoid the prying German eyes peering through cracks and keyholes.

Half an hour later the Germans left and sometime after that Alphonse came in to see them. His face looked grave and furrowed. "They found your hiding place, Jean-Marc," he said. "With all that shit and stink of pee they know someone had been hiding there for a while."

Merde, Jean-Marc thought, realising how badly this might reflect on his neighbours and hoping it would not bring misfortune upon Alphonse.

"Bömers is angry about something and in an awkward position." He hesitated. "He has called a public meeting of all wine farmers tonight."

"But we are so busy," Federico protested. "It is the middle of harvesting."

"That's what I told him, but he would not take no for an answer. He said simply, 'It's me you'll deal with now, or someone like Göring later. Who would you prefer?'" Alphonse shook his head and placed a stubby finger heavily against his temple. He glanced warily at Jean-Marc and Federico. "You'll have to be extra careful. I cannot have him suspicious that I am concealing you. God knows what they would do to us." He glanced around towards the house. "To Marthe and the boys."

Jean-Marc bit his lip and looked over to the corner where baskets piled high with harvested grapes were stacked, waiting to be sorted.

"We'll start de-stemming tonight while you're at the meeting. It's all we can do to help you," Jean-Marc said submissively.

Alphonse nodded in appreciation towards Jean-Marc and Federico. "I will not abandon you, my friends. We will see this through together."

Chapter Fourteen

The meeting was well attended and buzzing with edgy apprehension. Bömers had called them to the *Mairie* where they assembled in the main meeting room beneath chandeliers and moulded fleurs-de-lys in the ceiling plaster. Vignerons held urgent and stilted conversations in small huddles of twos and threes, eyes always glancing around furtively. The conversation that Alphonse heard repeatedly was of the difficulties in procuring the harvest. Copper sulphate had been in short supply and consequently mildew had tainted much of the crop; despite the good summer, yields were down; labour shortages were hampering harvesting; the challenges of vinification were yet to be uncovered, but murmurs of a shortage of glass bottles were already rife. But above all else was the grousing about the Germans.

"Do you know, Alphonse," said an old man with a weathered face and bushy moustache, through broken, nicotine-stained teeth, "my cousin in Alsace tells me the Germans have forbidden them from wearing berets. Berets! Forbidden!" He made a throaty hissing sound and clicked his tongue.

Someone emitting clouds of Gauloises smoke from his nose and mouth turned to face them. "Yes, Georges, but imagine how much worse it could have been if not for Pétain. We can thank our lucky stars for the marshal."

Alphonse remained silently neutral. Marshal Pétain's policy of co-operation was a divisive subject and he was not going to be drawn into it.

"Lucky, are we?" challenged the moustached man. "My cousin's two boys – just out of school in Colmar – have been drafted into the Wehrmacht to fight against the Russians. They are French, not German, and when I last looked Alsace was in France, not the Reich. And what does Pétain do about that? Huh? Is he French, or is he German?"

As in many intimate huddles, tempers flared quickly. People were tense, frightened, unhappy. Bömers, flanked by armed soldiers, walked in briskly wearing his SS uniform. As he sat down at the desk he removed his cap and placed it on the desk, sweeping fingers through his hair with a flick of his wrist, re-establishing the perfect coiffure. Silence descended on the crowded room.

"*Heil* Hitler!" boomed the loud voice of one of the soldiers as he and his colleague saluted with straight arms.

Bömers did not salute as he studied the papers held in his grasp, and his eyes did not rise to meet those of the eager crowd as he began to speak. "As you may know, I have been given delivery quotas for Bordeaux wines. My colleagues in Champagne and Burgundy have their own quotas to deliver." He looked up slowly and scanned the faces of those gathered before him. "These quotas are dictated by Berlin."

Alphonse tried to keep out of his line of sight, seated as he was two-thirds of the way to the back of the hall and hiding behind George's enormous head.

"For the present I will be buying one million bottles of your best red wine every month to be transported back to the Reich by train."

A murmur spread across the room like a ripple on a smooth pond.

"I know your last few vintages have been poor, and even though this year seems better you are struggling with manpower shortages." Bömers studied the faces intently, almost in a game of daring: who would falter first? "I cannot help with any of these things, I'm afraid. But this does not stop my superiors from expecting a constant flow of wine. If necessary, you will have to work harder." He twirled a hand in the air as though conjuring a spell. "Work weekends if you have to."

In response to a muted murmur that vibrated through the room, Alphonse lowered his head and sighed. Bömers' bold rhetoric now seemed a far cry from the conversation he had held with his old merchant friend back in July.

"I needn't remind you that Reichsmarschall Heinrich Göring is a great lover of red Bordeaux wines. If he could, I believe he would simply annex this whole area and ship every bottle back to his private cellar."

Another burble of dismay infected the room, very briefly.

"This is unlikely to happen as long as he trusts me to deliver what I am expected to. If I fail, then he will come here in person, of that I'm certain. So, my friends, you will have to co-operate with me as I do my best to act as an intermediary between you and Göring."

Alphonse knew that Göring's love of Bordeaux was only one aspect of this process. Not only were the senior figures in the Third Reich filling their cellars with fine wines, but by controlling the market and export of French wine the Reich intended to profit massively from all of this wine-grabbing.

"I will buy every bottle of wine that we take from you and pay for it in French Francs. I have been given plenty of Francs to do this," Bömers continued.

"Yes, but they are worthless now that you have devalued them," a bellicose man beside Alphonse grumbled under his breath.

"All bottles to be exported to Germany must bear a red stripe with the words *Reserved for the Wehrmacht* on the label – to distinguish them from others."

Bömers looked around the room, appearing to expect an affirmative response. Not a sound, not a whimper.

"Please remember I have been buying wine from you for many years and I know what every vintage tastes like. I will conduct regular and random quality checks to ensure that the wine I have bought is what you are sending to the rail trucks in Bordeaux."

The audience erupted into contained outrage at such a suggestion of deception and dishonesty. Bömers remained unmoved and held up a piece of paper.

"What does he take us for?" shouted the bellicose man, right into Alphonse's ear.

Alphonse smiled back at him, realising just how astute the new *weinführer* was.

"I have here, gentlemen, an anonymous letter sent to me – quite possibly – by someone in this room." Bömers held aloft a crumpled sheet of paper as he let his words settle on the audience. Silence once again prevailed, all eyes on the letter.

Sideways glances were cast between vignerons: who amongst them would dare to be a turncoat and write to the *weinführer*? And what might they have written about?

"I will read it to you." Bömers put on a pair of small, round reading glasses and cleared his throat. "*You should be aware that some wine producers are hiding their best wines; some producers are being deceptive in what they present to you and what they package for transport; some producers are a disgrace to the good name of the Bordelais.*"

72

Bömers removed his glasses and placed the letter on the desk, smoothing it out with one hand. The silence in the room was tangible. Not even a sniff or the slightest tickly cough broke the oppressive stillness.

"What am I to make of this?" Bömers said accusingly to the audience, rising and leaning forwards, his knuckles pressed onto the desk. "Am I to believe that you would collectively be so foolish as to try and deceive the Third Reich, to deceive me, a winemaster and long-standing wine merchant who was been buying Bordeaux wines for over twenty years?"

Silence. Alphonse felt his mouth drying up. He had labelled one hundred cases of his poor 1939 vintage as 1935 and sold these to Bömers, honestly believing that there was very little to distinguish the two awful vintages in bottle. He knew also that he was not alone. Everyone was trying to offload their worst vintages of the '30s to the Germans and keeping the best back. It was a dangerous game of brinkmanship.

"So, what should I do about this?" Bömers said, picking up the paper and sneering at it. "What would Reichsmarschall Göring do about this, do you think?" He looked around the room, forcing eye contact with as many vignerons as he could. "Well, I'll tell you what I'm going to do." He began to tear the paper into fragments, becoming more feverish as he progressed. "I despise those who rat on their own kind. But I also do not like people who try to deceive me. Make sure that you are neither of these two kinds of people and we will get along just fine." He swept the shredded papers off the desk with a violent sweep of his arm. "Do I make myself clear?"

Alphonse breathed a sigh of relief. He knew that Bömers had just cut them some slack, or had he simply given them more rope? Those who were not very careful would surely end up hanging themselves.

73

Chapter Fifteen

They were all there in Alphonse's absence, working like packhorses, sorting the grapes and discarding poor fruit, de-stemming the bunches, an arduous and finger-breaking exercise completed eventually in silence as they were too exhausted to engage in further idle conversation. Jean-Marc and Federico took the lead in fruit selection, being experienced in this matter, though Gregoire had much to say about his father's fruit that ended up in the waste bin.

"There is nothing wrong with this," Gregoire complained, turning a discarded bunch over in his hand. "This would make a second wine many Bordelais would kill for."

Jean-Marc and Federico exchanged a weary glance. "We do not have the manpower nor the time to manage a second wine as well," Jean-Marc said.

"We could put these in with your harvest, then," Gregoire replied.

Jean-Marc glared at Gregoire with such venom that he feared he might swear in front of the women.

"Gregoire, please help me with the de-stemming. My fingers are nearly raw," Marthe said, holding up her hands, stained red from berry juice. Sitting between Angelica and Olivier, she looked up at Jean-Marc and her eyes conveyed empathy.

74

"I am too tired to work," Gregoire exclaimed irritably, standing up slowly as his body unwound from its cramped position, huddled over crates of grapes.

The seventy-year-old Federico looked up at him but said nothing, lowering his head and pressing on, picking up one bunch after the next for experienced eyes to examine.

"Marthe, you and the boys go off and wait for Alphonse. We'll finish up," Angelica said.

There was tension in the air, like static electricity, caused only partly by exhaustion. In truth they were also troubled by what may have transpired at the meeting called by Bömers and from which Alphonse had not yet returned.

The cellar felt cool and Jean-Marc shivered. He walked over to the lagar and surveyed the mass of purple-black fruit, the culmination of a year's preparation in the vineyard and bounteous hours of sunshine. "Should we tread tonight or tomorrow?" Jean-Marc said.

"I don't think Alphonse treads his grapes before maceration," Federico said without looking up.

Jean-Marc turned to gaze upon the old man, still working his way through the final basket of fruit between his knees.

"Whole berry fermentation?" Jean-Marc questioned.

Federico looked up at him. "Don't you?"

"No... er, how long does he leave skin contact, then?"

Federico pulled a face and stretched his neck as if easing a cramp. "Quite long. I think he said up to six weeks if he can keep the temperatures down."

Jean-Marc was stunned. This was twice as long as he did. "Is that what you do?" Jean-Marc said.

Federico tilted his head in a non-committal way. "Tuscany is different. This cellar is beautifully cold," he said, pausing and looking around. "Perfect for long, slow maceration."

Alphonse did have the most perfect cellars, gouged into the limestone hillside. For the first time Jean-Marc considered that his enforced incarceration away from the occupying Germans might prove useful to him; that he might learn some new winemaking tricks from his much-vaunted neighbour.

For a time after that, things were quiet. The days grew shorter and the nights cooler. Alphonse was barred from entering Château Cardinale after they had harvested Jean-Marc's crop and was therefore unable to provide any further vineyard maintenance for his neighbour. Down the rows of his own vines he and the boys cleared weeds, pruned and tied back stems ready for the following spring. Jean-Marc missed that time outside in the crisp, frosty air, the distinctive smoky smell of fires burning the vine cuttings at the end of rows, and the subtle warmth they provided. He missed the winter sun, low in the sky and always shrouded in pastel shades. Pascal would have been at his side, chasing birds, chasing his own shadow. Isabelle would call him in for a hot beef ragoût with *cèpes*, and a bottle of his most recently bottled vintage to sample. All that normality – almost unbelievably – was his life, less than one year ago.

The only warmth that he and Federico got on these cold days was the immersion in the must as they punched down the cap of grape skins covering the macerating juice. Sinking down into the exothermic mush, wearing just his shorts and clinging to chains suspended from the cave ceiling above the lagar, Jean-Marc released an invisible burst of carbon dioxide.

"Last year a boy at Château Villemaurine died during *pigeage*," Jean-Marc said, his arms straining to keep himself from sinking into the dangerous quagmire of fermenting fruit.

"It happens," Federico said with a doleful nod of his head as he gingerly lowered himself into the second lagar.

"My boy, Claude, wanted me to let him help with *pigeage*, kept asking me, 'Please, Papa, this year?', but I was afraid he was too young still – you know, not strong enough to hang on," Jean-Marc said. His thoughts floated back to his missing family.

"Do you regret not going with them?" Federico said with measured sensitivity.

Jean-Marc bit his lip and pressed down with both feet on an unbroken section of the cap. Of course he regretted it, but how could he abandon Château Cardinale in the face of so distant a threat? If he had known then how things would turn out, it might have been different. Perhaps his protective leadership might have prevented their detention and imprisonment. Perhaps not, and he too might at this point be in a camp full of unwanted Jews facing an uncertain future.

"Of course," Jean-Marc said quietly. "Every day.

Federico's skin was coloured purple up to his neck; his face strained from the waves of pungent gas released from beneath the cap, his veins bulging from the effort.

"Take a break, Federico," Jean-Marc said, "I'm not diving into your lagar to fish you out."

Both men laughed.

Due west, barely twenty-two miles away at Gare Saint-Jean in Bordeaux, a freight train was being loaded on track nine, some distance from the passenger platforms in the goods and heavy cargo section. Even though the front freight carriages were being loaded with crates stacked high with wine bottles and fifty-gallon wooden barrels, not everything boarding the train was cargo.

Stationmaster Jean Thibault walked up and down beside the train, his flat black cap perched askance on his balding head. Clamped between his lips, a battered cigarette left a trail of smoke behind him. Isabelle watched him as he barked orders at the men loading the wine; officious, wanting to appear in control; aware that he was being watched constantly by the multitude of armed Wehrmacht soldiers in their grey tunics.

The soldiers were present more for the human cargo, but nevertheless exerted an overall authority that no Frenchman would dare to challenge. The hard atmosphere of coal smoke, grease and billowing steam over unforgiving stones underfoot accentuated their alien predicament.

"*Bewegen!*" a soldier shouted, motioning with his arm for the long line of bedraggled humans to move forward towards their point of embarkation.

Isabelle was beyond tears, totally cried out for her lost children whose whereabouts and safety were unknown to her, a heartbreaking plight for any mother. How could she worry about herself knowing that her children were somewhere out there, alone, possibly facing danger and starvation? She was numb, staring at the dirty yellow Star of David tacked onto her sleeve and that of every other person standing before and behind her. Disbelief swelled from within her. Beyond the emptiness of separation from her son and daughter, Isabelle had barely any emotion left to contemplate her circumstances. She had scarcely thought about her husband and their argument over fleeing France. Where was Jean-Marc? Was he perhaps there too, boarding this cattle truck bound for the dark heart of Germany? Cattle trucks indeed! It was inconceivable. Nobody had told them anything, but she had heard the stationmaster, standing beside a crate of wine barrels, saying something about Berlin as he wrote in his ledger. It made sense that the wine would be destined for the Reich, so presumably they were going to the same destination. What awaited them? Would she perhaps be reunited with Claude and Odette?

"*Schnell!*" another soldier shouted as an old man lost his footing scrambling aboard the cattle truck. He was pulled roughly to his feet and pushed aboard, sprawling across the splintered wooden floorboards.

Suddenly it was her turn. Stepping reluctantly into the packed, malodorous truck, Isabelle turned around and looked

78

out across the vast expanse of the iron lattice roof that covered Gare Saint-Jean, beneath which other passengers went about their ordinary lives. It was a structure that symbolised everything honourable about being French, but a world away from where she stood at that moment: a world away from her nightmarish predicament. How had this happened? Her country had betrayed her, thrown her to the occupying Germans like an animal. She wondered if she could ever look upon that very proud Gallic symbol, Gustav Eiffel's Gare Saint-Jean roof, in the same way again. And then she wondered if she would even live to see Bordeaux again.

In that instant her gaze drifted downwards and met that of the stationmaster, who had been counting wine bottles and barrels. He seemed momentarily mesmerised by the sight of these unwanted Jewish prisoners boarding the train. His eyes locked intensely with Isabelle's, even though his face remained expressionless, impassive. In an instant her view was obscured by embarking prisoners being pushed into the remaining gaps.

Sensing a swirl of light-headedness enveloping her, Isabelle clutched at the sleeves of those around her in vain, crumpling to the floor of the dusty cattle truck.

Chapter Sixteen

Turning the sturdy wooden lever to tighten the screw press was hard work. Jean-Marc pushed against the lever with his chest, one hand braced on either side of his body. He felt like a mule. With every revolution the press was pushed down an inch, squeezing out deeply purple juice through the wooden slats. Frothy juice the colour of cherry blossoms flowed into wooden barrels on either side, filling the air with aromas of sweet black fruits. Despite the low ambient temperature, Jean-Marc – shirtless and with his loosened braces hanging down around his knees – paused to wipe sweat off his brow. He marvelled at the intense colour of Alphonse's must. Again, a pang of envy shot through him, together with a determination to make some changes to his own winemaking techniques.

"I am not used to this basket press," Jean-Marc said.

Federico was pushing the lever of a second press beside Jean-Marc. The sinewy old man, despite veins bulging to bursting point in his face and neck, seemed to have limitless stamina, Jean-Marc observed, and it spurned him on to labour without complaint beside the older man.

"What do you use?" Federico asked.

"My feet." Jean-Marc chuckled.

"I don't know many winemakers who still tread their grapes," Federico observed. "That is a true labour of love."

"I think it's far easier than turning this basket press." Jean-Marc slapped the wooden lever with the palm of one hand.

"Did your wife used to help you?" Federico asked with a definite note of empathy in his voice.

Jean-Marc felt a pang of regret in the centre of his chest. He had never allowed her to tread the grapes, an old custom handed down from father to son that women might turn the wine sour. Last year Claude had helped him for the first time, just about heavy enough now to be effective. When would the boy return to the farm and be able to help him with a vintage again? There was so much he wanted to teach his son about the time-honoured art of crafting Saint-Émilion's fine wines, to make amends for countless failed opportunities.

Can I help you squash the grapes, Papa? he could hear Claude saying as he lingered hopefully at the cellar door.

You are not big enough, my boy, he could still hear himself reply. *Wait a few years.* Well, there had not been a few years. And where was Claude now?

"What do they use in Champagne and Burgundy these days?" Federico asked, thankfully changing the subject as he leaned against the lever and paused for a rare breather.

Jean-Marc considered how to respond. He knew he was lagging behind with modern technology at Château Cardinale and that the basket press was in widespread use, even in the ancestral heartlands of France. The fact that he could not afford to buy one was beside the point.

"It is only the Bordelais who still use lagars." Jean-Marc shrugged and sniffed. "We are traditionalists."

Federico groaned as he leaned into the lever, the tendons in his arms snapping taut like bowstrings. "Nothing wrong with that." He tapped his forehead with a finger. "It's what's in here that makes a good winemaker."

"Uh-huh," Jean-Marc agreed, "and in here." He pressed a balled fist against his chest. "You know, this will be the first harvest since I was a boy helping my papa that I will not bring in my own grapes. It doesn't feel right."

Jean-Marc wondered for a moment what Federico might be feeling, perhaps thinking about his own vineyard back in Tuscany, abandoned, with unharvested fruit rotting on the vines.

"You are fortunate to have such a good friend as Alphonse," Federico mused.

Jean-Marc nodded in silence, watching the deep red juice flow out between the staves of the press. He was fortunate. Where would he be now without his neighbour? Alphonse had obtained permission from Weinführer Bömers to access his land, to pick his grapes. How could he repay such a debt to his friend? The least he could do was sweat and strain against the barrel press lever that secreted the ripe and superior juices of Château Millandes' fruits. Tomorrow, or the next day, he would have the limited satisfaction of at least pressing his own grapes, even if he would be using someone else's equipment.

Every year the harvest marked the crowning of a year's labours in the vineyard in a speculative partnership with the weather. It always filled him with excitement and joy, always had, ever since he had watched his father beam with satisfaction as he tasted the first samples out of barrels in the cellar.

This year was different. He had not tended his own vines; he was not picking his own fruit, nor was he even treading his own grapes in the usual way. All because of the damned Germans living on his property. His thoughts once again turned to Isabelle, Claude and Odette. He tried to imagine their plight at that minute, interned in hostile camps miles from him, helpless and afraid. He shut his eyes and forced his thoughts back to the smell of the fresh juices, the hopes and optimism of a new vintage.

82

Alphonse burst into the cellar, closing the door deliberately behind him. His face looked grave and he would not initially make eye contact with Jean-Marc, who sensed that something had happened.

"What is it?" Jean-Marc said.

Alphonse sighed. "We have heard that the camp at Merignac has all but been emptied."

Jean-Marc's heart skipped a beat. Isabelle.

"A train bound for Germany was seen being loaded with Jewish prisoners."

Federico closed his eyes and bowed his head as his lips mumbled a few Hebrew words. He looked up. "May HaShem protect them."

"But... where..." Jean-Marc mumbled, his mind spinning.

Alphonse moved closer and laid a hand on his shoulder. "I am sorry, Jean-Marc. That is all I know."

Jean-Marc lifted his eyes from the floor, stained with splashes of red juices, and looked into Alphonse's face. "How do you come by this information?" Jean-Marc asked.

Alphonse shrugged. "There are people out there, undercover, working behind the Germans' backs."

"Who are they?"

Alphonse narrowed his eyes and shifted uncomfortably. "Hard to say – it is not organised in that way."

Jean-Marc paused for a moment, wiping his brow. "I want to meet them, I want to find out what they do."

"You are a Jew, Jean-Marc. If the Germans catch you..." Federico said.

"So what? My family is gone – I have no idea where they are or if I will ever see them again. I cannot spend my days in this cellar hiding like a coward."

Angelica emerged from the shadows, still holding corks that she had been washing.

Jean-Marc felt a sudden pang of remorse as he felt Federico and Angelica's eyes upon him. "I'm sorry, I didn't mean it like that," he said to them.

"I know it is a shock, Jean-Marc, but just think about what you are saying, give it a few days. I don't know where these people are, let alone how to contact them. We just hear things." Alphonse opened his palms in a helpless gesture.

Jean-Marc nodded and turned around, applying his weight to the press lever with a groan as he strained to turn it through another revolution, concentrating his frustrations on that central pivot, willing himself to overcome its inertia.

"I want to find them. I want to fight back against *les Boches* bastards."

"I know where they are," said Gregoire. Alphonse's head spun around, unaware that his son had entered the cellar.

"No, Gregoire," Alphonse said.

Gregoire approached them and Jean-Marc stopped pushing the lever, turning to join the huddle of men, his eyes eagerly searching Gregoire's young and precocious face.

"Papa, listen to me. The Germans are rounding up young men, men like Olivier and me, and forcing them back to Germany to work for the war effort."

"What?!" Alphonse said.

Gregoire sighed. "It is true, Papa. Laval has ordered it – STOs, they call them, and Olivier and I will be forced to go."

"I will forbid it!" Alphonse said, flushed in his face.

"You cannot, Papa. It is the law," Gregoire said.

"Damn the Vichy law, damn Laval and... Pétain!" Alphonse spat on the ground.

"Most young men are not going, Papa, they are going into hiding."

Jean-Marc stepped forward slightly, sensing where this was heading. "You know some of these people?"

Gregoire nodded.

"Where are they?" Jean-Marc pressed, leaning forward in his eagerness.

"Everywhere – in the mountains, the forests. Many hide out across the demarcation line in the *zone libre* around Bergerac."

Alphonse emitted a loud, guttural sound of disapproval.

"Is it safe in the *zone libre*?" Jean-Marc said.

"No, of course not!" Alphonse blurted out. "It isn't safe anywhere."

"The Milice control the unoccupied zone. I hear they are terrible," Gregoire said, his eyes hard.

"Gregoire, I cannot run the farm without you and Olivier. I have no labour left," Alphonse said, turning his gaze from his son to rest on Jean-Marc.

"I know, Papa, and I am sorry, but we have no choice. It's either go to Germany and work in their factories, or…"

"*Merde!*" Alphonse said, turning and walking away to one side, a fist held up to his mouth. "I should speak to—"

"You cannot speak to Bömers about this, Papa – avoiding STO is illegal," Gregoire said. "You do not want to be involved."

Jean-Marc listened to the exchange with mounting enthusiasm, his gaze flicking from Gregoire's excitement to Alphonse's frown. "I want to be part of it," Jean-Marc said.

Gregoire met his eyes and nodded. Turning, with a finger raised in the air, Alphonse spoke thoughtfully.

"I have miles of cellars in this hillside here." He gesticulated into the depths of the cavern. "I am already concealing three, you and Olivier can hide in here too."

Gregoire lowered his head and shook it. "Papa, I want to do something positive, not just hide. I am young, my life ahead of me, we young people all want to fight for our country, for our freedom."

"Such easy words to say." Alphonse walked towards Gregoire, shaking his head. "But what will you do, eh?" he said, almost derisively, his shoulders heaving up convulsively.

"You will be amazed, Papa. They are fighting back – sabotage, spying, everything." Gregoire was animated in his excitement, eyes dancing from one face to another, hands grappling with the cold air before him.

Alphonse hesitated, bowing his head down, almost as if in surrender. "Does your mother know about this?"

"No."

Alphonse pursed his lips and thought for a moment. "When will you go?"

"As soon as they tell us we have to go to work in Germany." Gregoire softened. "We will keep contact, Papa, we will not just disappear."

Silence enveloped the men, broken only by the echoing sound of wine dripping slowly from the basket presses into barrels. Jean-Marc shivered and felt a rash of goose pimples across his shirtless body. Standing still in the cool air was suddenly unpleasant, and he rubbed his arms briskly.

"I will help you as long as I can, Alphonse, to finish this vintage." Jean-Marc flicked his gaze towards Gregoire. "But when you have made contact I want you to come back and tell me. I want in," he said with determination in his voice.

Gregoire nodded to him with flawless eye contact and Jean-Marc felt a new bond developing between Alphonse's son and himself, beyond their petty differences, a bond forged out of their shared convictions.

Alphonse and Federico looked at each other dolefully, seemingly united in apprehensive trepidation, perhaps a weariness borne out of history repeating itself once again.

"I don't like this," Alphonse said quietly.

Chapter Seventeen

Evening drew nearer, painting Monet's dreams onto a lightly clouded pastel sky. Jean Thibault paced up and down beside the freight wagons, cap on his head, whistle and watch dangling on the end of a silver chain from his tight black waistcoat, and clipboard clutched in his stocky grasp. The cattle trucks had been closed and although no human suffering was overtly visible, writhing hands and fingers protruded through the slats in the woodwork accompanied by a cacophony of muted whimpers and sobs. Desperate calls for help floated eerily and unanswered across the cool autumn air. Thibault gritted his teeth to block the wretched sounds from his mind. These were his own people, some perhaps even his neighbours or from his own street – God forbid – yet he was powerless to do anything.

An armed Wehrmacht soldier stopped Thibault and asked what he was doing there so late. Thibault, a veteran stationmaster accustomed to belligerent train drivers and haughty passengers, fobbed the German off, derisively saying that he was ensuring that the freight he had signed for left the station with the train at eight o'clock.

"Hauptsturmführer Kühnemann's orders," Thibault added, stabbing his index finger at the clipboard in his hand.

The mention of Kühnemann was enough to silence the private, who walked on past the moaning that emanated from the cattle trucks.

"Water, please, we need water!" a man's voice called out from within.

"*Ruhe!*" shouted the soldier.

Lengthening shadows resembling evil spirits crept inexorably across the rough track ballast, zigzagging from one angular surface to another. An owl hooted from the shadowy bushes beside the track. Thibault stopped to check for the soldier, lifting his watch to his face. The owl hooted again. He moved across towards the bush furtively and pretended to check the freight on the wagon. A pair of eyes within a face smeared with coal dust peered out from beneath a dark beret.

"It is much cooler in Paris," whispered a voice.

Thibault froze and bit his lip. The German soldier was nowhere in sight. "Bordeaux can be warm in November," he replied without turning around.

"There is frost in Paris."

Thibault breathed a sigh of relief. "There is no frost here."

The bush rustled and parted slightly. The blackened faces of two men and one woman surfaced from the shadows.

"Stay out of sight, there is a soldier patrolling," Thibault warned.

"Any news?"

Thibault licked his lips, smoothed his moustache and continued to talk, facing the boxes of freight on the train.

"Shipment of fifty thousand bottles of wine and sixty barrels of distilled alcohol to Berlin."

"Anything else?"

"A few hundred Jewish prisoners – probably from Merignac."

A brief pause.

"Who is the wine for?"

Thibault felt himself frown at this question. What did it matter, he wondered, who ultimately drank it in the Reich?

"The bottles are labelled *For the Wehrmacht*. It's a new rule," he said, pretending to tick the form on his board.

"Nothing else?" asked a female voice from the bushes.

Thibault thought about this. What did they want to hear about? German troops, weapons? He knew this information went back to London.

"One thing," Thibault said, rubbing his chin. "The wine for the next two shipments is being specially packed for hot conditions, by order of Kühnemann. He said to make sure the wine would be able to withstand very high temperatures."

"Thank you, Jean. Keep your eyes open," said the man's voice in the bushes. "When is the next shipment?"

Thibault began to move off, pocketing his pen and swinging his whistle on the end of its chain. "There is a train every other day."

And with that he walked back out into the open space between the tracks, removed his cap and ponderously scratched his balding head for a few languid moments as he whistled Charles Trenet's *La Mer*.

With practised agility and surprising quietness the trio slunk away from the trackside bushes down the embankment and into the throat of deepening shadows. Once obscured behind a stone wall beneath a gnarled walnut tree, they regrouped quietly. Underfoot, walnuts lay everywhere, the rotting fern-green husks peeling away from the walnut stones.

"Not only are they stealing our wine, but our people as well," Patrice said tersely, hunkered down over his pistol.

"Where do you think they're taking them?" Anton asked.

Patrice shrugged.

"Jews?" Anton added.

"Let's hope they are," Patrice replied, his face lowered as he released the safety on his pistol and thrust it into his trousers. "Otherwise we've all got more to fear than we think."

"We must get Thibault's information about the wine back to London," said Monique as she settled down on her haunches, her taut, elongated frame coiled like that of a leopard. "Where do you think it could be headed?

Picking up pebbles, which she weighed in her hands and then moved from one to the other, she glanced at her two comrades, crouched beside her in the murky light of dusk. Patrice shrugged, his deeply pocked features accentuated by the hastily applied coal dust that made his face look like the lunar surface in the feeble light.

"Not Germany, not Poland." Patrice spat on his hand and began to wipe away the coal dust.

"It can't be anywhere in Europe," Anton said.

Anton was short at five foot six, lightly built and burdened by a lazy eyelid on the left that made him look inattentive and bored.

"Definitely not Russia either," Patrice said.

"Shall I go to our contact in Bordeaux and get a coded message sent?" suggested Monique. "It could be important."

"No!" Patrice said sharply and shook his head. "I mean, we must report it, but not you – your accent is too… northern." He shrugged. "They will be suspicious of you. I'll go, they know me."

"And me?" Monique protested.

"You and Anton return to Bergerac."

"Too northern? I'm from Normandy, what do you expect?"

"These are times of war, Monique, people don't trust anybody, let alone someone who is not a local. Think about it," Patrice said.

Anton nodded in agreement. "It is better. I will take Monique to Louis' place, we will wait there for you."

Monique suppressed frustration. She didn't think her northern French accent was that bad. "You never let me join in. Why?"

"I know, Monique," Patrice said. "Trust takes time. You're new here, and…"

Monique exhaled in exasperation and tossed the remaining pebbles against the stone wall. They clattered and ricocheted about.

"Ssshhh!" Patrice hissed.

"I can do more than you let me," Monique said, almost sulkily.

"Your turn will come." Patrice smiled and moved closer to wipe dust off Monique's face with one of his fingers.

Monique pulled back, uncomfortable under Patrice's leering eyes. Patrice stiffened, looking hurt.

"Let me come with you then," she pleaded.

Patrice dismissed her with a hard face. "Go with Anton, it is much safer."

Monique sighed loudly and looked down at the ground where rotting walnut husks covered the dry soil. "Ask him to tell London that the wine might be destined for North Africa."

Patrice turned, his eyes thoughtful. "North Africa? Could be."

"In excess of fifty thousand bottles is a lot to send to the middle of nowhere without good reason," Monique said. "They must be planning something."

"OK, Monique. You two be careful now. See you at Louis' tomorrow night." With that Patrice darted off into the engulfing blackness.

Monique picked up a walnut shell and hurled it to the ground in frustration. "Shit! Why won't he let me do anything?" she hissed. "He does all the interesting stuff."

Anton smiled and nudged her elbow to get her up, nodding his head to indicate they were off. "You know, Monique, there

91

are only two kinds of soldiers: arrogant ones, and old ones."
He paused and she felt his eyes upon her face until she met
them with her own. "I have never met an arrogant old soldier,
have you?"

"What are you trying to say?" Monique said ungraciously,
getting up reluctantly, as though she was being admonished
like a schoolgirl.

"Don't wish yourself into harm's way so soon, we are in
enough danger as it is. Let's go."

They would have to be careful returning to Bergerac,
Monique knew that; taking back roads with their bicycle lights
off. The good news was that the further east they went, away
from Bordeaux towards the demarcation line, the fewer
Germans they were likely to encounter. But there was another
enemy in the east, though. Vichy.

Chapter Eighteen

"What is the meaning of this?" Alphonse fumed as he tossed a pamphlet onto Bömers' desk.

Bömers glanced at the pamphlet without unclasping his hands beneath his chin, a flash of irritation crossing his face. "I have seen you as a personal courtesy, Alphonse," he said calmly.

Alphonse stabbed his finger at the picture of a man carrying a sledgehammer set against a background of barbed wire. "How are we supposed to run the vineyards if you take all the young men away? Can you tell me that?"

"Sit down, please," Bömers said, opening a silver cigarette case and offering it to Alphonse.

"This is ridiculous!" Alphonse said, refusing a cigarette.

"Would you care for wine?" Bömers said amiably.

"No!"

Bömers leaned back and let Alphonse steam silently. "It is your Prime Minister's idea, Laval, nothing to do with us," Bömers said, lighting a cigarette with an engraved silver lighter.

Alphonse stared at Bömers with an intensity that stung his unblinking eyes. He felt both furious and helpless, all at once.

93

"I can understand that you worry about your boys – where they might go, will they be OK?" Bömers said. "You're a father, it's natural."

"Of course. And they are my only help on the farm."

"It is just labour, you understand, strong, able-bodied young men to work in the German factories. They will be quite safe, even earn a little money," Bömers said in a reassuring voice.

"The war factories," Alphonse hissed.

Bömers shrugged indifferently and drew on his cigarette.

"And who will help me pick grapes?" Alphonse said, leaning forward. "You want a million bottles a month, it will not happen."

Bömers inhaled deeply and leaned back in his creaking chair, enveloped in smoke. "As I understand it, the STOs are in exchange for prisoners of war, so you may get some labour back." Bömers raised one eyebrow.

Alphonse breathed heavily, unsure what to say. He knew full well neither Gregoire nor Olivier had any intention of complying and he did not wish to attract undue attention to his affairs at Château Millandes.

"Can you guarantee that the Bordelais will get labour back?" Alphonse said.

Bömers pulled a face. "No. How can I do that?" He paused. "But I could at least contact High Command and see if I can influence things a little. I will speak to General von Faber." Bömers leaned forward and picked up a gold Schäffer fountain pen, pulling off the cap and making a quick note on the pad in front of him, the scraping of the nib the only sound audible in the smoky room.

Though it stuck in his throat, Alphonse rose and conceded a thank-you. At the door he stopped and turned around. "One more thing. We are very short of glass bottles. There will not be enough to go around."

Bömers nodded in silence and again made a note on the pad. As Alphonse was about to pull the door shut, Bömers stood up. "There is something you can do for me too, Alphonse."

Alphonse hesitated and thrust his face back into the room.

"I'm afraid you'll have to look deeper in your cellars for an alternative to meet the quota. I simply cannot pass on the dreadful 1939 vintage to Berlin."

Alphonse did not know what to say. He knew that every Bordelais vigneron was saddled with the 1939 vintage, wine so poor that no Frenchman would drink it. They had all been hoping to offload these, even at basement prices, to the vast, faceless German Wehrmacht.

"I understand," Alphonse said quietly.

"I'm sorry."

Alphonse stormed down the corridor escorted by an armed soldier. His heart was pounding in his chest. Would he, just like Jean-Marc, end up unable to protect his own children from this war?

Chapter Nineteen

They sat playing a game of Polignac around a battered rectangular table, crumbs and food fragments visible between the warped oak slats. A candle in a pewter holder flickered in the centre. Anton smoked, a Gauloises heavily pregnant with ash dangling from the corner of his mouth, his left eye droop always worse at night. Nicolas, fair-haired with blue eyes and high cheekbones, was slicing and eating a red onion off a wooden board beside him. Wordlessly he offered an onion slice on the paring knife to Louis beside him, but was waved off. Louis wore a mane of brown hair which partially obscured thick rolled scars the colour of salmon on his upper cheek and neck. All three men were unshaven with bushy moustaches.

Monique surveyed her companions from the window where she sat on a low pew bench, knees drawn up beneath her chin. Occasionally and very cautiously she parted the sunflower-yellow curtains to peer outside. She could see her dark hair reflected in the window and as a matter of constant vigilance found herself checking her roots for any sign of blonde hair. In the far corner of the dimly lit room, beside the dark oak door and opposite an open hearth in which several logs crackled and hissed as orange flames licked around them, stood a shotgun and hunting rifle.

"Capot!" shouted Anton excitedly, startling Monique.

"That's the third time," Louis objected, throwing his cards on the table, scattering cigarette ash. "You think he's asleep behind that closed eye, but..." Louis smashed a fist into his hand.

"You deal this time, Nicolas."

Monique checked her watch. It was 7.30pm, half an hour to curfew. The hamlet of La Besage was silent except for the occasional bark of a dog. Outside the night was as black as space; the expanse that should be visible as Bergerac, beyond the turrets of Château de Monbazillac, was dark and invisible – like a crater – its citizens bound by the curfew and hidden by the ban on any form of lighting.

"We should go looking for him," Monique said, leaning against the wall and casting an eye over the distracted gamblers.

"Are you missing him?" Louis cackled salaciously as he exchanged suggestive looks with his companions.

"Don't be stupid!" Monique responded quickly.

"He'll be here soon," Nicolas said absently without looking up, shuffling the cards in his hand. "He's very reliable, Patrice."

"*Merde*, I prefer it when Anton deals," Louis grumbled, tossing his cards onto the table and subconsciously rubbing the jagged pink scar that connected his right ear to his prominent Adam's apple.

"I see capot, again!" Anton laughed before breaking into a wheezy coughing spasm, spilling the long worm of cigarette ash onto the table in a powdery splash.

"Wait!" Monique said, raising a hand for quiet. The card game froze. "I see a blue light."

Louis snuffed the candle and he and Anton walked to the door to grab their weapons. Nicolas pulled a pistol from his coat pocket and stood up unsteadily, slowed and always leaning to the right as a result of the shrivelled limb he kept as a memento of polio.

"It's a bicycle, I think, a single flickering blue light. It might be Patrice," Monique said with cautious excitement.

Through the parted curtain she could just make out the silhouette of a man wobbling along on a bicycle beside an avenue of trees. Above the faint light, dulled by obligatory blue paint, a spot of red glowed briefly. Louis cocked his shotgun. The bicycle stopped and a man alighted, approaching with such stealth that his footsteps were almost inaudible. There came the sound of an owl hooting, once, twice, three times, then a knock on the door. Louis' battered face broke into a smile and he unbolted the door. Patrice entered, pushed his way in and pulled off his beret.

"Thank God!" Monique said, standing up awkwardly, thrusting her hands into her trouser pockets. "We were worried."

Louis, Anton and Nicolas all gathered and shook his hand.

"Monique was worried about you, Patrice," Louis said lasciviously.

"Oh shut up, Louis," Monique said and turned away.

"Any problems?" Nicolas asked, shuffling unsteadily back towards the table.

Patrice shook his head and sat down at the table, splashing wine eagerly into a glass tumbler.

"Did you send the message to London?" Monique asked.

"Of course."

"Any news?" she asked.

"Yes, but not from London. We have work, my friends," Patrice said, gulping down the wine and looking around at his companions. "What is this?" He held up his empty glass and examined it with a look of deep suspicion.

"It's from Cahors, my cousin lives there," Anton said.

98

They all pulled up a chair and Nicolas relit the candle with a match that was quickly seized upon by Anton to light a cigarette.

"There are two British airmen at Château Lascombes, shot down just north of Libourne," Patrice said, his hands outstretched on the table, still clutching his cigarette.

"Brutinel has them?" Louis said.

"Uh-huh. They need safe passage to Bayonne for a boat out of France," Patrice said.

"When?" Monique asked from the pew at the window, feeling a frisson of excitement surge through her.

"Friday."

Silence as each man examined his hands around the table: dirty fingernails, calloused working palms. Monique understood their quiet contemplation. It was dangerous smuggling downed enemy airmen across occupied Bordeaux, and if they were apprehended it was punishable by immediate execution.

"Who asked?" Nicolas said.

"It came via the contact in Bordeaux," Patrice said.

Monique's heart was pounding and her mouth dry, but these were the moments that she had dreamt of, that she was hungry to experience. This was why she had come to Bordeaux.

"When do we leave?" she asked, searching Patrice's face.

He turned to meet her eyes and pulled on his cigarette. "As soon as I've eaten, under cover of darkness."

Chapter Twenty

Jean-Marc sat quietly beside a long wooden table used for the tasting and blending of wines prior to bottling. Scattered untidily across the coarse surface were glass beakers, pipettes and flasks, resembling a school science laboratory. His eyes were closed as he drummed his fingers rhythmically up and down the edge of the table, eliciting a soft, staccato thumping sound, the melody confined to the silence of his imagination. As his nose filled with the familiar smells of a wine cellar in the throes of vinifying a new vintage, his mind drifted to thoughts of his lost family, his abandoned house and his state of virtual imprisonment.

"What are you doing?" Angelica asked softly.

She had walked up behind him so quietly that he had not heard her, or perhaps his ears were simply filled with the imagined harmonies of the *Prelude*. Jean-Marc opened his eyes and turned to smile at her.

"I am playing my piano," he said, and tapped his temple with one finger before returning all ten fingers to the tabletop. "Debussy's *Prelude*."

Angelica smiled. "Ah, I love Debussy too. Which one?"

Jean-Marc leaned into the wooden surface and gently lifted his fingers off the heavily grained wood as he played with great feeling.

"*Suite Bergamasque.*" Jean-Marc looked at her again.

Angelica nodded and he could see in her eyes that she understood, that she possibly heard the same music that he did, felt it, and was moved by it.

"You have a piano at home?" she asked, moving to stand by his side.

Jean-Marc shrugged, trying to disguise a shiver of apprehension. "*Les Boches* have it now." He looked at Angelica, her watery brown eyes set in a friendly, wrinkled face framed by curls of grey-white hair. "Do you play?"

Angelica nodded. "I had to leave a very special piano behind too, belonged to my father." She paused, staring into the distance, then angled her head. "Ironically, it is a German piano, a Bechstein."

"Mine is French, a Pleyel grand. Come, Angelica, play with me, I am about to start the *Menuet*."

Angelica smiled and sidled closer. "I'm not sure I'm as good as you," she said, chuckling nervously.

Jean-Marc smiled. Unsaid words passed between them as they tapped the table, absorbed in their individual thoughts, imagining beauty and harmony, wishing it back. The door burst open and Alphonse and Federico entered. Jean-Marc turned and saw the puzzled look etched onto his host's face.

"What are you doing?" Alphonse said.

Angelica turned and smiled at her husband. "We're playing Debussy, can't you hear?"

Alphonse stared with bemusement for a moment and then approached. "Listen, Jean-Marc, Federico and I have a plan. Tell me what you think."

Jean-Marc stopped drumming his fingers and spun around on the wine cask.

"I have barrels of worthless 1939 wine sitting here. Nobody wants it. Bömers doesn't even want it," Alphonse said with intensity written into his face. "Most of the wine we sell to the

Reich probably goes to the Wehrmacht – and what do they know about wine?" He glanced at a nodding Federico for support. "It's the *Grand Crus* that will end up on Hitler's banqueting table at Platterhof, but for the rest..."

"So?" Jean-Marc said.

"We bottle the '39 and label it... '38." Alphonse paused, expecting a response from Jean-Marc. "'38 was equally bad."

Jean-Marc winced and rubbed his chin. "What is your '39 like?"

"Dishwater," Alphonse said.

Jean-Marc chuckled. "Like mine, then."

"Why not blend it with the '38 to give it a little more body and also make it less distinctive and recognisable?" Federico said, his eyes flitting from Jean-Marc to Alphonse. "We do a lot of non-vintage in Italy."

"Have you tasted my '38?" Alphonse said, giving Federico a dubious look.

Jean-Marc nodded. "This could be dangerous."

Alphonse made a guttural Gallic sound.

"Is anyone else doing it?" Jean-Marc asked.

"Everyone else is doing it," Alphonse burst out.

"*Sacré bleu!*" Jean-Marc said, shaking his head and inhaling through pursed lips.

"We don't talk about it openly, but yes, I'm sure they are. Everyone wants to protect their best vintages and get rid of the rubbish," Alphonse said. "Wouldn't you?"

Jean-Marc wondered what was happening in his cellar since the Germans had discovered his hideaway. Undoubtedly they were pilfering all the accessible wines and he could only hope that those good vintages that he had bricked in, at Alphonse's suggestion, remained undiscovered. The thought of all that wine, including those made by his father and his grandfather, beyond his protective reach and at the mercy of the occupier, was tormenting him. Through the open cellar door Jean-Marc was aware of the peaceful solitude of the courtyard. Aside from the chickens there was barely a sound, just the occasional cooing dove.

"Where are Gregoire and Olivier? I haven't seen them all day," Jean-Marc said.

Alphonse's shoulders slumped and his eyes dimmed. "They left today, gone to make contact with some people they know."

"Resistance?" Jean-Marc asked as a jolt of excitement gripped him.

Alphonse hesitated. "Marthe is beside herself with worry. She thought..." He caught himself. "She hoped we could sidestep the war." He looked down and bit his lip off centre. "I suppose, so did I."

Jean-Marc felt the painful strike of this comment, right in his heart. That is how he had felt when Isabelle had first confronted him with her wild talk of leaving France. But he knew now how naive he had been. Since then he had seen everyone's lives unravelling around him, including his own, living as a virtual prisoner in Alphonse's damp cellars. It was vitally important to have a goal for each day – a task – to keep himself sane, to prevent his mind from contemplating the fates of his family. Now Gregoire had given him new hope, the aspiration of joining the resistance movement against the occupiers. But he knew this would have to wait until the boys returned. For now he was trapped in Alphonse's cellars with Federico and Angelica.

"It will be alright," Federico said, placing his hand on Alphonse's shoulder.

"Well then, let's get blending. I say anything from '36 to '39 is in the frame for a special 'Wehrmacht' blend," Jean-Marc said.

Alphonse lifted his head. "Just good enough to convince Bömers it's not the '39 – if he samples it," he said and chuckled.

Jean-Marc nodded. "Exactly."

The three vignerons set to work around the blending table, cackling like the witches in Macbeth. Jean-Marc hadn't had so much frivolous fun since before Isabelle left and he felt his troubles briefly lifting enough to feel normal, even though he was well aware of the latent dangers of their chicanery.

Chapter Twenty-One

The journey to Château Lascombes on the west bank of the Gironde took several hours as they had to cross the river at Pont de Pierre on the northern aspect of Bordeaux. Cycling without lights along small roads and lanes, not daring to use even their dimmed wartime-blue lamps, and pausing frequently to reconnoitre for hidden German patrols, Monique knew that to be captured would most likely mean death. Both she and Patrice had papers valid only in the *zone libre* and they did not have an *Ausweis* to cross the demarcation line, while Anton, Nicolas and Louis were all on the run from STOs. If that was not enough, they were all breaking the curfew.

But the excitement of doing something positive was exhilarating and smothered her fear comprehensively. Monique could not wait to be involved in some real action. That, after all, was what she had signed up for.

They reached the modest but elegantly proportioned château, with its hexagonal turret towering asymmetrically to the right of the gabled entrance, as the weakly resplendent winter sunrise accentuated the russet ivy enveloping the entire building. They dismounted carefully, hot breath misting instantly in the crisp air, their vulnerability as uncomfortable as public nudity. Nervously, they surveyed the flat landscape beyond rows and rows of bare vines.

Monique jumped as the château's front door creaked open. To her surprise a man in a wooden Dupont wheelchair emerged clumsily, bumping into the door frame as he deftly manoeuvred the wheelchair with its dual front hand cranks. He motioned with one hand.

"Get the bicycles inside, quickly!"

Rotating both hand cranks simultaneously, he moved beyond the doorway to allow them space to wheel their bicycles past him. Monique stared at him: he was neatly groomed with combed black hair tinged with grey, small round glasses and surprisingly meaty thighs nestling beneath his loose clothing. She thought he could be approaching sixty and she wondered why he was in the wheelchair, a contraption that closely resembled a dining chair on castors.

"Welcome, Patrice. I see you have brought your friends this time," the man said, shaking Patrice's hand vigorously.

"Brigadier-General Brutinel, may I present my comrades, Louis, Nicolas, Anton," each stepped forward to shake the general's hand in turn, "and Monique."

Brutinel smiled warmly and took her proffered hand in both of his, kissing the back of her knitted brown gloves. "You are all Maquis?" he asked.

Patrice nodded, as did Monique, extracting her hand from the general's warm grasp.

"You have taken enormous risks getting her from Bergerac and I am very grateful," Brutinel said, turning his wicker-styled high-back wheelchair by rotating just one hand crank.

"We do it for France," Monique said.

Brutinel turned his head. "But of course."

A clock chimed in the background. They followed Brutinel into a large, warm kitchen that housed a deeply gouged oak table surrounded by six chairs. Copper skillets and pans hung from hooks on the walls.

"Where are the British airmen?" Patrice asked, tapping out a cigarette and lighting it.

Brutinel wheeled himself across to the cast iron cooking range, and opened a fire door to reveal glowing red logs within before checking on a blackened kettle on the stovetop.

"There is no coffee, I'm afraid, but I can offer you hot toasted barley mixed with chicory." He glanced across at them. "It doesn't taste too bad if you sweeten it."

"You have sugar?" Anton said, blinking his lazy eye as though something was irritating it.

"Thank you, Raymond," Patrice said, walking over to help him at the range.

Monique exchanged a furtive glance with Patrice, recognising the apprehension in his eyes. He always took charge, effectively and without question, but he too was displaying signs of his interminable stress. Long seconds ticked by as they stood and shuffled their frozen feet on the worn flagstone floor, trying to thaw their bodies from the long, cold journey. Monique exhaled onto her cupped hands to revive her blue-tinged fingers while Brutinel busied himself with mugs and hot water. The unspoken words hung heavily on everyone's faces. They had risked their lives travelling across Bordeaux to reach Château Lascombes and now Brutinel was being evasive.

"The airmen, General?" Patrice repeated as he carried mugs of steaming brown liquid to his comrades.

Brutinel sighed. "There have been... developments."

Monique sensed a flutter of nervousness ripple through her comrades as they shuffled their feet. One thing she was becoming accustomed to was that nothing ever seemed to go according to plan in a war. Nicolas limped over to the table and took a chair to ease his discomfort.

"A German platoon has taken up residence in a nearby Château... er... Palmer... just yesterday. They are still settling

in, quite enthusiastic, getting used to movements and so forth."
Brutinel paused, having spun his wheelchair around again to
face all of them, his eyes clearly troubled. "We can't risk
moving the airmen just yet, they are too conspicuous and they
speak no French."

Monique suppressed the urge to question why their safety
had not been considered before they left Bergerac.

"What about the boat from Bayonne?" Anton said.

Brutinel flicked his eyes across at Anton, and then gradually
over each member of the group, lingering on Monique. "We
are set for pick-up on Sunday… so we have four days."

"Four days!" Patrice said. "We can't hide here in the
occupied zone for four days."

Monique was surprised to witness his outburst as Patrice
was usually so calm and controlled. She knew he was tired –
having cycled all night to cover the distance – but she also
realised that being trapped in the occupied zone for four days
was far from optimal. Brutinel nodded in acceptance.

"It is not ideal. But…" He paused upon hearing the creaking
of footsteps descending the staircase. Two young men entered
the room wearing woven jackets and black berets. They looked
as if they had just woken up. Monique sensed her comrades
stiffen as they studied the intruders suspiciously. Brutinel
smiled and lifted both arms in a gesture of welcome. "I may
have a solution, though. Chicory, gentlemen?" he asked the
newcomers.

They nodded, both pushing their hands deep into coat
pockets self-consciously, glancing at the room full of unkempt
strangers from beneath lowered eyebrows. They were young,
Monique could see, even younger than she and Anton and
Louis, and they looked alike, something about their noses.

"Gregoire, Olivier, meet my comrades from the *zone libre*
who have come to rescue the two crashed British airmen. This
is Patrice, er, Monique… er, I'm sorry, please introduce

yourselves, gentlemen." Brutinel turned away with a shrug to the range and poured two more mugs of steaming black liquid.

Everyone shook hands with Gregoire and Olivier and introduced themselves.

"Gregoire and Olivier have refused the STO and are seeking to join a local *maquisade*," Brutinel said, seeking out Patrice's eyes.

Patrice shook his head and studied the floor. "We are already five, General, and we know each other so well."

"Their father is Alphonse Sabron, he has Château Millandes in Saint-Émilion, not far away," Brutinel said.

Patrice shrugged dismissively.

"Château Millandes has miles of underground tunnels and caves in a limestone hillside." Brutinel lowered his head and studied Patrice over his glasses as if to emphasise his point. "If you are to continue helping me with these airmen who keep getting shot down, then having a local safe house in the occupied zone will be invaluable."

Patrice walked to the window, rubbing his chin thoughtfully. He swallowed some chicory, making a face, and then pulled on his Gauloises, emitting a cloud of blue smoke through his nose and mouth as he sighed. Monique knew what he would be thinking: Patrice did not like loose ends and complications that threatened the safety of his small outfit.

"My father is concealing three Jewish winemakers in the caves. They are vast and..." Gregoire said, perhaps sensing Patrice's reluctance.

"Are there any Germans stationed nearby?" Patrice shot back, turning just his head to study Gregoire.

Gregoire hesitated. "There are about a dozen on Jean-Marc's farm, Château Cardinale, the property next door to us."

Patrice exhaled with a guttural sound and raised both arms.

"But they have never bothered us," Olivier said hastily.

"You have only just become an illegal person in the *zone occupée*, it is only now that you will begin to feel whether they bother you or not," Patrice replied icily.

Monique stepped forward and laid a hand on Patrice's arm. "Look, we haven't slept and we're all tired. Can we rest somewhere, General, and then we can talk about this again later?"

Brutinel liked this and smiled his approval back at Monique. "Of course, of course. Gregoire, Olivier, show these gentlemen to your room where they can sleep for a few hours. Monique, er, would you like...?"

"No, no, it's fine, General, I will sleep on the floor with my comrades," Monique said with a cursory smile.

Brutinel nodded. "I have been promised eggs today by Madame Marty, so if she delivers, and she usually does," he smiled as if amusing himself alone, "I will wake you for omelettes at midday."

They placed their mugs on the uneven kitchen table, mumbling thanks, and followed Gregoire up the creaky staircase, Nicolas clinging to the banister with every laboured footstep.

"Is he a real general?" Anton asked as they walked across the landing.

"He fought for the Canadians in the Great War," Patrice explained, nodding.

"Is that why he is in a wheelchair?" Monique said.

Patrice shrugged and they looked across at Gregoire, who sensed their attention.

"I don't know," Gregoire said, frowning. "But I have seen the general walking, though he does not know that."

They were led into a reasonable-sized bedroom with three single beds in it. Monique decided it was too cold to remove her coat and scarf, unlike Nicolas and Louis.

"Two to a bed, you can have your own, Monique," Patrice said.

At the door Gregoire hesitated and turned back to face them all. "I really want to join the Maquis. I cannot spend my days watching the Germans take over our lives, afraid even to go out of my house," he said in impassioned voice.

Patrice nodded as he slumped onto the deep mattress beside Anton. "We'll speak later."

Chapter Twenty-Two

Alphonse, Jean-Marc and Federico stared at the crate of bottles that had been delivered from the co-operative in Saint-Émilion. Alphonse circled the pack like a cat sniffing out the scent of an intruder that had dared to enter its territory. Jean-Marc stood stiff and silent, one finger brushing across his lips as he studied the pale green bottles derisively.

"What the hell is this?" Alphonse said eventually. "We can't bottle red wine in these."

Federico pulled an empty bottle from the crate and held it up to the dim light in the cellar. The glass was so pale, so washed-out and insipid, more turquoise-blue than verdant green.

"We can for the Germans," Federico said tersely.

"*Grand Cru* in... in... it's almost clear glass!" Alphonse protested. "I will have it out with Bömers."

Outside the sound of tyres crunching to a halt on the gravel silenced Alphonse. Federico moved cautiously to a slit in the door and peered out. "You may get your wish sooner than you think," he whispered.

"What?"

"German soldiers!" Jean-Marc said in a tight voice as he peered through another slit. "We must hide."

Federico handed the bottle to Alphonse and hastily followed Jean-Marc into the darkened depths of the cellar. "Angelica, come, quickly," he called out. They disappeared down the central of three tunnels, the sound of their footsteps diminishing into the echoing distance.

Alphonse waited until he could no longer hear them above the sound of a soldier knocking impatiently on the château's front door, and then exited the cellar into bright sunshine. Two Wehrmacht soldiers stood beside a Stabswagen; one held his helmet in the crook of his elbow as he scratched his head, peering around the courtyard.

"Monsieur Sabron?" the soldier said, stiffening.

"What is it?"

"Hauptsturmführer Bömers wants to see you right away."

Alphonse paused, looking behind him to check that the cellar door was shut before striding towards the house. "I will get my coat and tell my wife."

Château Millandes was situated on the outskirts of Saint-Émilion and a journey into the town – past the old Roman walls and down the cobbled roads that led to the market square – did not take long. The town was practically deserted, but for occasional pairs of wandering German soldiers.

Bömers was seated at his desk scrutinising papers through small glasses perched on the tip of his nose. On the edge of his desk stood an engraved silver tray on which had been placed an uncorked bottle of wine and two crystal glasses. It looked very premeditated.

"Alphonse," he said cheerily, gesturing to the empty armchair in front of the desk. "One moment."

He continued to peruse the papers, making the occasional mark with his fountain pen. The air smelled of fresh cigarette smoke and Alphonse's eyes fell upon a smoking cigarette butt in the ashtray beside Bömers.

Finally Bömers looked up and pulled the glasses off his face with a flourish. "When Göring demands I cannot ignore it, you know," he said with a helpless shrug of his shoulders, placing the fountain pen down with deliberate firmness.

"What do you want, Heinz?" Alphonse said, squeezing his beret between his hands on his lap, as though he was rubbing a dog's ears. "I am trying to bottle the 1938 vintage – not easy without labour."

"Mmmh... yes," Bömers said, drawing his eyebrows together and tapping his lips with an extended finger. "No point hanging on with the '38, is there, it has no longevity in it. Might as well be bottled and drunk. I didn't even visit for barrel tasting the '38... well... war had already started for us in any event, too..." His voice trailed off as he perhaps sensed Alphonse's abject display of disinterest. "No matter," Bömers said, standing and moving to the elegant bottle of wine on the tray, "this won't take long."

Across the label, like the slash of a sabre, was printed the mandated red stripe: *For the Wehrmacht.* Alphonse's eyes drifted down to the bottle and, although he didn't know why, he felt instantly uncomfortable, and swallowed.

"1939 was quite a challenging year for you Bordelais, wasn't it? I cannot remember, as a merchant, such a poor vintage since the early '30s." Bömers looked up to Alphonse, who remained initially silent.

"The 1930s were packed with disastrous vintages, you know that. Then there was the depression, prohibition, the revolution in Russia – no one was even buying any wine," Alphonse muttered dejectedly.

"Tell me, how is the current vintage shaping up?" Bömers asked.

"A lot better, just down on yield. Not enough labour, not enough copper sulphate..."

"Ugh," Bömers said with theatrical empathy and raised hands. "The inconveniences of war." He met Alphonse's eyes. "Wine?"

Alphonse nodded. He sensed it was not an invitation to refuse. "The bottles we have received are very pale green in colour, not adequate for red wine," Alphonse said.

Bömers poured wine into each glass, raising one to his nose, which he buried in the bowl, inhaling deeply.

"Ah, Château Palmer 1934. What could be better?" Bömers said, passing a glass to Alphonse. "To your health, and mine."

Bömers raised the glass to his lips and took a deep gulp, swilling it around his mouth, aerating it at his lips and then swallowing as he sat down. Alphonse could not read the expression on his face – a seasoned wine merchant and taster, Bömers gave nothing away.

"Yes, the green bottles, I have heard. It is scandalous, I agree, but nothing I can do, I'm afraid, that is what we're getting if we get anything at all. Wartime shortages," he said, pulling a face and opening his silver cigarette case. "I will be issuing an order to Berlin that all empty bottles are to be returned for reuse. No bottles, no wine. There will most certainly not be an endless supply of glass during the war."

Alphonse grunted, accepting that the subject of the pale green bottles was at an end, beyond their control. Lifting the heavy crystal glass to his face he sniffed the bouquet of the wine: thin, tart and unappealing. He could feel the hairs rising on the back of his neck as his eyes met those of Bömers, who was staring at him with a silly, expectant grin on his face. Something was wrong.

"Cigarette?" Bömers asked, holding out the case.

Alphonse shook his head and took a sip. Expecting something quite different from the insult which jarred his palate, he was unable to prevent a ripple of distaste from corrupting his face. It certainly did not taste as he would expect of Château Palmer 1934.

"What do you think?" Bömers said, leaning forward as he lit his cigarette and reached out for the bottle, showing the label to Alphonse.

Alphonse tensed. The wine was awful and Bömers was no fool.

"Well?" Bömers persisted, goading Alphonse.

Alphonse shrugged and put his glass down.

"It is shit, isn't it?" Bömers erupted suddenly, like a firework exploding. His face became suffused with colour and his eyes bulged. Picking up the bottle, he studied the label with disdain. "Château Palmer 1934? Never, not in a month of Sundays!"

Alphonse swallowed again, the wine having left an unpleasant aftertaste on his palate, like *vin ordinaire* diluted with dishwater.

"Can you imagine Reichsmarschall Göring opening that bottle in Berlin, or the Führer at his guesthouse in Plattehof? Mmmh? Can you? Do you want to know what would happen to Monsieur Verne from Château Palmer if Göring drank this... this...?" Bömers was on his feet, pressing his knuckles onto the desk, veins bulging on his forehead.

Alphonse looked down. He knew what had happened, for he was plotting the same: labelling poor wine such as the 1939 with a superior provenance and fobbing it off as something better than it was, hoping and expecting that *les Boches* would not notice.

"I have Göring contacting me all the time: 'Where is the Pichon '28, where is the La Tour '29, where is the Duhart-Milon '34?' And you expect that I can send this shit to him?"

Alphonse was concerned for his own well-being too as he thought about his best wines, bricked up in the depths of his cellars away from prying German eyes, and he knew many of the Bordelais had done the same. Indeed, he had encouraged them. How much of this did Bömers know?

"What have you done with him?" Alphonse said eventually, quietly.

Bömers shot a derisive look at Alphonse, turning and walking to the window where he planted his feet apart and pushed his hands into his tunic pockets.

"What, Verne? I have had him arrested. He will be lucky if he only spends the rest of the war in prison, a message to all the Bordelais that I will not tolerate such..." he withdrew one hand and clenched it into a tight fist, his skin blanching, "such... insolence, daring to insult me." He spun back to meet Alphonse's eyes. "I did not run Reidemeister & Ulrichs for all these years without being able to spot bad wine. Do people not realise that?"

Alphonse looked down, hoping that Bömers did not suspect him and, more importantly, could not detect the guilt he was trying to hide.

"If Göring was here he would have had Verne shot, I'm sure of it," Bömers said, calming slightly.

Visible through the tall mayoral window a blue sky highlighted silhouettes of bare trees and smoky chimneys across Saint-Émilion. Momentarily, it seemed so normal that Alphonse deliberately looked away.

"How did you come to move from Reidemeister to the SS, Heinz?" Alphonse said quietly without looking up, thinking back to the days when he and Bömers would chat and discuss the nuances of each vintage over lunch at Château Millandes. He remembered Bömers' visits to Saint-Émilion, being feted by the top châteaux where he had come to know the winemakers personally. They had become friends in addition to selling their best wines through Bömers' import business. It was not that long ago and yet it felt like a lifetime as he sat in Bömers' office, intimidated by his military demeanour and SS uniform.

Alphonse began to regret his insolent question, instantly feeling that he may have overstepped the mark.

"It is no secret that Göring hates me," Bömers began quietly, much to Alphonse's surprise, though he continued to stare out of the window. "My father was a senator in Bremen when Göring was Prime Minister in Saxony." He paused. "They did not get along. In truth, my father despised Göring and he knew it."

Bömers returned to his sumptuous leather seat, sinking into it without looking at Alphonse. "My father publicly snubbed Göring once and the man never forgot it. After my father died Göring forced me to join the Nazi party or lose the business." He hesitated and then his eyes met Alphonse's. The pain was visible. "I could see what was coming and that war was inevitable. You have to do what is necessary in a war to survive, no?" He looked at Alphonse for long seconds. "We are all doing it." His eyes drifted down to the bottle of Château Palmer '34.

Bömers extracted another cigarette from the case and lit it with the impatient flick of a match. Alphonse felt pity. Not for the occupiers and certainly not for Germans, but for his old friend. He realised that Bömers was potentially in a more precarious situation than even he was.

"If a bottle of wine like that landed on Göring's table…" Bömers shook his head. "He is no fool when it comes to wine, you know, not like many Germans, and he is not forgiving, and he certainly does not forget."

Alphonse realised that Bömers was afraid too, afraid of retribution from Berlin, from heavyweights in the Nazi elite.

"Is that all?" Alphonse said, grabbing the armrests in preparation for standing.

"Make sure everyone knows what happened to Monsieur Verne, and why," Bömers said, steely eyes fixed on Alphonse.

Alphonse drew a deep breath and nodded, regretting that he and Federico had blended 1939 wine into the 1937 bottling. At least that was less obvious than trying to pass such inferior wine off as the glorious 1934 vintage, which was simply arrogant and foolish. In a normal world he would rather have chewed his hand off than risk his coveted promise of *Grand Cru* status with bad wine behind his label. But this was not a normal world.

"One more thing," Bömers said as Alphonse's hand touched the brass doorknob.

Alphonse turned slightly, clutching the beret tightly in his right hand.

"Do you know what happened to Monsieur Valadie?"

Alphonse's heart skipped a beat. "Jean-Marc, my neighbour at Château Cardinale?"

Bömers nodded his head with a steady beat.

Alphonse shrugged. "He fled as soon as he heard of the German invasion."

Bömers continued to nod, maintaining eye contact with Alphonse. "Where did he go?"

Alphonse pulled a face. "Spain, I think."

Bömers shuffled papers on his desk, searching for something. "Ah." He picked up a sheet. "You see, we have information that his wife, Isabelle Valadie, was deported from the internment camp at Merignac."

Alphonse's heart was beating in his throat, impeding his attempt to swallow. Though he knew about Isabelle he was well aware that he was not supposed to be privy to the information.

"And his children?" Alphonse said.

Bömers twisted his mouth and tapped the paper. "There were Valadie children deported to Paris and then from there back to Germany – they could be his." He looked up. "Two boys?"

"A boy and a girl," Alphonse said, his mouth dry. "Why are you telling me this?"

"General von Faber is a meticulous man, you see, being in charge of Bordeaux, and he has brought this to my attention."

Alphonse felt the colour draining from his face, his eyes losing their point of focus. "Brought what to your attention?"

"That there is no record anywhere of Jean-Marc Valadie. Would he not have been with his wife and children?"

Alphonse felt like a cornered animal, perspiration soaking his armpits. "Why did he tell you this?" Alphonse feared that his former wine merchant friend may now have turned rat-catcher.

Bömers shrugged casually. "I suppose because I know so many of the Bordelais, perhaps he thought I might have heard something."

"Well there are soldiers garrisoned at Château Cardinale, so you know he is not there," Alphonse said with no attempt to soften the irritation in his voice.

Bömers inhaled on his cigarette and nodded. "No, he isn't there, not anymore."

Alphonse wondered if this was a veiled reference to the discovered evidence of Jean-Marc's concealment in the cellar at Château Cardinale. Was he therefore under suspicion, as Jean-Marc's neighbour, merely by association?

"So you have no idea where he is?" Bömers said.

Alphonse hesitated. He knew that he was being tested and he could not come up short.

"I am shocked to hear about his family and I sincerely hope he is safe," Alphonse said, looking down.

"So you don't know?"

Alphonse looked up at Bömers and shook his head.

"No."

Chapter Twenty-Three

Monique slept for several hours, waking all alone in the darkened bedroom with achingly cold feet. She could hear her comrades downstairs, muted masculine voices locked in grave discussion.

Slipping on her solid leather boots she made her way down to the smoky smell of the *salon* where she found everyone gathered in front of a spitting log fire in the open hearth. On the table were two unlabelled bottles of red wine, the flickering glow of orange dancing on them frivolously, and a few lumps of soft white cheese on a wooden board. They all looked up as she entered the room.

"Ah, you're awake," Patrice said, motioning her to approach.

"When did you…?" Monique asked.

"Not long ago. Come, we're discussing when to leave."

"Leave?"

Brutinel was facing her in his wheelchair, his back to the fireplace, wearing a burgundy robe and slippers, clutching a glass of red wine in one hand. On the wall opposite Monique a large gilt-framed oil painting of Château Lascombes dominated between floor-length blue curtains.

"We're going to spend three nights in Monsieur Sabron's cellars," Nicolas began, nodding towards Gregoire and Olivier.

"And then return here to pick up the two airmen on Sunday and deliver them to a cargo ship in Bayonne," Anton finished, cutting a corner off the *chabichou* and popping it into his smiling mouth.

Monique accepted a glass of wine from Louis and looked from one unshaven face to another. Gregoire and Olivier resembled eager pups – keen for anything – sitting forward with hands clasped together on their knees. They looked like excitable schoolboys.

"Have you considered that your plan requires four more journeys across occupied Bordeaux?" Monique said.

They all stared at her and Monique suddenly felt like a coward, the odd one out.

"It will be dangerous," Brutinel acknowledged, holding Monique's gaze, "you are right, Monique. But we think that staying here, so many of you, with a new German garrison close by, is a greater risk. It's not just your safety, remember, it is the whole network we have established for smuggling out British airmen that would be at risk."

Monique looked down, ashamed for being so short-sighted and declaring her sense of self-preservation so publicly. She too desired action, to be part of something that bore positive fruits, or at the very least hurt the Germans.

"I also think that we should meet Monsieur Sabron and explore his cave cellars. They may provide an excellent base for us, much closer than Bergerac," Patrice added.

Anton was nodding, smoke curling around his face from a glowing Gauloises; Louis tucked into the cheese; Gregoire nodded enthusiastically.

"You will like the caves at Château Millandes, they are long and tortuous. No one will ever find you in there," Gregoire said.

Monique nodded as she began to consider some of the beneficial possibilities. "Will we be able to set up a radio from there to keep in contact with, say, London?"

Patrice frowned, and Anton pulled a face.

"It would save us having to take the risk of entering Bordeaux to meet our contact," Monique said.

"I'm sure we could," Gregoire said. "I know the local school science teacher who has access to radio components."

"How will we get there?" Monique said, finally succumbing to the cheese, her hollow stomach growling audibly.

"You'll take my car and travel tonight," Brutinel said, tapping his legs. "I have no use for it."

Olivier and Gregoire exchanged a furtive look with subtly raised eyebrows that Monique did not miss, but when she glanced at Patrice he nodded, and she felt a little more at ease.

Brutinel's car was a black, hearse-like Citroën, devoid of hubcaps and as dirty as a ploughing horse. Bolted to its rear end was a black drum from which smoke escaped constantly. A sturdy metal pipe protruded from the drum and snaked its makeshift way over the roof of the car to a radiator mounted on a cylinder in front of the Citroën's corroded chrome grill. Monique had never seen anything remotely like it before and thought that she might, in a different time and place, have mistaken it for a mobile distillery.

"You know how to work a gasogene, Patrice?" Brutinel said from his wheelchair at the front steps.

Patrice nodded.

"There are bags of chipped firewood in the back, enough to get you to Saint-Émilion," Brutinel said.

"Thank you, Raymond. We will be back on Saturday night." Patrice shook Brutinel's hand and descended the steps two at a time to the car. The darkness was broken only by the twinkling of stars and the sliver of a new moon rising over Château

Lascombes' sleeping vineyards. "Monique, Gregoire and Anton, you come with me."

Nicolas grabbed Patrice by the coat sleeve. "Be careful."

Patrice grinned. "See you soon, my friend."

Once inside the car, cold and smelling overpoweringly of damp upholstery and rubber mats, Patrice pulled off quickly. As soon as he reached the road he turned off the blue-tinted headlights.

"What the hell is this thing?" Monique asked, pointing to the thick pipe descending the left side of the windscreen down to the radiator in front.

"There is no petrol," Patrice said, leaning forward to squint into the darkness. "The gasogenes run on wood-gas." He turned and looked at her, his eyes narrowing quizzically. "Our family used one after the Great War as well, lots of people did. You've never seen one before?"

Monique regretted asking the question. She had given too much away and for the second time that afternoon felt the eyes of everyone upon her. Her inexperience was putting her at risk.

"It's a bit of a home-job this one, isn't it?" she said mockingly, trying to divert attention from her foolish admission.

Anton snorted in the back seat. "It's not the most professional conversion I've seen."

Monique laughed, relieved, sensing an opportunity. "Me neither."

Patrice seemed to know the back roads of Margaux well. He drove cautiously down the D2 past Château Cantenac before taking the lesser and windier D209 at Labarde. Monique could see perspiration on his upper lip and forehead even though the unheated car was like an ice chest. His eyes never left the purple-black road as they negotiated between rows of vineyards left and right of them. Once they had crossed the

Louise River heading ever closer to Bordeaux, Monique knew that this was where the greatest danger lay, as German presence in the city was considerable. They controlled the port and defended the coastline, barely forty miles due west of Bordeaux, using the city as their headquarters and operations room.

The most perilous part was once again going to be crossing the Garonne on the Pont de Pierre. Heavily guarded and within a heartbeat of central Bordeaux, there was no easy way to approach it. Patrice headed east again down Avenue de Labarde as it snaked through vineyards parallel to the Garonne, providing the option at least of diverting quickly into the vineyards in the event of a roadblock or approaching patrol.

Anton smoked nervously, and Patrice was never without a cigarette dangling out of his mouth. Gregoire accepted a few from Anton but seemed to cough more than savour them. Monique figured he was simply trying to fit in. She looked down at the heavy metal lump, the MAS pistol she held for Patrice, nestled against her heavy woollen slacks and warmed by her body. She hadn't fired a gun since her training and wondered how easily she would be able to shoot at an enemy soldier if confronted. What if a patrol rounded the corner in front of them? She would have to fire at them while Patrice steered the car into the vineyards. Kill or be killed.

"I'm going to pull into the Parc Floral so that we can fill the burner with wood. I don't want to run out when we're crossing the *pont*," Patrice said.

The car's tyres began to crunch on gravel as they left the tiny Avenue de Labarde, trundling down a lane lined with bare, wintry trees. Monique squinted through the grimy windscreen, trying to see where they were heading in the pitch blackness. Patrice guided the car into a copse of bushes beside the silvery oblong lake. With the engine off they sat in silence for several minutes, observing the surroundings carefully, looking for movement, the flash of a light or a glowing cigarette.

"How far to the bridge?" Monique said.

"It's very close," Patrice replied, glancing at her and then down into her lap. "Is it loaded?"

Monique lifted the pistol, slid the magazine out and checked that it was full before clicking it back into the handle. She nodded to Patrice. In the back seat she heard Gregoire and Anton doing something similar.

"Do we cross in the dark?" Anton said from the back.

"That's what I'm wondering. If we're spotted during the curfew we're dead. At least in daylight we may not be stopped," Patrice said.

"But in daylight…" Anton began.

"Why don't we cross on foot like we did last time? It gives us more manoeuvrability," Monique suggested.

"And the car?" Patrice said.

"Leave it here for when we come back," Monique said. "It's not far from here to Saint-Émilion. We can walk it."

"She's right," Gregoire said. "We'll be more invisible on foot."

"We should have come by bicycle again," Anton muttered. "We are too conspicuous in this car."

Patrice considered this in silence, biting his lip on one side. Monique studied her wristwatch. Midnight.

"No," Patrice said eventually, opening his door. "I don't like it. Let's fill the burner and keep going. If we leave the car it will be taken. Gasogenes cost a fortune to convert."

Monique met Anton's eyes in the rear-view mirror. He looked as uncomfortable as she felt. Patrice emptied two bags of wood chips into the smoking burner and clamped it shut. Soon they were off, in silence, driving down the darkened road and turning off quickly into small side roads that weaved their

126

way between sleeping homes as they slowly approached the main route crossing the Pont de Pierre.

Within sight of the bridge, they stopped in Rue de la Rousselle and watched movements carefully. Two armed soldiers guarded the Bordeaux end of the bridge, standing together, smoking cigarettes. The road looked deserted.

"What now?" Monique said. "They weren't here yesterday."

Just then headlights strafed the bridge, illuminating the two guards, who cast long shadows across the road. Patrice cut the engine and they instinctively ducked their heads. It was a military truck approaching from the west, and it stopped right in front of the two guards on the Pont de Pierre. Monique could feel her heat beating, could smell the sweat of primal fear in the cramped car, mixed with gun oil from the MAS pistol clutched in her right hand, inches from her face. Minutes ticked by.

"Now what?" Anton said.

"We wait," Patrice said.

"Jesus, they came out of nowhere. We could have been halfway across the bridge," Gregoire said.

Patrice interpreted the fearful outburst as criticism. "No one said it was failsafe. Sneaking around is dangerous," he said tersely.

Soldiers alighted from the rear of the truck and stood around on the bridge lighting cigarettes, rifles slung over their shoulders. Sounds of their gruff conversation and laughter wafted on the breeze to reach the car.

"Shit, this is crazy," Anton said, sitting back heavily and covering his stubbly face with one hand. "If they don't hand us over to the Gestapo they will shoot us."

Suddenly a muffled boom echoed through the air. The soldiers sprang into action, clutching their rifles, dropping glowing cigarettes. The silent night air filled with animated voices in an unfamiliar language.

"Something's happened," Patrice said, leaning forward on the steering wheel and watching the bridge with narrowed eyes.

"Where did that come from?" Monique said. "It sounded like an explosion."

"I'm not sure," Patrice said. "But I hope it was this side of the river."

Soldiers began to climb into the truck, which reversed off the western end of the Pont de Pierre with a grinding of gears, and then roared off down the main road heading into Bordeaux, billowing clouds of engine fumes swirling behind it. As the truck passed the end of Rue de la Rousselle everyone in the car instinctively shrank from sight.

"The guards are gone. Let's go!" Anton whispered urgently.

"Just wait a moment," Patrice said, his eyes glued to the bridge.

One minute, two, three – it seemed like an eternity.

"There's nothing, let's go!" Anton hissed again.

Patrice started the car and they eased cautiously onto the main road, turning to face the Pont de Pierre, staring down its barrel-like thoroughfare, flanked by cast iron lamp posts shouldering lights that glowed feebly in the Stygian atmosphere. There was no going back now. Monique felt sick with fear, her pulse thudding somewhere beneath her tongue as they crossed the bridge. They could not in that instant have been more exposed and vulnerable, devoid of any possible escape plan should a patrol round a corner either in front or behind them, something that could happen in a heartbeat. Within seconds they had crossed the bridge and at the very first turning, tyres squealing, Patrice headed sharply off the main road onto Rue Calvimont and then Rue de la Benauge and Faure and Cours Gambetta, sticking to the smallest, windiest little roads.

No one spoke, though with every passing kilometre optimism grew. There could be no celebration though, not until they had reached their destination safely.

Chapter Twenty-Four

Jean-Marc swirled a calibrated glass beaker, one quarter full of Merlot, before thrusting his nose into it and inhaling deeply. Closing his eyes, he took a mouthful and immersed his palate in its smooth, plummy red-fruit flavours languorously. He lowered his head and made a note with a crudely sharpened pencil, his cheeks still filled with wine. Pushing the beaker aside, he picked up another labelled *Cabernet* and repeated the ritual, savouring hints of chocolate, black pepper and tannin.

"Blending your wines before *élévage?*" Federico said, leaning over Jean-Marc's shoulder and studying his notes.

Jean-Marc shrugged and reached for the third beaker of deep red, almost purple juice: Malbec.

"I have always blended after at least a year in barrel," Jean-Marc said, "but now that I see what Alphonse does…"

"You think it's better to blend early?" Federico said, raising his eyebrows to expose heavily veined eyes.

"Well, Château Millandes is almost *Grand Cru*," Jean-Marc said, unable to strangle his envious tone. "What do you do?"

The old man smiled. "I blend early, but only with half my barrels."

Jean-Marc chuckled and turned back to the beaker of Malbec. "Keep your options open, eh?"

The older man sat down beside Jean-Marc on a rough wooden stool. "What is your blend?"

Jean-Marc puckered his lips and decanted a little from each of the three beakers into a dirty wine glass. "My initial thought is sixty per cent Merlot, thirty per cent Cab Franc and ten per cent Malbec. What do you think?"

Federico took the glass and inhaled the bouquet, long and thoughtfully. Jean-Marc watched his face and eyes for subconscious reaction. The old man took a mouthful and appeared to rinse his teeth with it. He angled his head and placed the wine glass down and slid it across the table towards Jean-Marc, who repeated the same actions. The two men sat in silence, enveloped in the musty aromas of damp stone, oak barrels and spilled red wine, analysing the wine as it warmed in their mouths.

"The Malbec is not very ripe," Jean-Marc said eventually.

Federico nodded, perhaps waiting diplomatically for Jean-Marc to initiate criticism of his own blend.

"I would put more Merlot in the blend, no more than five per cent Malbec," Federico said.

Jean-Marc opened his mouth but did not reply. Outside the gloomy cellar the sounds of a commotion burst forth. A vehicle had come to a halt on the gravel and numerous footsteps crunched on the pebbles, intermingled with excitable voices.

"Soldiers?" Federico whispered, frowning.

"No," Jean-Marc said quietly, raising a hand. "They are French…"

"Milice?"

Jean-Marc listened intently, moving to a crack in the door and squinting through it with a cupped eye. Upon hearing Alphonse's voice he suddenly realised who it was.

"It's Gregoire!" he said, raising his voice and moving to open the cellar door, sliding the heavy bolt across and heaving the enormous door to one side.

Bursting into the bright crispness of an early dawn, he was met by the sight of Alphonse embracing an unshaven Gregoire beside a large black gasogene-converted Citroën.

Marthe emerged from the doorway with uncharacteristic haste, dabbing her eyes with her upturned, flour-dusted apron as tears streamed down her cheeks. "My boy, my boy…" And then, glancing around at the gathered entourage, "Where is Olivier?" she said.

Jean-Marc's eyes were drawn to the figures of three strangers: a man in a brown coat and black beret with pocked facial skin and curly hair; a squat man with hands pushed deep into a leather jacket, his beret pulled down close to one half-closed eye; and a young woman with black hair, turquoise-blue eyes and flawless skin, her figure keenly masked by baggy, stout woollen slacks. Protectively cocooned in a thick green scarf, her fine cheekbones and demure lips accentuated a delicacy that Jean-Marc found compellingly beautiful.

"Mama, Papa, may I introduce my comrades, Patrice, Anton and Monique," Gregoire said, pulling from his mother's embrace and rushing over to drag his friends by the arm to meet his parents.

They shook hands without exchanging a word, lots of nodding and cautious smiles. Jean-Marc could see Alphonse was scrutinising them, trying to ascertain the sort of company his son had stumbled upon.

"You travelled during the curfew?" Marthe said, the censure evident in her voice.

Patrice lowered his head slightly and nodded. Jean-Marc stepped forward.

"I am Jean-Marc, vigneron there at Château Cardinale," he said, gesticulating perfunctorily towards his property beyond the trees and extending his hand eagerly. "Are you…" he hushed his voice, "Maquis?"

132

Patrice shook his hand, but looked back suspiciously. "Is that where the Germans are garrisoned?" he asked, glancing across towards Château Cardinale in the distance.

"Let's go inside, Papa, please, we need coffee and food," Gregoire said excitedly.

Patrice turned to consider the black Citroën. "We should conceal the car," he said.

"Absolutely," Monique agreed, her eager eyes scanning the courtyard.

"In the barn," Alphonse said, walking across the courtyard towards the wooden gabled building that partly obscured Château Cardinale from view. He opened a creaking timber door to reveal the inside of a poorly maintained roof, devoid of a great many tiles through which light streamed.

With the gasogene safely stowed, the warmth of Château Millandes' kitchen welcomed the newcomers as they stamped their frozen feet on the flagstone floor and took seats around the Provencal-styled oak table. Marthe presented them with steaming mugs of chicory.

"No coffee, I'm afraid. But we do have a few freshly laid eggs I can boil," she said, making eye contact with Monique.

"Thank you, *madame*, that would be most kind," Monique replied in an accent that Jean-Marc found curiously northern.

Monique's fresh dissimilarity to the rest attracted Jean-Marc as he stared at the woman, her warm smile and sincere gaze seemingly at odds with the ragtag band of Maquis gathered distrustfully in their midst. They all appeared closed, guarded and unlikely to reveal much.

"Why did you take such a risk, travelling during curfew?" Alphonse asked the assembled group.

"Papa," Gregoire began, "we need your help, in matters of great importance against the Germans."

"Where is Olivier?" Alphonse said.

"He is staying with General —"

133

"No, no names!" Patrice cut in, raising a cautionary finger in Gregoire's direction.

Gregoire stared back with bovine eyes and even Alphonse was visibly struck by the abrupt caution.

"No names," Patrice repeated.

"He is quite safe, *monsieur*, with more of our colleagues," Monique said softly, smiling at Alphonse and then at Jean-Marc in turn, as though trying to mollify them both after Patrice's insensitivity.

"We have heard that you have very long cellars ideal for concealing things," Patrice said, pulling out and lighting a Gauloises, his eyes fixed on Alphonse.

"Things?" Alphonse said, caution audible in his voice. "Like what?"

"Us, Papa," Gregoire said. "Us!"

Alphonse looked at his son, rubbing his stubbly chin with calloused fingers. "What about Olivier?" Alphonse replied.

"Yes, Olivier too," Gregoire said.

Patrice exhaled a cloud of smoke. "There are five of us, Monsieur Sabron, plus your sons. We just need a place to hide out for a few days, now and then."

"Where do you live?" Alphonse asked.

"We are from the *zone libre*," Patrice replied evasively.

"So you have no papers to be here," Alphonse said, sighing.

"No. Some of us are avoiding STOs... like Gregoire," Patrice said, gesticulating towards Gregoire with his glowing Gauloises.

"Are you Jews?" Jean-Marc said without thinking.

Their eyes collectively spun around to meet his. "No," said Patrice, as if denying a slur.

Silence.

"Eggs are ready," Marthe said, bringing an oval plate to the table with half a dozen hard-boiled eggs on it, surrounded by hunks of baguette.

"Thank you, *madame*," Monique said, touching Marthe on the arm and smiling broadly. Jean-Marc liked her voice, her unusual accent and her disarming eyes.

"I am already living in the cellars," Jean-Marc said, picking the shell off an egg. "Can I join you?"

Patrice ignored this question, but Monique smiled at him.

"What do I get from taking such a risk?" Alphonse said.

"The chance to fight back, *monsieur*," Anton said, raising the eyebrow above his good eye.

"We may be able to help you with supplies now and then, whatever we can take from *les Boches*," Patrice said.

"Do you realise there is a garrison of German soldiers next door in Jean-Marc's property?" Alphonse said, turning away thoughtfully to consider his new predicament.

"Yes, that's what worries me," Patrice said.

Alphonse stopped in front of the warm cooking range and placed both hands on the chrome rail. Marthe walked over and placed one hand on his shoulder.

"It worries me too," Alphonse said.

"We could have both boys back home, Alphonse. Would that not be worth it?" Marthe said quietly.

Alphonse drew a deep breath and sighed. "I know the *weinführer* in Saint-Émilion and he has been known to call or send his men here without any warning. You will have to stay out of sight, as Jean-Marc does," Alphonse said resignedly, his eyes meeting Jean-Marc's.

"Do you want me to show them the cellars and caves?" Jean-Marc asked, feeling a shiver of anticipation ripple through him.

"Please, that would be most helpful," Patrice said, rising immediately and draining his mug of chicory, businesslike to the core.

Alphonse raised a hand in a helpless twirl above his head without turning around. "Make yourself at home."

135

"Thank you, *monsieur*," Monique said. "You are doing a wonderful thing for the cause, for the fight to liberate France."

"You dream of liberating France, do you?" Alphonse asked.

"What else can one dream of, *monsieur*?"

Alphonse turned and nodded wearily towards Monique. Jean-Marc caught her eye and his heart jumped as she looked right at him, lingering. Patrice and Anton had followed Gregoire out into the courtyard and Jean-Marc waited for Monique. Up close she did not smell as sweet as she looked; long hours and perhaps days on the road, the life undercover, in hiding, in danger.

"That is your wine farm next door, *monsieur*?" Monique said, pointing past the barn as they stepped onto the crunching gravel.

"Château Cardinale. It has been in my family for four generations."

"The Germans just kicked you out of your house?"

Jean-Marc nodded. It was both saddening and humiliating to admit it to a stranger.

"Your family?" Monique said.

Jean-Marc lowered his eyes. "Deported."

Monique hesitated. "To Germany?"

Jean-Marc shrugged and immediately Monique gasped, raising a hand to her mouth, her eyes locked on his face, the skin beneath them creased as if she was in pain. "Were they… are you…"

Jean-Marc nodded. Her mouth fell open just enough to reveal small white teeth. "My God, I am so sorry." She took a few ponderous steps towards the cellar. "I have seen it, you know, trainloads of people being deported from Bordeaux, bound for Berlin."

Jean-Marc sensed from her reaction exactly what he himself feared: that he would never see his wife and children again. They crunched their way across the courtyard to the mighty cellar door, the entrance to Alphonse's great winemaking enterprise and the cave tunnels beyond.

"Are you from Normandy?" Jean-Marc said, intrigued by her accent.

Monique smiled and inclined her head slightly. "More or less."

"You're a long way from home," he said.

She smiled back at him as they entered the semi-gloom of the cellar, enveloped by the dank smell of limestone, oak and fermenting grapes. Gregoire, Patrice and Anton were in a huddle in the centre of the cavernous room, looking about at wooden barrels stacked high at one end and presses and lagars dotted about. Monique was drawn to the blending table upon which Jean-Marc's wine samples and handwritten notes still lay amongst glass pipettes, flasks and test tubes.

"What is this?" she asked, running her hands across the roughly textured surface, spreading her arms out wide and taking it all in.

"I am blending varietals for this year's harvest," Jean-Marc said, walking up beside her.

She lifted the scrap of paper with his notes scribbled on it. "Looks complicated."

"I could explain it to you, but then I'd have to kill you. Such are the secrets of Bordeaux."

She turned her smiling face to him and they both laughed. Monique tilted her head back, revealing the creamy skin of her slender neck beneath the scarf. He couldn't remember when last he had laughed in this way, even in his own house, even before the occupation when Isabelle had fled with his children. It felt emancipating, infectious. But, more than that, the laughter was intoxicating.

"Jean-Marc!"

It was Alphonse, stern, leaning into the entrance of the cellar. Jean-Marc cleared his throat and guided Monique by her elbow towards the group in the centre of the room.

"Excuse me, Monique. Gregoire will show you the rest," Jean-Marc said.

She nodded to him and he watched as she melted away into the shadows in the company of the men, his moment basking in her natural energy spent. Jean-Marc could see by Alphonse's face that he was troubled.

"What is it?" Jean-Marc said.

"I need to speak to you. Come."

Alphonse led him out of the cellar and into the château.

Chapter Twenty-Five

Alphonse did not stop until both he and Jean-Marc were in the *salon* of Château Millandes. Alphonse held one hand up to his face for several moments, as though it held back his inner thoughts, before lifting his eyes to meet Jean-Marc's.

"What do you think?"

Jean-Marc shrugged. "About what?"

"Them." Alphonse jerked his head in the direction of the cellar.

Jean-Marc had not given any thought to this, not in that way. So far, he had enjoyed their company and basked in the excitement of their dangerous lives. "Why do you ask?"

"I need to know what you think of them, the people Gregoire and Olivier have taken up with."

Jean-Marc felt the intensity boiling off Alphonse, as though unexpressed concerns had been simmering and needed airing.

"They seem OK, Alphonse. I mean, I barely know them, but..."

"Exactly – what do we know of them? They could be criminals, gangsters, or worse," Alphonse said, leaning closer to Jean-Marc until he could smell the old man's breath.

"What is worse?" Jean-Marc said, recoiling slightly.

"Communists."

"What?"

"I don't want their minds bent by twisted propaganda. You know how vulnerable and impressionable they are right now."

Jean-Marc stifled a snort, which he regretted. "We're at war."

Alphonse shook his head and turned away. "And I don't much like that Patrice."

Jean-Marc knew what Alphonse meant, for he too had not warmed to Patrice in their brief introduction. There was aloofness about him, a distant detachment that imbued him with a sense of danger, and eyes that seldom met and held his own.

"Do you think he is the leader?" Alphonse added.

"It looked that way. You know, they are guerrilla fighters, Alphonse, they spend their days hiding, not knowing who to trust." Jean-Marc shrugged his shoulders. "Perhaps we should give them a chance, eh?"

"Perhaps."

"Monique seems a very level-headed woman."

"Yes," Alphonse said in a ponderous tone, "Monique..." He turned to face Jean-Marc again. "A northerner, though."

Jean-Marc wondered how far from Saint-Émilion Alphonse had ever ventured in his life. Even he had not journeyed beyond Poitiers.

"Keep your eyes and ears open for me, Jean-Marc, please. I want to know that my boys are in the right company."

"Of course."

Silence descended on the two men.

"I am very worried about the number of people I'm suddenly concealing on my property. If they catch us..." Alphonse began, shaking his head disconsolately.

Jean-Marc placed a hand on Alphonse's shoulder. "I will make sure we all stay out of sight. Thank you, Alphonse."

Alphonse suddenly frowned. "What if they discover the gasogene?"

"Tell them…" Jean-Marc said thoughtfully, "tell them it's mine and you're using it as I've disappeared."

Alphonse stared at him, unconvinced.

"How will they know?" Jean-Marc raised both arms.

Alphonse's expression was unreadable, his watery eyes looking every bit their fifty-eight years of age. Older men were not built to withstand the punishment of war, Jean-Marc thought, before wondering whether indeed he was.

"I have a bad feeling about all this. But I don't know what else to do: I have a duty to protect my sons and my friends – the Masis."

Suddenly he grabbed Jean-Marc's hand and sandwiched it between both of his, the intimacy of his warm but calloused vigneron's skin quite unfamiliar to Jean-Marc.

"You will help me, won't you?"

Jean-Marc emitted a gentle chuckle, as if to alleviate some of the palpable emotion. "Of course I will."

Chapter Twenty-Six

"*Merde!*" Patrice said loudly, crumpling the scrap of paper in a balled fist.

Moments earlier the note had been brought into the cellar by Alphonse, announcing that he had received it from an unknown man who had appeared from nowhere.

"He said only five words to me: 'Alphonse Sabron?' followed by 'For Patrice, urgent.'" The man had then retreated just as surreptitiously into the shadows that obscured his face, tightly wedged as it was between a black beret and a voluminous scarf.

"Who was it?" Patrice demanded, visibly paling as he took the note from Alphonse.

"I have never seen him before. He had a bushy moustache, that's all I could make out," Alphonse replied, "and a gruff voice."

They were all gathered in the cellar around two upturned barrels upon which misshapen candles encrusted in molten wax tendrils rested, surrounded by several enamelled mugs. Anton sat on the floor and whittled a piece of wood with his Laguiole bone-handled knife, squinting at his work with his good eye; Gregoire was reading François Mauriac's *Les Anges Noirs* while resting against the basket press and biting his fingernails; Monique stood beside Patrice, studying a map, her face betraying her anxiety.

"Who knows that you're here?" Jean-Marc said over his shoulder, his hands still firmly applied to barriques that he was gently and methodically rotating through thirty degrees.

Chalked onto the barrel ends beneath Jean-Marc's fingers were the year, details about the wine contained within and its vineyard provenance: *'38 – Merl – SF1/4*. This was Alphonse's wine he was tending – all his own wine maturing in barrels was abandoned at Château Cardinale and probably being consumed ungraciously by the soldiers.

Patrice shot a thoughtful look at Jean-Marc. "Olivier, the rest of our group, and..." Patrice hesitated, "the general."

"Who is 'the general'?" Jean-Marc asked.

Patrice ignored this and ripped the envelope open with dirty fingernails. His eyes appeared to burn holes into the notepaper. "*Merde!*"

Anton stopped whittling and Gregoire lowered his book.

"What now?" Monique said, her face draining of colour as her eyes darted eagerly across the notepaper in Patrice's grasp.

Jean-Marc approached with growing curiosity, his eyes drawn to the note, but Patrice quickly crushed it and pushed it into the candle flame, turning it to ash. Patrice then turned away and began to walk around the upturned barrels like a moon orbiting its planet, one hand pressed to his chin.

"Fuck!" Patrice said.

"We have to go back," Monique said.

"We can't, it'd be suicide," Patrice shot back.

"What is going on?" Anton asked, standing up and walking towards Monique.

Jean-Marc felt their covert glances in his direction, as though he was untrustworthy, an intruder, and undeservedly privy to Maquis business.

"Is Olivier alright?" Gregoire asked.

"Yes, he's fine," Monique said, turning quickly to reassure him with a flash of a smile.

"Is the mission off?" Anton said, upturning both palms.

Patrice stopped walking and stared at Anton, eventually nodding his head.

"But what about Nicolas and Louis?" Anton said.

Patrice sank down onto a wooden box filled with empty wine bottles up against a limestone wall. "That is the problem," he said, closing his eyes in despair.

"And the airmen?" Anton persisted.

Patrice glared at Anton and then at Jean-Marc, who sensed Patrice's innate distrust, and suddenly, it angered him. "Oh come on, I'm in here with you, up to my neck in your business, hiding from *les Boches* just like you. I want to join you, for God's sake, not turn you in!" Jean-Marc exploded.

"Tell him," Monique said quietly, looking sympathetically at Jean-Marc and smiling ever so slightly, as if in apology.

Anton nodded. Gregoire's opinion seemed not to count as nobody cast an eye in his direction.

"Where is the old man?" Patrice said, looking around cautiously.

"Federico and his wife are asleep in one of the tunnels," Jean-Marc said irritably.

Patrice nodded. "Careless talk costs lives, you understand – the fewer people that know, the better. It's not that I don't trust you or anything…"

"Sure," Jean-Marc said sarcastically.

Patrice sighed. "Our mission is to deliver two airmen who have been shot down to a port for safe passage out of France."

"British?" Jean-Marc ventured.

Patrice nodded. "An attack by the British on the port of Bordeaux a few nights ago caused considerable damage and -"

"The explosion we heard?" Anton said, angling his head keenly.

"Anyway, the Germans have increased their numbers and beefed up security. They have occupied more wine farms, roadblocks everywhere..." Patrice rubbed his eyes wearily and then stared vacantly into the air.

Monique slid down the side of the wine barrel until she was squatting on the floor, knees under her chin, leaning against the barrel, the flicking candlelight from above haphazardly illuminating her head. Her face was still pale and her eyes floated like saucers within it. "Did they capture the airmen?"

"No, they are all at..." Patrice checked himself, glancing at Jean-Marc. "They are all together, but they cannot be moved. No one has papers."

"We cannot just leave Louis and Nicolas there," Anton said.

"We all know the dangers," Patrice said quickly. "They are experienced operatives, it will be safer if each one makes his own way on foot back to the *zone libre*. We will meet them in Bergerac."

"What about Olivier?" Gregoire protested. "He is barely nineteen."

"Well, he got himself there safely," Patrice countered tersely.

"And what about the airmen?" Monique said.

Patrice shrugged, his arms hooked around his knees.

"When do you have to deliver the airmen?" Jean-Marc said, looking from Patrice to Anton, his eyes coming to rest on Monique's face.

"Sunday," Monique said.

"Which port?"

"Bayonne."

In the background Jean-Marc saw Patrice lower and shake his head disapprovingly. "Fuck it, Monique, tell him everything, won't you?!"

Jean-Marc rubbed his face with an open palm. He had wanted this ever since he found himself hiding in his own cellar, listening to the Germans destroying his house, drinking his wine; after they killed his beloved Pascal and especially after hearing that Isabelle, Odette and Claude had been deported. This was his chance to fight back, an opportunity for revenge.

"I will go," he heard himself say.

Monique looked at him intensely and he basked in the feel of her eyes upon him. What did they reveal: surprise, admiration, affinity?

"No!" Patrice said. "You don't know what you are doing, and it's far too dangerous."

"I know Bordeaux like the back of my hand. I was born here," Jean-Marc countered.

Patrice spat on the floor between his boots. "It's suicide. The Germans are crawling everywhere."

"My brother is trapped there," Gregoire said, standing up and moving towards Jean-Marc. "Don't you see? If they find him it will lead *les Boches* back to us. I will go too." Gregoire and Jean-Marc nodded in solidarity.

Anton looked indecisive, caught between old loyalties and this surprising display of youthful valour.

"I will join them," Monique said, standing up, turning to face Patrice, her hands planted on her hips.

"I will not allow it. Not only will you be caught, but when they torture you the entire network will be at risk," Patrice said.

"What network?" Jean-Marc said, mocking.

Patrice stood up, affronted. "There is more to this than personal egos, Jean-Marc. We are a team and we have to look after each other. They will interrogate you and, believe me, you will talk."

"I know nothing about your network," Jean-Marc said, "so you are safe."

"Neither do I," said Gregoire, flicking a pointed index finger into his chest.

"You know where the airmen are," Patrice said belligerently. "That puts other lives at risk."

"I am not your enemy, Patrice. I want to strike back just as much as you do," Jean-Marc said in a mollifying voice. "Perhaps even more so."

Patrice shook his head. "I cannot allow it."

"I'm not asking for your permission," Jean-Marc said, surprised at his own fiery defiance, feeding off the camaraderie he felt from Monique and Gregoire.

"What about you, Anton?" Monique said softly but clearly.

Anton hesitated, one eye drooping like the tail of a hyena. "Patrice is right: it is a suicide mission. We should lie low until it quietens. The general will take care of the airmen, and of course, Louis and Nicolas."

"It may not quieten. This is a war," Jean-Marc said. "It has just started."

Patrice took a step forward, emboldened by Anton's support. "Assuming you make it that far, have you thought about how you would smuggle two British airmen – who speak no French – past German roadblocks?" His fierce eyes were fixed on Jean-Marc, darting about like those of a predator.

Monique, Anton and Gregoire all turned to face Jean-Marc. The candle flickered atop the barrel, creating haunting shadows on the angular cellar walls and accentuating the unwashed glisten of the men's faces.

"In fact, I have," Jean-Marc said. "Does the general have a lorry, or a tractor we could use?"

Patrice leered at him and made a face implying disinterest. Monique smiled, the warmth of her admiration making Jean-Marc's heart race.

Chapter Twenty-Seven

"You do not have a pistol?" Jean-Marc said, astonished.

Monique seemed uncertain as she glanced at Patrice.

"We will all need weapons," Jean-Marc said, making firm eye contact with Patrice as if to say, *She's your comrade and you haven't even armed her.*

Patrice sighed and pulled a worn MAS pistol out of his jacket, flipped it around and held it out, handgrip first, towards Monique.

"Is it loaded?" Jean-Marc asked.

Monique slid the magazine out and counted five bullets. She looked up, first at Patrice and then Jean-Marc.

"I have no more here," Patrice said, his mouth hanging open in abeyance before he continued. "You don't have to do this, Monique, it's not your fight."

Monique seemed to bristle. "It very much is my fight, and I want to do this."

They left at dusk, their breath fogging the cold air that stung their soot-covered faces exposed beneath black berets. It had been Patrice's idea but Jean-Marc felt that their dark facial complexions merely emphasised the lunar white of their eyes.

"Be careful, Gregoire, and bring your brother back safely," Alphonse said in muted tones, standing in his doorway with hands pushed deep into baggy woollen trousers. "When you get back we will fine the '38 for bottling, Jean-Marc."

Jean-Marc glanced at Alphonse and nodded. "You'd better start saving eggs, then."

"The moon is high tonight. Take care," Patrice said, leaning against the cellar door, ankles crossed, arms folded, head hung low like a defeated dog.

Jean-Marc took no pleasure from seemingly usurping Patrice, but he did enjoy the surge of adrenaline that pulsed through his frame as they trudged off into the deepening shadows. They headed north, away from his property, moving quickly and quietly, boots crunching on the gravel, Jean-Marc's shotgun slung over his shoulder as though he was going pigeon shooting.

"What do you need eggs for?" Monique whispered to him.

"We use egg whites to fine the wine… er, to remove small particles that make the wine cloudy," he explained.

Monique's eyes opened wide, like two marshmallows in her blackened face. "I never knew eggs were used in winemaking."

Jean-Marc narrowed his eyes at her. "You come from Normandy. What do you use to fine cider?"

"Not eggs." She looked away abruptly, as if embarrassed, and Jean-Marc found himself considering both her question and her reaction.

"Why did Patrice say this is not your fight?" Jean-Marc said, keeping his eyes on Monique's partially averted face.

She shrugged, protruding her lower lip.

"Where are we headed?" Gregoire said, breaking the silence.

They lumbered on as Jean-Marc fumbled in his coat for a cigarette, pulling it out eagerly and inserting it between his lips.

"Is that wise?" Monique asked.

Jean-Marc sighed and replaced the cigarette in his pocket. "I suppose not."

"Why didn't we take the gasogene?" Gregoire said, his tone challenging.

"You really want the three of us – all without papers – to travel across Bordeaux in that big black monstrosity?"

"Patrice did it," Gregoire said.

Jean-Marc emitted a guttural dismissive sound. "It's safer on foot."

"What's your plan then?" Gregoire asked, hunching his shoulders violently to reseat the shotgun slung across his body.

"I think we should skirt around Libourne, avoiding all roads, and then head south-west down to the Dordogne."

"How will we cross the Pont de Pierre?" Monique asked.

"We won't. It'll be too well-guarded."

"How will we reach Bordeaux?" Gregoire said, panting slightly to keep up with Jean-Marc's strides.

"We don't."

"What, then?"

Jean-Marc walked on.

"Patrice is not here. Why should you be in charge?" Gregoire said insolently.

"Because," Jean-Marc stopped and turned to face Gregoire, "I want to survive this and return home."

Without hesitation Jean-Marc walked off and quickly lengthened his stride, enjoying the opportunity to experience the wide outdoors again having been cooped up in the cellars for so long, unable to take his customary strolls through his vineyard, Pascal by his side, sniffing at the worms.

"Tell me about the general," Jean-Marc said.

The sky was a shade deeper than purple-black and the moon had not yet risen, though the clear sky beckoned. The darkness was suffocating. Gregoire drew level with Monique and Jean-Marc as they trudged between rows of vines, pruned back to the stems, ready for new growth when spring opened her eyes. The soil was damp and clung to their boots in great unwieldy clumps.

"He is not young, I would guess around seventy," Monique said.

"He is a war hero, you know, not that he says much about it," Gregoire said. "Decorated in the Battle of Arras at Vimy."

"The Canadians fought at Vimy," Jean-Marc said, as though thinking aloud.

"And he is in a wheelchair," Gregoire added.

"A wheelchair?"

Gregoire nodded. "A fancy one with crank handles, never seen such a thing before."

"War injury?" Jean-Marc ventured.

"Perhaps," Gregoire said. "He can walk, though."

Jean-Marc exchanged eye contact with Monique, who pulled a face.

"So he's not paralysed," Jean-Marc said.

"Olivier and I saw him one night," Gregoire said.

Jean-Marc shook his head as he tried to fathom this. "You trust him?" he asked, looking at Monique, drawing out her female intuition.

"Maybe he uses the wheelchair to make himself appear frail in the eyes of the Germans," Monique said, "as a cover."

"Does he regularly smuggle airmen out of France?" Jean-Marc said.

"Apparently. Patrice is very protective of the network."

Jean-Marc chuckled. "I noticed."

They rounded Libourne near Marchesseau, keeping to the fields, walking either through vineyards or orchards, cursing the cloying mud. Not a light burned anywhere, the blackout seemingly highly effective as the curfew hour drew nearer. An owl hooted and swooped, grappling with a small bundle in its claws. Jean-Marc looked at his watch. Seven o'clock. They had been walking two and a half hours and the moon was rising, a swollen, creamy orb hanging in a glittering sky. A short while later they reached an expanse of water.

"L'Isle," Jean-Marc said.

"How wide is it?" Monique asked.

It was so dark that the distant bank was not delineated.

"It's just an old waterway," Jean-Marc said.

"Do we follow it?" Monique asked.

"No, it runs right through Libourne. There'll be locks – if we walk south we'll find one and cross," Jean-Marc said.

Once they had crossed over a slimy and slippery lock, water dripping silently through its leaking gates, they headed west again towards Saint-Aignan.

"If we follow the river all the way we'll still be walking this time tomorrow," Gregoire muttered. "And we'll still be on the wrong side."

Jean-Marc exchanged a wry smile with Monique, but said nothing. Once they were within sight of Port de Tressac they hid amongst a tangle of bramble vines in an overgrown hedgerow, observing the riverbank. Satisfied eventually that there were no patrols or lights, they crept down to the water's edge, bent over like hunchbacks.

"What are we doing?" Gregoire hissed.

"Look for a canoe," Jean-Marc whispered back.

"We're going on the water?" Monique said.

"You're mad," said Gregoire.

"The water's black, and the Dordogne takes us right past Ile du Nord at Margaux where we can sneak ashore. Lots of places to take cover."

"So we totally bypass Bordeaux?" Monique said as her face lit up with hesitant expectancy.

Jean-Marc nodded, his eyes flicking from Monique to Gregoire, both of whom studied his partially moonlit face intently, as he determined their level of conviction.

"It's a good plan," Gregoire said, seeming convinced suddenly and springing forward in search of a vessel along the muddy bank, ripe with the sound of frogs and the odour of rotting vegetation.

Jean-Marc smiled at Monique. She smiled back. "This is fun," she said.

"We're not there yet."

Having located a boat covered with a cracked, pale bluish tarpaulin, they quickly unwrapped it and inspected the hull.

"No oars," Gregoire muttered.

"It's dry," Jean-Marc said. "We'll keep the tarpaulin in case we need to hide beneath it."

Jean-Marc ripped a short length of plank off a rotten mooring jetty and they pushed the boat into deeper water before escaping the smooth, soft mud and cold water by jumping in. The current was swift, swollen by winter rainfall and a higher than usual water level, and the boat began to drift downstream immediately. Jean-Marc paddled a few times to straighten the boat as they settled into it, Gregoire in the bow, Monique in the middle and Jean-Marc paddling and steering from the stern.

The muddy smell of the river was strong, the silence broken only by the gentle sound of the boat caressing the water's surface. The moon was rising ever higher and its candescence was casting a dappled reflection across the vast expanse of water, including their vessel.

"That damned moon is like a spotlight on us," Jean-Marc cursed. "Keep your eyes on the banks. Any sign of activity or lights, we're all down flat in the boat with the tarpaulin pulled over us."

"We're moving quite quickly," Monique observed, dragging a hand in the water.

As they glided around a bend towards Asques the ambient light diminished.

153

"What's on the banks?" Monique asked.

"Vineyards," Jean-Marc said.

Around the next bend a blackness that stretched across their field of vision began to block out stars. As the current swept them closer it grew larger.

"What is that?" Monique asked.

"It's a bridge, the same road that crosses at the Pont de Pierre," Jean-Marc said quietly, his eyes searching the bridge for signs of activity.

"I see two red dots!" Gregoire said. "Cigarettes!"

Jean-Marc saw them, close together in the centre of the bridge. "Down!" he hissed with urgency as they scrambled into the cramped floor of the boat, stretching the smelly oilskin tarpaulin over their bodies. "Not a sound."

The boat floated along on the current, helplessly, drifting ever closer to the bridge and the two German guards smoking together at the stone parapet.

"*Schau*," one of the guards said, turning and pointing to the boat.

Jean-Marc could just make out Monique's eyes, staring fearfully towards him. He put a finger to his lips.

"*Ein Boot*," another voice said.

"*Halt!*"

"*Es ist leer*," one soldier said.

Then they heard the sound of a weapon being cocked, followed by two loud cracks splitting the nocturnal solitude above their heads. Jean-Marc heard one bullet tear through the tarpaulin and exit the bottom of the boat – splintering the wood – and began to feel for the hole with an extended finger, probing the growing wetness.

"*Ach, lassen Sie es*," said one of the soldiers with a chuckle.

The boat drifted on silently, just the sound of water lapping against the hull and their rushed breaths as they lay huddled beneath the claustrophobic tarpaulin. Jean-Marc found a hole punched into the hull, jagged with splinters. He pushed his hand against it to stem the flow of icy water. Minutes ticked by slowly and Jean-Marc knew that they were drawing water as the puddle enlarged and seeped through his trousers.

Suddenly the boat scraped on something and then twisted gracefully as it ran aground. Gregoire peeped cautiously from beneath the tarpaulin. "We're up against the bank," he hissed.

Jean-Marc manoeuvred himself and lifted the tarpaulin with his foot to gain a rear view. "I don't see the bridge," he said.

"Fuck, that was close," Gregoire said, lifting the tarpaulin off his head. "You nearly got us killed, Jean-Marc!" The venom in his voice boiled over.

"Be quiet!" Monique said with irritation in her voice as she straightened in the centre of the boat, the moonlight silhouetting her face and a solitary silvery tear down one cheek. "There are Germans everywhere."

"You OK?" Jean-Marc asked, pushing against the soft mud with the makeshift oar to free the boat. A few more thrusts with the jagged plank and they began to float with the current again.

"My leg is burning," Monique said, "and it's wet."

"Mine is wet too, let me see," Jean-Marc said, moving towards her in the boat. "Come and put your hand over the hole, Gregoire, we've got about two inches of water in the bottom of the boat already."

"Yes, sir," Gregoire said sarcastically.

Monique rolled her legging up and Jean-Marc ran his fingers across the pale flesh of her calf until he felt something wet, something sticky. Monique flinched and drew breath sharply. Their eyes met in silent comprehension. "I think I'm hit."

Jean-Marc strained his eyes to see in the moonlight.

"I think it just grazed your leg, broke the skin, but not much more." He sensed her relieved eyes softening. "You're lucky."

155

"Where's the other hole?" Gregoire said.

"I think it missed the boat," Jean-Marc replied.

"Where are we?" Monique asked, pulling her trouser down and looking around at the water, glistening its ragged trail of silvery moonlight that failed to light up the dark and secretive riverbanks.

"I don't know yet. When we reach the first islands in the Dordogne up ahead, then I'll know," Jean-Marc said.

"Are there any more bridges?" Monique asked.

"No," Jean-Marc assured her.

"This was a stupid idea," Gregoire said. "We are helpless in the boat, sitting ducks."

Jean-Marc twisted his head to meet Gregoire's mutinous eyes, his hand still submerged and plugging the hole. "And what would you have done? Driven the gasogene straight into a German roadblock?" Jean-Marc said.

"We'll sink anyway, long before we reach Château Lascombes."

Jean-Marc looked out across the water, at the moon high in the sky, at his breath fogging the air. He wanted to light a cigarette, but he knew he dare not even suggest it, remembering how they had seen the German soldiers smoking from such a distance.

"It's not that far. When we reach the first land point we must head straight for the bank of Ile du Nord, it's close. Then we could even drag the boat around on the bank before we need to cross at Ile Margaux."

Within thirty minutes they had reached their objective and Jean-Marc began digging the plank into the brooding waters to steer them towards the western shore. The boat was heavy in the water with at least eight inches of murky liquid swilling around their soaked feet. Monique held the two shotguns across her lap to keep them dry. As soon as they had run aground on the sandy bank they hastily disembarked the vessel and crouched down on dry land.

"What's on this island?" Monique asked.

"Vineyards," Jean-Marc said.

"How do you know this place?" Gregoire asked.

"I was born in Bordeaux, I pay attention," Jean-Marc said, tapping the side of his nose.

"Does anyone live here?" Monique asked.

"No. Come, we must tip the water out and then drag the boat around to the other side for the final crossing," Jean-Marc said.

Dragging the boat was a labour but the island was only a few hundred yards across. Monique carried the shotguns as they pushed and heaved their way through the silty soil of a vineyard.

"Look, Gregoire, these vines have buds already," Jean-Marc said, examining the pruned vines as they passed. "The new vintage has begun."

Once across Ile du Nord they floated downstream in the boat for a few miles and then navigated crudely with the plank across to Ile Margaux, a sliver of land in the water.

"We must look out now. Across from this island is the western bank of the Gironde, and only a mile or two further west is Margaux. There will almost certainly be *les Boches* about," Jean-Marc said.

"How far to Lascombes?" Gregoire said, glancing at his wristwatch.

"What time is it?" Jean-Marc asked.

"Eleven thirty."

Jean-Marc nodded. "About another two hours, depending on how much crawling we have to do along drainage ditches."

"The boat is sinking again," Monique observed, lifting her feet onto the side of the boat.

They approached the western shoreline cautiously. It was quiet as they scrambled ashore hastily, only the dappled splashes of their feet in the shallows audible in the darkness.

Monique stumbled. "You OK?" Jean-Marc asked, placing a steadying hand on her arm.

"It hurts – but I'm OK."

"Keep to the vineyards," Jean-Marc said.

The moved stealthily between rows of vines, their wet boots squelching like plumbers' plungers, Jean-Marc's shotgun slung awkwardly over his shoulders, digging into his spine. Monique brought up the rear with a noticeable limp. They had reached a road and as they crouched between vines, poised to cross, a Kübelwagen with its headlights tinted blue suddenly swung into view.

"Down flat!" Jean-Marc whispered sharply, quickly freeing the shotgun from his shoulder, his heart pounding in his throat.

The Kübelwagen passed them and pulled over a hundred yards further down. Four soldiers alighted and urinated on the vines before lighting cigarettes, chatting as though on vacation.

"Bastards," Gregoire hissed angrily. "*Boches'* piss on the grapes."

After considerable time – Jean-Marc's legs freezing against the damp cold soil – the soldiers pulled away, the scent of their cigarette smoke still wafting across on the air and teasing him. Jean-Marc gesticulated and they hurried across the road. Monique struggled and fell on the verge, rolling over. Jean-Marc rushed to her and pulled her up, virtually dragging her away into the next vineyard and towards the safety of a drainage ditch, one of many that criss-crossed the vineyards towards the Gironde.

They had no sooner settled into the drainage ditch than an Opel Blitz truck carrying more than a dozen soldiers drove by, the stench of its diesel fumes causing Gregoire to stifle a coughing spasm. The truck slowed and then turned up a track between the vineyards towards the main house.

"They must have occupied the château," Jean-Marc observed. "We'll have to detour and stick to the drainage ditches."

This meant trudging through icy water and mud that often reached up to their knees, hunched over as they were to minimise their protruding profiles.

"God, they are everywhere," Gregoire cursed as yet another Kübelwagen with four soldiers passed close by. "How will we get back?"

The three of them lay pressed into the muddy side of the ditch, their legs in the water, watching the Germans disappear into the distance.

Monique was shivering, her teeth clattering into each other. "I can't believe this marshy, flat landscape is home to the world's best wines," she muttered through clenched teeth, eyes half-closed.

"It used to be a bog before these drainage canals," Jean-Marc said, peering cautiously over the rim of the ditch. "Can you still walk?" he asked Monique.

She nodded, groaning as she straightened up. "How far?"

"Close."

At three o'clock in the morning they quietly crept up to the front door of Château Lascombes. The building's stonework glowed in the moonlight as if radioactive, its leafless vine stems cutting jagged pathways across the walls, like arteries feeding the structure.

"Now what?" Jean-Marc said, studying the darkened windows.

"Where did we sleep, Monique, was it up there?" Gregoire said, pointing up to a window on the first floor.

But Monique slumped to the gravel in a graceful heap despite Jean-Marc's chivalrous charge to support her.

"We must get her inside," Jean-Marc said.

Gregoire began to throw stones at the first-floor window, striking it several times, calling out Olivier's name. Eventually a pair of cautious eyes peered out through the creosote glass.

"Olivier, it is me, Gregoire! Let us in!"

Chapter Twenty-Eight

Jean-Marc had drifted into a fitful sleep, mesmerised by the pendulous yet polite intrusion of the Antoine Brocot grandfather clock standing dutifully in the corner. Monique's sudden, sharp inhalation startled him such that his head slipped off its supporting hand.

"Where am I?" she gasped, eyes wide and staring around the dimly lit room.

Jean-Marc stood up quickly – blinking forcefully to clear his gritty eyes – and in two strides was by her side where she lay on a threadbare chaise longue the colour of starling eggs. A woven brown blanket covered her legs and was pulled up to her chest. Curled up beside her feet a large, red Persian purred contentedly.

"We're at Château Lascombes with General Brutinel." Jean-Marc paused, tenderly placing his hand against Monique's forehead. "Remember?"

Monique turned her head as she took in the room: the empty hearth, cold and sooty; a grand piano behind a trio of Louis XVI sofas upholstered in crimson velvet. Her eyes stopped on the cat.

"That is Oscar, the general's cat. He's been with you all afternoon," Jean-Marc said, moving forward to stroke the appreciative cat behind its ears.

Monique frowned and glanced at the piano. "Was it you playing earlier?"

Jean-Marc smiled and looked down, slightly embarrassed. "I'm sorry if it disturbed you, I tried to do it quietly. I haven't had a piano to play for months."

"No, it was beautiful. Chopin?"

"Debussy."

"Ah yes, *Clair de Lune*," Monique said and shut her eyes, as if remembering the delicacy of the notes.

The cat lifted its head, staring at Jean-Marc indifferently with eyes like bronze fifty-centime coins, and then stretched, catching Monique's leg with a claw.

"Ouch!" Monique moved her leg stiffly away from Oscar.

"How does your leg feel?"

Monique peeled back the blanket to reveal her right leg bandaged below the knee. "It throbs." She palpated the bandage and winced instantly, recoiling. "Where is Gregoire?"

"They are all asleep upstairs."

"Who did this?" Monique asked, indicating the bandage, and surreptitiously checking that her slacks were done up.

"The general helped me," Jean-Marc said with a shy grin. "We applied a poultice – the wound was soiled from all that dirty water."

"Thank you." Monique shivered violently and lay down, drawing the blanket up to her chin. "God, I'm starving."

"I will tell the general you are awake and fetch you some food," Jean-Marc said, rising and walking towards the large double door behind the piano.

"What time is it?" Monique asked.

"You have slept all day."

As Jean-Marc was about to slip through the enormous doorway, Monique called him back. "Will you play again for me?" she asked.

Jean-Marc looked down and nodded. "Of course."

162

In the kitchen Jean-Marc found Brutinel slicing a large *pain de campagne* into quarters and then eighths beside a diced *saucisson* and a bottle of unlabelled red wine.

"She is awake," Jean-Marc said.

"Good."

"And hungry."

"Also good."

Jean-Marc surveyed all the food. "How many are you feeding?"

"The two airmen are here now, sheltering in the basement."

Jean-Marc's heart beat a little faster as the reality of their mission jumped significantly closer. There was no escaping it now. The men were there, at Château Lascombes, and they had to be moved.

"Does she speak any English?" Brutinel asked, gesticulating towards the *salon* door with the bread knife.

"I don't know. She says she's from Normandy," Jean-Marc said, pouting his lips and shrugging. "I don't understand a word of English."

Brutinel emitted a throaty sound and pulled a face. "Me neither. Will you call them for me, please?" He pointed down towards the floorboards.

The two English airmen looked dishevelled: unshaven; drowning in ill-fitting clothing that they had no doubt been given to help them blend in; unwashed and smelling faintly of urine. They expressed what must have been gratitude to Jean-Marc as he waved for them to follow him up the stone stairs, making eating movements with his hands and his mouth as he led the way.

"Poor bastards," Brutinel muttered as the airmen emerged behind Jean-Marc out of the musty cellar, shielding their eyes from the brightness. "No one to talk to for two weeks, cut off from the outside world and even the light of the sun."

Jean-Marc identified with their plight, for he too had tasted the unnatural and inhuman existence of hiding in a cellar for months now, prevented from enjoying the satisfaction of a gentle breeze through his hair and the invigoration of sunshine on his face.

"When does their ship sail?" he asked.

"Sunday night."

Brutinel clicked the cellar door shut and paused in the wide hallway, empty of furniture with only the portrait of an ancestor and a mottled mirror hanging against the cream wallpaper. "I have no papers for them," he admitted ruefully. "*Les Boches* have this place locked down at the moment – they are everywhere. I don't know how we will get them to Bayonne."

"I... may have a plan," Jean-Marc said.

Brutinel nodded thoughtfully, manoeuvring his wheelchair towards the kitchen. "Call the others, we'll talk."

When Jean-Marc returned to the warm kitchen, heady with the aromas of wood smoke and salted meat, he found Monique seated at the table chatting to the airmen whose faces were now animated and bright, their eyes dancing in stubbly faces. Brutinel was wedged against the table at the far end, nursing a glass of red wine, his face a study in bemusement. Behind him Jean-Marc heard the clomping of boots on the oak stairs as Gregoire, Olivier, Louis and Nicolas descended sleepily.

"You speak English?" Jean-Marc said as he caught Monique's eye, pausing in surprise on the bottom step.

"Uh-huh." She nodded, turning back to the airmen, who tore into their food like starving prisoners.

Jean-Marc remembered how hungry he had been in between food parcels delivered by Alphonse while hiding in his cellar, waiting day after day in the hope that his neighbour would brave the German presence. Even a scrap of old, warm sausage and stale bread could taste out of this world.

"Monique!" Louis said as he entered the kitchen. "Are you OK?"

He approached with arms outstretched and kissed her on each cheek, followed by a limping Nicolas. Gregoire and Olivier, in close conversation with each other, merely acknowledged her without interrupting their muted conversation.

"I'm fine, really, fine," she said, projecting a brave face.

They all sat down noisily, the scrape of wooden chairs on the stone floor punctuating the murmur of muted and incomprehensible greetings between the Maquis and the two British airmen.

"They want to thank you for helping them," Monique explained to her assembled comrades.

"Tuck in, everyone," Brutinel said, sweeping his arm across the table. "There is no more bread but there is more wine. Jean-Marc, tell us, what is your plan?"

Jean-Marc explained his idea of hiding the airmen inside empty wine barrels, which could be transported past the Germans, right under their noses.

"Barrels?" Louis said disrespectfully, a large chunk of bread visible in his mouth, the remainder clenched in his hand.

"Gregoire told us about your crazy idea that nearly got you all killed," Nicolas said derisively, shaking his head, his lips apart sufficiently to reveal a piece of grisly *saucisson* as he chewed. "Floating down the Dordogne." He emitted a throaty sound.

"It got us here safely, didn't it?" Jean-Marc replied, aware of Louis' and Nicolas' eyes upon him. Gregoire kept his head down over his food and Olivier shuffled uncomfortably in his chair.

Jean-Marc could feel their diffidence, could see their doubt, and he knew that their allegiance was to Patrice. To them he was merely a vigneron, an interloper and an unknown quantity.

"Safely, eh?" Nicolas said, gesturing towards Monique with a chunk of bread. "When Patrice finds out he is going to..."

"At least I had the guts to come back to fetch all of you," Jean-Marc said, as anger welled up within him. He stared at his untouched food.

"It's barely a scratch," Monique said, attempting to lighten the atmosphere by laughing a little.

The two airmen chewed silently, lips pressed together thinly, their eyes flicking about the faces of those at the table, the men responsible for their safety, men who were clearly at loggerheads about something.

"You did not have to fetch us," Nicolas sneered, wiping his nose with the back of his hand and sniffing loudly.

"No, we can make our own way back," Louis added, nodding in unison with Nicolas.

"Gentlemen, please," Brutinel interjected, exhaling impatiently before taking a gulp of wine. "The airmen," he said, opening his hand towards the two British men, "have to be in Bayonne in two days."

"It's too dangerous," Louis said, pushing back from the table.

Nicolas nodded.

"That's what Patrice said, and yet, look, we are here," Gregoire said meekly, failing to meet the fiery eyes of the doubters.

"What about Jean-Marc's plan?" Monique said.

Nicolas released a burst of air and food fragments. "You mean the barrels?"

"Yes, I think it is a good plan," Monique said, her face unmoved and earnest.

Louis, Gregoire and Nicolas stared at her blankly for a moment, perhaps astonished by her failure to support them.

"It could work," Brutinel said in his baritone voice, "but we'd have to take the barrels apart to get them inside." He looked at everyone around the table. "Who here has any experience as a cooper?"

Louis and Nicolas shrugged and pulled faces. "This is what I'm saying," Nicolas said, shaking his head.

"Exactly," Louis said with a dismissive gesture of his hand.

"I do," Jean-Marc said.

Silence. Monique's eyes met his and held them. Louis and Nicolas looked crestfallen.

"My father made me spend six months learning how to make barrels at Tonnellerie Bordelais before I blended my first vintage."

"You can do it?" Brutinel said.

Jean-Marc nodded, looking slowly from one dissenting and averted face to the next. "Of course."

"Good," Brutinel said, slapping his hands down on the wooden armrests of his Dupont as he began to crank the handles and manoeuvre away from the table. "There is no time to waste, then."

"Wait," Louis said, a solitary hand raised in the air.

Brutinel turned back to face the table.

"Who is going to drive these wine barrels past *les Boches*?" Louis said, an air of triumph forming behind his sultry eyes. "I have no papers to be in the *zone occupée*."

"Neither do I," said Nicolas.

"I have none and I have refused an STO," Gregoire said. "They will arrest me."

Brutinel's face fell as he manoeuvred his wheelchair round to face the table. "Monique?"

Monique shook her head. The silence at the table was tangible. Brutinel glanced at Jean-Marc, but he didn't even ask the question. Jean-Marc lowered his eyes and sighed, sensing Louis' gloating stare burning a hole in him.

"I can drive," Olivier said. "I haven't officially been served an STO notice yet, I don't think."

Gregoire looked up in horror. "No, Olivier. Papa —"

"We agreed to do this to make a difference. Jean-Marc risked his life to come here – are we to sit back and do nothing?"

"But *les Boches…*" Gregoire protested.

"I am only nineteen and I have my scholar papers still."

Monique smiled and put her arm around Olivier, seated beside her. "You are a born Maquis," she said. "Brave and smart."

Olivier blushed bright puce and beamed with pride. Jean-Marc felt both elation and apprehension. The plan might well work, but Olivier was just a boy caught up in a man's war and for a brief instant he imagined having to face Alphonse if anything happened to Olivier. Just as quickly, he shut his eyes tightly to banish the thought.

Chapter Twenty-Nine

Kimmel stood six foot three, a blonde colossus with hair cropped very short; pale, almost milky eyes squinting in the sunlight beneath bleached eyebrows. Alphonse watched him warily through the kitchen window, standing beside the Stabswagen and flicking at the leggings of his black uniform with leather gloves held tightly in one hand.

"Who is it?" Marthe asked nervously, resting a hand on Alphonse's shoulder.

Alphonse shrugged and swallowed. "I hope it's not about the boys." Stepping into the courtyard and greeted by the crow of a cockerel, Alphonse walked towards Kimmel, who spun around to face him.

"Monsieur Sabron?"

"Yes?"

"Untersturmführer Kimmel," the officer said, snapping his heels together.

Alphonse smiled and extended his hand, to be rebuffed with an unsmiling sneer.

Kimmel turned to the large cellar doors bordering the courtyard and waved his gloves at them. "I have come to search your wine cellar."

Alphonse's heart skipped a beat as he hoped that either Federico or Patrice was watching, and that they would at that moment be fleeing down one of the dark passages to their place of shelter, deep in the hillside caves. Discovery now would bring catastrophic consequences upon all of them. He knew that the black uniform signified the SS, and that to be caught sheltering Jews and Maquis would mean a bullet.

"Does Bömers know that you are here?" Alphonse asked.

"Who?"

"Heinz Bömers, *weinführer* of Bordeaux?"

Kimmel sniffed and rocked on his heels, slapping his gloves against an open palm. "I answer to Reichsmarschall Göring."

Alphonse felt a ripple of fear surge through his body, nausea welling up from the pit of his stomach. He turned to his open front door and, even though he could see Marthe watching from the shadowy hallway, he shouted to her, loudly.

"Marthe, I'm just taking Untersturmführer Kimmel into the cellar. Can you bring my keys, please?" He hoped Federico or Patrice would hear his warning, and react appropriately.

Moments later Marthe emerged and waddled across the courtyard, taking small steps, glancing nervously at Kimmel. She pressed a bunch of keys into Alphonse's hand, and held on for a moment longer. Her chest heaved as she looked into his eyes.

"*Schnell!*" Kimmel said.

Two more uniformed soldiers emerged from the Stabswagen and hitched rifles up onto their shoulders. Alphonse fumbled with the keys at the cellar door and eventually it creaked open.

"What are you looking for?" Alphonse said.

Kimmel glared at him. "Wine, of course. What do you think?"

"But I supply Bömers every month according to the quotas that have been established. It is he who buys the wine for Germany."

Kimmel stepped across the dusty threshold into the stone cellar, his boots clipping the floor and echoing through the vast chamber. The smell of oak and wineskins was thick, the air cool and still. Alphonse looked around nervously, expecting to see an incriminating piece of Angelica's clothing or a personal item of Federico's, overlooked in their hasty retreat.

"I am not buying, *monsieur*. I am here under orders to locate the best wines that you are all withholding from the Reich."

Alphonse planted his hands indignantly on his hips and made a guttural sound.

"Come, come, *monsieur*, don't play games. Take me to the..." Kimmel impatiently extracted a piece of paper from his tunic, unfolding and studying it closely, "the 1928s, '29s, '34s, even the '26 if you have." He turned to the soldiers and motioned for them to enter, barking something at them in German. They began to search every stack of bottles, every shadowy recess, opening crates and pulling back tarpaulins.

"Where do these tunnels lead?" Kimmel asked.

"They extend for miles underground. I do not use them."

Kimmel looked at Alphonse and angled his head in disbelief.

"Well why do you have them, then?"

"I didn't make them."

"Who did?"

"The Romans."

Kimmel hesitated, staring at Alphonse, seemingly searching his mind for a riposte. "So, this is not the first time you have been occupied then, *ja*?" His gaze faltered and he turned to call his men. One produced a torch and they moved towards a tunnel entrance.

"After you, *monsieur*," Kimmel instructed, ushering Alphonse in with a sweep of his black gloves.

Lining the tunnels – illuminated by the occasional arc of torchlight that swept over dusty and cobweb-covered walls –

171

were stacks of wine bottles. Kimmel picked up a few and turned them over, wiping the dust away with his gloves.

"There is no label."

Alphonse pointed to the chalked sign on the ground beside each stack. "These are recent vintages."

"*Ja*, probably the shit you are selling to the Reich." Kimmel dumped the bottle back roughly. "Keep moving."

Alphonse hoped that the others were well out of sight, deep in the tunnels, and that they had not left any signs of their presence. The mere thought of stumbling across evidence of human habitation caused a swell of nausea within Alphonse's chest, and sweat to soil his armpits. He was fairly sure that the Germans would not venture too far; the cave tunnels were dark, damp and quite daunting.

Kimmel stopped beside a bricked-up hole in the tunnel, covered in cobwebs and hidden behind upturned wine barrels. "What is this?" he demanded, examining the brickwork.

Alphonse shrugged. Behind it was a treasure trove of his finest vintages, tens of thousands of bottles hidden in a branching tunnel and ingeniously camouflaged with spider webs and carpet dust.

"I don't know. It has always been like that." He tried to look Kimmel in the eye, not difficult given the gloomy ambience and flickering quality of the torchlight.

Kimmel peered at the bricks up close, snorted and kicked at the barrels, full of wine. "What is in here?"

Alphonse moved closer and revealed the chalk scrawl on the barrel top. *38:ouest:3éme remplissage.* "It's the 1938 vintage. Not bottled yet."

"Proceed." Kimmel pointed down the tunnel.

Twenty yards further they came upon a small stack of bottles, about a hundred, dusty and webbed. Kimmel picked one up. 1934. "Ah. See, this what I want," he said. He barked orders to the soldiers, who began to carry the bottles out.

"Who is paying for those?" Alphonse said.

Kimmel stepped closer, his chin clearing the crown of Alphonse's head. "Reichsmarschall Göring says, '*Danke*'. You are, after all, an occupied country – just be grateful I'm not taking more."

"But these are my last '34s, my livelihood. What am—"

"I'm sure you make enough money selling that other shit to Weinführer Bömers. You're lucky he pays you anything for it."

He walked down the narrow tunnel with Alphonse, finding nothing, and losing interest after a hundred yards or so. Alphonse breathed a sigh of relief that his friends were out of sight.

Kimmel removed all one hundred bottles and several cases of other wines he came across without uttering another word. Anger burned within Alphonse and he felt betrayed by Bömers, if indeed he had anything to do with this. This was a breach of their gentlemen's agreement to trade with the Reich under civil terms. But Alphonse also felt immense relief despite the plundering. He had left those 1934s exposed because he knew that one day someone might come to search his cellar, and their loss was minimal compared to what might have been.

Still, he felt violated, and vulnerable. That the SS could simply turn up unannounced on his doorstep was unsettling, demonstrating that the long reach of a monster like Göring extended all the way from Berlin into the heart of Bordeaux. Having someone like Bömers in authority in Saint-Émilion was all very well, but he too was clearly powerless to prevent such heavy-handed intrusions.

Alphonse locked the cellar and retreated into the château, sitting beside Marthe in silence for some considerable time in the *salon*. What was there to say? He had no control over his life anymore.

Chapter Thirty

Jean-Marc knocked the outer two metal cerclage rings off two used wine barrels, splaying the oak staves on one end of the barrel sufficiently to remove the round oak disc that sealed the end. The interior of the barrel, stained the colour of Cabernet Franc after several fills, appeared inhospitably cramped.

But the two British airmen, eager and determined to escape occupied France, managed to contort themselves into a squatting position inside the barrels, enabling Jean-Marc to hammer the two cerclage rings back into position, pulling the staves back into shape and sealing the disc firmly in place at the top of the barrel.

The hole at the barrel's girth, used to fill and empty the barrel as well as sample wines, became the entombed airmen's air supply. The two barrels containing the human cargo to be smuggled out of France were placed in the centre of twenty barrels stacked on the flat loading surface of Brutinel's Renault SXB truck. Jean-Marc felt for the two airmen, trapped in the centre of a wooden house of cards: not for the claustrophobic; not for the weak at heart. War did not suffer the faint-hearted.

The inadequate morning sun was rising reluctantly, tipping the dormant vines with pale saffron. Frost crunched underfoot and breathing misted the crisp air. Olivier ground the stiff and unyielding gearbox several times before becoming accustomed to the unforgiving clutch. Finally, they were ready, the route agreed, the purpose of their journey clear for every German roadblock they would encounter: their cargo, easily identifiable as empty wine barrels, destined for export via the port of Bayonne to the Jerez region of Spain where they would be used for sherry.

"You should go with Olivier," Nicolas said, shifting his weight from his weak and shortened polio leg to his stronger limb.

"I agree," Jean-Marc said, meeting Brutinel's steady eyes. "Perhaps your presence as a disabled man, confined to a wheelchair, will make your passage past checkpoints easier."

Brutinel nodded thoughtfully. "Perhaps."

"We should place your wheelchair on the back, strapped to the barrels, make a show of it," Monique said.

Brutinel looked at Olivier, so young, fresh-faced and inexperienced, yet eager to place his life in danger. "Yes, help me up," he said.

"The rest of us will wait here until you return," Louis said.

They helped Brutinel into the Renault cab beside Olivier, who once more ground the gears ferociously.

"Godspeed," Jean-Marc said, rapping the rusty door twice. He felt a presence beside him, close to him; it was Monique, resting a hand on his shoulder as she waved them off, misty-eyed and clutching one hand to her mouth. Jean-Marc turned and embraced her and sensed the emotion simmering beneath her warm skin. "It is getting light, we must get inside and lock up," he said.

"When should they be back?" Monique said, wiping her nose.

Louis shrugged and turned indifferently. "Tonight, before the curfew."

They slept whenever nagging anxiety permitted; they ate little when awake, listening to the endless ticking of

175

Lascombe's grand Brocot clock counting down the seconds to the next danger as the curfew loomed ahead like a curtain of death. When darkness descended in early evening Jean-Marc crept down to the *salon* where he found Oscar curled up on the grand piano. The house was cold, but they dared not light any fires while Brutinel was out because of the smoke.

Jean-Marc sat down at the piano and found his fingers caressing the keys, *pianissimo*, his head bent forward until his angled cheek almost touched the frame. He played slowly, mournfully, a man alone in a cold house amongst strangers, unable to walk freely outside at any time of the day or night. Where was Isabelle, where were his children? He didn't like to think about them because he feared he would never see them again.

"That is beautiful," Monique's soft voice said from behind him.

Jean-Marc started and turned into the gloom. Oscar jumped down from the piano and padded across to the chaise longue where Monique lay beneath her blanket.

"What is it?" she asked.

"Debussy."

"I don't recognise it."

Jean-Marc played on, massaging sorrow out of each cadence, letting notes hang in the cold, still air. Oscar's purr became audible in the longer pauses. "It is the *Prelude* from his *Suite Bergamasque*, the first piece of four..."

"Ah, *Clair de Lune* is..."

"One of them, yes. Number three."

When Jean-Marc closed his eyes an unpleasant image of his beloved Pleyel piano back at Château Cardinale formed in his mind. He imagined it being abused by German Wehrmacht to hammer out crass drinking songs, suffering disfiguring stains from glasses and spilt drinks, perhaps cigarettes and guns placed carelessly on top of it. He hoped no worse than that.

"You play with sadness," Monique said.

Jean-Marc shrugged and felt his fingers sink into the ivory, melting away his frustration and his anger.

"Do you think of your family?" Monique said.

Jean-Marc drew breath sharply. "I try not to."

Thereafter Jean-Marc played on without speaking, through the *Minuet*, *Clair de Lune* and only when he had begun the *Passepied* did they hear the clatter of a diesel engine and the crunch of tyres on the courtyard gravel. By the time they had reached the kitchen door – slowed by Monique's hobbling – Louis, Nicolas and Gregoire were already poised, shotguns and rifles in hand, lurking in the shadows beside the unlit hearth. It seemed to take forever before they finally heard keys scratching at the door and Brutinel's tired, gruff voice.

"Don't shoot, it is me, Raymond."

They had made it. But the initial elation that throbbed through the cold, dark kitchen was tempered by the sight of Olivier's ghostlike complexion, his eyes staring emptily ahead. Brutinel edged his way through the doorway, his face tense and concentrated.

"Everything alright?" Jean-Marc asked, sensing the strained atmosphere.

"Close the door," Brutinel said, spinning his wheelchair around to face everyone as he reached the table.

"What is it?" Nicolas said. "Did you not reach Bayonne?" He craned his neck to peer through the window at the truck outside.

"No, that all went according to plan. We delivered the barrels and the airmen must be on the ship heading for Spain now," Brutinel said tersely, his eyes downcast.

Olivier seemed to be trembling and Gregoire moved across to him, murmuring something in his ear. Jean-Marc met Monique's troubled eyes, her eyebrows angled down towards the delicate bridge of her nose, the corner of her lower lip curled up under one of her teeth.

"I think we've been followed. At the last checkpoint, just outside Castelnau, there was a very suspicious *unteroffizier*."

"What are you saying?" Monique asked, her body stiffening beside Jean-Marc.

"Was it your papers?" Louis said, glancing at Olivier, who had begun to shiver, a delayed reaction to the shock, perhaps.

"No. He just said, 'I think we should come and search your cellars.'"

They all stared at Brutinel, slumped in his wheelchair. Suddenly light flashed across the windows and they heard the deep sound of throbbing diesel engines. Nicolas ran to the window and peered out cautiously.

"Soldiers!" he hissed.

Brutinel became animated in the wheelchair. "There is a back door leading out into the vineyards. Hurry, take all your things. Leave nothing behind."

Louis and Gregoire ran upstairs to clear the bedroom. Monique stared at Jean-Marc with frightened eyes, her mouth slightly agape. He knew what she was thinking.

"We'll return to the river, it's the most direct route, the shortest," Jean-Marc said, placing a reassuring hand on Monique's arm.

"I am not going along the river. We will take the bicycles and go back the same way we came," Nicolas said defiantly.

"Across the Pont de Pierre?" Jean-Marc said in disbelief.

"We have done it twice before," Nicolas argued, challenging Jean-Marc. "Come with us, Monique, you'll be better on a bicycle with that leg."

Jean-Marc studied Monique's reaction. She was clearly uncertain, chewing her lip and studying the floor.

"You must hurry!" Brutinel said, becoming more agitated.

Louis and Gregoire clomped down the staircase, three steps at a time, carrying items of clothing in their arms. "The room is clean," Gregoire reassured Brutinel.

They rushed through to the back of the château where the bicycles rested against one wall in the unlit passageway. Louis pushed the door open and they exited as smoothly as possible into the cool, dark night.

"There is a bicycle for you, Monique," Nicolas said. "Come!"

"There isn't one for Jean-Marc," Monique said.

"He wants to go along the riverbank," Nicolas said.

Monique hesitated while everyone mounted their bicycles.

"Good luck, I must close up. They are at the front door!" Brutinel whispered urgently. "Go, quickly!"

Jean-Marc peered into the darkness, deciding which route to follow into the vineyards to circumvent the German threat and reach the river as directly as possible. "This way," he said.

"No!" Louis said. "We're going that way." He began to cycle away, followed by Gregoire and Olivier.

"Monique, come!" Nicolas urged.

"No. I'm going with Jean-Marc," Monique said, and limped towards him.

Nicolas flung his arms upwards in a gesture of utter despair and emitted a throaty sound. The cyclists disappeared into the darkness, struggling across the lumpy soil heaped between the dormant vines. Jean-Marc grabbed Monique's warm hand and pulled her along with him between rows of vines, heading for a drainage ditch. He turned briefly, seeing lights going on in the château, imagining the clatter of boots searching every room. He hoped they had not left behind any evidence of their presence. Above all he hoped Brutinel would not be harmed.

When they reached the first drainage ditch, cowering beneath the lip, Monique lay right beside him, her staccato breath misting the air. "How long will it take us?" she asked, rubbing her leg and grimacing.

Jean-Marc watched her, trying not to think about what lay ahead of them. "Perhaps you should have gone on the bicycles with your bad leg."

"No. You are right, Pont de Pierre is too dangerous."

"We have to be safe by sunrise." He glanced at his wristwatch. "We have about ten hours."

"Can't we use the boat?"

Jean-Marc shook his head. "We have to go upstream and the current is too strong. We'll have to walk, in the shadows and under the trees along the riverbank." He looked into her vulnerable eyes, detecting doubt and fear.

"I will slow you down."

"I will carry you if I have to."

Chapter Thirty-One

Alphonse marched down the cobbled road leading towards the market in Saint-Émilion, his balled hands pumping up and down at the end of rigid arms like clubs. His eyes flicked towards a large *Revolution Nationale* poster pasted against a cracked concrete wall in front of which stood two Frenchmen wearing berets, muttering and gesticulating. Alphonse stopped and inched closer.

One of the men, unshaven and leaking wispy grey smoke through his nose and crooked, yellowed teeth, turned to Alphonse. "Pétain is a disgrace!" he growled.

The poster depicted a tumbledown house built on burning foundations standing beside a proud and perfect French house supported on solid foundations: *Travail; Famille; Patrie.*

"The work we do," the wizened man snorted with a guttural sound, "is all for *les Boches*. We have no family, all the young men are prisoners of war or taken away on STOs."

"And the talk of Fatherland," scoffed the second man, shaking his head without turning around, "it's insulting."

Alphonse walked on, shaken and upset by the images he had seen and the betrayal he felt at the hands of their hero, Marshal Pétain. He was lost in thought by the time he reached the paved entrance to the *Mairie*, flanked by ornate cast iron flowerpots containing geraniums shrivelled by the winter frosts. The doorway was guarded by two armed Wehrmacht soldiers standing to attention. Appearing startled by his bold approach, one stabbed an open hand at Alphonse.

"*Halt!*"

"I have come to see Weinführer Bömers," Alphonse said, a little out of breath and brimming with contained anger.

"*Sprechen Sie Deutsch?*"

Alphonse sighed and stiffened his arms by his sides, clenching his fists until his knuckles ached. For the first time he felt overwhelmed by the humiliation and resentment of having to speak German outside his own *Mairie*, built from his own taxes and the taxes of his forebears.

"Weinführer Bömers, *bitte!*" he said, spitting the last word out of his mouth.

An officer strolled out of the doorway, cap on his head, gloved hands, holstered Luger on his hip. "*Was gibt's?*" he said calmly, his eyes moving from the faces of the soldiers – who immediately stiffened and saluted – and settling on Alphonse.

"I need to see Weinführer Bömers," Alphonse said.

The officer angled his head, almost in bemusement.

"You cannot seriously think you can just walk in here and demand to see Hauptsturmführer Bömers." His voice was laced with condescension.

"It is a matter of extreme importance," Alphonse said, staring into the officer's narrow, dark eyes, daring him to look away first.

The officer smiled and looked down as he tapped his shiny leather boot on the stone path. "Who are you?"

"Tell him Alphonse Sabron wants to speak to him urgently. He knows me."

The officer looked up at Alphonse again and considered him closely, rocking on his heels. His mouth opened, as if to speak, but he appeared to be considering his words before finally replying. "The *Hauptsturmführer* has been summoned to Berlin

182

on important business. You'll have to come back another day."
The officer clicked his heels together. "*Adieu.*" Turning on his
heel, he strode back into the *Mairie*, leaving Alphonse
bewildered and deflated. The soldiers' faces hardened and one
gesticulated with an outstretched arm for Alphonse to move
on.

"*Machen Sie das Sie wegkommen!*"

Alphonse turned away and lowered his head, defeated. He
had been plundered by Göring's thugs, heard not a word from
Olivier or Gregoire, and been denied access to Bömers. He felt
a knot of tension twist his stomach as he walked thoughtfully
along the quiet cobbled streets, with not a tourist in sight in
any direction.

Chapter Thirty-Two

Trying to avoid the worst of the sucking, soft mud, yet still remaining hidden beneath the protective canopy of arched trees and shrubs that hung over the riverbank, Jean-Marc and Monique trudged on, predominantly in silence. Above them a waxing moon hung in the frigid night sky, casting jagged slivers across the gentle waters of the Dordogne that flowed beside them. Monique was falling behind.

"I have to rest," she said, bending over and placing her hands on her knees. "I'm sorry."

Jean-Marc turned and cast his eyes around, looking for any signs of life: a light, the glow of a cigarette. There was nothing but darkness. "We can't stop."

"It's too painful," Monique said, apologetic eyes meeting his.

"Come," Jean-Marc said, bending down in front of her, "jump on."

He hoisted Monique onto his back, her arms and legs wrapped around him as they continued. She was surprisingly light, her baggy clothing concealing a smaller frame than anticipated, no doubt trimmed down even further by the food shortages, Jean-Marc thought.

"Where did you learn to speak such good English?" Jean-Marc asked, recalling her animated conversations with the

184

British airmen at Lascombes, and her apparent enjoyment of their company.

"My mother is English," Monique said.

"She lives in Normandy?"

"Yes."

"With your father?" Jean-Marc said, his breath coming a little faster as he struggled on with the extra burden.

"Of course." Monique shifted her weight on his shoulders. "We have a house near Boulogne, a tiny village called Mont Violette."

They walked in silence for a while, just the wet sounds of Jean-Marc's boots in the soft mud.

"I have never been north of Poitiers," Jean-Marc admitted.

The stars above them shimmered, the world below bathed in milky blue lunar light. They moved quietly, embracing the spidery shadows until, finally, they reached the formidable Pont de Pierre. Huddled together beneath one of many elegant iron posts from which trios of lamps hung like fuchsia flowers, a group of German soldiers stamped their feet and smoked cigarettes in the yellow light. Seventeen arches split the strong current and Jean-Marc and Monique had to creep around the enormous curved buttress straddling the bank, holding hands tightly as they pushed against the raw current, pressed against the damp stone, digging their fingernails into the gaps for purchase.

Above them Jean-Marc could clearly hear the German soldiers talking, spitting, smell their cigarette smoke and taste the bitter bile of his own fear. The cold water felt like a thousand needles in his legs, pain that threatened to paralyse him. He looked anxiously at Monique, concerned that her injured leg would not withstand the challenge. But her eyes, fixed and grey in a determined stare, and her mouth, clenched in defiance, told him she would endure.

There were more soldiers now, and the occasional truck rumbling past on the Quai Richelieu. They had to be very careful, tiptoeing, as it were, through the heart of German domination in Bordeaux. Jean-Marc held a finger up to his lips as he and Monique cowered in the shadows to allow the worst of the cold water to drip off their clinging clothes. His legs ached as circulation returned and tried to warm the frozen flesh. Enormous relief surged through him as Monique began to limp forwards, because he knew that his legs could not yet support her weight again so soon.

Making painfully slow progress, they crept through the mud, putting distance between themselves and the guarded Pont de Pierre.

"How will the others ever cross the river?" Monique whispered.

Jean-Marc shook his head. "Never on their bicycles."

A dark structure loomed ahead, flat and featureless, devoid of lighting. Jean-Marc strained his eyes until – as they neared – it became apparent that they had reached Gare Saint-Jean station. His heart suddenly leapt with excitement.

"We may be able to cross here at the railway bridge. I don't see any guards," he said.

Crouching in the shadows, they studied the bridge and the surroundings, searching for weaknesses and dangers. Jean-Marc saw a way up the steep embankment to access the tracks, very much aware of the sky awakening in the east as the dawn approached. Their protective shroud of darkness would soon be gone and they were still some distance from Saint-Émilion.

"Come, hold my hand," he said, leading the way.

Virtually dragging Monique up the crumbling bank, they sank to the ground near the summit, sharp with scattered track ballast rocks and heavy with the smell of grease. Their rapid breaths fogged in the air, illuminated suddenly by an approaching light, a split second before they were deafened by

186

a locomotive's steam whistle. The chug and whoosh of the approaching engine – billowing steam sideways into the clear night – seemed almost comforting, a sound of normality, loud and unmistakeable, a relief from the whispered silences of their night's journey.

Sheltering behind a scrubby bush, they watched the train roll by slowly, its speed increasing gradually and without haste as it clanked its way leisurely over the bridge, as though it was unaware that there was a war on. Jean-Marc studied the freight wagons and felt sick.

"Look at all that wine!" Monique hissed beside him.

Jean-Marc's eyes bulged at what they saw. Behind the slatted freight trucks he could see cases and cases of wines boxed in wood, being transported to the dark heart of the German Reich: Château Pichon Baron, Château Leoville Barton, Château Haut-Brion, Château Palmer, Château Figeac, Château Pétrus, Château d'Yquem. He felt tears prickle his eyes and anger burn his heart. Several flat wagons passed, laden with barrels.

"I cannot watch," Jean-Marc said, turning away, haunted by thoughts of the labours of his father and his grandfather and those before him, working the land of Château Cardinale, making the most of what it had, only for its resplendent fruits to be plundered. He could not bear to think of this happening on such a grand scale right across Bordeaux: pillaging and looting justified in the name of war.

"There are no soldiers. We could jump on," Monique said.

To the rear there were only a few wagons left emerging from the freight yard of Gare Saint-Jean, most of the train now clicking its way over the bridge towards the right bank.

"OK," Jean-Marc said, suddenly animated, shaking off his self-pity and adjusting his feet in the gravel. "We'll grab on to the last wagon and jump off as soon as we're clear on the other side."

187

The final three wagons were slatted cattle trucks and Jean-Marc breathed a premature sigh of relief, hoping that he would not have to stare at Bordeaux's finest wines leaving in the occupier's clutches.

"Now!" he shouted, helping Monique forwards as she faltered on her injured leg.

She grabbed on to the back of the carriage, slipping her feet onto the greasy couplings. Jean-Marc slid in beside her, pushing his fingers into the gaps between the weathered wooden slats. He looked at her and they exchanged a smile. It had been surprisingly easy, and in just a few minutes they would be on the right bank of the Dordogne.

"Help us!" The barely audible, pitiful voice of a young woman from within the truck poured ice into Jean-Marc's veins.

He focused his eyes through the narrow slats into the filleted darkness of the cattle truck and saw huddled figures of people crammed together, some crying, some wailing, others gazing in disbelief into nothing.

"Please, help us!" she said again, imploring, pressing her face against the wooden slats, inches from Jean-Marc's face.

He looked into her brown eyes, rank with terror, dark with despair. Suddenly, the woman's face transformed into Isabelle's and he found himself staring into her eyes, and then, inexplicably, searching beside her for his children, Claude and Odette. He turned sharply to find Monique's eyes fixed on him, tears streaming down her face.

"Call the police, please – do something," the woman pleaded from within.

"Where are they taking us?" a more confident male voice behind the woman asked. "Is this train bound for Germany?"

Jean-Marc realised that many eyes were staring at them, hoping they might represent a last chance of salvation. "I... think so... I'm so sorry," Jean-Marc said in a thick voice.

Where indeed had they taken his family? Where was Isabelle now? Were his children frightened? Were they safe? Were they even still alive?

"Oh God, please, let us out!" shrieked another woman's voice.

In that instant Jean-Marc saw children huddled between the dirty folds of a mother's skirt, urine pouring down the legs of a little girl and splattering on the wooden floorboards, spraying her dusty brown shoes, like rain. He closed his eyes and squeezed them shut tightly, screaming inside his head to banish the awful images. Was this how his own family had been torn from him? Was this the indignity and terror that they had had to endure?

He felt Monique's hand on his shoulder and looked into her wide eyes, and then began to sob.

Chapter Thirty-Three

Jean-Marc and Monique clung to the back of the rear cattle truck for as long as they could, tortured by the desperate pleas for help from within, helpless to do anything but look out for their own safety. As the sky became pinker – glowing with growing intensity through shades of orange and ochre – they tumbled off the carriage onto the unyielding track ballast and rolled into the cover of trackside undergrowth. They managed to cover about two miles before Monique was no longer able to walk, forcing them to shelter in the leeward shadows beneath a single-span stone bridge crossing the River Laurence, just outside Pompignac.

Leaning against each other, Monique's head resting warmly on his shoulder, sleep came quickly for Jean-Marc, but he dreamed, haunted by visions of Isabelle in that same cattle truck, of Odette urinating on the floorboards out of sheer terror, of Claude's face inches from his own, imploring him to set them free. The whole experience had left him shaken and empty.

Hunger came and went, thirst lingered and eventually they both succumbed and drank from the river, which seemed clean and tasted sweeter than sugar. No one disturbed them and Jean-Marc hoped that no one could even see them, tucked down low behind a thorn bush. As dusk banished shadows and welcomed in the camouflage of darkness they began to move again. Monique limped at first, but soon Jean-Marc lifted her onto his shoulders where he felt her head rest against him. She was exhausted.

"It's not far now. We should be there in a few hours," Jean-Marc said.

The moon was fuller but partially obscured behind cloud, creating silver-edged monuments in the sky. Allowing himself to rest only once, Jean-Marc finally reached Château Cardinale just before 2am. Having been out on foot, evading capture during the curfew, brazenly entering the heart of occupied Bordeaux without any papers, he felt imbued with a certain degree of immortality as he decided to make his way across to Château Millandes through his own vineyards. His house was plunged into darkness with no signs of habitation or activity. Perhaps the Germans had moved on, he thought optimistically.

"This is where I live," Jean-Marc said as he negotiated a path between rows of vines. "Or lived," he added.

He felt Monique lift her head briefly and mumble something.

"Look at the state of my vineyard," he muttered, kicking at weeds that grew boldly between his vines. "It is a sacrilege."

He bent down slightly, adjusting his grip on Monique, to inspect the vines up closer.

"There are buds already. I must get into the vineyard to clean it up."

"You can't," Monique mumbled into his coat. "Too dangerous."

Château Millandes was in darkness when they arrived. Gently laying Monique down on the gravel against the wall, Jean-Marc began to knock on the door, and then the windows, calling out in hushed whispers for Alphonse. Eventually a candle flickered from within the house and a suspicious-looking Alphonse, wearing a nightcap on his head, opened the door.

"Come in, quickly!" Alphonse urged, snuffing out the candle.

Monique struggled into the house, leaning heavily against Jean-Marc's shoulder, before collapsing into a kitchen chair.

"Water, please, Alphonse," Jean-Marc said.

"Are you hurt?" Alphonse asked, his face creased in concern as he poured water into two glasses.

"Monique has a flesh wound on her leg. Are the others…?"

Alphonse nodded, handing over the water. "They came yesterday. Where have you been?"

Jean-Marc buried his face in the glass, downing it and asking for another. Monique tried to be more ladylike at first but quickly succumbed to her thirst and swallowed the water in great noisy gulps. Alphonse refilled their glasses in silence.

"We had to hide during the day." Jean-Marc drank again. "Do you know, the vines have buds already, Alphonse, but there are weeds growing everywhere, choking the vines, and I saw mildew on the stems."

"Jean-Marc, listen to me —" Alphonse began.

"It will be a disaster unless we clear the soil and loosen it, and we need copper sulphate, now. Can you not speak to —"

"Jean-Marc!" Alphonse said, raising his voice.

Monique laid a hand on Jean-Marc's arm and raised her eyebrows slightly.

"Why were you separated from the others?" Alphonse asked.

Jean-Marc opened his hands in a vague gesture of helplessness. "They would not come with us."

"You should have stayed with the boys," Alphonse said.

Jean-Marc was about to protest when he caught a glimpse of the look in Monique's eyes and kept his mouth shut. When he looked back at Alphonse, silhouetted in the darkness, he saw the gravity lining his friend's face, as if his skin was being pressed down by the weight of his nightcap.

"Olivier was shot," Alphonse said quietly.

"What?" Monique said.

"Is he...?" Jean-Marc asked, hesitantly.

Alphonse nodded and turned his head into the house. "He is here... with Marthe and me."

"Oh thank God for that," Monique said.

"He needs a doctor, he is not well."

"Well, I will take him for you," Jean-Marc said quickly.

"I can't take him around here. People talk, I'm not even sure who to trust, and if the Germans hear about a gunshot wound or find out anything..." Alphonse paused, biting his lip before looking up to meet Jean-Marc's eyes. "Patrice wants to take him to a doctor in Bergerac, a Maquis sympathiser," he said.

Jean-Marc blew through his lips in exasperation. "How?"

"The gasogene," Alphonse said quietly.

Monique shook her head. "There are German soldiers everywhere."

"But they are mostly around Bordeaux, not so much further east," Jean-Marc said.

"That's what I've heard," Alphonse said.

"But there is Milice in the east," Monique said. "Some of them are worse."

Jean-Marc nodded in concession. There was no safety for someone on the run from the authorities, not even in the *zone libre*.

"What do you think, Jean-Marc?" Alphonse said, looking at him plaintively, seeking support.

"They should have listened to me, I told them it was too dangerous to cross the Pont de Pierre," Jean-Marc said, guilt welling up within him under Alphonse's gaze.

"He did try, *monsieur*," Monique said, placing a hand on Jean-Marc's arm.

"But yes, I think Olivier must go to a doctor. Patrice knows Bergerac, it is his territory." He sighed deeply. "We must trust him, Alphonse. I will go with them."

"No, I cannot risk anyone being caught and traced back to me. You must keep your head down now for a while," Alphonse said, placing his hands on the back of a chair, squeezing it until his knuckles blanched. "I was searched a few days ago, Göring's men came with orders to seek out the best wines, which he believes we are hiding from them."

"What did they find?" Jean-Marc asked.

"They didn't find anybody, thank God, but they took about ten cases of my 1934 – and some others."

"Bömers?" Jean-Marc said accusingly.

Alphonse shrugged. "I don't know."

Jean-Marc thought back to the multitudes of cases of wine he had seen on the freight train at Gare Saint-Jean, leaving Bordeaux for the banquet tables and private cellars of the Third Reich. "There must be something we can do," he said, glancing at Monique, believing that she shared this belief.

Alphonse emitted a throaty sound and turned away. "What can we do? I am going to bed. Here are the keys to the cellar."

"Thank you, *monsieur*," Monique said, and then with soft empathy, "I am sorry to hear about Olivier. He was very brave in Margaux."

"Stay out of sight," Alphonse barked as he left the room.

Chapter Thirty-Four

Monique sat on the cellar floor beside a rack of damson-stained barrels, leaning against the cool stone wall that was peppered with saltpetre crystals. She was devouring the contents of *La Petite Gironde* – the newspaper of Bordeaux – while she listened with one ear to the conversation between Jean-Marc, Alphonse and Federico in the background. The three men were standing around racks of wine barrels, pouring charcoal into each as they sipped red wine. Jean-Marc constantly scratched his legs and his back.

"Won't the charcoal affect the taste of the wine?" Monique said, lowering the newspaper.

"A French woman who does not understand winemaking," Jean-Marc said, shaking his head as he rolled his eyes to the heavens. "*Sacré bleu.*"

"I am from Normandy," Monique protested.

"So you say," Jean-Marc replied and smiled wryly.

Alphonse turned to her, like a father to his child. "The charcoal removes unwanted particles and clears the wine. Normally we would use eggs."

"I still can't believe there are no eggs. Have you ever used charcoal before?" Jean-Marc said.

Alphonse pulled a face as he worked. "Every time there is a war, my friend."

Federico chuckled in agreement. "*Cosi vero.*"

"But how do you know how much charcoal to add to a barrel?" Jean-Marc said, his fingers blackened from handling the charred fragments they had made earlier.

"Depends on the tannin levels," Alphonse said. "This being the '38 – not very ripe fruit, low to moderate tannin levels all pointing to early drinking – what do you think Federico, a cup or two?"

Federico straightened and wiped a hand across his nose, leaving a smudge. "A cupful per barrel to start, we check after a few days, eh?"

Alphonse nodded. "That's what we did during the Great War. It worked perfectly."

"It doesn't...?" Jean-Marc began, gesticulating.

"No, it even eliminates some bad flavours," Alphonse said, looking furtively at Federico, "which can only help the '38."

"Though some would regard that as cheating," Federico added with a nonchalant shrug and a malevolent twinkle in his eye. He chuckled throatily with Alphonse, as though the two were sharing a private joke.

Monique watched Jean-Marc working his way down the row, pulling out the cork stopper on top of each barrel and carefully pouring in a cupful of fragmented charcoal. This was in fact the true essence of the man who had guided her safely through German lines in Bordeaux: tending his wines passionately as they aged in oak. Her eyes followed the movements of his hands: strong yet delicate; casual but measured.

"My vineyard is a mess," Jean-Marc complained. "There are weeds growing wild between all the vines, which are in desperate need of pruning, and there is mildew everywhere. It will be a disaster!" He glanced at Monique. "You saw it, didn't you?"

"I too have problems in my vineyards," Alphonse said, "and mildew."

"Well, who is going to help clear out the weeds?" Jean-Marc continued as though Alphonse had not spoken. "I am stuck here in this cellar all day, and all night."

"And what must I do?" Alphonse said, shrugging his heavy shoulders. "I cannot even care for my own vineyard, let alone tend to yours. My boys are not here, there is no labour, I am at least a month behind."

"Then I will go out," Jean-Marc said petulantly, "at night."

"No!" Alphonse said. "You will put us all in danger."

Jean-Marc hung his head and blew through his lips in exasperation. "This vintage will be a catastrophe if I do nothing. Have you no spare copper sulphate for the mildew?"

Federico laid a calming, blackened hand on Jean-Marc's shoulder. "There is no copper, Jean-Marc, you know that. It is the same right across Europe."

"Well, how do *les Boches* expect us to make good wines under these conditions?" Jean-Marc said, scratching the skin of his back and legs vigorously, his thumb bent like a fish hook and leaving a trail of black smears on his clothing. "Just look at us... pouring charcoal into wine instead of egg whites."

"You are scratching a lot, my friend. Have you got lice?" Alphonse said.

"*Mon Dieu*, no! It is that homemade soap, my skin is like sandpaper. What does Marthe put in it?"

Federico shuffled self-consciously. "Angelica makes it with what little fat we can get and caustic soda," he said.

Jean-Marc rubbed his eyebrow, embarrassed, and Monique smiled to herself as she observed his awkwardness, and his now-blackened forehead, lowering her eyes to the newsprint before he saw her.

"I cannot make wine under these conditions!" Jean-Marc blurted out, frustration boiling over through his facial expressions.

"We have a quota to meet," Alphonse said matter-of-factly, his voice drained of passion. "We have to."

"Quota! *Merde!* We are working for Berlin," Jean-Marc said, disgruntled.

"Listen to this." Monique folded the paper, emitting a loud rustling sound that turned heads. "The pigeons in Bordeaux's squares are all gone." She tapped the paper with a finger.

"What?" Jean-Marc said.

Monique watched the three men – hands blackened like pandas, faces adorned with sooty smudges – craning around to look at her. She could see that even they had lost weight, trousers encasing sinewy legs, belts pulled tight and collars hanging spaciously around bony necks.

"They are starving in the cities," Monique said, "and the people have eaten them."

"All the pigeons?" Alphonse said with disbelief twisting his lined features. "In Bordeaux?"

"Perhaps we should be planting vegetables in the vineyards to help," Monique suggested.

Jean-Marc dismissed this suggestion with a twirl of his hand and a throaty sound. "Vegetables will not grow in the gravelly soils of vineyards." He rolled his eyes heavenwards. "They need pampering, rich soil, water."

"And vines?" Monique said.

"They need to be stressed, of course," Jean-Marc said with contained irritation. "Poor soil – do you know nothing about making wine?"

"At least we all still have wine to drink," Alphonse said.

"Not if Pétain gets his way," Monique replied quickly, holding the newspaper up.

"What do you mean?" Alphonse grumbled.

198

"It says here – page three – he is introducing wine-free days in the week to stretch supplies. With the Germans taking so much and the harvest volumes decreasing there is not enough to go around," Monique said, her eyes flicking from the article in the newspaper back to their astonished faces.

All three men raised their arms in hostile and vocal protest, stamping their feet and shaking their heads in a discordant cacophony of dissent.

"Let me see that," Jean-Marc said, moving towards her.

Monique held out her hand and he grabbed it, pulling her to her feet, holding on to her hand longer than necessary as he smiled at her. "Here," she said, holding out the paper, before wiping the charcoal dust off her hand onto her trousers.

Jean-Marc grabbed the paper and opened it impatiently to find the article. "So the French must go without wine to feed the fat belly of Berlin," Jean-Marc said. "What next?"

"There," Monique said, stabbing her finger onto the page.

She thought back to the freight trucks they had seen leaving Gare Saint-Jean station as she walked over to where Alphonse and Federico stood.

"You know, when we reached the railway line we saw cases and cases of the finest wines being shipped off in a freight train." She paused. "Thousands of bottles and dozens of barrels."

"This is an outrage!" Jean-Marc blurted, smacking the paper. "The French have always drunk wine, why don't the Germans just continue to drink beer?"

"A million bottles a month is a lot of wine to supply," Alphonse said.

"And with harvest yields down by nearly a half…" Federico muttered.

Monique could see dejection written on the faces of the winemakers. The gross unfairness of it all struck a chord within her. "We must do something."

"What can we do?" Alphonse said plaintively, curling both hands into claws.

"It's true! *Merde*. Here it is, there are no pigeons left in Bordeaux's squares," Jean-Marc said, almost in disbelief, staring wide-eyed at the newspaper.

Monique picked up Jean-Marc's glass and drank liberally from it. "Have you heard from Olivier?"

"Not yet," Alphonse said.

"Do we know when Patrice and the others might be back?"

Alphonse turned away and sighed.

"Is Olivier better?" Jean-Marc said, looking up from the paper.

Alphonse shrugged.

"Can he... I mean... his legs...?" Jean-Marc stammered.

Alphonse shook his head almost imperceptibly, his eyes sad and watery.

"I have an idea," Monique said quietly, "a way to stop some of this gross injustice. But we need more people."

"I'm not sure I want to hear this," Alphonse said, refilling his wine glass.

"We won't involve you," Monique said as Jean-Marc joined them, thumping the paper down onto a barrel in disgust.

"Please, don't do anything stupid," Alphonse said. "Don't draw attention to Château Millandes." He looked tired suddenly.

"We can't just sit back and let them plunder all the wine," Monique said. "*Your* wine."

"Bömers pays for all the wine he takes," Alphonse said defensively.

Jean-Marc guffawed. "What, at twenty Francs to the Deutschmark? That's robbery."

A silence enveloped them, the smells of fermenting and ageing wine and oak barrels and limestone calcite suddenly amplified.

"This," Monique said, sweeping her arm around the gloomy cellar, "this is a way of life, and I cannot just stand and watch it being raped and... stolen." She paused, conscious of their eyes on hers. "I have an idea."

Alphonse and Federico exchanged a wary glance, old men who were weary of youthful ideology in times of war. Perhaps, Monique thought, they had seen too much in the past.

"Tell me," Jean-Marc said, his voice taut and his eyes dancing over her face. "I want to hear it."

Chapter Thirty-Five

Alphonse was summoned to the *Mairie* in Saint-Émilion within a matter of days. There was no wine on Bömers' desk this time, no cigars on offer, and he detected in the former *maire*'s office a distinctly cool atmosphere that gave him goosebumps.

Bömers sat rigidly behind his desk, tapping on it with his gold Schäffer pen, his body bouncing slightly as though his leg was moving rhythmically beneath the desk. The muscles of his temple and jaw tightened constantly, flanking hard eyes that banished even a flicker of acknowledgement that Alphonse had entered and sat down.

"Heinz?" Alphonse said with a polite nod of his head.

Bömers stared at him without response, effectively unsettling Alphonse, who began to squirm in his hard chair.

"Do you know where I've been?" Bömers said eventually.

The sound of the pen tapping on the desk was beginning to erode into Alphonse's head: constant, probing, relentless.

"Berlin?" Alphonse said, unclasping his hands briefly.

Bömers sat, rocking, nodding slightly. "Do you know why?"

Alphonse shook his head and watched Bömers stand up stiffly and move to the window that overlooked white peach blossoms drifting across the gravel garden below.

"I was summoned by Göring to High Command, to be dressed down, threatened…" He paused, bending slightly to enable him to lean on his knuckles on the windowsill.

Alphonse found the smell of oak panelling and linseed oil suddenly nauseating. Usually it was masked by tobacco smoke, but for some reason Bömers was not smoking.

"Do you want to know why?" Bömers barked, turning around to glare at Alphonse. "Because I am not obtaining enough of the very best wines from you and your winegrowing Bordelais, who are quite evidently hiding it from me." His voice rose sharply.

Alphonse swallowed and tried to maintain resolute and unflinching eye contact.

"I have tried to be reasonable with you but it seems you have all decided to play me for a fool. Göring is demanding answers. Göring is demanding action." Bömers was beginning to form spittle on his lower lip.

"I came here several days ago to tell you that some SS men came and stole wine from me under Göring's orders," Alphonse said.

Bömers nodded, as a headmaster nods at a hapless, cornered pupil waiting to be disciplined. "And what did they find of interest to… er… 'steal'?"

Alphonse was beginning to perspire under Bömers' intense scrutiny, regretting his decision to put on a heavy woollen coat. He had never seen his former friend like this before, not in all the years that they had shared the excitement of each new Bordeaux vintage together. It was clear that someone had got to Bömers, most likely Göring. "A few cases, the last cases in fact, of my 1934," he said.

"How convenient," Bömers said, deeply sarcastic. "Strange that this should have happened at every château they visited." He walked around to face Alphonse directly, placing his hands on the armrests of Alphonse's chair, leaning in as he spoke.

"Do you think Göring is stupid? Do you think I am stupid? Huh?"

Up close, his breath smelled of stale tobacco and onion. Alphonse searched the face of his former business colleague, now a man tasked with the impossible. He did not know what Bömers was looking for but hoped simply that his own facial expressions were not giving anything away. Bömers pulled away and moved back to his chair, slumping into it with a heavy sigh, as if in surrender.

"We sell our wine to *you*. We simply cannot have SS thugs wandering into châteaux as they please, plundering wine to order for the Nazi elite," Alphonse said with surprising conviction, perhaps sensing a weakness in Bömers' armour.

"Oh, so *you* are giving the orders now," Bömers said, mocking.

"I thought you were in charge, not Göring."

Bömers did not rise to the provocation, instead appearing to measure his words before speaking. "It's not just about the wine, you know. There is a bigger agenda at play here." Bömers reached into a drawer and extracted his silver cigarette case, flipping it open and hastily lighting a Bremaria without offering one to Alphonse. After drawing deeply on the cigarette, he continued. "There are suspicions of resistance activity amongst Bordeaux's vignerons, Alphonse, subversive actions being carried out with their knowledge and even their help." He hesitated, drawing his hands up to his face, placing his thumbs beneath his chin and tapping his fingers together in front of his nose. "You wouldn't know anything about this, would you?"

Alphonse felt his bladder weaken and forced a chuckle. "This is absurd, Heinz. What are you suggesting?"

Bömers laughed insincerely. "Absurd, absolutely. Tell me, Gregoire was called up for STO, was he not?"

Alphonse felt his heart skip a beat and hoped he had not paled visibly.

"He never reported," Bömers said.

Alphonse shrugged pathetically, lost for words, frightened.

"Where is he?" Bömers demanded.

Alphonse stared through burning eyes at Bömers, not daring even to blink. "He would not be the only young French man to refuse STO."

"And how would you know?" Bömers said, leaning forward slightly, his eyebrows lifting with curiosity.

"People talk."

"And what about Olivier?" Bömers emitted a cloud of smoke. "Where is he now?"

Alphonse felt his stare falter. This was a low blow, and a very raw wound for him still. "He is only a boy, Heinz, you know that, too young to be caught up in this war."

"Perhaps," Bömers said, leaning back, "but there are sixteen-year-olds fighting on the eastern front against the Russians."

"That doesn't make it right."

"But it's OK if they are French and fighting *against* the Germans?" Bömers shot back quickly. "Is that it?"

Alphonse felt his shirt begin to stick to his sweaty skin as a trickle of perspiration ran down his back. He needed to urinate and yet his mouth was as dry as a cactus flower.

"Let me be blunt, Alphonse: Göring is breathing down my neck and leaning on me with all of his considerable bulk. I can only do one thing, and that is to watch all of you very closely and ensure that the *Reichsmarschall* gets what he wants, or it's my neck."

Alphonse nodded.

"I have no intention of losing my head, and in any case if I don't give him what he wants he will simply take it anyway," Bömers made a face, "as you have already discovered."

"So now what?" Alphonse asked.

Bömers stared at him, spinning the pen around absently on his desk with an index finger. "Things could get very nasty if we are not all extremely careful, Alphonse. No more games."

Alphonse stared at his old friend, trying to read his eyes, his face. He rubbed a hand across his stubbly cheeks. He knew they were being given an ultimatum: for the Reich, or else.

"Understand?" Bömers said, lifting his eyebrows menacingly. "No more games."

Alphonse pushed his chair back and stood up. Bömers picked up his pen and began to tap it rhythmically on his desk once again as Alphonse walked to the door.

"Do I make myself clear?" Bömers said firmly.

Alphonse paused with his hand on the polished brass doorknob. "I shall spread the word."

Chapter Thirty-Six

Jean-Marc and Monique lay side by side in the darkness, shrouded by the tiny yellow spring blossoms of a common gorse bush. In the moonlight her pale complexion glowed around the smudges of coal dust they had applied for camouflage.

"Where will we get explosives from?" Jean-Marc asked in a hushed whisper.

A steam locomotive emitted a loud hiss of steam in the distance across several lines of empty railway tracks.

"I have a contact in Bordeaux. Patrice knows him too," Monique said, her eyes just inches from his face, the pleasant odour of her breath warming his skin.

"And where does he get them from?"

Monique smiled. "What, do you think those British airmen bring over in their aircraft?"

"Ah, so that's why you were so keen to rescue them: a supply of explosives."

"And guns. Sten guns, revolvers, ammunition – radios too."

"British army?" Jean-Marc said.

Monique shook her head. "SOE, special operations – there are agents all over France."

Jean-Marc looked at Monique, long and intensely, as her eyes scanned the seemingly deserted railway goods yard. Her nose was sculpted, almost perfect, the *alae* moving ever so slightly with each breath; her lips, violet in the moonlight, thin and delicate. He had never met a woman from Normandy but she was unlike any woman he had known before, both beautiful and dangerous.

"Someone's coming," Monique whispered and crouched lower in the gorse.

Lumbering, unhurried footsteps approached, the crunch of hard-soled boots on track ballast. Jean-Marc felt his jaw tighten as he pressed his face against the cold earth, warmed only by Monique's breath. Jean-Marc looked up to see a corpulent figure nearing their position, a silver chain hanging from his waistcoat glinting in the moonlight. He meandered casually towards the bushes where they lay hidden. Suddenly, Monique emulated the sound of an owl hooting, once, then again. The man coughed, tobacco phlegm, cleared his throat and then returned the call.

"It's Thibault," Monique whispered into Jean-Marc's ear. "It is much cooler in Paris," she said in a hushed tone.

"Bordeaux can be warm in April," said the man, bending to tie a bootlace.

"There is frost in Paris."

"There is no frost here."

Monique sat up so that her face was exposed, drawing Thibault towards them.

"Who are you?" Thibault hissed, his eyes then finding Jean-Marc and widening. "Where is Patrice?"

"Patrice is in Bergerac, tending a wounded colleague," Monique said.

Thibault rubbed his chin and cast a suspicious glance at Jean-Marc.

"When is the next shipment of wine leaving?" Monique said.

"Thursday night."

"Anything interesting... for London?"

Thibault rubbed his chin. "There is a large consignment marked for the Luftwaffe in Juvincourt."

"Juvincourt? Where's that?" Jean-Marc asked.

"North of Paris, Picardy I think," Monique said before turning back to Thibault. "Any prisoners?"

Thibault shrugged and looked over his shoulder furtively. "How should I know? There was a truck full of them just the other day, so probably not."

"Are there soldiers on the trains?" Jean-Marc asked.

Thibault eyed Jean-Marc cautiously. "Not usually, no."

In the distance orders shouted in German could be heard, jarring consonants uttered in anger, floating eerily across the still and cool night air.

"I must go. Good luck, whatever you're planning," Thibault said, retreating as stealthily as he had approached, whistling *La Mer* slowly and out of tune.

Monique and Jean-Marc wasted no time in withdrawing from the trackside, slithering down the embankment to the gully at its base. Lying in a twisted heap on rotting walnut husks they waited to ensure that no one had seen or heard them.

"I must go to my contact, tell him about Juvincourt and get explosives," Monique said.

"What about Patrice and the others?" Jean-Marc said, getting to his feet and brushing mud off his trousers.

"They are not here," Monique said, shrugging. "I see no sense in delaying."

Thursday night was overcast and a light drizzle hung in the air, defying gravity. Jean-Marc followed Monique, who had seamlessly assumed control, making her way like a trained professional from one shadowy vantage point to the next: here a flaking gatepost pillar, there an unpruned row of vines. She

209

moved like a panther, only the occasional sideways glance revealing her milky facial skin partially smeared with coal dust.

The canvas rucksack – Royal Air Force issue, no doubt, dropped by British airmen along with weapons – dug uncomfortably into Jean-Marc's ribs, the straps too high for comfort and the buckles awkwardly positioned. Inside his rucksack was half the amatol explosive Monique had procured from her contact, sealed in brass tubes. The rest was in her rucksack, together with detonators and wiring.

They had set off early as soon as darkness fell, heading for an area north-east of Saint-André-de-Cubzac, where the railway line headed north towards Angoulême. Moving without any rest breaks they covered ground remarkably quickly and Jean-Marc found himself in awe of Monique's physical agility and confidence in the absence of Patrice's dominance. As they circumvented Libourne through the flat and uninteresting landscape of Pomerol, Jean-Marc felt increasingly depressed by the good state of the exalted vineyards they passed through, even though Pomerol had only been officially delimited as an *appellation* some fifteen years before. The weeds had been cleared, the vines pruned, and even though he did find evidence of some mildew here and there, he was struck by the dramatic contrast between his own vineyards and these of Pomerol. It left a bitter taste of resentment in his mouth and he spat on the ground. The fact that he had never received recognition from the new authorities for his commitment to quality at Château Cardinale, let alone the efforts of his forebears, still rankled, made even worse by the anticipated elevation of Alphonse's Château Millandes to *Grand Cru*.

By the time they reached the *terroire* of Fronsac and the Libournais district the increasingly dishevelled state of the vineyards began to assuage his disgruntlement. In these

210

humble winegrowing areas there was evidence of as much neglect in the vineyards as he had observed in his own. He could see that many ordinary winegrowers were struggling with the wartime restrictions. Jean-Marc glanced up to see Monique several strides ahead of him, totally unaware of his preoccupation with the state of the vineyards they were passing through.

"Do you think Patrice will be pissed off?" Jean-Marc said, trying to catch up to Monique and hungering for breath.

"What for?"

"You going ahead on such a dangerous mission without him?"

"I don't care. He is not my master," Monique replied without looking around or stopping. "How much further do we have to go?"

Jean-Marc stopped, stabbing his hands onto his hips, and looked around for orientation. "Less than a mile, I would say – that will take us close to Marsas."

Monique studied her wristwatch. "It's 10.30 already. We'll have to hurry."

They set off with renewed vigour, covering the terrain with speed and purpose. On foot the furrowed fields and vineyards offered welcome cover and invisibility, but the going was brutal underfoot.

"How is your leg?" Jean-Marc asked, out of breath.

"Which one?" she retorted, turning to reveal a cheeky grin.

For some strange reason the finality of reaching the railway line seemed to spark a sense of vulnerability in Jean-Marc. He realised that crouching over the exposed tracks, engaged in illicit activity, with nothing but two glistening parallel lines stretching away to either side, was inherently dangerous. Their journey to Saint-André, through the *zone occupée* without papers, after the curfew, with explosives strapped to their backs, had been exciting. Yet now, climbing the elevated

211

embankment to the tracks and strapping brass tubes filled with amatol to the tracks using adhesive tape screamed 'dangerous activity punishable by execution' at him.

Monique worked with practised precision, her fingers seemingly knowing exactly what they were doing. Could she have done this before, Jean-Marc wondered? Was this the same woman he had guided back from Lascombes?

"Just watch me," she said, strapping a tube to the side of the cold railway track. "Push the detonator in *very* slowly, amatol doesn't like sudden movements, then expose the wires with your teeth." She bit the wire and pulled off the insulation, spitting it out. "Connect it to the detonator and run it away under the tracks so the wheels don't cut it."

"Where did you learn all this?" Jean-Marc said as he watched her. "Patrice?"

Monique scoffed and continued working. "Patrice would never let me do anything."

"Is that why you want to do this on your own?"

Monique shrugged. "Perhaps. But this is not about me, or about Patrice, it's about the battle for France."

In Monique's purposeful and focused presence Jean-Marc found himself comforted by her confidence and determination. As drops of moisture from the drizzle dripped off the end of his nose he secured a tube of amatol to the track and repeated her instructions, glancing up to check that he was doing it right. It felt good. It felt empowering, as though he was doing something to secure the future of his beloved Bordeaux, far better than hiding in Alphonse's damp cellar, cowering from the neighbouring garrison of German soldiers.

A distant train hooted and Jean-Marc was startled, fumbling with a detonator and wiring.

"Careful," Monique said.

Staring down the disappearing tracks he could see nothing but sleepers carrying the relentlessly straight, wet steel away into the distant void. He strained his eyes into the murky haze but could not make out any movement.

"You can feel it coming," Monique said, pressing her cheek to the rail. "Hurry, feed the wires out as we go."

They retreated with the entrails of detonator wires being laid across the chocolaty earth. Hiding behind a mound of damp earth at least two hundred yards from the tracks, Monique deftly exposed the wires with her teeth, twisting them into positive and negative strands, and looped them through the detonator box terminals.

"Ready?" she said, looking at him.

Jean-Marc's heart was racing and he was suddenly unable to speak, nodding instead, swallowing bile and suppressing the urge to urinate. Here he was, a fifth-generation winemaker from Château Cardinale, about to make war on the Germans. He wanted to pinch himself to confirm it was not a dream.

"Can you see anything yet?" Monique said.

Jean-Marc squinted through the binoculars, water from the incessant drizzle hanging in his eyebrows and fogging the eyepieces. Focusing the image, he saw freight wagons and flatbed wagons stacked with barrels of wine.

"I see lots of wine," he said.

"Any prisoners?" Monique said.

Jean-Marc scanned the train, forward and back. It wasn't easy in the darkness.

"Look towards the rear of the train," she suggested.

"I can't see anything."

He lowered the binoculars and their eyes met. She lifted the plunger on the detonator box.

"Would it make any difference if there were prisoners?" Jean-Marc said. "I mean, at least this way they would have a chance to escape an otherwise certain fate."

Monique shrugged and adjusted her fingers on the T-handle of the detonator, apparently measuring the texture of the handle that would soon unleash the fires of defiance. Jean-Marc studied her resolute, cool face, a gentle bite on the outer edge of her lower lip the only sign of any nervousness.

"You done this before?" he asked.

"Only in training."

"Training?"

"Concentrate," she said.

The train approached, the chugging whoosh of steam and billowing grey-black smoke getting louder. His heart was pounding in his chest, his mouth dry, his fingers trembling, and yet his soul was soaring with exhilaration. The train crossed the point where they had placed the amatol. Monique waited. Jean-Marc glanced at her anxiously. Suddenly she grimaced and pushed the plunger down. A burst of light and orange flames heaved freight wagons into the air with a deafening boom and the tearing screech of metal.

The noise was incredible and Jean-Marc instinctively covered his ears as wagon after wagon lurched off the fractured tracks and smashed into the wet ground below, sending plumes of mud into the air. It only lasted about half a minute before an eerie quietness began to return. The rear wagon clung to the tracks, as did the locomotive in the front, motionless where it had stopped some distance down the line.

Monique jumped up and down, her face lit up with ecstasy, balled fists pumping the air. They jumped into each other's arms and he felt her embrace, firm and strong, pulling her into him – the softness of her breasts, the prominences of her pelvis – he felt it all. She withdrew slightly, her face exuding manic pleasure.

"We did it!" she whispered.

Suddenly their lips touched, gently at first, followed by the moistness of her delicate tongue, probing, caressing. Surprise and pleasure rippled through his body. He did not know how it had happened, who had initiated it, and he didn't care. His

214

nostrils were filled with the acrid smell of smoke and chemicals while his mouth bathed in the sweet taste of her.

She stopped kissing him, touched his face tenderly with one finger, tracing it down his cheek, then turned to survey the scene of carnage.

"I smell wine," she said.

"So do I."

Wine leaking from shattered bottles and ruptured barrels ran in languid rivulets across the uneven ground, snaking towards them, seeping back into its wet earthen cradle. They watched in horror for several moments.

"What a waste of good wine," Monique lamented.

"At least *les Boches* will not drink it," Jean-Marc said, licking his lips and yearning for the taste of Monique again.

Two men jumped down from the locomotive and ran away into the temporary refuge of night, leaving the untended engine hissing steam onto the tracks and smoke billowing from its chimney. Jean-Marc watched the scene in stunned silence: overturned freight wagons with their doors broken open, splintered boxes of wine, smoke rising from the shattered wreckage, everything, everywhere, fractured, twisted and mangled. He had never seen such devastation before: the ravages of war.

"We should go," Monique said. "Help me to pull in the wiring."

Within minutes they were gone, moving quickly and cautiously through the same shadows as before, retracing their footsteps back to the safety of Saint-Émilion before all hell broke loose.

Chapter Thirty-Seven

Olivier was back. Gregoire carried him into the château like a sleeping child with limp legs, Olivier's emaciated arms wrapped around his brother's neck as he clung to him like a gecko. Marthe wept into her red and white chequered apron. Jean-Marc and Monique watched, side by side, from the open door to the cellar as Patrice unfolded his lanky frame from the driver's seat of the dusty gasogene. Only Anton had accompanied them back from Bergerac, his lazy eye somewhat accentuated by the late hour in the day.

"Thank you, Patrice. I owe you a debt of gratitude," Alphonse said, emotion straining his face as he stepped forward to grab Patrice's hand.

"You owe me nothing," Patrice said, catching sight of Jean-Marc and Monique.

Alphonse followed Gregoire into the house, eager to see his invalid son and settle him in. Patrice and Anton ambled over to the cellar door, hands pushed into baggy trousers.

"Monique," Patrice said. "Jean-Marc." His eyes did not miss the intimacy of their proximity to each other.

"How is Olivier?" Monique said.

Patrice shrugged and rubbed his stubbly face, heavy with dark hair. "He is paralysed." He pulled a face.

Jean-Marc turned away and cursed silently. What a disastrous outcome from an entirely avoidable confrontation. Guilt wormed its way to the surface of his skin through every pore. He knew Olivier's predicament was not his fault, but his own conscience and Patrice's accusatory eyes filled him with doubt.

"It's not your fault," Monique said warmly.

Patrice emitted a dismissive guttural sound and smiled conspiratorially at Anton.

"They crossed the Pont de Pierre like you did and that's why he was shot," Jean-Marc said defensively, irked by Patrice's implication.

"Oh, so it's my fault now?" Patrice mocked.

"If they had stayed with us he would still be OK," Jean-Marc said. "I'm fairly sure of it."

"And what do you know about these things, wine man?"

"That's enough," Monique interrupted, glaring at Patrice. "Any other news?"

Patrice and Anton glanced at each other, Anton peering out cautiously from beneath the canopy of a puffy eyelid. "Did you not hear about the train at Marsas?" Patrice asked.

"A train packed with wine destined for Berlin – blown off the tracks!" Anton said with sudden enthusiasm.

Jean-Marc just stared back at them impassively, and then Monique's eyes met his and she winked at him. He felt a surge of electricity between himself and his new accomplice.

"That was us," Monique said.

Patrice's face was a study in astonishment. His jaw hung open slackly and his skin pulled taut, expressionless.

"You two derailed a German goods train?" Anton said with a derisive snigger, shifting his weight on his feet.

Jean-Marc nodded back and felt Monique take his hand. Her warm, smooth fingers slid between his and squeezed.

"I don't believe it," Patrice said. "I don't fucking believe it!"

217

"We're going to do it again," Jean-Marc said.

Patrice stepped forward and stabbed a dagger-like finger into Jean-Marc's chest, repeating the motion twice. "Who the hell do you think are you, suddenly?"

"Stop it!" Monique said, stepping forward. "You're behaving like a child. We're at war – every man who can, must do."

Patrice stepped back and shook his head, breathing heavily. "What's this then?" he said, casually gesturing towards their held hands.

"What of it?" Monique said.

Patrice stared at Jean-Marc, eyes icy and provocative, as though he was looking for any reason to step forward and punch Jean-Marc in the face.

"Patrice," Alphonse said from the doorway to the château, trying to keep his voice down. "Please hide the gasogene in the barn."

Patrice nodded and turned back to face Jean-Marc. "You are a vigneron, not Maquis," he hissed. "Remember what you are good at."

"We're at war, Patrice. *Les Boches* live in my house, I am not a proper vigneron under these conditions."

Patrice stared at Jean-Marc, his face deadpan though his eyes burned like white-hot discs. "Is it because you are a Jew, do you simply want revenge... is that it?"

"Stop it, Patrice. Damn it! Have you been drinking or something?" Monique cut in.

"Fuck this. I'm going back to Bergerac," Patrice muttered and turned away. "You coming, Monique?"

"We're fighting the Germans here, Patrice, stopping them from taking every last bottle of wine from Bordeaux. What are you doing in Bergerac?" Monique said.

Patrice turned back to her and grinned mockingly. "You are going to get yourself killed, Monique, which is a pity, because... I like you."

With that he climbed into the gasogene and waited for Anton who seemed frozen to the spot, staring at Monique.

"Tell Louis and Nicolas what we're doing, Anton. We could do with good help to keep the Germans away from our precious wine," Monique said.

Jean-Marc squeezed her hand in his and felt her press against him. Though he had not expected Patrice to be overjoyed about their activities, he had not expected such a venomous reaction from him.

"Come on, Anton," Patrice barked with his hands clasped on the steering wheel.

"Think about it, Patrice. We are doing what needs to be done. I'm sure you know that," Jean-Marc said. "Join us."

The gasogene pulled away before Anton had even closed his door.

"Idiot!" Monique said, retreating into the cellar and burying her face in both hands, smothering a muted scream as she shook with apparent rage.

"Were you and Patrice...?" Jean-Marc asked.

Monique laughed. "In his dreams."

Jean-Marc stood with his arms hanging limply at his sides. "Did he try?"

Monique cocked her head and raised one eyebrow. "Does it bother you?"

Jean-Marc approached her, preparing to envelop her in his arms when Federico emerged from the shadows, yawning and seemingly oblivious to their presence. Monique smiled at Jean-Marc's embarrassment.

"Is Olivier back?" Federico asked.

"Yes, he's in the house," Jean-Marc said.

Federico grunted and continued shuffling, looking older by the day.

"I am going to fetch more amatol tomorrow night. You coming?" Monique said quietly.

Jean-Marc placed a hand on each of her shoulders, watching surreptitiously as Federico ambled out through the cellar door.

"Just where did you become such a soldier girl?" With his face inches from hers, he felt her hands around his waist, smelled her breath on his face. "And why did you hide it for so long?"

"Kiss me," she said, "while he's gone."

Chapter Thirty-Eight

"What are you doing?" Jean-Marc said irritably, emerging from the darkness of the tunnel in which he slept to find Alphonse piling pots, pans, electrical cables and old water pipes onto a clashing heap.

In addition to the intrusive noise Jean-Marc had to shield his eyes – not long awake to the new day – from the bright light streaming in through the open cellar doors.

"I'm collecting copper," Alphonse said, lobbing a tarnished U-bend pipe onto the pile where it clanged against a pot.

Jean-Marc gestured in frustration with his hands and then planted them squarely on his hips. "Why?"

Aware of his puzzled gaze, Alphonse stopped and straightened. "The mildew is getting worse in my vineyards. I have heard that there is a school science teacher who makes copper sulphate – if you get him the copper."

"Where?"

Alphonse shrugged and continued foraging in the corner of the cellar. "Libourne."

Jean-Marc nodded, forcing his eyes open wide in an attempt to wake up quickly. "This is good. Will there be some for my vines too?"

Alphonse stopped again and gazed at him. "Find me more copper and I will keep some for you."

221

Jean-Marc nodded. "OK. How is Olivier?"

"Not good."

"His legs...?"

Alphonse shook his head, sadness across his lined face. "He is paralysed. One night of madness and that is my son's life, forever."

Jean-Marc felt the guilt, unsure whether Alphonse was insinuating anything, but very much aware of the informal expectation that he would protect his neighbour's young sons.

"You are keeping him here, at the château?" Jean-Marc said.

"What can I do? He is not well enough to sleep in the tunnels with the rest of you," Alphonse said.

"But if they find him?" Jean-Marc said, regretting his vocalised thought as soon as it left his lips.

Alphonse simply nodded, holding Jean-Marc's gaze knowingly. They both understood the danger. If the Germans were to discover Olivier, paralysed from a recent gunshot wound to his spine, it would raise more questions than Alphonse could possibly hope to answer.

"He is my son, what else can I do?" Alphonse said, his eyes appearing swimmy. "In war you do what you must, that's what an old friend told me."

"Do you know what we are doing?" Jean-Marc said.

Alphonse nodded, slowly, gravely. "The train at Marsas."

"Yes," Jean-Marc replied cautiously, unsure how Alphonse would react.

"Good."

"You don't want us to stop?" Jean-Marc said, surprised.

Alphonse shook his head such that his jowls quivered. "Send them to Hell." He picked up another twisted pipe. "But first, help me find more copper."

222

Chapter Thirty-Nine

Alphonse and Federico were satisfied with the result and no further charcoal was added to the barrels of 1938 Château Millandes, which they began to bottle a few days later. The war-issue pale green glass bottles were insipid, cheap-looking substitutes to hold his coveted Saint-Émilion wine. But they consoled themselves in the knowledge that most of this wine, from a mediocre year, would end up either in Germany or in a German forward offensive unit, being quaffed by pimply foot soldiers, most likely with a preference for Pilsner. The wine in these cheap bottles would never adorn the shelves of discerning wine merchants in New York, or London, and most likely not even Paris.

For Jean-Marc the most frustrating point, though, was thinking of his own 1938 vintage sitting in barrels in his cellar, unfinished, spending too long in oak, spoiling. Unless – he shuddered to imagine – the German soldiers had already plundered it during one of their numerous drunken orgies. All he could do was close his eyes to banish these thoughts. Not once in all his years of helping his father, as well as running Château Cardinale himself, had he failed to see a vintage through to its preordained conclusion: from soil to vine to bottle.

It was a relief when Monique once again dragged him away one dark night, with rucksacks of amatol strapped to their backs. This time they would be heading further north than Marsas to evade German patrols that had been increased in number and extended in range around the environs of Bordeaux. The German response to the bombing had been swift and substantial and on their second mission Jean-Marc and Monique had to be far better prepared.

In addition to amatol Jean-Marc carried food: *saucisson* and *pain de campagne*, and two bottles of wine; Monique had also packed a Welrod pistol and two hand grenades obtained from her contact in Bordeaux.

"Where will we hide during the day?" Monique said as they walked briskly through the darkness of vineyards, flush with fledgling foliage that, in the reflected moonlight, looked the colour of clay.

"Everyone has mildew," Jean-Marc commented, pausing to examine the new growth on the vines, fondling the shoots. "Untreated, it is going to destroy this vintage."

Monique chuckled. "You're impossible."

"What?"

"Can't you put winemaking out of your mind for one minute?"

Jean-Marc emitted a wheezing protest. "This is like asking a Catholic priest to forget the Virgin Mary."

Monique turned and laughed at Jean-Marc. "No it's not."

"You cannot ask a priest such a thing, can you?"

"As I said, you're impossible. Now, where will we spend tomorrow?"

"Ah," Jean-Marc clucked his tongue, "we must stay out of sight."

"I know that." Monique rolled her eyes. "Where?"

"We'll find an empty barn somewhere."

The air hung heavy and quiet, pregnant with unsaid implications. It would be the first time that Monique and Jean-Marc had been truly alone since that first passionate kiss had ignited something between them, free from the distant snoring of Federico, or Angelica's coughing. Jean-Marc was well aware of it, and he hoped Monique felt it too.

Monique stumbled in a ditch and lurched forward suddenly, face first into a hedgerow. "Shit!" she hissed, perhaps louder than she had intended.

Brambles had scratched her cheeks and drawn blood, leaving broken thorns embedded in her woollen hat. Jean-Marc stared at her and drew closer to check her face.

"You OK?"

She nodded, brushing the thorns off and sucking the wiped blood off her hands. Jean-Marc tenderly ran a finger across her facial skin.

"You swear in English," Jean-Marc said.

"Did I?" Monique replied evasively. "I'm fine. We must keep moving." She walked on, putting distance between herself and Jean-Marc.

"What's the hurry?" Jean-Marc asked.

"Thibault said he thought the train might leave earlier, remember," Monique said. "The Germans are jumbling the train departures, making them less predictable."

Jean-Marc watched her walking from behind, her long legs striding effortlessly. The wounded calf had healed well and left no discernible limp. How old was she, he wondered? Had she been married? Did she have children waiting for her somewhere in France? Had she been separated from them, as he had been from Odette and Claude?

"What made you come down here, from Normandy?" Jean-Marc said. "It's a long way."

Monique did not turn around. "I thought I already told you."

"No, you didn't."

She walked quietly, just her heavy breathing and the trudging sounds of their boots audible. "I wanted to fight the Germans."

"There are no Germans in Normandy."

"I needed to get to the *zone libre* and join the Maquis. So I headed for Bergerac."

"And met Patrice," Jean-Marc finished.

"And met Patrice, and Louis, and Nicolas and Anton."

"Your parents?" Jean-Marc said.

"They fled."

"Where to?"

She hesitated, just momentarily. "England."

Jean-Marc felt a ripple of surprise move through him. "But you stayed," he mused.

Monique nodded. "Uh-huh."

"Husband?"

"No."

"Children?"

"Stop it!" Monique said, a little too forcefully, and then covered her mouth and hunched over, glancing around furtively. "Sorry," she whispered. "Would I be down here fighting with the Maquis if I had responsibilities?"

Perhaps, perhaps not, Jean-Marc thought to himself. *Everyone has their own reasons.* He considered his own, hardly honourable, reasons – his stubborn refusal to flee with his family – that had led him to this point.

"Everyone is motivated by something, aren't they? Gregoire is avoiding STO, so are some of the others. I have my reasons, as you know," Jean-Marc said, letting his sentence hang.

Monique turned and smiled at Jean-Marc playfully, raising an eyebrow and revealing a rash of dark bramble thorn scratches on her cheek in the cerulean moonlight. "Oh, I have my reasons too."

She said no more and Jean-Marc did not pursue it. By dawn they had covered most of the distance and found themselves on the southern outskirts of Saint-Yzan. To the right of the tracks, fields of vineyards stretched away across the flat landscape. To the left, a line of dense shrubbery and trees formed a natural flanking obstruction.

"The railway line splits just after Saint-Yzan. We must set the explosives this side," Jean-Marc said, and Monique nodded.

In the early morning gloom they surveyed the landscape, hands on hips, breath fogging the fresh air. A pale sun threatened to peer over the cold, flat horizon at any moment. They moved off to the right of the tracks through rows of vines, Jean-Marc slowing frequently to examine the growth, study the techniques of pruning, of training the vines to the trellises, occasionally picking up handfuls of soil and crumbling it between his fingers before tasting it.

"What are you doing?" Monique said, pulling a face.

"I'm tasting the terroir," Jean-Marc explained. "You know, my soil is quite different even to Alphonse's, right next door to me."

Monique said nothing.

"Maybe that is why his wines are almost *Grand Cru*." Jean-Marc discarded the soil. "I know what the soil tastes like in every section of my vineyard," he added, feeling that he needed to convince Monique.

"You'll catch worms," Monique said.

"*Merde*! There is mildew here too," Jean-Marc said to himself, studying one of the vines.

Unpruned, with remnants of last year's shrivelled fruit still clinging to the twisted stems and choked by a profuse growth of weeds and wild flowers, the vineyard reminded Jean-Marc of his last encounter with his own vineyards at Château Cardinale. They were in a pitiful state.

227

"I don't think anyone has lived here all winter," Jean-Marc said.

Ahead of them stood a barn of weathered wood and neglected roof tiles, nestled beside an abandoned property. Not even chickens roamed around. Moving quickly, they entered the barn and gained access to the loft floor using a ladder that was missing several rungs and squeaked and protested ominously with every step. From this elevated position they could see the distant railway line through a round, glassless window, framed with cobwebs and tiny spiders. Dried straw lay scattered around the barn in untidy clumps and rusted farm implements leaned against the walls. They did not appear to have been used for some time. In one corner a barrel press in a poor state of repair had become home to a group of wood pigeons and was smothered in their excrement.

"The house looks empty," Monique said, surveying the property through substantial spaces between the wooden planks.

"Let's eat," Jean-Marc said, opening his rucksack eagerly, knocking the brass explosive tubes together.

"Careful – the amatol!"

They ate in silence, hungry from a long night's walk covering the forty-five kilometres from Saint-Émilion over rough, vineyard terrain. Leaning against disintegrating bales, the smell of dust and hay filling their nostrils, they drank in turns straight from the unlabelled bottle, washing down the bread. Jean-Marc was intensely aware of Monique beside him, her long legs crossed at the ankles, almost touching his. She smiled frequently as she chewed on the fatty *saucisson*. Every time they exchanged the bottle their fingers touched, sending electricity down Jean-Marc's spine. Was it his imagination or were her fingers lingering longer each time?

"I *love* this wine!" Monique said. "What is it?"

"It is Saint-Émilion," Jean-Marc said, swelling with pride.

"So much ripe fruit... smooth... it's like... velvet in my mouth," Monique said, struggling for the words.

"What you are tasting is from a Merlot-dominant blend with maybe... ten per cent Cabernet Franc. Merlot is always smooth – plums, black fruits and cherries, and in this wine I also get..." he smacked his tongue against his palate, "mocha, and... tobacco... and... a hint of vanilla from a little time in oak barrels."

Monique giggled. "You can taste all that?"

"Of course!" Jean-Marc said indignantly. "I make these wines."

"Well, I think it is delicious. Is it your wine?"

Jean-Marc looked away. "It is from Château Millandes, Alphonse's wine." He grimaced and drank from the bottle again. "But I agree with you, it is good."

Monique smiled and punched Jean-Marc playfully on the arm. "I'm sure your wines are just as good."

Jean-Marc was silent, unsure where to rest his gaze, swimming in Monique's company and yet feeling guilty. "It feels... strange... being alone with you," Jean-Marc said eventually, picking food from between his teeth. "I have been with Isabelle for over twenty years, you know."

Monique smiled and angled her head. "Don't worry, I don't bite."

"Do you think I'll ever see her again?" he said, looking up at Monique, searching her eyes, though unsure how he hoped she might answer. What sort of man could not wish his wife back?

A train's whistle interrupted their thoughts and they leapt towards the dirty round window. The sound of the approaching steam locomotive became louder and louder until it passed in front of their line of vision, pulling freight cars, great plumes of smoke rising against a vibrant pink sky aglow with the promise of sunrise any minute. The rumble of the wheels clacking on the tracks vibrated the barn and shook dust down from the rafters.

"Soldiers!" Monique said quietly.

Sitting around a heavy-calibre machine gun behind sandbags on the roof of one of the central freight cars were four Wehrmacht soldiers. Jean-Marc felt his heart quicken. The trains were meant to be unguarded. They were not prepared for such an encounter.

Unable to get comfortable on the unforgiving wooden floorboards, covered in straw and dried chicken droppings, Jean-Marc and Monique ventured into the empty house in search of a bed. The door had been forced previously and stood ajar, the interior ransacked. Broken crockery lay strewn across the floor, a mangled Menorah upside down in one corner, empty wine bottles on the table, some on their sides amid powdery red patches of dried spilled wine.

In the *salon* was an upright Érard piano with a few white keys missing in the upper register. Jean-Marc was drawn to it and sat down, sweeping the dust off the keyboard with his sleeve. He sneezed as the dust was drawn to him like iron filings to a magnet. Closing his eyes, he began to play the *Prelude* to *Suite Bergamasque*, softly, quietly, almost as an apology to the evicted houseowners. The delicate harmonies floated through the empty house like ghosts of a past life, conjuring up for Jean-Marc memories of his own home, violated by the invader who was most probably perpetrating careless acts of wanton indifference upon his cherished possessions at that very moment.

Jean-Marc became aware of Monique standing behind him, her breathing just audible in the pauses, her presence feeding into his playing, guiding his fingertips and measuring his tempo. It seemed as if the slower he played, the more he hungered for air. The *Prelude* ended and he paused briefly before moving straight into the *Menuet*.

"You play beautifully," Monique said.

Her feet slid across the dusty floor, closer to him. She rested her hands on his shoulders, limply at first, before moving her fingers ever so slightly – a tremble – the pressure they exerted on his skin very subtle, yet tingling all the way down his spine. His breathing deepened, his eyes closed, his head tilting back.

He felt Monique's hands work their way gently towards his neck, challenging his concentration. He leaned back and met the soft warmth of her body, which she pressed against him. He reached the end of the *Menuet* and stopped.

"You like *Clair de Lune?*" Jean-Marc said.

Monique twisted around and sat beside Jean-Marc, pressed against him on the narrow stool, her back to the piano. He shuffled across slightly and began to play, distracted by her face just inches from his, her eyes studying his.

"I don't like it, I love *Clair de Lune*," she replied, and slipped one hand down the inside of his thigh.

A bolt of electricity immobilised Jean-Marc's hands and he turned to her. Suddenly they were entwined, her kisses deep and hungry, unquestionably surrendering to him. Her back pressed against the keyboard, eliciting a discordant protest from the piano. They both smiled simultaneously, their lips still touching.

"Let's go upstairs," Monique whispered huskily, her warm breath filling his mouth.

Jean-Marc had not felt so aroused for years, and led Monique up the dusty staircase to find a bed, any bed. Finding a mattress stripped of bed linen in a dusty bedroom, they made it their whole world for an hour, eventually falling asleep in each other's arms, exhausted from a sleepless night and their sapping passion. When they awoke they made love again as though for the first time, as though in a dream, in a strange house ransacked by the perpetrators of war in the midst of a dangerous mission in occupied territory. Jean-Marc had never felt so alive since the Germans had invaded his world. Was this what war had done to him? It had stripped him of everything familiar, dependable, comfortable, and thrust him into living on the edge where the rarely encountered fruits were so much sweeter than ever before. The surges of wanton adrenaline heightened his senses like a drug.

Lying side by side, the daylight beginning to fade behind ripped white linen curtains, her smooth, flawless skin pressed against his body, they stared at the cobwebbed brass light dangling from the flaky ceiling.

"You are not French, are you?" Jean-Marc said quietly, his arm behind her neck, his hand stroking her exposed shoulder.

Monique did not react, her breathing slow and deep, her fingers playing with the line of hair that traversed his umbilicus and disappeared beneath the sheet they had found.

"Why do you say that?"

"It's just a feeling I get. You are so... polite."

Monique lifted her head off his chest. "Polite?"

They both laughed. "You are English, aren't you?"

She laid her head down on his chest again and he could see her biting the inside of her cheek. "I have lived long periods in France." She lifted her head to look at him. "In Normandy."

He said nothing and she rested down again.

"My parents are English." She hesitated. "I was born and went to school in England."

Jean-Marc ran his fingers through her hair. "You pass... almost flawlessly... as native French."

Monique took a deep breath and shuddered.

"Does Patrice know?" Jean-Marc said.

"Nobody knows."

Jean-Marc paused. "Are you with the British, the SOE?"

232

Monique lifted her head and held his gaze intensely. "You must not tell anybody. Promise me?"

"I promise," he said, pressing a finger against her lips.

"It could endanger the entire network, other people living undercover."

"I would never do anything to put you in danger," he said, drawing her chin towards him as he pouted his lips for a kiss.

She closed her eyes and kissed him, looking like a great burden had been lifted off her shoulders. Outside, dusk suffocated the dying light and Jean-Marc realised that their blissful hours together must end. It was time to move.

Chapter Forty

Patrice sat smoking a Gauloises on the rough edge of a stone trough filled with soil and geraniums that were not quite in bloom yet. To his left sat Anton and squeezed together on his right, Nicolas and Louis. Monpazier's Place des Cornières was enveloped in darkness and filled with people who had come for the *cinema plein air* screening of Marcel Pagnol's *La Femme du Boulanger*. Glowing cigarette ends danced frivolously across the crowded square, like fireflies, as the huge white screen erected against a stone wall was lit up by the flickering images of a Pathé newsreel. The burble of chatter and anticipation in the marketplace quietened.

"It's always German news," Anton grumbled.

"*Les Boches* control everything," Nicolas said.

Patrice crossed his ankles and said nothing, watching images of German soldiers intercepting and opening cases of French wine, clearly marked from Bordeaux. Inside they find not wine but rifles, pistols, grenades and explosives. Case after case reveals the same contraband contents.

"Can this be true?" Louis said, rubbing the scar on his neck.

"Of course not!" Patrice said, waving his cigarette irritably.

German soldiers storm into a wine cellar and confront resistance fighters hiding inside, finding concealed weapons behind barrels and racks of wine. They are all marched outside, hands on top of their heads – looking like coat hangers – and lined up against a wall.

"This is intimidation, pure and simple," Patrice muttered. "Nazi propaganda."

"I've never heard about any of this happening," Nicolas said, shaking his head as he watched.

The narrator speaks of wine producers collaborating with the resistance being rounded up and sent to concentration camps as trains are shown steaming out of Bordeaux's Gare Saint-Jean, pulling freight wagons crammed with people.

"Do you think Brutinel and Alphonse...?" Anton began tentatively, concern on his face.

"We should be there," Louis said, stabbing a finger towards the screen. "That's where the fight is, not here in Bergerac."

The screen fills suddenly with images of winemakers tending their vines, smiling, happy, watching trucks loaded with their wine leaving the châteaux. French women stand holding happy, well-dressed children beside their legs. The farmers are treated well by the Germans, the narrator says, who buy all the wine from the French at a fair price.

"*Foutaise!*" Anton yelled, gesturing dismissively at the screen.

"Be quiet!" a voice yelled from the crowd.

"Shut up!" from another.

"We should be with Monique and Jean-Marc," Nicolas said, flicking his cigarette into the flower trough. "Sabotaging that train at Marsas was pure... genius, wasn't it, Patrice?"

"Give one to *les Boches*," Anton said, raising his lazy eyelid with excitement. "I'm sure they could do with extra help."

Patrice felt irritation at Jean-Marc – his subordinate protégé and a mere vigneron – now being admired by his men. He walked away and turned around to face them. "We are fighting a war, there has to be discipline, like a military unit, or everyone is at risk."

"Sssh!" Louis cautioned, putting a finger to his lips.

Three men sauntered down the edge of the Place des Cornières beside the vaulted arcade, wearing khaki shirts, black ties and black berets. Holstered pistols rode high on their hips and they slapped truncheons into the palms of their hands as they walked, their eyes turned away from the screen and scanning the crowd.

"Milice," Anton whispered, unable to contain the venom in his voice.

"I know that one, he was at school with me, always a snitch," Louis hissed, his eyes narrowed.

One of the Milice stooped over a balding man sat in the square, laughing at the images on the screen, and knocked a bottle of wine out of his hand, cuffing the man across the head.

"No wine! Today is a wine-free day. Tuesdays, Thursdays and Sundays – remember!"

"*Merde*! Look what you've done," the man protested, hands held up in a gesture of helpless frustration. "Not even Hitler can drink it now!"

"Shut up, you old fool!" The Milice man brought his truncheon down on the man's back with a sickening thud.

Louis coiled himself like a leopard about to launch itself at the Milice, a look of hatred etched into his face, but Anton held him back and shook his head wordlessly. Patrice watched in angry silence until the Milice had moved away sufficiently to be out of earshot, his Gauloises dangling forgotten from the corner of his mouth.

"Traitorous bastards," Patrice said.

"Is that how you want to live?" Nicolas asked.

"Come on, Patrice," Anton said. "Why should we be prevented from drinking our own wine by these little black-shirted shits, while it is all sent back to Germany? We should be there in Bordeaux blowing up German trains."

"I agree," Nicolas concurred. "Look at the crap these *Boches* are feeding us in the cinemas." He gestured behind his back towards the screen. "Are we to let them run every aspect of our lives, *and* steal our wine? What are we doing about it?"

Feeling the heat of his comrades' eyes upon him, Patrice turned around to face the screen, now showing images of Russians being bombarded by German forces on the eastern front. German victories, Russian defeats, that's all it showed. Then German soldiers swanning around in Paris, occupying the best tables in restaurants along the Champs-Élysées, drinking champagne and burgundy and cognac and grand Bordeaux wines; smiling as if on holiday with their friends, smoking, laughing, entertaining pretty girls in their laps: French girls.

"What would you have us do?" Patrice said, turning to face them again.

"We go back to Château Millandes, hide in Alphonse's caves and join in with the sabotage of German freight trains," Nicolas said. "Trains supporting *that* lifestyle," he added sharply, jabbing his finger at the screen.

Patrice breathed deeply, surprised by the depth of feeling amongst his comrades, and by the level of support and admiration for Monique and Jean-Marc's insurrection.

"And what about Jean-Marc?" Patrice said.

"What about him?" Anton shot back.

Patrice exhaled smoke through his nose and looked down. "He is a Jew, you know, a wanted man, and an amateur to top it all. He is a risk."

"*Merde*, Patrice, we were all amateurs when we started. He is passionate, and committed, and French. What more do you want?" Louis said.

The Pathé newsreel ended and the opening credits for *La Femme du Boulanger* illuminated the screen, accompanied by Vincent Scotto's whimsically playful harp and violin score, echoing from tinny speakers around the Place des Cornières. The crowd clapped and erupted into spontaneous whistles of approval. The promise of a light-hearted escape from the drudgery and suffering of occupation lifted the audience.

"Let's remember who the enemy is here," Nicolas said, his eyes riveted to Patrice's face.

Patrice emitted a guttural sound, folded his arms and spat on the cobbles.

"Are we not watching the film?" Louis grumbled. "It's got Ginette Leclerc in it." He made lewd gestures with cupped hands over his chest.

Patrice blew through his lips. "What must I watch a film about a baker whose wife runs off with a shepherd for?"

"This is about Monique, isn't it?" Anton said, staring at Patrice with a stupid grin.

Patrice ignored the remark.

"It is. It's about you and Monique," Anton goaded.

"Fuck you!" Patrice shot back.

"Shut up!" someone hissed from the crowd, accompanied by 'shooshes' and the clicking of tongues. "Watch the film or piss off."

"You always told us that no one person is bigger than the cause," Anton said.

"They can help us and we can help them," Nicolas said.

Patrice didn't know how to respond to the challenge from his comrades in arms. His authority had always been absolute, unchallenged, until Monique came along. No, it wasn't Monique as much as Jean-Marc who had changed things. Monique had always been content to follow his command as he gradually introduced her to the life of a *maquisard*.

"Come on, let's go and give it to *les Boches*," Louis said. "Six is better than two."

"Seven," Anton added. "Don't forget Gregoire."

238

Patrice stared at them, tapped another Gauloises from the packet and without offering them around, lit one and inhaled deeply. "Do what you like," he said bitterly and began to walk away, stopping after a few paces and turning around, pointing the glowing Gauloises at each of his comrades in turn. "Just remember: this is not a game, this is war, and war always ends in tears."

Chapter Forty-One

Monique made certain that the amatol was attached to the tracks over a much longer distance this time, ensuring that the blast would be spread across more wagons. She and Jean-Marc worked quickly as they carefully taped the brass tubes – closely resembling shell casings – to the sides of the steel tracks. Darkness had descended rapidly due to thick cloud cover obscuring the moon. Jean-Marc was worried that he might make a fatal mistake with the detonators in his haste in such poor visibility.

"Quickly!" Monique said. "I hear something."

She laid her ears on the tracks, pressing her cheek onto the cold steel, her alert eyes darting about. "It's coming."

"Will it not be obvious that we might be hiding in the barn?" Jean-Marc said as they hastily attached wires to the detonators and fed these under the tracks.

"We have no time, and we have to be a safe distance away," Monique said, unwinding wiring from the spool. "Are they all attached?"

"Yes, I think so."

"Check them!"

"I'm sure they are."

"Check them again," Monique insisted.

Jean-Marc recoiled slightly at the order but did as instructed while Monique began to feed the wiring down the embankment away from the tracks and down to the rows of vines. By now the chugging of a distant steam locomotive was faintly audible.

"What if there are soldiers guarding it?" Jean-Marc said, suddenly aware of nauseating fear in his stomach, conscious that in five minutes they would unleash their attack, the consequences of which could not be predicted.

"We must hurry," Monique said, backing up steadily as she fed the wiring out, one armful at a time, between the rows of overgrown vines, suffocated by profusions of dandelions and tufts of grass.

By the time they had reached the barn the rising plume of smoke from the approaching locomotive was steaming into view. Jean-Marc's heart bounced in his chest, threatening to burst through his ribs. The prospect of armed Wehrmacht soldiers on the train, machine guns and God knows what else, was suddenly uppermost in his mind.

"Jesus, I'm scared this time," he admitted, studying his trembling hands.

Monique kept her head down, biting the insulation off the wires and attaching each to the electrodes on the detonator box.

"Get your binoculars out and look for soldiers," she said.

Jean-Marc fumbled in his rucksack and extracted the field glasses. Squinting through them into the infinite darkness, it took several minutes before he located the smoke plume. "If they realise we're here, we're dead ducks," he said.

"Our explosives are in line with that telephone pole on the other side of the tracks. See it?"

Jean-Marc scanned the tracks. "Yes."

"Are there any soldiers?" she asked again, checking the wiring.

Jean-Marc strained his eyes, willing more light to fill the lenses. But the night was so dark, not even the whites of Monique's teeth and eyes stood out.

"I can't see the wagons properly yet." The puffing of the train was louder now and the whistle blew as it approached the Saint-Yzan signals.

"What can you see?" Monique said.

Jean-Marc hesitated. "Nothing."

"The locomotive is approaching the telephone pole," Monique said with urgency tightening her voice. "Are there any soldiers?"

"Damn it, Monique, I'll tell you as soon as I see any."

"We haven't time. I need to know now."

The whistle blew again. Jean-Marc panned the binoculars left and right across the freight wagons, dim shades of grey, charcoal and black in his eyepieces.

"The locomotive is past the telephone pole," Monique said. "I'm ready any second now."

"Nothing," Jean-Marc said.

His eyes burned from the strain. And then, just a mere glimpse, but he saw the red glow of a cigarette on top of a wagon.

"I'm going to blow it," Monique said.

"Wait! Soldiers!"

"Where?"

"One, two, three… middle of the train, more or less," Jean-Marc said.

"How many?"

"I can't see them, just their cigarettes."

"Shit!" Monique hissed.

"Do we abort?" Jean-Marc said, lowering the binoculars to look at Monique.

She hesitated for the briefest of seconds. "No. Tell me when the soldiers are at the telephone pole."

"What?"

"We must ensure that they are eliminated."

Jean-Marc clamped the binoculars to his face and stared intently, first to locate the wagons, then the soldiers.

"I can make them out now, faintly. About six of them, I think," Jean-Marc said.

"Tell me when, I can't see anything," Monique said.

"Three... two... get ready – now!" Jean-Marc hissed the last word like a cornered goose defending its young.

He heard the sound of the plunger driving down and making contact, followed by bright white and then orange light bursting into the black sky, illuminating the rows of parallel vines pointing back towards the barn. A second later an ear-splitting explosion shook the barn and forced Jean-Marc to cover his ears instinctively.

Steel screamed and fractured, sparks cascaded into the starless night, wooden freight wagons splintered and shattered. One after another, wagons hurtled off the tracks, down the shallow embankment and smashed into others already lying on their sides. Jean-Marc wanted it to stop, the relentless noise of destruction, carnage on the railway line. Something deep within him knew that this massive scene of devastation would result in consequences. There was no exuberance, no celebration like last time. This freight train was long and the wagons just kept coming, tumbling off into the abyss of the night in a forgotten and neglected vineyard.

The smell of detonated explosive, of fire and scorched metal, reached their nostrils, followed by the sweet smell of spilled wine.

"We've done it!" Monique said, clenching a fist and reaching forward to hug Jean-Marc. "Let me see."

He passed the binoculars to her and she scanned the scene, now well lit up by the fires of war.

"Any soldiers heading our way?" Jean-Marc said, partly joking but filled with dread.

"No signs of life. The locomotive has steamed off to Saint-Yzan."

"They'll raise the alarm," Jean-Marc said, feeling a surge of adrenaline hit him, "in just a few minutes. We should go."

Their eyes met. "I must pull in the wiring," Monique said.

"Leave it. Let's go – now," Jean-Marc said, standing and pulling on his rucksack. "We have to be home before dawn."

Monique seemed caught between her training, her duty and a desire for self-preservation.

"But they'll find – " Monique began.

"You think they don't know that this is the work of Maquis? A few wires will make no difference," Jean-Marc said, holding out a hand to pull her up. "Come!"

She grabbed his hand and they started running into the cover of darkness.

Chapter Forty-Two

Bömers sat stiffly behind his desk, a cigarette smouldering in a walnut ashtray littered with butts. His hands, clasped together on an open dossier, kneaded each other constantly, as if wringing out washing. A loud knock at the door stirred him from his deep thought.

"Come!"

A uniformed soldier stepped into the room, saluted with a perfectly synchronised click of his heels, and waited. Bömers beckoned him forward with a subtle motion of one hand. The soldier, tall and lanky, strode forward and held out a cream envelope.

"Hauptsturmführer," he said.

Bömers took it and nodded, dismissing the man who left without a sound, closing the door quietly behind him. The envelope was of good quality, embossed with *Gmund* on the flap and bearing a watermark. He knew where it was from even before turning it over and settling his eyes on the postmark.

His name and address were typewritten on the envelope in black ink: precise, to the point, unequivocal.

Hauptsturmführer H. Bömers
Mairie

245

Saint-Émilion
BORDEAUX

Picking up an ivory-handled letter opener he slit the envelope end to end and extracted a single, heavy-grain sheet of paper, also typewritten. Unfolding it, he sighed and placed one hand over his mouth as he read.

From the office of Reichsmarschall H. W. Göring
  Das Luftsfahrts-Ministerium
  Wilhelmstrasse
  BERLIN

To Hauptsturmführer Heinz Bömers,
  You are required to present yourself to these offices at the Reichsministerium for an urgent meeting with Reichsmarschall Göring and Hauptsturmführer Kühnemann to explain and discuss the ongoing insurrection and sabotage in Bordeaux. Immediate measures to crush the activities of the local French resistance are paramount.
  A Junkers will be sent for you on Friday 23ʳᵈ at Merignac airport. Heil Hitler.
  From the desk of Oberst-Gruppenführer Karl Köller
  Chief of Staff to Reichsmarschall H. W. Göring

As he let the letter fall to the desk, Bömers was conscious of a tremor in his hand that reached forward to open the silver cigarette case. In spite of the unsmoked cigarette lying in the ashtray, smoke curling up from its lengthening ashen tip, he lit another with an unsteady hand before inhaling deeply and leaning back in his desk chair.

"*Scheisse!*" he said quietly, knowing it would not be a pleasant weekend in Berlin.

How he longed for the comfort of his family back in Bremen; for the familiarity and predictability of Reidemeister & Ulrichs, his wine importing business that used to bring him to Saint-Émilion in civilian clothes to meet with his Bordelais friends in their châteaux; being the toast of the town, wined, dined and fêted by vignerons hoping for lucrative export deals to Germany. Now, just a few years into this Godforsaken war, they all hated him, and who could blame them? Even his superiors back in Berlin hated him. He could please no man. He was friend to no one.

What a miserable predicament, he thought, losing himself in a fog of cigarette smoke. The only positive side was that he got to spend the war in his favourite home from home, Bordeaux, doing what he loved, tasting and enjoying good red wines. He knew it could be far worse. He could have been sent to the horror and misery of the eastern front where Operation Barbarossa had already turned into a nightmare of never-ending proportions.

Chapter Forty-Three

Alphonse and Federico were bottling wine, a tedious and repetitive process that strained every sinew in their arms and backs. Each bottle had to be filled to the same level and then a cork driven into the neck of the bottle using the Pinel hand-levered corking device. Alphonse only had one corker and so Federico was put in charge of filling the bottles while he monotonously depressed the wooden-handled iron lever on every bottle. Angelica and Marthe chatted in the background, washing the newly corked bottles and stacking them on racks ready for labelling. The dulcet tones of their conversation were regularly punctuated by the sound of Alphonse drawing down the lever every fifteen seconds. The cellar doors were open, the bright warmth of a spring day flowing in on long shadows, bringing with it tiny butterflies and flying insects, drawn to the sunbeam like bees to pollen.

"What is taking them so long?" Gregoire said, entering the cellar from the courtyard.

"They cannot travel by day, it's too risky," Alphonse said. "I'm sure they'll be back tonight."

"I should have gone with them. You should have let me, Papa," Gregoire said.

"Look at your brother, and remember what can happen. Do that to your mother, would you?"

"My back is killing me, Gregoire, come and take over please," Federico said, rubbing his lumbar area and arching his back.

Federico patted Gregoire on the shoulder and stepped outside, turning his face to the sun. "God, I miss being outside," he lamented, inhaling deeply. Something caught his eye and he froze, head angled to one side. "Alphonse!"

"What?"

"Come and see," Federico said.

Both Gregoire and Alphonse hastily joined Federico and saw the dusty trail behind two lorries heading towards Château Millandes.

"Inside, quick! As far as you can down the tunnels," Alphonse said. "Marthe, join me here with the bottling."

Federico, Angelica and Gregoire disappeared down one of the cave tunnels, taking with them hats and coats left lying about.

"Hurry!" Alphonse yelled.

"What about Olivier?" Marthe said, her frightened eyes looking up at Alphonse.

Alphonse hesitated. "I doubt they will have any reason to enter our house, let alone our bedrooms." He began to fill another bottle. "It's the wine they're after."

Two flatbed Renault trucks – caked in dried mud around the wheel arches – crunched to a dusty halt on the gravel. They were the colour of faded grey gunpowder, the doors badly eaten by rust. On the load bed of each truck stood a large, cylindrical galvanised metal tank. Alphonse was taken aback. They were not German. These men wore civilian clothes and looked exactly like local Frenchmen.

"Monsieur Sabron," said a tall, slender man in loose-fitting brown trousers and jacket who had lowered himself from the passenger door of the truck.

249

"Yes?" Alphonse said, wiping his wine-stained hands on a red and white checked cloth that was pushed into the waistband of his trousers.

"We are representatives of the local Vichy government, do not be alarmed."

The tall man had a pencil moustache along which he ran his index finger, one side; then the other, before adjusting his navy blue beret.

"Do you want to buy wine?" Alphonse said with a half-hearted chuckle, a nervous laugh. "I am bottling the 1938 as we speak."

The tall man was unmoved by this. "We are here under Marshal Pétain's orders to requisition alcohol for distillation." He extracted a notepad and pencil from his coat pocket and began flicking through the pages.

"You are mistaken, *monsieur* – I am a wine producer, I do not distil any alcohol here," Alphonse said with a smile and casual hand gestures.

"No mistake, Monsieur Sabron, it is your wine we are after."

"But... we are..." he chose his words carefully, "certain to be *Grand Cru!*"

The tall man exhaled wearily and began to scribble in his notepad with a blunt pencil. "*Monsieur*, the country needs alcohol as fuel for vehicles, for heating. In such times wine is a luxury."

"Not to the Germans it isn't."

"We are taking five hundred litres from every property in Bordeaux this month," the man continued, scribbling in his notepad without looking up.

"This must be a mistake."

"No mistake."

"What is it, Alphonse?" Marthe said, stepping through the cellar doors and squinting as she emerged into the sunshine.

"Go inside, Marthe," Alphonse chided her, waving his hand.

"Who else is here?" the tall man asked, glancing about the courtyard.

"No one, just my wife and me."

Several men had alighted from the cabs of the two trucks, all wearing dark berets and jackets. They stood about, quietly but confidently, smoke curling from cigarettes protruding from their unshaven faces.

"What wine do you wish me to take?" the tall man said.

"But... are you serious?" Alphonse protested.

"Shall I choose?"

"No. No. Take the 1939, the most recent vintage. It is still in barrel."

"Show us, please," the tall man said, beckoning his men over.

They all entered the cellar, crowding around a frightened-looking Marthe who tried her best to fill bottles of wine without interruption. Alphonse walked over to a rack of 225-litre wine barrels with '39 chalked on them.

"Two will do," the tall man said before glancing sideways at Alphonse, "for now."

"The oak barrels cost a lot of money," Alphonse said, stepping forward protectively towards the wine barrels.

"We will siphon the wine out, of course," the man said. "We are not unreasonable, *monsieur*."

A red rubber pipe was dragged in and pushed into the barrel of wine, and the other end taken towards the tank on the truck.

"How are we to survive?" Marthe said, her voice quivering. "The Germans take our wine, Vichy takes our wine, and there is not even anyone to help us make it."

The tall man scowled at her. "Do you not think Marshal Pétain has your best interests at heart, *madame*?"

"Hush, Marthe," Alphonse said, walking towards her and placing two comforting hands on her shoulders. He looked at the tall man and smiled. "Take what you need."

"The tanks are full, Roger," shouted a man from outside.

"*Merde*. OK, bring the oil, please," the tall man said, apologetically gesturing for his men to roll up and remove the rubber piping.

A can was brought to him. He opened it and walked to the barrels of '39 wine.

"What are you doing?" Alphonse said, aghast, as the man poured pale yellow fluid into the barrels.

"It is heating oil, to ensure that you do not use this wine for anything else. We'll be back for it," the tall man said with an insincere smile.

"But that oil, it will ruin the barrels!" Alphonse pleaded, moving to the barrels and placing his hands on them, as though caressing his pregnant wife's belly. "I will never be able to age wine in them again!"

"Is that a complaint?" the tall man goaded, screwing the cap back onto the can slowly, and smirking.

Alphonse gritted his teeth and clenched his fists as anger washed over him. He felt Marthe's arms around his shoulders and her comfort helped him to keep quiet, to avoid saying something that could provoke the officious Vichy man into unpleasant action.

"I thought not," the tall man said. "We'll be back in a few days to collect."

Alphonse did not turn around to see them drive out. Squeezing his eyes shut, he gritted his teeth and shook with pent-up frustration. As the sound of the trucks receded, Gregoire's energetic footsteps echoed their way up the tunnel.

"What was that, Papa? You OK?" Gregoire said, his eyes flicking about the cellar, searching for anything out of place.

Alphonse breathed slowly and deeply, his gaze meeting the pained, watery eyes of his long time-friend Federico, as he too emerged from the tunnel.

"Have they taken wine, Papa?" Gregoire said.

"Never mind the wine, Pétain's Vichy bastards have just ruined two of my oak barrels with heating oil," Alphonse said quietly. "Why do such a thing?"

"Damn Pétain to Hell!" Gregoire said.

"Gregoire!" Marthe protested.

"It's true, Mama, what is he doing for us? Pétain has betrayed the French. We are alone, we must fight our own way now."

"Gregoire, please don't talk like that... your poor brother..." Marthe said.

"That is another reason, Mama – for what they did to Olivier!"

Chapter Forty-Four

Jean-Marc and Monique spent a second day sheltering in a barn outside Saint-Georges. Although they were so close to Saint-Émilion, they could not risk the final few kilometres in daylight. The Germans had roadblocks placed liberally around Bordeaux and with each new attack on their freight these seemed to increase in number. Jean-Marc and Monique had scrambled up into the loft amongst old boxes and used wine barrels. Beneath them a brown stallion chewed lazily on hay and flicked his tail at persistent flies. Monique lay in Jean-Marc's arms as they listened to the familiar sounds of activity outside. Muffled voices floated through the wooden walls and mingled with the unhurried sounds of the stallion's daily rituals.

"What are they doing?" she whispered.

"They are going to work in the vineyards," Jean-Marc explained.

"So early in the summer? What will they do?"

Jean-Marc's mind conjured up fond memories of his former life on his beloved wine farm, now a distant memory blighted by the Germans.

"They will clear the weeds away from the vines, tie up loose shoots to the wooden trellises, ensuring maximum sunshine to the leaves. Most likely they will prune the tips of new growth shoots and remove all rootstock shoots."

"Sounds mundane," Monique said.

Jean-Marc emitted a guttural sound. "It's very important. Good wine starts with the vines. And of course there is the mildew that has to be sprayed, if they have any copper sulphate, that is."

Monique nestled into the base of Jean-Marc's neck. "You miss it, don't you?"

"By this time I would have planted asparagus and strawberries, while daffodils, tulips and narcissi would be in bloom at the end of each row of vines. The air..." He inhaled deeply. "The air will be fresh and perfumed from all the flowers."

"Sounds idyllic."

"My father would kill me if he could see what a state my vineyards are in," Jean-Marc said.

"Well, rather him than *les Boches*," Monique said playfully.

"You didn't know my father."

"Do you have any photos of your family?"

Jean-Marc inhaled deeply. "No."

"Your children?"

He shook his head.

"Your wife?"

"I do not own a camera, Monique. How would I get photos of everyone?"

Silence amplified the sounds from outside: the clank of metal equipment and the scuffle of boots on the gravel interspersed by muted voices.

"I have a photo of my parents and my sister," Monique said, digging into her pockets and retrieving a crumpled monochrome picture.

Jean-Marc took it and studied it. A middle-aged man, balding from the front, wearing a tweed jacket with elbow

255

pads; his wife, wearing a floral scarf around her head, pressed against him. A younger girl stood beside her father, holding his hand, her feet pointing inwards.

"Where is this?"

"We were on holiday at Saint-Valery. 1935," Monique said wistfully.

Jean-Marc turned the photograph over: *Henri Boillot Photographie, Boulogne-sur-Mer.*

"That's my younger sister, Charlotte," Monique said.

"Where is she?"

"In England, with my parents. She's only nineteen."

Jean-Marc emitted a throaty sound. "Just like Olivier."

He studied the photograph, mesmerised by the image of the happy family it had captured, perhaps envious, even. He had no such memories of Isabelle, or Claude, or Odette. As he stared into the faces of Monique's family he began to doubt his recollection of the finer details of his own family's faces. After all, he had not seen them for two years now. Would they look different when he was reunited with them again? *If* he was reunited with them again, he checked himself.

"What is your real name?" Jean-Marc said, running a dirty finger across the photograph.

Monique hesitated. "Monica."

"Ah," he said warmly, kissing her forehead. "I think I am in love with you, Monica."

He felt her hug him tighter, pressing her body against his, the tender bulge of her breasts, the firmness of her pelvis.

"Is that wrong?" he said.

She took the photograph from him and slid it back into a pocket. "What is right in war, Jean-Marc? I don't know. We must live for today – tomorrow might not come, as long as... as long as you do not hurt anyone."

Once the sounds of the vigneron and his family had ceased and they were presumed to have entered the vineyards, leaving the farmyard abandoned and quiet, Jean-Marc and Monique made love, slowly, tenderly, and above all, quietly, interrupted only by the occasional snort from the stallion below. When they fell asleep, Jean-Marc was haunted by the photograph, seeing the faces of Isabelle, Odette and Claude superimposed onto Monique's family photograph, staring at him. They had never had a holiday together anywhere. Their entire lives had been lived out on Château Cardinale. Where were they now? Were they still alive? Was it wrong that he had found such unexpected happiness in the midst of all this misery? How would he be judged when they returned? Again he found himself contemplating that hollow uncertainty which always followed this thought: if they returned.

Chapter Forty-Five

The inside of the Junkers Ju52 was cramped, draughty and deafeningly noisy. As the entire structure was vibrated by its three BMW engines, Bömers struggled futilely to find a comfortable position for his head, which percussed constantly against the uninsulated corrugated fuselage like a woodpecker's beak. Even though Hauptsturmführer Kühnemann sat opposite him, his knees just inches away from Bömers', conversation was impossible above the reverberating drone. Not that Bömers had any desire to talk, nor did he have much to say to his superior officer in Bordeaux. They successfully avoided each other's gaze, taking turns pretending to be asleep even though the noise and penetrating cold made this impossible.

Göring had been brutal, giving them a stark ultimatum with a menacingly pointed finger, as fat and round as his belly. France was an occupied country, he said; it had surrendered in its entirety to Germany. He regarded it as a *milch kuh*: a milk cow existing only to be plundered. Everything France possessed and produced could be claimed by the Reich, and wine was certainly no exception. Wine was needed for entertaining, for uplifting the morale of the troops and for its international market value, which should benefit the Reich and not France.

But he did not want Bordeaux's leftovers. He wanted the best vintages from the best vignerons and would settle for nothing less. His ultimatum, however, was directed at the matter of French resistance activity. In this regard he would accept nothing short of savage reprisals: two eyes for an eye. "Subdue them," he said, "destroy them, or I will find someone else to do it for me." Bömers had been particularly concerned about the plan to send German troops, battle-weary and traumatised by their savage experiences on the eastern front, to Bordeaux for periods of alleged recuperation. These soldiers had been desensitised to the normal humanity of civilised society. The conditions and brutality they had suffered and most likely meted out during Operation Barbarossa were unimaginable, if reports were to be believed. Bömers did not want them in France, let alone in Bordeaux. Göring and the senior rank and file saw things differently.

Kühnemann had been no support to Bömers whatsoever, eager to please Göring and plainly indifferent to the plight of the ordinary vignerons, the lifeblood of Bordeaux. The aircraft lurched suddenly, dropping from the sky, hurling both men about in their harnessed, steel-framed seats like mannequins, arms and legs flailing uselessly. They glared at each other briefly when it was over, and then looked away. The only other passengers in the square fuselage were half a dozen Waffen-SS. Probably Göring's henchmen, Bömers thought to himself.

The actions demanded by Göring to quell the resistance were almost certainly going to cause discontent, perhaps even stir up revolt. Bömers could foresee that and he had no stomach for it, but he knew that Kühnemann did. What would be required of him was intense diplomacy and stewardship of the Bordelais, to steer them away from the brink of a conflict that he feared might live on beyond the war, generating an atmosphere simmering with resentment. He had to keep the

Bordelais from inviting Kühnemann's retribution, delivered with Göring's blessing.

Göring did not care in the least for the vignerons. His chilling and non-negotiable self-interest was all too apparent to Bömers, who knew that the *Reichsmarschall* would not let anyone stand in the way of his goals.

But Bömers recognised that the war would not last forever, and that when it was over one day, France and Bordeaux would return to normal. With some luck, so would Germany. He wanted desperately to be part of that normality and he did not care much for having to wait for the war to end first. He desperately wanted it now. He was tired of being hated by everyone. He was not an odious or unpleasant man; he regarded himself as friendly and fair – an astute businessman, yes, but not a monster. Unfortunately, if Göring and Kühnemann prevailed, his stature amongst the Bordelais would be degraded along with that of every other German.

He opened his eyes and stared at Kühnemann, who appeared to be asleep. The cold was making Bömers' teeth chatter and filled him with an increasing desire to urinate, something he would have to suppress. How on earth had he got into this situation, he wondered? Was there a way to escape the looming inevitability of confrontation?

Bömers realised that he could no longer feel his toes as he moved them in his shiny black EM boots, trying to reconcile himself with the knowledge that, if his posting had been to the eastern front, such physical discomforts would have been an everyday sufferance. He reminded himself that he was inordinately lucky to be in Bordeaux.

Chapter Forty-Six

"What the hell are you doing?" Patrice hissed urgently, crouching down below vine level.

Jean-Marc spun around, secateurs dangling in abeyance in one hand, paralysed with fear. He felt for the Welrod pistol tucked into his belt but realised that if he was to use it, despite its cunningly built-in silencer, German soldiers would certainly come pouring out of his house.

"Are you crazy?" Patrice said, revealing his face from behind an adjacent row of vines.

"Patrice!" Jean-Marc said with relief, the tension melting instantly from his shoulders as he released his tentative grip on the pistol.

The moon was obscured behind cloud and a light drizzle dampened everything into a sheen of featureless grey. Jean-Marc wiped his face and the coal dust Monique had smeared onto his skin came away on his wet hand.

"Have you lost your senses?" Patrice sibilated venomously.

"I'm just pruning and tidying up," Jean-Marc said defensively. "No one has attended these vines for so long, it's disgraceful. It's a mess."

"You are fifty yards away from a German garrison," Patrice said, stabbing his arm in the direction of Jean-Marc's house. "No papers, after curfew, and you're a Jew... a stupid Jew."

"It's two in the morning, Patrice, and they had a drunken party last night, we could hear them from the cave."

Patrice clenched his fists in frustration and emitted a growling sound. "I don't give a damn if they catch you, but have you given a moment's thought to everyone else around you?"

"I am alone here," Jean-Marc said, returning to pruning the new shoots.

"If they catch you they will be all over the neighbouring properties like a rash in a brothel, Jean-Marc. What would happen to Alphonse, huh, to Monique?" Patrice's eyes widened. "They will find Olivier, wounded from a gunfight with German soldiers; Gregoire, hiding from an STO; two Jewish winemakers being sheltered. You know what they will do: they will shoot Alphonse. Is that what you want?"

Jean-Marc bit his tongue and said nothing, waiting for Patrice to calm down. He realised that Patrice was probably right and, remembering his argument with Isabelle on their last night together, he cursed his stubbornness. He moved down the row of vines with remarkable dexterity and speed, his fingers working independently of his brain, accustomed to this task he had performed for dozens of vintages, since he was a boy helping his father.

"Do you see down there, Patrice?" Jean-Marc said, raising his arm and pointing without lifting his head. "*Les Boches* have uprooted rows of my vines – it looks like half of my Cabernet Sauvignon plantings – just to make a shooting range."

Patrice shrugged, incredulity evident on his face.

"A fucking shooting range!" Jean-Marc said. "In my vineyard!"

"Keep your voice down," Patrice hissed. "This is what I don't like about you, Jean-Marc: you have no discipline. You are not a military man. You are... you are... a farmer."

"But yet you decided to come back?" Jean-Marc said. "Why?"

Patrice exhaled and pushed his hands into his coat pockets. "The boys wanted to join in with the sabotage," he said.

Jean-Marc bristled at the term 'boys': Patrice, ever the authoritarian, the leader, patronising those around him. He wondered how Louis, Nicolas and Anton would feel about being referred to as 'Patrice's boys'? Why did they tolerate him?

"How did you know where to find me?" Jean-Marc said.

"Monique told me."

Jean-Marc stopped and surveyed the lines of vines. "Well, I have managed to do half of this south-west corner, my oldest and best Merlot plantings. It's better than nothing."

"We must go inside now," Patrice urged.

"Sunrise is two hours away. I can get a lot more done yet," Jean-Marc said.

"*Merde!* Are you listening to me?" Patrice growled.

"I am careful, this is not the first time."

"That is what worries me: you are getting too cocky, too confident, and you are endangering everyone," Patrice said.

Breakfast, consisting of a hot roasted barley brew suffused with a touch of chicory and stale *pain de campagne* with a scraping of butter, was a tense affair. Louis kept asking about the train sabotages, Nicolas about when they would attack again and Anton listened like an obedient sniffer dog, hanging on every word. Monique held the floor, discussing tactics: how the supply of armaments for the Maquis was reaching Bordeaux through British air drops; the importance of helping downed airmen who were risking everything to arm the resistance; where they might strike at the German freight trains next. Patrice's disapproval and indifference hung over the conversation like a funeral shroud, like a purple storm cloud building to an inevitable thunderous climax, his averted body language and petulant facial expressions almost comically exaggerated.

"I can get all sorts of weapons from my contacts," Monique said, her elbows resting on the upturned wine barrel as she broke the hard bread in her fingers, spraying crumbs. "Sten guns, Welrod pistols, explosives..."

"Is the Welrod the one with a silencer?" Anton said with boyish bewilderment.

Monique nodded. Jean-Marc pulled his Welrod pistol out of his deep, baggy trouser pocket and held it out for Anton to examine with curious, envious eyes.

"Oh, I want one of those," Anton said.

"Who are your contacts?" Louis asked. "British?"

"Can't say," Monique replied, looking at Jean-Marc and raising one eyebrow as if to remind him.

"What sort of explosives?" Nicolas asked, adjusting his stance to rest his weak leg.

"Amatol," Monique said.

"That is good," Anton said, nodding as he chewed. "It must be from the British." He glanced at his comrades around him, lifting his eyebrows. "No?"

"There are also lots of German MP40 machine guns around now, captured from *les Boches* and circulating amongst the Maquis," Louis said, looking at Patrice, who appeared to be sulking. "We can get hold of some, can't we, Patrice?"

Anton chuckled. "I hear they are now almost as common as hookers in Paris."

Louis had lit a Gauloises and emitted a cloud of blue smoke. "The MP40s are getting more action, though," he said, and erupted into a chesty cough as he laughed.

The others all joined in, except for Patrice, whose sour face suddenly lifted to confront them. "Listen to yourselves, you're like children. This is not a game. We are talking about the

264

German Wehrmacht here, not Les Scouts de France! If we wake the sleeping giant all hell will break loose, and your handfuls of MP40s and silly British pistols will be pitiful in retaliation."

Jean-Marc watched as the others lowered their eyes one by one, but he said nothing. Monique shot an icy stare that could freeze alcohol in Patrice's direction.

"I have heard that other *maquisards* have begun sabotaging German freight trains further north. Two more were derailed last week," Monique said. "The resistance is gaining momentum, with or without us."

"And confidence," Jean-Marc chipped in.

Nicolas nodded. "You have started something good, Monique."

Patrice emitted a throaty wheeze.

"What?" Monique said, looking at Patrice.

"You will get us all shot," Patrice muttered under his breath.

"I am very proud of what Monique is doing," said the baritone rumble of Federico's Italian voice.

Heads turned to watch the greying man emerge from one of the tunnels and shuffle slowly and stiffly towards the barrel on which their shredded bread was strewn around a pewter pot.

"I salute what she is doing to the Germans and even though I know she is putting my life at risk, and Angelica's too, I feel it is a risk worth taking," he continued. "No one is ever far enough from the long reach of war that they can claim to be safe from it. It surrounds everyone... and touches everyone."

Anton and Nicolas nodded, while Patrice shifted his feet on the stone floor.

"They have taken our wine farms, they live in our houses, they plunder our wines and demand more while leaving us with no means to manage each new vintage," Federico said, pouring black liquid from the pewter pot into an enamelled mug. "Do you simply want to sit back and watch them take all your best wines back to Berlin?" He drank from the mug and

QUENTIN SMITH

grimaced. "Do you want to drink this... this shit for the rest of your life?"

Federico moved to Monique's side and placed an arm around her shoulders, embracing her like a daughter. "This brave woman, together with Jean-Marc, has achieved the impossible. They have got under the Germans' skin." He raised a clenched fist, gnarled from arthritis and blanched by impassioned resolve.

"Just wait until they bite back," Patrice muttered.

"This is war, of course they will fight back. Is that a reason for you to give up? Surely that is just what the enemy wants?" Federico looked into the eyes of Anton, Louis, Nicolas and Patrice in turn. "Are you mice or are you Maquis?"

He squeezed Monique tightly and kissed her forehead, a tiny smile creasing his unshaven, lined face as. "If I was a younger man..." his lip trembled, "you give them hell, for me, for Angelica and for our vineyards we had to flee in Tuscany, a life we had to leave behind, all because of the Germans."

"Thank you, Federico," Monique said, resting her head against his shoulder.

"*Mia cara*," Federico said, "I am so proud of you. Don't ever stop what you are doing on my account."

Jean-Marc took joy from watching Patrice's discomfort: unsure where to look, how to stand, humiliated by Federico in front of 'his boys'.

"You too, Jean-Marc," Federico added, nodding in his direction.

"I too have lost my farm – Château Cardinale – my home, my wife and my children, my right to make wine out of my own grapes, my freedom to move about in the fresh air – all of this because of *les Boches*. Fighting back gives me a reason to live, not a desire to die." Jean-Marc felt Monique's hand slip into his and tighten her grip around his fingers.

"I want to fight back too," Anton said, blinking his eyes.

266

"Me too." Nicolas nodded.

"And me," Louis said.

Monique's eyes met Jean-Marc's, a sparkle glinting in their vitality, making his knees weak. He squeezed her hand and she squeezed back. He felt as though he was sixteen again, courting Isabelle, only more alive than he had felt in years.

"What about Gregoire?" Patrice said sourly, looking around the cellar.

"Gregoire is with us," Jean-Marc said confidently.

"Then we are seven. Now all we need is a truck," Monique said.

A small but rousing murmur of assent filled the viniferous air of the cellar. Patrice stood still, like a statue, hands clenched at his sides, outmanoeuvred and considering his options. Jean-Marc felt invigorated, vital, with renewed purpose to his otherwise mundane days, and without thinking he leaned over and kissed Monique. Even before he saw it he felt Patrice's stare.

"We will get hold of MP40s, won't we, Patrice?" Anton said excitedly.

"Yes, we all deserve some action," Nicolas joked, pulling a crumpled packet of Gauloises from his coat and offering them around. "Not just the Paris prostitutes."

"Where should we attack next, Monique?" Louis asked, tearing into the bread.

Monique pouted her lips and gently removed her hand from Jean-Marc's grasp, before walking in contained circles around the barrel.

"There are a lot of *maquisards* derailing German freight now, and the number of soldiers patrolling and also guarding these trains is increasing by the day," she said thoughtfully.

"My point exactly," Patrice said, extending a hand.

"So, I have a new idea. The best part is that they may not even know we are doing it," Monique said.

267

"Not for a while, anyway," Jean-Marc interjected as their eyes met – partners in war, partners in collusion, partners in life.

"Not for a while, anyway," Monique chuckled.

"Tell us, Monique!" Nicolas said. "Tell us. What is it?"

Chapter Forty-Seven

Hauptsturmführer Jan Korten paused in front of a printed notice secured with flax to a wooden lamp post on the main square in Saint-Yzan. He removed his SS cap as he read, his lips moving soundlessly as he wiped sweat from his brow with a starched white handkerchief. The midday heat rose in languid waves off the gravel, stinging his eyes.

Eight German soldiers were murdered in a brutal and unprovoked attack on a freight train outside Saint-Yzan. For the guerrillas and those who helped them there is punishment. Forty guerrillas will be hanged and their dead bodies thrown into the river.

By order of Hauptsturmführer J. J. Korten, Kommandant 3rd Panzer Division.

Korten sniffed and walked on to a group of officers seated around a table beneath the green canvas awning of Café Vitie. Several bottles of wine, glasses and a Berliner gramophone filled the round table. The men stood up, stiffened and saluted him.

"At ease, gentlemen," Korten said, pulling off his cap and dropping it beside the gramophone. "What have you brought today?"

"Mozart," one of the men said.

Korten nodded. "Opera?"

"*Le Figaro.*"

"Good choice," Korten said. He glanced around the empty square, through which a light breeze gently swung dozens of gaping rope nooses hanging from lamp posts, trees and balconies. "Where are the prisoners?"

Sturmführer Lammerding stepped forward. "We have rounded up over a hundred men aged under sixty, sir. The mayors of Saint-Yzan and Saint-Savignac were also told to point out known partisans and... er... were permitted to nominate a handful of people essential to the normal running of the towns to be considered for exclusion."

"Good, this is what Göring demanded," Korten said. "No women?"

"No, sir."

"And no children?"

"No one under sixteen, sir."

Korten clasped his hands behind his back and turned around to survey the square with its ghostly nooses hanging in macabre anticipation.

"How many nooses?"

"Fifty, sir."

Korten was satisfied and nodded, moving to sit down in one of the rattan bentwood chairs. "Well, we may as well start the music and open the wine while we wait."

Opposite the café a priest dressed in a long black cassock and white collar emerged from the church – shaped like a bleak sarcophagus with a stubby apology for a tower into which a black bell had been inserted – and walked towards Café Vitie. Just then the first grumbling truck lurched around a corner beside the *boulangerie* and swung into the square, raising a cloud of dust mixed with diesel fumes, which wafted over towards Korten and his men, accentuating the stifling nature of the oppressive heat. The priest drew nearer, a silver crucifix swinging like a pendulum on the end of a long chain around his neck. He was almost completely bald, save for wispy dander above his ears and bushy grey eyebrows, above which a permanent frown etched his lined forehead.

"Who is this, then?" one of the officers said, lifting a lead crystal glass filled to the brim with red wine.

Korten and his men studied the priest with bemusement as he approached, dust fouling his robes and covering his cracked black shoes.

"May I speak to the commanding officer, please?" the priest said, clasping his hands together beneath the crucifix.

"Hauptsturmfürer Korten at your service," Korten said without standing. "And who are you?"

"I am Father Espinasse," he said, turning and gesturing towards the church.

"Have you come to deliver last rites, Father?" Korten said.

Espinasse glanced around at the waiting nooses. "I have come to ask that you not execute these men by hanging," Espinasse said. "This... this is brutal and inhumane," he continued, waving his arm around.

"It is punishment, Father, for the similarly brutal and inhumane slaughter of German soldiers," Korten replied.

"But not by hanging – show some mercy," Espinasse said, clutching at his crucifix.

"Would God prefer that we shoot them?" Korten said.

Espinasse shrugged and unclasped his hands.

Korten exhaled and placed his wine glass on the table. "Let me tell you something, Father: we have developed this practice of hanging on the Russian front, as punishment, as a warning to dissident locals. We have hanged thousands already in Kharkov and in Kiev. Fifty more is nothing."

"Fifty?" Espinasse gasped, his eyes widening.

"It could be more," Korten said. "My superiors demand ten partisans be executed for every German soldier killed."

271

Espinasse swallowed and looked down.

"Do you want to know how many German soldiers were killed?" Korten continued, taking pleasure in taunting Espinasse.

Behind him the soldiers had opened the tailgate of the truck and were herding prisoners out roughly, jabbing them with the butts of their rifles and shoving them about abusively. The prisoners had their hands tied behind their backs and stared around the square fearfully as they saw the nooses.

"Divide the prisoners into three groups, Untersturmführer, I want to come and inspect them," Korten said.

The youngest of the officers jumped to his feet. "Immediately, sir."

"Let's have some music now, shall we?" Korten said.

"Of course," Lammerding said, unfurling the gramophone horn, cranking the handle and swinging the tone arm around to place the needle on the rotating record.

"Search your hearts," Espinasse said, taking a pleading step towards Korten.

Korten looked up at the priest. "Oh we have, Father. We mourn the senseless death of eight of our colleagues."

A second truck pulled into the square and soon disgorged its ragtag contents of dishevelled men, some with dried blood on their faces and eyes swollen shut. Untersturmführer Geissler herded the men into three groups, shouting orders. One partisan made a run for it, heading towards the church. A short burst of gunfire brought him crashing to the ground in a cloud of dust.

"Mother of God," Espinasse whispered, aghast, and signed a cross over his chest.

"We are ready, Hauptsturmführer," Geissler called out.

Korten inhaled the sharp smell of cordite and stood up. "Stay here, Father. You may watch, but not another word from you," Korten said, wagging his finger in Espinasse's face. "Until it's over, then you may do as you wish."

Korten walked down the line of prisoners with Lammerding and Geissler by his side. "Unshaven, dirty clothes," Korten said of a few men, gesticulating with his thumb after which the soldiers grabbed these men to one side. "Unpolished shoes, grass in his hair."

Each of the three groups was divided in this way, Korten choosing those whom he suspected of being partisans, underground resistance, living rough, fighting back against the German occupation.

"One group at a time," Korten shouted, signalling for the first to move towards the nooses. "Everyone else watches."

Scuffles broke out and the soldiers swiftly beat the prisoners down with rifle butts and paralysing kicks to the knees. The prisoners were forced up ladders placed beneath the nooses, their heads shoved into the nooses, and the ladders summarily kicked away. The hanging men kicked and jerked. One panzer soldier grabbed hold of a prisoner's ankles and pulled him down with his body weight, laughing as he did so. The body began to spasm and writhe. Another soldier stepped forward and fired two shots into the victim's back.

Korten, Lammerding and Geissler sat at the table and drank wine as the melodious notes of *Le Figaro* echoed out through the tinny gramophone horn. The rest of the prisoners, those selected for execution and those uncertain what their fate might be, stood around in terrified huddles surrounded by armed soldiers, watching in horror. One prisoner vomited onto his shoes.

Espinasse tried to intervene several times, pleading for clemency as prisoner after prisoner was cruelly strung up and hanged slowly by the neck, often beaten while jerking death spasms racked their bodies.

273

"In God's name, put an end to this savagery," Espinasse said.

"Soon, Father," Korten said, swaying to the melody as he sniffed the wine. "Rather good, this wine, don't you agree?" he said to Lammerding.

"I have never drunk Château Lafite Rothschild before," Lammerding said. "It is... incredible."

Korten studied his glass, turning it around to appreciate the wine's intense colour as he licked his palate. "Apparently, Rothschild is a Jew. Who would have thought it?"

"We probably shouldn't drink it, Hauptsturmführer," Lammerding said uncertainly, recoiling from his glass.

"Or, drink it but not celebrate it," Korten said with a mocking chuckle, plunging into another mouthful.

Forty-five French men from Saint-Yzan and neighbouring Saint-Savin were hanged in two hours. The rest were beaten, bundled back into one truck and driven away. The bodies of those executed were left hanging from their nooses after the Germans packed up and left, leaving behind only footprints in the dusty square and half a dozen empty bottles of Château Lafite Rothschild 1934.

Father Espinasse walked around the square, stopping beneath each body and praying as he gripped his silver crucifix in both hands, pausing only to kiss it intermittently, tears streaking his dust-caked face, like rivulets breaking a long summer drought in Avignon.

Chapter Forty-Eight

"Who was that?" Jean-Marc asked suspiciously.

Nicolas limped back into the cellar, pressing his palm against the thigh of his inadequate leg, as if soothing an ache, and pulled the door closed behind him. "We never ask their name."

Everyone was crowded around Jean-Marc and Monique, who were poring over a map spread out on the wine-stained blending table, adorned untidily with glass flasks and pipettes. The map's four corners were held down with empty wine bottles, their labels streaked with red wine tears.

"Well?" Anton said impatiently, staring at Nicolas over his shoulder.

"It was from Brutinel. He has another downed pilot to be rescued," Nicolas said.

"Those British should learn to fly better," Gregoire chuckled, his voice inflected with the immaturity of his attempt at humour. No one responded.

"Only one?" Monique said.

"The other one was killed."

"Same plan as before?" Louis asked.

"Same as before – he liked the wine barrel idea of yours, Jean-Marc."

Jean-Marc rubbed his fingers over the rough stubble on his face, unshaven now for three days. "When?" he said.

"Friday."

Feeling Monique's fingers squeeze his forearm, he turned to face her. "You know, Brutinel has a truck," she said, letting her words hang in the air.

"So he does," Jean-Marc said, enjoying the nods of support from each member around the blending table: Nicolas, Louis, Anton and Gregoire. Only Patrice was absent.

"OK, so we go to Château Lascombes, transport the pilot to safety, and then requisition Brutinel's truck for our first raid," Monique said, glancing around at everyone, testing their resolve.

"Do you think he'll let us take it?" Anton asked.

"When he hears our plan he will not refuse us," Jean-Marc said.

The cellar door burst open, startling Jean-Marc, whose hand sank into his trouser pocket to close around his pistol. Patrice fell through the doorway, sweaty, wide-eyed and breathing heavily. Everyone turned to face him. Patrice shut the door and leaned his back against it, staring ahead at the stone walls.

"Are you hurt?" Anton said.

Patrice held up a hand and shook his head. "No," he managed through a stifled swallow.

Silence descended on the cellar, broken only by Patrice's breathing and the fresh sounds of spring audible beyond the wooden doors. Patrice lifted his eyes to those watching him and Jean-Marc could see in them a nervous, overactive edginess.

"What is it?" Anton asked.

"Do you know that Brutinel has another airman to be transported to Bayonne, Patrice?" Nicolas said. "Friday."

"We may be compromised, I'm not sure," Patrice managed to say between breaths. "My contact in Bordeaux has been arrested and shot by *les Boches.*"

"What?" Monique said sharply as her body stiffened beside Jean-Marc. "Leveque?"

Patrice nodded.

"*Mon Dieu,*" Jean-Marc said quietly. "When?"

"Have you not heard?" Patrice said, looking at them with disbelief evident across his face.

Jean-Marc sensed darkness in Patrice's tone, a gravity that he had not witnessed before. This was not Patrice's usual petulance or grandstanding, nor his arrogance. He had been shaken by something.

"The Germans executed forty-five men in Saint-Yzan yesterday, hanged by their necks in the market square until they stopped kicking, like chickens." Patrice's face was ashen.

Monique and Jean-Marc exchanged a brief glance, enough to confer a shared thought: was this to do with the train they had sabotaged?

"That is not war, that is murder!" Anton yelled.

"Bastards!" Nicolas said.

"We will kill forty-five of them – no, a hundred and forty-five!" Gregoire said, his voice rising with emotion as the peachy skin of his youth flushed.

"Please, everyone," Monique said, raising her hands. "Tell us what you know, Patrice."

Patrice breathed in deeply and sank down to the dusty floor of the cellar, his head slumping forwards on his chest. "They posted a notice in Saint-Yzan, declaring punishment for soldiers killed by partisans in train sabotage." Patrice paused. "They rounded up a hundred men from Saint-Yzan and Saint-Savin and hanged half of them. The rest haven't been seen since."

277

Jean-Marc felt his pulse thumping in his neck and searched beside him for Monique's hand, but she was as stiff as a board.

"Oh my God," Gregoire said, pressing a fist against his mouth. "Papa has cousins in Saint-Savin, they have family…"

"I'm sure that there is very little chance…" Jean-Marc began in a pale attempt to reassure Gregoire.

"They are not big towns, the loss of forty-five men will affect almost every family," Gregoire said. He stared at the ground, his eyes unable to rest. "I must tell Papa."

"Leveque and dozens of others were apprehended. I heard that a few winemakers are amongst them, too," Patrice said.

"*Merde!*" Jean-Marc said quietly.

"I am afraid they may be on to us; Maquis like us hiding out in wine cellars and caves," Patrice said.

"They are simply trying to intimidate us," Monique said defiantly, stepping forwards to face those around the blending table. "They cannot know where we all are. Don't let yourselves be frightened by them. They are the enemy and they will not rest until they have everything, until they have you and all of France completely under their control."

Jean-Marc felt the tension in the dank cellar, like static electricity sparking in the cool air.

"Don't you see? These deaths, these executions, are because of *your* sabotage of the trains!" Patrice said, directing his venomous gaze at Monique.

"We did not invite the Germans into our country, Patrice," Monique said. "Nobody here wants to live as a slave."

"But people do want to live," Patrice said, rising up onto his feet and approaching her.

"I don't want to live my days hiding in this cellar like an outcast," Jean-Marc said, protectively stepping towards Monique. "They have taken everything from me and I'm damned if I'm going to spend the rest of my life hiding from the world!"

278

Patrice fixed his eyes on Jean-Marc with a cold glint. "You can choose to do what you want, Jean-Marc, but the people of Saint-Yzan did not invite such slaughter upon themselves, did they?"

"Neither did we," Monique said.

"No?" Patrice said, mocking as he circled her. "You never gave a moment's thought to the possible consequences of your actions, did you?"

Jean-Marc could see Monique's shoulders slumping as her head bowed forwards. Patrice had scored a direct hit with his attack.

"You never thought that the Germans would kill ordinary people as a direct result of your—" Patrice began.

"Every war has innocent casualties, unfortunately," Jean-Marc said in a quiet and almost apologetic tone. "That fact should not deter us from our goal to drive out the occupiers."

Patrice stopped right in front of Jean-Marc, close enough for Jean-Marc to smell the raw alcoholic vapour of Armagnac.

"And your derailing of wine supplies to Berlin is going to drive out the Germans, is it?" Patrice said through clenched teeth.

"When the Allies drop bombs on the Germans they too kill innocent people, innocent French men, women and children. Would you have them stop?" Jean-Marc said, unflinching.

"And what good is it doing?" Patrice said, raising his hands.

"Do you want them to give up already?"

"Many people in northern France might think so – they are the ones being killed," Patrice said.

"The truth is, Patrice, that the Germans want to intimidate the Maquis into submission, into hiding. They cannot control a whole nation that is fighting back," Jean-Marc said. "We would overrun them if we all stood together."

Jean-Marc looked to Monique for support, but her head was down. He feared that her conscience might be filled with regret.

"If they divide us they will conquer us," Jean-Marc added. "Is that really what you want?"

"He is right," Nicolas said, stepping forward awkwardly on his unsteady leg. "Now is not the time to stop. It is easy to give up, anyone can do that. But beating *les Boches* at their own game takes courage, willpower…"

Patrice's head snapped in Nicolas' direction, a fiery look of censure burning in his eyes.

"Tomorrow we should go to help General Brutinel," Louis said. "After that our mission goes ahead as planned. They can't hang all Frenchmen."

Patrice was stunned by the show of unshakeable support for Monique and Jean-Marc from his colleagues, men who had previously obeyed his every command. Jean-Marc could see the bitterness festering within Patrice as he narrowed his eyes, darting about with incredulity, and bit his lip.

"You will be responsible for the destruction of an entire village at this rate," Patrice hissed, his clenched fists shaking by his sides. "Who knows the limits of their retribution?"

"Do you want to let people capable of such atrocities live on, unchallenged, in your country?" Monique said, her head lifting.

Patrice turned, narrowed his eyes, and closed in on Monique, like a cat rounding on a cornered mouse. "*My* country, or *our* country?" he asked, his face twisted, just inches from Monique's.

Jean-Marc stepped in quickly and grasped Monique by the shoulders, turning her away from Patrice. "Enough of this petty shit. There is a war on out there, and in case you've forgotten, the enemy is the Germans, not anyone in this cellar.

Now, we have a job to do." He turned to face each one in turn. "Who is in, and who is out?"

"I'm in," Nicolas said without hesitation.

"Me too," Louis and Gregoire said simultaneously.

Anton hesitated as he and Patrice locked eyes. "I am very sorry about Leveque, Patrice, but I am definitely in."

Patrice turned away abruptly and shook his clenched fists. "Fuck! You people are crazy." He walked away towards the far wall before spinning around suddenly. "Fucking crazy! But I will not give you the satisfaction of leaving me out. Brutinel is *my* contact."

"No, Patrice," Monique said calmly, "he is *our* contact."

Chapter Forty-Nine

Brutinel welcomed them into his kitchen enthusiastically, manoeuvring his wheelchair deftly in between the throng of bodies as he set about brewing a pot of chicory and barley on his cast iron range. Beside the blackened pot rested a greasy skillet of half-eaten *Pommes de Terres Sarladaises*, frozen in congealed goose fat. Jean-Marc's empty stomach rumbled but he realised that the dish would probably feed Brutinel for a week.

Dawn was in its infancy, still a suckling babe, casting the colours of Monet's passions in a rising arc across the sky. They had journeyed all night on foot, ventured up the finger of land separating the left and right banks and crossed the Garonne at the southern tip of Île Cazeau. Patrice boisterously took charge of their journey. Incredibly, they never even saw a single German patrol.

"All seven of you... for one airman?" Brutinel said with a wave of his arm as he tended the pot of chicory from his wheelchair.

Patrice drew a chair up to the kitchen table noisily and slumped into it. "You may well ask, General."

"We have a plan," Jean-Marc said before gently pushing Monique into view, resting his hands on her shoulders. "Monique has a brilliant idea."

"Oh," Brutinel said with amused curiosity visible on his face.

Monique told him of her plan, mentioning that Château Lascombes, being closer than Château Millandes, could provide them with safer refuge for the next week or two. Casually, but crucially, she raised the matter of the truck. Brutinel listened intently, handing out mugs of steaming black liquid apologetically.

"I'm afraid it's not coffee," he said, but never interrupted Monique once.

In the background a clock chimed six times and the first lazy shadows of morning began to appear in the kitchen.

"Have you heard about Saint-Yzan?" Patrice said in the silence that ensued.

Brutinel manoeuvred his wheelchair to the table. "Of course."

Jean-Marc knew that Patrice would once again declare his opposition to their plans and he sighed and prepared for it, winking at Monique in solidarity.

"I fear that further actions against the Germans at this time will result in more retaliation," Patrice said. "Like Saint-Yzan, perhaps worse."

Brutinel pursed his lips, placed his widespread fingertips together and nodded. "It probably will."

"Continued loss of innocent lives will turn the people against what we are doing," Patrice said.

Brutinel pulled a face. "They are not all innocent, you know, many of those executed in Saint-Yzan were singled out as members of the Maquis. They would be considered legitimate targets by the Germans, but I take your point." He hesitated.

Jean-Marc looked away, unable to watch. Was the general about to douse the flames of their ideology? He could not bear to see the self-satisfaction on Patrice's face.

283

"The people have lost faith in Marshal Pétain, they hate Vichy, they hate the Germans, and the British can do very little at the moment," Brutinel said slowly, measuring his words. "They need to believe that someone is fighting their cause, they need a reason... to hope."

Jean-Marc looked up and found Monique staring at him, her eyes expectant and surprised. He smiled at her.

"But this plan..." Patrice began, gesticulating towards Monique.

"I like it," Brutinel said. "I like it a lot."

Jean-Marc wanted to punch the air and shout out, but instead he instinctively leaned forwards and hugged Monique. Patrice looked away.

"I will give it all the support I can, including the truck, and you can hide in my cellar during the operations," Brutinel said, smiling at everyone in turn.

"Where can we store the wines without risking discovery?" Jean-Marc said.

Brutinel pressed an index finger to his lips and tapped it for several moments. "There is a disused cinema in Bordeaux, it belongs to a good friend of mine. Perhaps...?" He looked across at Monique for her reaction. "It would raise no interest amongst the Germans and it is also close to Gare Saint-Jean."

"We also need a driver, General – none of us has papers for the *zone occupée*," Monique said.

This was an obstacle they had yet to overcome; of this Jean-Marc was well aware as he looked at everyone in turn. Louis, Anton and Nicolas were all from Bergerac, as was Patrice. He was a Jew in hiding and Monique... no, that was far too risky.

"Gregoire?" Jean-Marc said.

Gregoire looked at him blankly.

"You are from the area, and you are still young enough to pass under the radar, perhaps," Jean-Marc suggested.

"But I am dodging an STO," Gregoire said. "I will be arrested in an instant and deported to Germany."

"I can get you papers," Brutinel said. "I know someone."

They all turned to face the general, who drank from his mug, one hand resting on the lever of his armchair, tapping the brass knob rhythmically. He raised his eyebrows while looking at Gregoire.

"I think you are the best man," Brutinel said softly, raising the mug to Gregoire.

In silence all eyes were directed at Gregoire. Suddenly he slammed his mug onto the table, spilling chicory. "*Merde*! I'll do it, for Papa's murdered relatives in Saint-Savin, for Olivier, for France!"

A muted cheer rang out through the kitchen as everyone slapped Gregoire on the back. Monique squeezed next to Jean-Marc and he revelled in her warmth as she hugged him and then raised her lips to his.

"I salute you all," Brutinel said. "You are very brave. But first, we need to get the British airman to Bayonne. Jean-Marc," he said, gesturing for Jean-Marc to follow him, "I have a barrel ready for you."

The mission to Bayonne went smoothly. Gregoire got his papers and was accompanied by Brutinel as they transported a load of empty wine barrels to the port in Bayonne, with the British airman crouched uncomfortably inside one barrel at the centre of the load. This time a German soldier examined the barrels at the port, tapping them in turn with the butt of his *machinenpistole*. The resounding hollow echo seemed to reassure him. Back at Château Lascombes the rest prepared wine barrels, puncheons, tanks, pumping equipment, and weapons.

Contact with Thibault had provided them with the date and time of the next rail shipment of wine. Sunday evening was blessed with clear skies and long, forgiving shadows of dusk that played tricks on the human eye, providing a myriad of options for the camouflaged saboteurs to exploit.

Dressed in black with soot-covered faces and matching black berets, they were all but invisible in the thickly leafed bushes that flanked Gare Saint-Jean's freight yards. Brutinel's truck was parked two hundred yards away, loaded with large wooden wine barrels – puncheons and vats. Jean-Marc surveyed the freight wagons on the tracks near to them. He could see cases of wine through the wooden slats and large puncheons on the flatbed trailers. He elbowed Monique and pointed. She nodded, lifting a pair of camouflaged field glasses to her eyes.

Jean-Marc pulled his sleeve back and looked at his watch. It was 8.30pm. "Where is he?" he whispered to Monique.

She shrugged and pulled a face. To their left and right in the gorse lay their comrades, staring towards the railcars, waiting. Just as the first stars began to burn their way through the darkening sky, the crunch of footsteps on track ballast and the familiar sound of Thibault whistling *La Mer* drew nearer. It was difficult to discern him in the blackness that now blurred everything in the freight yard, but an inverted triangle of white above his short black waistcoat revealed his position.

Three hoots of the owl from Patrice, returned, and repeated by Thibault. "It is much cooler in Paris," whispered Patrice.

"Bordeaux is warm in July," Thibault replied without turning around.

"There is frost in Paris."

Thibault breathed a sigh of relief and hurried over to the bushes. "There is no frost here."

"Where have you been?" Jean-Marc hissed, tapping his watch.

"Schedule changes," Thibault said, out of breath. "The train leaves in about forty-five minutes."

"*Merde!*" Jean-Marc said.

"We have very little time," Monique said.

"The coast is clear. I will keep watch and keep whistling. If I stop, get out of here," Thibault said and sauntered off casually, swinging his pea-whistle on its chain and continuing his languid renditions of Charles Trenet tunes.

Monique looked at Jean-Marc, then past him to the others. "Let's go!" she whispered sharply.

They sprang into silent action. Jean-Marc made straight for the flatbed freight trucks together with Nicolas and Louis, scrambled onto the rail truck and reached down for the stout pipe held aloft by Nicolas. Climbing to the top of the puncheon, he levered off the cork stopper and fed the pipe into the barrel. Nicolas uncoiled the rest of the pipe back through the bushes where Gregoire was waiting to connect it to the puncheons on the back of Brutinel's truck.

Jean-Marc made a circular motion with his hand in the air and hissed, "Go!"

Gregoire began to grapple with the hand-cranked pump to siphon wine out of the puncheon on the train. It squeaked every now and then, like a trapped field mouse, and made Jean-Marc wince, fearing it would alert German soldiers.

Monique was helping Louis crack open the locks and chains on the closed freight truck. They slid the door open quietly and Louis climbed inside and began to pass wooden cases of wine out along a human chain; first Anton, who walked twenty paces and passed it to Monique, who did the same and handed it to Patrice. With muted grunts Patrice hoisted and packed each case onto the truck beside the two puncheons.

Jean-Marc uncoiled another hose and fed this into a second puncheon on the freight car, leaving Nicolas to operate another hand pump beside Gregoire. Jean-Marc surveyed the area from the top of the puncheon and then searched for Monique. He could just make out her figure, bent beneath the weight of a box of wine that she carried to Patrice. Jean-Marc signalled positively to her. All was good: he could hear Thibault whistling in the distance, and very little else.

Jean-Marc jumped off the wagon and walked over to relieve Monique. "I'll do that. You get onto the freight truck and keep a lookout. You can hear Thibault better from up there."

They worked solidly until Thibault stopped whistling and Monique raised the alarm. In the distance the distinctive piercing emissions of steam from the locomotive could be heard, and quickly they began their retreat to the truck, dragging the hoses with them and relocking the freight wagon. Everyone huddled together in a breathy mass behind the truck, crouched low, heads out of sight.

"Do we leave with the noise of the train, or wait until it's quiet?" Nicolas said.

"Good question," Jean-Marc said, glancing at Monique, and catching a supercilious look from Patrice.

"Don't you have all the answers?" Patrice said sarcastically.

"What do you think, Patrice, now or wait?" Monique said, pointedly ignoring his barbed remark.

"Now," Patrice said.

In an instant everyone was aboard the truck. The train's whistle blasted deafeningly in the background and the locomotive began to chug and wheeze slowly, pulling the freight cars with a lurch and clank of metal. Gregoire started the truck and they moved away cautiously, heading for the darkened roads leading to Rue Delphin Loche, away from Gare Saint-Jean and away, they hoped, from danger.

It took just four minutes to reach their rendezvous. Brutinel was right: it was very close to the station and perfectly situated. Juliette Felgines was waiting for them and swung the disfigured metal gate wide open for the truck. Gregoire cut the lights and in an instant they were off the map, hidden in the small courtyard behind the old cinema as the gate was shut behind them. A rusted metal staircase scarred the cracked and dishevelled rear wall of the old, dirty building.

Juliette had short dark hair and wore a red beret with matching jumper gathered in above baggy brown trousers and leather boots. She moved fluidly but with the confidence of a man, taking command, opening the rear door to the cinema – marked *sortie* in white paint on brown cement – and ushering them inside. With barely a word exchanged they had unloaded the truck in thirty minutes.

Inside the cinema the cases of wine had been stacked in front of a small, ornate stage, decorated with faded red, blue and gilt carvings, separating the screen from the first row of plush maroon velvet seating. The cinema smelled of dust and stale cigarette smoke and the enormous rectangle of white facing the rows of seats hung emptily, perhaps longing to entertain again.

When it was done they all shook hands and slapped each other on the back, and Monique and Juliette embraced. Even Patrice seemed pleased.

"You don't use the cinema?" Monique asked.

Juliette shook her head, her eyes revealing a glimpse of sadness. "When I tried to screen *La Grande Illusion* and German soldiers stormed in, ripped the copy of the film out of my projectors and destroyed it, I knew I faced a choice, and I didn't want to show German news reels and propaganda – you know, films approved by Goebbels."

Jean-Marc admired the dormant architecture of the old cinema; rows of tiered seating rising to three small projection windows high on the rear wall, each creatively framed by plaster pastiches of the *Coeur de France* coat of arms.

"Stay in here tonight and don't leave before 8am," Juliette said in a husky smoker's voice that reminded Jean-Marc of Edith Piaf. She glanced around at the haul of wine that would have graced tables and cellars in the heart of Germany, and smiled. "You have done well tonight. Raymond will be proud."

And with that, she was gone.

"I thought we were meeting a man," Louis said, scratching his head.

The others laughed. "No, Louis, Juliette is definitely a woman," Anton mocked.

Jean-Marc found Monique and embraced her, pressing himself against her firmness, unconcerned about their open display of affection amidst expressive relief that it was over, safely and successfully.

"I am so proud of you," he whispered into her ear, inhaling the scent of her hair as she squeezed him.

She pulled away, holding onto his elbows. "Look, Jean-Marc."

"What?"

"In the corner, a piano!"

Barely visible behind a stack of wine cases, partially covered by a linen sheet, was an upright piano. Jean-Marc felt his heart leap.

"What would a cinema be without a piano?" he said, rushing over and pulling the sheet off, revealing a very dusty Érard piano.

There was no piano stool so he drew up a case of wine and stood it on end as he opened the fallboard to reveal yellowed ivory keys. As if extinguishing birthday candles he blew across the keys, raising a cloud of dust into the air.

"You play?" Anton said, limping over and leaning his shoulder against wine cases.

"A little," Jean-Marc replied, testing the piano with a few chords and arpeggios.

"He's very good," Monique said, moving in behind Jean-Marc and placing her hands on his shoulders.

Jean-Marc began to play Edith Piaf's *Mon Legionnaire* in a coquettish bluesy style. Nicolas began to slap his thigh rhythmically, but Monique ruffled his hair.

"No, play my favourite... please."

Jean-Marc turned and smiled at her, enjoying the tender pressure of her fingers caressing his neck, and began to play *Clair de Lune*. Everyone gathered around in silence and soaked up the tranquillity in a fog of cigarette smoke. Only Patrice sat on his own in the first row, smoking a Gauloises, his legs crossed at the knee, staring at the blank screen.

Thibault estimated that the freight trains might normally take up to a week to reach Berlin. This would give them a window to exploit before the wine theft was uncovered, before the Germans inevitably unleashed measures to complicate their efforts. Monique's energy was inexhaustible and she pressed them to target every nocturnal shipment of wine that left Gare Saint-Jean in the ensuing week. Some trains left in the middle of the night and the work was exhausting and, of course, executed under constant fear of discovery. Sleeping awkwardly in Juliette's cinema seats or on the unforgiving hard floor between rows was not conducive to restful recovery.

But the fruits of their labours were substantial: hundreds of cases of Bordeaux's finest wines; classed growths, Crus Bourgeois, table wines and everything in between. One thing they did not lack in their lonely hours of hiding was access to good wine, wine that tasted even sweeter in the knowledge that it had been rescued from heartless, distant Nazi mouths.

As Jean-Marc slumped in his cramped cinema seat, caressing Monique's head resting fast asleep in his lap, he surveyed the stockpile of wine with satisfaction. He considered that each case might represent one French Jew deported to Germany, to an unknown but almost certainly unpromising fate. Amongst them would be a case for Isabelle, for Odette and for Claude. Glancing down at Monique's peaceful face, strands of hair crossing her ear and cheek, he was filled with pangs of guilt and remorse, followed by anger and helplessness. All that he could do was what he was doing; the Maquis had become his life. Every day he risked certain death but it was the only thing that made him feel alive. His vineyards and the only life he had known since boyhood were now beyond his reach; his daily contact with the soil, the vines, assessing the weather, tasting in the cellar, blending, experimenting – all forcibly denied him.

He had never considered that he could be anything other than a winemaker, nor indeed had he ever wanted to do anything else. Yet look at him now: unshaven, sleeping rough, no fixed abode, no regular meals, a Welrod pistol jammed into his leather trouser belt, surrounded by comrades who had become his surrogate family, plotting insurgency every morning when the sun rose secretly beyond their four concealing walls.

That morning, as they ate crusty baguettes left by Juliette in silence, washed down with Château Batailley for good measure, Jean-Marc became aware of Patrice's eyes upon him.

"It won't be long before Gare Saint-Jean is crawling with more Wehrmacht than Stalingrad," Patrice said. "There is no way we will be able to continue stealing wine. It would be suicide."

"Patrice is right," Anton said through a mouthful of bread, spraying crumbs onto his hands.

"I have been thinking about this too," Monique said. "We should stop now, change tactics altogether."

Patrice's face twisted into a frown.

"Do you have any contacts further north, Patrice?" Monique asked.

Patrice hesitated. "Perhaps."

Monique stood up and walked around, stretching her back with arms straightened above her head, studying the piles of wooden wine cases stacked upon each other.

"We have done well, but we could do even better," she said. "Jean-Marc and I disrupted entire shipments of wine when we used explosives, but the wine was destroyed." Monique inhaled deeply. "I think I may have a better way to increase our efficiency."

Jean-Marc turned to face her. "Don't tell me you want to steal the whole train!"

Silence hung over them; mouths stopped chewing.

"I do," Monique said.

"You could never do that," Patrice spat.

"How?" Nicolas said.

"Surely it's impossible?" Louis said.

Patrice laughed derisively. "This should be good. Go on, Monique, entertain us, this is a cinema after all."

The others chuckled half-heartedly.

"We would need the help of another *maquisard*, perhaps several, further up the line. But we can target trains well away from Bordeaux where all the German security will very soon be concentrated," Monique said confidently.

"Go on," Jean-Marc urged.

"We divert the train at a nondescript junction, sending it down the wrong line..."

"By switching the points?" Jean-Marc asked eagerly.

Monique nodded. "Exactly. We send the whole train down a side line into a trap, where our comrades up north will help us unload the wine and hide it."

Jean-Marc slapped his thigh. "I love it!"

"You would, lover boy," Patrice hissed. "It's a stupid idea. The Germans will never fall for such a thing."

"It has nothing to do with the Germans," Monique said, rounding on Patrice.

"The train drivers are usually French anyway – they wouldn't care, if they even noticed," Jean-Marc said.

"What if there are German soldiers guarding the train?" Anton said.

"If there are any, the local Maquis snipers should take care of them. They will always be outnumbered," Jean-Marc said.

Monique nodded enthusiastically. "Absolutely. What do you all think?"

There followed a great deal of deep sighing, averted eyes and biting of lips.

"I think it could work," Nicolas said, the first to look up tentatively.

"You are going too far, Monique," Patrice said. "You will anger the entire Nazi establishment, humiliate them. It'll be like standing on the lion's tail."

"Isn't that exactly what we're trying to do?" Monique countered. "War is fought on many levels, Patrice. It is not just about bombs and trenches and flanking manoeuvres, it is also about psychology, eroding their morale and self-belief. We want to make them hate being in France."

Patrice stared at her, his mouth moving noiselessly as though he was chewing. "How do you know so much about all this?"

Monique dismissed him with a casual wave and a snort. "I pay attention." She moved back to her seat beside Jean-Marc, but Patrice's eyes never left her.

"We should contact... er... what's his name up near Jonzac... Poujol?" Nicolas said, waving a finger lazily at Patrice.

"Poujade," Patrice said tersely.

"And... er... Vincent er... in Brossac, Vincent...?" Anton said, clicking his fingers.

"Teulières," Patrice said. "Vincent Teulières."

295

"Didn't we hear that Vincent had started derailing trains south of Angoulême, like Monique did?" Louis said. "This might well interest him."

"I say we do it," Nicolas said. "We can go back to Château Millandes, on the right bank. I much prefer it there to Brutinel's dark cellar."

Jean-Marc decided to strike immediately, to seize the perceived air of optimism. "Right, who's in?"

They all raised their hands without hesitation, except for Patrice, who slowly, resignedly nodded his head. "OK, I'm in."

Chapter Fifty-Two

The dampness of the vast stone chamber provided a welcome coolness in contrast to the stifling dry heat outside. Alphonse did not remove his beret and smoked pensively as he waited. Footsteps crunching on the earthen floor echoed throughout the cavernous underground cathedral, situated just off Saint-Émilion's marketplace, gradually becoming louder. Alphonse listened: only one person's footsteps.

Bömers rounded one of the substantial solid square columns of limestone – four on each side – left by the stonemasons to support the ceiling, and approached Alphonse. He was not in uniform but wore a black suit and homburg hat that reminded Alphonse instantly of the Gestapo. Alphonse turned away to look at candles flickering indifferently on the stone altar.

"Thank you for coming, my friend," Bömers said.

He stopped beside Alphonse and craned his neck as he admired the crude yet astounding architecture of the cathedral. Alphonse felt himself recoil at the words 'my friend'.

"Why here?" Alphonse said, and then, unable to resist a barb, "Are you planning to shoot me?"

Bömers turned on his heels, scraping the earth, stretching his arms out wide as he looked up at the chiselled ceiling. "It's an incredible place, isn't it – a cathedral carved out of a single massive rock, nine hundred years ago." He paused. "Do you know, I used to come here every year on my buying trips? I love it, one of Saint-Émilion's greatest treasures – apart from the wines, that is," he laughed, perhaps hoping to amuse Alphonse and lighten the atmosphere.

Alphonse sighed, feeling irritable. "And now you can come here whenever you like. Are we here to pray for the new vintage?"

Bömers laughed heartily again, leaning backwards as he did so. "How is the vintage shaping up? Lovely weather again, isn't it?"

"Another good summer, yes, but you know very well we cannot take advantage of it. Vineyards are in a mess, mildew is rampant, we have no copper sulphate, there is no one to maintain the vines, to clear the soil, many vineyards stand abandoned..." He turned to face Bömers. "Only you know where the owners have been taken."

"It is not easy, I know," Bömers said. "Cigarette?" He offered his open silver cigarette case to Alphonse, who accepted and extracted one.

They both lit up and smoked in silence. The German tobacco was so refined, though Alphonse would rather choke before admitting it.

"Yields are down to half what they were before the war, you know," Alphonse said.

"Alphonse, I am under immense pressure from my superiors, from Göring, to deliver the quota."

"We cannot produce any more wine, Heinz. Even the French are forbidden to drink it on certain days now to conserve supplies."

"I know, it is unfortunate, but not what we are here to speak about."

Alphonse inhaled on his cigarette and then studied it, a smooth and pleasant Brinkman Bremaria, Bömers' favourite.

"There is increasing guerrilla activity against German supply trains," Bömers said.

Both men, standing side by side, looked ahead at the candlelit altar, their eyes never meeting, as if communicating through the medium of glimmering candlelight.

"I am not aware of such things," Alphonse said.

"Oh come on, Alphonse, everyone knows about it."

Alphonse lowered his head and spat on the floor. "I had cousins in Saint-Savin, you know, they had sons, generations of winemakers, past, present and future."

"I am sorry about what happened in Saint-Yzan. I assure you that it was nothing to do with me," Bömers said. "Nothing."

"Forty-five men," Alphonse said tersely, turning for the first time to face Bömers.

"I hope you know me well enough to believe me, Alphonse?"

Alphonse stared into Bömers' watery eyes, the eyes of a middle-aged, overweight wine merchant from Bremen, out of his depth in a dirty war, trying to please too many people.

"Göring is ruthless, even Kühnemann frightens me at times. I never thought about the ugly side of war, you know," Bömers said.

"Well perhaps you should reconsider your position now."

"I am trapped, Alphonse, just as you are, trying to make the best of this situation until it's over."

"Do you want me to feel sorry for you?"

"I want to help you as best I can, but you need to help me too," Bömers said.

"There is nothing more I can do – you already take most of my wine, and Vichy takes the rest for distilling fuel alcohol," Alphonse said. "Three nights a week Marthe and I drink water with our food."

Bömers walked around slowly until he was facing Alphonse. "Göring believes that the vignerons are in league with the Maquis, helping them, hiding them."

"Göring is in Berlin, what does he know?" Alphonse countered.

"Come on, Alphonse."

"Do you also believe this?" Alphonse said, pointing his cigarette at Bömers' chest.

Bömers hesitated and lowered his eyes. "We both know it's probably true."

"Why do you need me, then?"

"Look, I don't want to make trouble, I am not a soldier. I told you all from the beginning, be fair with me and I'll leave you alone. Remember?"

Alphonse nodded.

"I don't want to be arresting my winemaking friends, sending Kühnemann after them. Can you imagine what would happen to people?" Bömers continued.

"No, Heinz, I can't. Tell me what would happen to them."

"Please, you are not involved in any of this, are you?" Bömers asked, a pained expression on his round face.

"Don't be absurd, I am an old man," Alphonse said dismissively, patting his sagging belly. "How dare you even suggest it?"

"Not even Gregoire, or Olivier?"

"I said no, Heinz. I am not in the Maquis."

Bömers walked slowly towards the altar before turning to face Alphonse again. "But I'm sure you probably know of those who are." He tapped the side of his nose with an index finger.

Alphonse flicked his cigarette away and approached Bömers. "Assuming I did know, and I'm not saying I do, do you actually expect me to turn people in to you, to be killed?"

"No," Bömers said quickly. "I do not want blood on my hands, and I would never expect you to either."

"What then?"

"Tell people to stop, Alphonse, before this goes too far and Göring takes a personal interest. I shudder to think what could happen then and it would all be so unnecessary, quite avoidable."

"Unnecessary," Alphonse snorted, waving his arms about excitedly. "There's a thought. The whole war, the occupation, all of this is unnecessary."

"You know what I mean."

"I cannot help. I know nothing of these matters."

"Think about it, Alphonse. Please. For the sake of the Bordelais, for the sake of Saint-Émilion."

Alphonse felt nauseous, the taste of German tobacco in his dry mouth making him gag.

"I am going to stay a while," Bömers said, lifting his eyes to the ceiling and admiring the ancient carvings. "One should never take for granted the incredible treasures that we cherish today."

Alphonse walked away towards the catacombs that led out onto the market square, his feet as heavy as lead. He heard Bömers light another cigarette.

"Think about what I said, Alphonse," Bömers said.

Chapter Fifty-Three

Jean-Marc siphoned deep ruby-coloured juice out of a wine barrel using a rubber bulb pipette, held it up to the weak cellar light and then released it into a wine glass in a splash. As he swirled the wine around he studied it closely, as one might examine a precious gemstone in the light, before thrusting his nose into the glass and closing his eyes as black fruit and sweet berries and cassis and vanillins filled his nostrils. He had missed being away from crafting wines.

"What are you doing?" Monique asked.

Jean-Marc tapped the side of the barrel, marked with chalk: '40/SW/3eme remplir/M.

"This is Merlot from the 1940 vintage, from a special sunny corner of my vineyards where *les Boches* barbarians have apparently dug up all my vines to make a shooting range," Jean-Marc said and took a gulp of wine. "Try it. There'll be no more of this - ever."

Monique took the glass and sipped the wine. "Mmmh. Oh, it's good, so fruity and rich."

"1940 was a good summer, but..."

"But what?"

"I had nothing to do with making this wine, the first vintage in my life I have simply had to watch. I didn't tend the vines, I didn't harvest..."

"It's still from Château Cardinale," Monique said, and emptied the glass.

"Well, I am going to rack it, I think it needs it now," Jean-Marc said, turning away and replacing the stopper in the barrel.

"We have found a few suitable railway junctions," Monique said.

"Where?"

They walked over to the upturned wine barrel that served as a table, around which Louis, Anton, Nicolas and Gregoire were gathered, poring over a map. Patrice sat a few feet away, leaning against the limestone cave wall, whittling a piece of wood.

"The first time the line from Bordeaux splits is just beyond Libourne, where we could divert the train onto a track that sweeps south of Saint-Émilion, taking it to Bergerac via Castillon," Nicolas said, stabbing dirty fingers with blackened nails at the map, before sweeping dropped ash from his Gauloises away with his hand.

"Bergerac is in the *zone libre* and we have lots of contacts there," Anton added.

"And Vichy Milice swarming everywhere. They would notice an unscheduled train," Patrice said without looking up from his whittling.

"He's right," Monique said.

"I know people in Castillon," Jean-Marc said. "It is a sleepy wine town with big warehouses at Le Chai au Quai. The *negociant* business is flat now because of the war, and many of these warehouses are probably empty."

They studied the map for a moment. Then Nicolas emitted a puff of smoke and continued. "The next time the line splits is at Coutras, here, about twelve kilometres after Lalande-de-Pomerol."

Jean-Marc leaned closer and traced his finger along the map. "That heads for Périgueux, winding along the southern aspect of the River L'Isle."

"Lots of places to ambush the train between stations, I would imagine," Anton said.

"Teulières can help us with that," Nicolas said, glancing at Patrice on the floor.

"I could ask," Patrice mumbled with a flamboyant sweep of his knife across the wood.

"And there is another split here, further north in the Charente, beyond Angoulême," Nicolas said, stabbing his finger onto the map and dislodging a splodge of cigarette ash.

"That'll be more in Poujade's territory, don't you think?" Anton said, glancing up from beneath his sagging eyelid.

"Are you really going to attempt this?" Patrice said, halting the whittling and looking up at them.

Jean-Marc could feel the intensity of Patrice's disapproval and wondered why he was still there with them. The door to the cellar squeaked open and Alphonse stepped in. He was greeted by a murmur of acknowledgement from within the cellar and nodded back in reply.

"I am going to rack my 1940 Merlot, Alphonse," Jean-Marc said. "Have you checked yours?"

Alphonse was clearly distracted, his forehead deeply lined as he approached the map on the barrel. "What's this?" he asked.

"Railway map of the south-west," Nicolas said, shifting his weight off his weak leg and lurching to one side.

"Do you remember the name of that *negociant* in Castillon, Alphonse, the one who operates from Le Chai?"

"Gilles Barjonet?"

"Ah, that's him."

"Why do you ask?" Alphonse said, squaring up to the map and squinting at it.

"We are going to throw the points where the railway splits at Libourne and divert a shipment of wine to Castillon, where we'll seize it," Monique said.

"Do you think Gilles will help us?" Jean-Marc said.

Alphonse hesitated and stared at the map, frowning deeply. "Who has a cigarette for me?" he asked.

Nicolas rocked forward awkwardly and held out a crumpled Gauloises packet from which one cigarette protruded. Alphonse took it with a small, grateful nod and accepted the proffered lit match from Nicolas. The smell of sulphur hung in the air for a few moments. After a languorous inhalation he emitted a cloud of smoke.

"Bömers has threatened me," Alphonse said eventually.

All eyes were now fixed on Alphonse. "Where is Federico?" Alphonse asked, glancing over his shoulder.

"Haven't seen him, he may be sleeping back there," Jean-Marc said, gesturing casually towards the tunnels disappearing into the limestone walls. "What did Bömers say?"

"They suspect that we – the Bordelais, that is – are hiding Maquis – like yourselves – and supporting the resistance activity against the Germans." Alphonse looked dejected and deeply troubled as he leaned forwards and placed both elbows onto the outstretched map.

"*Merde!*" Jean-Marc muttered.

"He suspects you," Alphonse pointed the glowing Gauloises at Gregoire, "and Olivier, the poor boy, of being complicit." Alphonse turned and walked away from the map, biting at a fingernail.

"I warned you," Patrice said from the floor. "This is what I said would happen."

"Oh shut up, Patrice," Monique snapped.

"Maybe we should head across to Castillon for a while," Jean-Marc suggested, "in case they…"

"And what about Federico, and Angelica, and Olivier?" Alphonse said, turning to face Jean-Marc.

"You have been very supportive letting us hide in your cave tunnels, Alphonse, but we should probably do as Jean-Marc suggests and leave for a while. Patrice has contacts around Bergerac that we can use too," Monique said, laying a supportive hand on Alphonse's shoulder.

"And you, Gregoire?" Alphonse looked at his son.

"I will have to go, Papa, I am a wanted man here," Gregoire said. "Should we take Olivier?"

"No," Alphonse said quickly, "he is too weak and, in any case, it would break your mother's heart."

"Do you think a widespread search is imminent?" Jean-Marc asked.

Alphonse nodded slowly. "I think he was warning me."

"We must go then, tonight," Patrice said, standing up and dropping his whittled wood on the floor as he re-sheathed the knife on his belt. "I need to warn Brutinel as well."

"I'm sorry, Alphonse," Jean-Marc said, stepping closer and seeing the full depth of his neighbour's concern buried behind watery eyes.

"Don't stop doing what you are doing," Alphonse said. "Give them what they deserve." He paused at the door. "I will rack the 1940 for you. Just... be careful."

Amidst the commotion that ensued after Alphonse left the cellar, Jean-Marc found himself confronted by Monique's guilty eyes. "I could not forgive myself if something happened to Alphonse," she said.

Jean-Marc nodded and then noticed Federico emerge from the darkened entrance to a tunnel. The old man smiled and waved as he always did in his amicable Tuscan way.

"You've just missed Alphonse," Jean-Marc said.

"Yes." Federico nodded. "I heard."

The two men stared at each other for a brief moment, Jean-Marc unsure what to say. How much should he reveal; how much had Federico overheard?

"We're going to cross the demarcation line tonight and operate from Castillon or Bergerac for a while," Jean-Marc said.

"Good," Federico said, grabbing Jean-Marc's hand in his leathery grasp and shaking it.

"Do you and Angelica want to join us?" Jean-Marc asked hesitantly, aware out of the corner of his eye of Patrice staring at him intently.

Federico squeezed his hand more firmly and pursed his lips. "Thank you, but your battles are for younger fighters than us. You go, with my blessing, and carry on for me and for Angelica."

Jean-Marc felt a lump in his throat as he stared into Federico's resolute eyes. For the first time it occurred to him that the fate of this dear old Tuscan winemaker, cruelly displaced by the Germans, might be determined by their actions. For the first time too he wondered if he would see Federico again when they were next at Château Millandes.

"What about you?" Jean-Marc said.

Federico chuckled throatily. "Old goats like Alphonse and me, we are tough. We survived the Great War, you know, and we'll survive this one too, don't worry."

Jean-Marc wanted to believe him, but he had seen trainloads of people being deported to the black heart of Germany, and he had faced the grim knowledge that his wife and children had suffered the same fate. This was not like the Great War. This one was different.

Chapter Fifty-Four

Gilles Barjonet was a small man; hairy jowls, round, viniferous belly and stumpy thighs. Hidden beneath a bushy moustache was a crooked set of deeply tannin-stained teeth.

"Of course I will help," he said to Jean-Marc as they surveyed the tranquil waters of the Dordogne flowing past the elevated quayside. Behind them Le Chai, in all its symmetrical golden sandstone magnificence, was imposingly situated. "Most of my customers were in America and England and, thanks to the Germans, business is dead."

"This is very fine wine," Jean-Marc remarked.

Barjonet refilled his glass and then stared at the bottle unsteadily, his eyes betraying his insobriety. "I am drinking the last of my good wines in stock. No one to sell to, and I'm damned if *les Boches* will get them."

With an unexpected flourish Gilles hurled the empty bottle of 1928 Château La Tour into the river, where it plopped in the water like a fish breaking the surface. "Damn them all!"

Two days later Gregoire, Louis and Anton left with plans to divert the Berlin-bound 8pm freight train just north of Libourne. They would incapacitate the signalman in his signal box and pull the levers to direct the train off the Angoulême line and onto the Bergerac line. No one but the signalman would be any the wiser.

"You will have to kill him," Patrice had said.

"He is a jobbing Frenchman, we cannot just kill him," Gregoire protested.

"I'm sure if you render him unconscious and tie him up before you throw the switches, he will be none the wiser," Monique said.

"What if he is Vichy?" Anton asked.

"There are no Vichy inside the *zone occupée*," Jean-Marc dismissed.

Two kilometres outside of Castillon, Jean-Marc, Patrice, Nicolas, Monique and a dozen of Teulières' armed men stopped the train on a wooded stretch west of Saint-Magne-de-Castillon just before the tracks crossed the River Lacaret and intersected with Rue de Mauperey, which was their transport route to Le Chai. Vineyards stretched away in every direction on flat, featureless land, except for a two hundred-metre stretch of woodland that flanked the tracks.

The surprised French train drivers alighted with their hands in the air and were encouraged to flee, but three German soldiers who started firing from one of the freight cars could not be persuaded to surrender. There were no casualties amongst the Maquis and no sympathy displayed over the bodies of the dead soldiers. But, staring at their blood-spattered uniforms and deathly pale faces, Jean-Marc knew that their deaths would bring further retribution.

"We should bury them to prevent discovery," Monique said.

"Over there, amongst the trees," Jean-Marc added.

Behind them the locomotive hissed steam rhythmically through numerous pressure relief valves as lorries arrived and parked up beside the tracks, ready to be filled with cases of wine. The air smelled of grease and coal smoke, which hung with a tangible, gritty presence in the stagnant air, and stung Jean-Marc's eyes.

"What do we do with the train?" Jean-Marc said.

Patrice shrugged. "Leave it here?"

Five thousand cases of wine and fifty puncheons were unloaded and transported to the cavernous warehouse at Le Chai.

"I hope Barjonet doesn't drink it all," Monique joked. "He seems to have quite an appetite for wine."

"Show me a Bordelais who doesn't," Jean-Marc chuckled.

Later, Monique and Jean-Marc were standing on the stone quayside outside Le Chai in Castillon as pink and orange hues of dusk reflected in the calm expanse of Dordogne water. A pair of swans swam gracefully upstream, rippling the melange of colour, and swallows swooped and glided over the water's surface as if tasting the sunset. Beneath them at the water's edge, empty, sun-bleached wooden *gabares* waited patiently for peace, so that they might once again fill their sails with wind and ferry wines and cheeses downstream to Bergerac and upstream to the port of Bordeaux. Jean-Marc put his arm around Monique's waist and pulled her closer.

"That went really well, didn't it?" Jean-Marc said. "It's nice when plans work out." He pushed his nose into her fine hair as he kissed her ear and savoured her familiar smell.

"Don't judge it before we see the extent of the reprisals," Patrice said tersely.

Jean-Marc turned around to find Patrice standing behind them, his expressionless face punctuated by a glowing Gauloises hanging out of the corner of his mouth, an opened bottle of wine in one hand and three stemmed glasses in the other. He poured amber-coloured liquid into each glass.

"To you," Patrice said, lifting his glass to his lips. "*Santé.*"

Jean-Marc looked at Monique and saw his surprise mirrored in her face. He took a sip, tentatively. Monique took her glass from Patrice and frowned.

"And this?" Monique said, regarding her drink with suspicion.

"I misjudged you," Patrice said quietly. "An apology."

Jean-Marc raised his glass to the fading light of the setting sun. Amber and gold hues mingled seamlessly as the dying light danced off numerous vertical radial tears of wine visible in the glass: the Marangoni effect. "What is this wine?"

"It is grown very close to where I live and grew up," Patrice said, lifting the bottle for them to read the label. "I found a few bottles of Château de Monbazillac in Gilles' warehouse."

Jean-Marc murmured his appreciation. "The 1924 was a very good year too. Gilles keeps good stuff."

"Like sweet bergamasque," Monique said, licking her lips.

"What's that?" Jean-Marc asked.

Monique shrugged coyly, her eyes sparkling playfully at Jean-Marc. "Pure hedonism."

He felt her fingers slipping between his: smooth, velvety, inviting, exciting – just like the wine.

Chapter Fifty-Five

The soldiers came at 6am, half a dozen of them, armed and boisterous. They barked at Alphonse and barged past Marthe as they surged into the château to search all the rooms. Alphonse, standing in his baggy, striped nightclothes, tried to console Marthe, who held her face in her hands and sobbed, nightcap askew on her head.

"Obergefreiter, there is someone upstairs," called a soldier to the officer who was watching Alphonse and Marthe in the kitchen.

"That is my son," Alphonse said. "He..."

"How old is he?" the officer asked, staring ahead at the window and refusing to engage with Alphonse as he rocked on his jackboot heels.

"He is... er... only eighteen." Alphonse cast a nervous glance at Marthe.

"Has he been called up for STO?"

"You see, he is—" Alphonse began.

"Is he dodging STO?"

"My son is paralysed," Alphonse said, unleashing a fresh wave of sobbing from Marthe.

"He has been shot, Obergefreiter," shouted a soldier from upstairs. "He cannot walk."

312

For the first time the officer adjusted his gaze to stare at Alphonse, lifting both manicured eyebrows simultaneously. "Shot?"

"It's an old... er... an accident from years ago," Alphonse stammered.

"A winemaking accident?" the officer said sarcastically.

The sounds of boots cascading down the wooden stairs heralded the return of the soldiers. One turned his head into the kitchen while the others searched the lower floors.

"He is thin and stiff with spasm, Obergefreiter. It looks like an old injury," the soldier said.

The officer sniffed and his face stiffened once more. "Very well. What is across there?" He pointed to the cellar doors across the courtyard.

"My wine cellars," Alphonse said, swallowing.

The officer rocked back and forth, peering through the windows across the courtyard with narrowed eyes, like a kestrel might study a sparrow.

"All clear, Obergefreiter," the soldier said as they all returned to the kitchen, crowding in around Alphonse and Marthe.

"Search the cellars across there, every inch. Take torches with you," the officer said, and then followed his men out into the courtyard.

Marthe dissolved into sobs as Alphonse held her, his own heart beating violently in his chest, his mouth dry as he waited for the soldiers to discover Federico and Angelica. Would they shoot them right there in his courtyard or would they take them away? And what about him and Marthe, and Olivier – would they be taken away too?

"Go up and check on Olivier," Alphonse said, guiding Marthe towards the stairs.

Cautiously and reluctantly he stepped out into the gravelled courtyard, his soft bare feet recoiling on the sharp stones. The

313

soldiers had broken open the cellar door and were stomping everywhere.

"There are tunnels, Obergefreiter," a soldier shouted.

"Check them, every one, every inch," the officer shouted back. He gestured towards the barn. "There is a barn as well."

Alphonse closed his eyes. The war had come home to him now; it could not come any closer unless he were a serving soldier. This was where the reckoning began. He breathed slowly and deeply and hoped that Gregoire was safe and that Jean-Marc would look out for him, for he did not know how the day might end.

Chapter Fifty-Six

On Wednesday night Jean-Marc, Monique and Patrice crept cautiously through the darkened recesses that surrounded the isolated signal box outside Coutras. Dressed in black, complete with berets and soot-smeared faces, they moved wordlessly, following Patrice's hand movement instructions: a closed hand held up meant freeze; a downward motion of an open palm meant crouch down and an open hand thrust towards them meant stop.

Jean-Marc had learnt an entirely new language of hostility and subversive engagement since being evicted from his life as a humble winemaker. But when he was crouched beside Monique, able to smell her and catch sight of her vivacious eyes, enjoy the warmth and intimacy of occasional contact, it felt more like an adolescent adventure to him than a war.

Patrice entered the signal box with stealth and hit the signalman – who was drinking something steaming out of an enamel mug – on the head with his Welrod pistol. Then he hit him again, and then a third time. Jean-Marc winced as the poor man groaned and then finally fell silent. Patrice signalled for them to approach and they proceeded to bind the unconscious, round, middle-aged man with flax rope before gagging his mouth with linen.

"Which lever is it?" Patrice asked, fingering each of four large steel rods covered with well-worn white and red paint.

Jean-Marc looked at Monique, who seemed equally unsure, inhaling the smell of grease and spilled coffee.

"Let's check the tracks and see which lever moves which points," Monique suggested.

She and Jean-Marc moved out into the exposed darkness and orientated themselves on the tracks.

"These lines come from the south, which must be Bordeaux," Monique said, holding a field compass in her palm.

Turning on their heels and facing north revealed that two sets of tracks continued straight ahead and two peeled off to their right.

"This must be the line to Périgueux," Jean-Marc said and then gesticulated for Patrice to see. "These are the points that we must move, here."

After some trial and error the points were set and all three retreated into the trees to watch the train approach. It was a long wait, over two hours, before the distant puffing of a steam locomotive became audible. Muffled sounds from the signal box indicated that the signalman was conscious and Patrice vocalised his dissatisfaction and pulled out his pistol.

"Don't kill him, Patrice," Monique said, placing a hand on his arm.

"I don't like loose ends," Patrice muttered, before rushing off and beating the man a few more times until he was silent.

They decided to tie him to a tree deep in the woods to delay his discovery. By the time this was done the train was already clanking past and Jean-Marc and Monique ran back to the edge of the trees to check their routing. The train veered slowly to the right and headed for Périgueux via Lalande-de-Pomerol, where Poujade and his men were waiting.

Jean-Marc punched the air with both of his arms – "Yes!" – and then fell into Monique's warmth. There were indeed moments in this awful nightmare of German occupation when he felt as though he was having the time of his life. But ever-present in equal measure was the disturbing reality of what he was now capable of doing. Before Isabel took the children and fled he had known nothing more than vines and soil and wine; today he carried a pistol, perpetrated insurrection against the enemy occupiers and had seen dead German soldiers at close quarters. What would tomorrow bring, he wondered?

Chapter Fifty-Seven

Alphonse was shivering in the cool morning air, despite rubbing his arms vigorously, his toes turning blue on the gravel. After what felt like an eternity the soldiers began to re-emerge from the cellars. With his heart pounding in his chest Alphonse waited to catch sight of Federico and Angelica being frogmarched out at the point of a rifle. But they never appeared.

"All clear, Obergefreiter," a young soldier with acne said as he emerged from the cellar.

Alphonse swallowed in astonishment. Where had Federico hidden?

The officer pulled out his leather gloves and began to pull them on methodically, like a woman putting on silk stockings. "It seems everything is in order, *monsieur*," he said, sniffing and keeping his eyes averted. He snapped his heels together. "*Heil* Hitler!"

The men returned to their Henschel troop carrier and in a stench of diesel fumes they pulled out of Château Millandes, sending wandering chickens flying in a panicked flurry of feathers and squawks. As the dust cloud behind the vehicle receded safely into the distance, Alphonse hurried over to the cellar and peered in. Everything appeared undisturbed.

"Federico!" he called out. "Angelica!"

Walking down the first few metres of each tunnel, he called out several more times – ever more loudly – being greeted by nothing more than a dull echo from the unyielding darkness. How thoroughly could the soldiers have searched, he wondered? They had certainly been at it for over an hour. Then he remembered Marthe and Olivier and returned to the house to find them cowering in Olivier's bedroom. Olivier, pale and sweaty, was still under his sheets and Marthe sat on the foot of his bed, the cuticles of her fingers bleeding.

"The soldiers have left," Alphonse said.

"Angelica?" Marthe said, her swollen pink eyes welling up again. "Federico?"

Alphonse shook his head. "They didn't find them." He shrugged his shoulders, mystified.

Marthe emitted a sound that blended a sob with a gasp of relief. She bit her knuckles, closing her eyes and signing the cross over her chest with the other hand.

"Where are they, Papa?" Olivier said, pulling the sheet down a little further, perhaps sensing that the danger had eased.

"I don't know, I can't find them either."

Chapter Fifty-Eight

The atmosphere in Bömers' smoke-filled office was cold and tense despite the warm summer sunshine across Saint-Émilion. Kühnemann paced up and down, smoking continuously, imbuing Bömers with the urge to say, *Sit down, for God's sake, you're making me nervous*, but he thought better of it. Sitting behind his desk, Bömers read the letter typed on heavy-grained, watermarked ivory paper.

From the office of Reichsmarschall H. W. Göring
Das Luftsfahrts-Ministerium
Wilhelmstrasse
BERLIN

To Regional Kommand, South-Western France

LG Kurt Feldt (Kommander Section III)
LG Moritz von Faber du Faur (529ᵗʰ)
Hauptsturmführer Ernst Kühnemann (Bordeaux)
Hauptsturmführer Heinz Bömers (Saint-Émilion)

It has been brought to my attention that the situation in German-occupied Bordeaux, with regard to insurgent activity from the French guerrillas, is totally out of control.

Wine shipments have been pillaged on numerous occasions at various sites between Bordeaux and Paris and the placement of armed guards on the trains has had no material impact whatsoever.

More recently, several trains have simply disappeared, hijacked by resistance fighters who remain free to exist and attack German forces with impunity.

The ministerium will not tolerate this situation any longer. You are hereby given notice that you have seven days to bring the perpetrators to justice and return military order and rule to every aspect of life and in particular German affairs in Bordeaux, which, I remind you, is occupied territory.

Failure to do so will result in your reassignment from Bordeaux to the eastern front. Do not underestimate my resolve in bringing this lawless situation to order, at any cost.

Heil Hitler.

From the desk of Oberst-Gruppenführer Karl Köller
Chief of Staff to Reichsmarschall H. W. Göring

Bömers opened the cigarette case and lit his fifth Bremaria of the morning. Kühnemann was staring out of the window, his short, slicked black hair glistening.

"How can three trains simply fail to arrive in Berlin?" Kühnemann said without turning. "Stealing wine off trains, siphoning wine out of barrels and refilling them with water, such petty thefts when our backs are turned I can understand, but how the hell can they steal an entire train?" His voice rose manically towards the end, in both pitch and volume.

Bömers exhaled a fog of smoke into the air and leaned back. He had underestimated the Bordelais and he had been naive in his dealings with them, this much he realised. But, he was a businessman, a wine merchant, not a cold-blooded killer, not a mercenary, nor a ruthless agent of the Nazi state. He could never have been such a person; it was simply not in his nature.

"We have arrested twenty vignerons, uncovered a dozen covert resistance groups operating from châteaux across Bordeaux, executed nearly forty Maquis guerrillas, and still it goes on," Kühnemann ranted. He turned at the waist and pointed his cigarette at Bömers. "You have been too lenient with all of them, especially that fellow, Sabron. Generalleutnant Feldt has told me that your friendship with the Bordelais constitutes a weakness on our part. He wants you to be more like Otto Klaebisch in Champagne."

"Klaebisch is a ruthless bastard who is destroying Champagne," Bömers objected.

"Exactly. This is about the Reich, not about France. What they have belongs to us. They are no longer your friends, Heinz, they are our enemies – can you not see that?"

Bömers could see that, but did not believe in the warmongering philosophy behind it. These were people whom he had known for decades, a way of life that transcended politics and affairs of state as it passed from father to son. He felt more part of this tradition than he did the Third Reich.

"Our intelligence suggests there is someone out there who is driving the insurgency against the wine shipments," Kühnemann continued. "A ringleader, a... *Kapitän* among men."

Bömers lifted his eyes from the misery of Göring's letter on his desk. "Do you have a name?"

Kühnemann turned and walked over, slumping into the padded seat in front of the desk. "No." He twirled his wrist effeminately in the air, disseminating smoke from his cigarette. "We suspect British... you know... spies might be involved, but there is no proof."

"I thought the Saint-Yzan executions would be a deterrent," Bömers said, vividly recalling the horrific details of that day's death toll.

322

"Have you not got any cognac or whisky?" Kühnemann said irritably.

"I have plenty of wine," Bömers said.

Kühnemann made a disapproving sound and waved his hand in the air. "I need something strong. I long for a schnapps."

"I can send a *Schütze* into Saint-Émilion to buy a bottle of cognac, or Armagnac," Bömers said. "What would you prefer?"

"This is your problem, Heinz – we are the rulers here, we have conquered these people and they surrendered their country to us, as Göring keeps reminding us. You do not need to buy their cognac, just take it," Kühnemann said, leaning forward and rapping his index finger on the desk.

"Do you want any?" Bömers said, struggling to control his annoyance.

"No, forget it. What are we going to do about these insurgents?"

Both men sat in contemplative silence, the air rank with smoke, perspiration beading on their lips and foreheads.

"We cannot arrest or execute everyone, that is simply impractical and will be counterproductive in the long run."

"How can it possibly be counterproductive to get Göring off our backs and restore law and order?"

"Who will make the wine?" Bömers said calmly, keen to address his fears that Kühnemann, or Feldt, might come up with a radical and bloodthirsty plan.

"We do not have enough soldiers in France to police every kilometre of rail track, and every station, and every siding and junction," Kühnemann said.

Bömers stood up and walked around his desk, stopping at the ornate Vitrine drinks display cabinet in the corner. Extracting a bottle and two glasses, he began to pour red wine. "Care for a Mouton-Rothschild?"

"Ugh!" Kühnemann said indifferently.

"It's the 1929 – *magnifique*." Bömers kissed his fingertips.

"Heinz!" Kühnemann exploded. "Focus, for God's sake."

Bömers returned with two glasses and set one down in front of Kühnemann. "To deal with the Bordelais you must first understand them, know what they believe in, what they value, what they are indeed capable of," Bömers said, closing his eyes and savouring the bouquet of his wine as he swirled the ruby liquid beneath his nose.

Kühnemann leaned forward begrudgingly to take his glass and swallowed a hasty gulp of wine.

"Isn't it spectacular?" Bömers said.

"Christ, Heinz, you are in the fucking Wehrmacht now – we need a solution or Göring will have us in Kiev where there is no French wine for you to sniff. You may be prepared to end up waist deep in Russian snow because of people like Sabron, but I sure as hell am not."

A timid knock at the door seemed to bring the blood to the boil in Kühnemann's face as tortuous veins across his forehead and temples swelled. "Tell them to leave us, this is vital business," he snapped loudly.

"Come!" Bömers said.

A nervous *Schütze* entered, saluted formally, clicking his heels, and marched swiftly to the desk where he handed an envelope to Bömers.

"Thank you, Tolmann, that will be all," Bömers said politely.

The *Schütze* retreated with a flush of relief evident across his face. Bömers slid a fleur-de-lys letter opener through the envelope and extracted a folded piece of paper, which he read silently at extended arm's length. The curiosity became too much for Kühnemann.

"Is it from Berlin?" Kühnemann asked, shifting in his chair.

"Alphonse Sabron at Château Millandes is in the clear," Bömers muttered with a flick of his eyebrows, dropping the paper onto his desk. He was both astounded and relieved, and tried to hide this from Kühnemann.

"You had his château searched?"

Bömers picked up his glass and savoured a mouthful of wine languidly. "Does that surprise you?"

"That still doesn't mean we shouldn't make an example of him. Didn't his sons dodge the STO?"

"One is too young," Bömers lied.

"Where are they? If they are not at home they will be with the Maquis."

"I have an idea," Bömers said quietly. "It does not involve widespread arrests, nor mass executions. But I think it will strike at the heart of the Bordelais."

"I am rather in favour of widespread arrests and executions," Kühnemann said. "So is Generalleutnant Feldt."

"We will never find this... *Kapitän*... with your methods, Ernst."

"What do you have in mind, then?"

"We must make them come to us, an ultimatum they cannot refuse," Bömers said. He sipped the wine again. "My God, this is good."

"Everything you have tried so far has failed," Kühnemann said disparagingly. "What makes you think you will succeed now?"

Bömers grinned, basking in the glory of the wine, one that he knew Göring would give almost anything to have. "Wait until you hear my plan, Ernst."

Chapter Fifty-Nine

"Alphonse!" called Marthe in a shrill voice. "Alphonse, where are you?"

Alphonse heard her footsteps descending the stairs rapidly, moving much faster than she normally did. He looked up distractedly from the notice that he held in his hand. "I am in the *salon*," he said loudly. "*Mon Dieu*, Marthe, have you seen this?" Alphonse said in disbelief, holding out the notice as Marthe entered the room. "The Germans are going to demolish the Monolithic Cathedral in Saint-Émilion."

"Alphonse!" Marthe said again, her voice faltering as her watery eyes stared emptily at Alphonse, her mouth slightly agape.

He stood up from the floral patterned sofa and held out the notice. Marthe didn't move; she just stared at him, tears running down her cheeks.

"What is it?" Alphonse said, lowering the notice to his side.

"It's Olivier, he's..."

Alphonse dropped the notice and rushed to his wife just as her knees buckled. "What?"

"He's unconscious, he doesn't respond even when I shake him. I think we should call the doctor."

Alphonse took a moment to collect his thoughts and then guided Marthe into the closest seat, an oak rocking chair with a pale blue cushion. "Sit here," he said and then rushed up the stairs as quickly as his ageing, stumpy legs could carry him.

The sight in Olivier's bedroom squeezed his throat and crushed the breath out of him. Olivier was lying with his head and outstretched arms on the floor and only his lower body, the paralysed half, still tucked beneath the bedding. His eyes were half-open and flickering very slowly from side to side.

"Olivier, my boy," Alphonse said, crouching down and lifting the young man's wasted frame back onto his bed with a muted groan. His warm, sweaty body felt like a ragdoll in Alphonse's hands as his head flopped back onto the pillow. "Can you hear me?"

He wanted to believe that Olivier's eyes reacted to his question, but in truth he knew that his wounded son was unresponsive. Hesitating briefly and placing his hand on Olivier's forehead, though he did not know why, he rushed back downstairs.

"Marthe, he is back in bed, sit with him and I will go and call Dr Fabre. He is burning with fever." Alphonse patted Marthe's hands between his until she looked into his eyes. "OK?" he said.

"First Federico and Angelica, and now my boy. I can't take much more of this," Marthe wailed.

Alphonse glanced at the notice on the floor, regretting that he had mentioned it under the circumstances. He echoed his wife's sentiments. Just how much could one family be expected to endure? Bending down, he picked up the notice, turned it over and placed it on the coffee table.

"Go to him, Marthe. I will be back with the doctor."

Chapter Sixty

Gregoire, Patrice and his men crept into the courtyard of Château Millandes shortly after 2am, first knocking delicately on the kitchen window for several minutes before Gregoire tossed a few pebbles at his parents' bedroom window. The moon bestowed on the partially obscuring clouds a glowing silver ripple, like the leading edge of a wave along a shoreline. Patrice walked over to the cellar and noticed that the lock was broken. He examined it and beckoned to Nicolas, who limped over.

"Something happened here," Patrice said.

"*Les Boches?*"

Patrice shrugged, then turned upon hearing the château door open to see Alphonse embracing Gregoire. Patrice and his men gathered in awkward silence a discreet distance away, the emotion evident on Alphonse's weary face.

"How is he, Papa?" Gregoire asked.

Alphonse held his son at arms' length, his face contorted, and shook his head subtly before glancing at Patrice. "Come inside, out of sight."

As they filed into the parlour Patrice paused beside Alphonse and laid his hand on the old man's shoulder. "Is everything alright, Alphonse? Is there anything we can do?"

Alphonse looked away and shook his head.

"I will call the doctor."

"Dr Fabre says there is nothing more that can be done," Alphonse said in a broken voice, wiping at his eyes. "Unless the fever breaks…"

"There is still hope then, Papa," Gregoire said.

"No, my son, not with the war on, there is no medicine."

"I don't know what to say," Patrice said, moved by Alphonse's resignation.

"What is there to say?" Alphonse said and turned back into the house, muttering, "Make yourselves some coffee."

Gregoire followed his father up the stairs into the dark, silent bowels of the great house. The rest of them stood in silence in the kitchen, listening to the gentle tick of the carved Bergere clock standing in the shadowy hall like a ghostly sentry.

"This is Jean-Marc's fault," Patrice said angrily, smacking a fist into his open palm. "He should have watched out for the boy."

Louis and Nicolas shuffled their feet. "That's not entirely fair," Nicolas said, eyes downcast.

"He is only a winemaker but he thinks and acts as if he is Maquis, of course it's fair."

"Keep your voices down," Anton said, lifting his head towards the floors above.

"Who wants coffee?" Louis asked.

"There is no coffee, it'll be roasted chicory and barley," Nicolas replied.

"I need sleep," Patrice said, opening the door and walking across the courtyard to the cellar.

The others followed, their footsteps crunching on the gravel and their heads illuminated by the moon as it hung, caught between a break in the clouds. Patrice was troubled, pausing again to examine the broken lock on the cellar door, realising that it most likely was the Germans who had searched the

329

cellars by force. He wondered what had become of Federico and his wife, drawing hope from the fact that Alphonse and his family had remained untouched. If Federico had been discovered, surely Alphonse would have been arrested too.

But morning light and a search of the cave tunnels revealed neither Federico nor Angelica. This left Patrice with a gnawing anxiety in his belly. Something was wrong. He leaned against the splintered cellar door, warming in the strengthening sunshine as he tugged on a Gauloises, his simmering resentment over Jean-Marc and Monique's intrusion into his resistance activities rising to the surface yet again. It was difficult not to feel that all of this had happened because of their stubborn refusal to listen to his advice. He understood how the Wehrmacht operated, they did not; he appreciated the dangers of reprisal, they did not. Even now, as Monique and Jean-Marc lay in wait of yet another German freight train laden with wine, somewhere in the Périgord Vert, preparing to divert it along a secondary siding, neither of them would be aware that German soldiers had entered and searched the sanctity of their Saint-Émilion safe house – the caves at Château Millandes – endangering Federico as well as Alphonse and his family.

The door across the courtyard opened and Alphonse appeared, terminating Patrice's ruminations. "Marthe has made eggs."

Patrice tried to read his face, his intonation: was he in mourning or simply exhausted? He called the others out of the cellar and made his way across to the parlour. A clutch of chickens cackled and retreated in a hysterical flap.

"How is Olivier?" Patrice asked.

Alphonse busied himself at the cast iron cooker, tending a pot of steaming hot chicory and barley. He shrugged his sloping shoulders. "He is very weak, but at least he is still fighting."

330

Pouring dark liquid into several mugs, he took two of them and turned to the staircase. "Marthe has put the eggs in the *salon*, you are welcome to sit in there and eat." With that he was gone, evidently afraid to be away from Olivier for too long.

The four of them ate in silence in the *salon*, the scrape of forks on fine crockery and the reassurance of the ticking Bergere clock the only sounds to be heard. Patrice was still hungry and could easily have eaten more egg. He began to lick his plate. Out of the corner of his eye he saw the notice lying on the wooden table, partly obscured by the egg platter. He reached forward and pulled it out.

"What is it?" Louis asked.

Patrice read quietly, the leaflet fluttering in his grasp. "*Mon Dieu!*" he said, barely audibly.

"What?" Nicolas said.

"It is far worse than I ever imagined," Patrice said quietly, blinking in disbelief at the notice in his hands. He looked up, aware that all his comrades had stopped chewing and were staring at him, open-mouthed.

"Read it to us," Anton said.

Patrice licked his lips and took a deep breath. "*By order of Section III Kommand in Bordeaux, notice is hereby given to all citizens of Saint-Émilion and surrounding Bordeaux environs. Due to ongoing guerrilla insurgency against the German forces and their property in Bordeaux, the ancient monument of the Monolithic Cathedral in the heart of Saint-Émilion has been packed with 500kg of explosives. Failure to surrender to the German Kommand, within three days, those individuals responsible for the ongoing sabotage, will result in detonation of these explosives and the consequent destruction of one of Bordeaux's greatest historical monuments on 25th August. The future of Saint-Émilion's historic legacy is in your hands. Immunity may be offered to those supplying information. Generalleutnant K. Feldt (Section III).*"

An icy silence froze the room and all of its occupants. Nobody moved as Patrice stared at the notice in continued incredulity, his eyes running over the words again and again.

"They will never do it," Nicolas said. "It would be a travesty against humanity."

"You would call their bluff?" Anton growled, leering at Nicolas through his good eye. "No decent human being would blow up the Monolithic Cathedral in Saint-Émilion."

"Who says the Nazis are decent human beings?" Louis snarled.

"It's an attack on God!" Anton said, holding out a clawed hand.

"It would be like destroying the Eiffel Tower," Nicolas said, waving his hand. "Who would do such a thing?"

"*Les Boches*," Louis said, nodding emphatically.

"You do realise that they want *us*, don't you?" Patrice said softly.

"Us?" Anton protested. "What about Jean-Marc and Monique?"

"And them. They probably don't know who we all are, but they sure as hell know we exist," Patrice said.

Everyone in the room looked about uncertainly, fear behind their eyes as they faced up to their ultimate accountability. Patrice looked at them, feeling his heart pounding in his chest, resentment and regret puckering his cheeks repetitively, like a bellows.

"We should never have got so involved, I knew it was a bad idea," Patrice said, looking at each of his comrades in turn. "But no one would listen to me."

"We must get warning to Monique, tell them not to return to Saint-Émilion quite yet," Nicolas said, his words attracting derisive looks from those around him.

"Warn them?" Patrice said. "Warn them of what – that it is their fault that the Cathedral in Saint-Émilion is about to be destroyed?"

"You know what I mean," Nicolas said contritely.

"No, I don't. This is all their fault, and right now he is probably fucking her in a barn somewhere while they wait to ambush another train," Patrice said, his venom boiling over. "I am not protecting them." He glared at his men, each in turn. "Are you willing to protect them with your life?"

After a moment's silence, Louis spoke. "We are all comrades in this, them and us – we have fought side by side."

"No, we are not all comrades," Patrice said, his voice rising. "We, here, *we* are comrades." He drew a circle with his hands. "Jean-Marc is a wine farmer, and Monique, where does she come from, huh? Who is she?"

"What do you mean?" Nicolas said, meeting Patrice's gaze.

"Ask yourself, where did she come from? Out of the blue she arrived in Bergerac from Normandy. Why? Where does she get all the amatol from, huh? The Welrod pistols, the Sten guns? They are all British military, my friends." Patrice stared at them. "Have you thought about that?"

Alphonse appeared at the door, unseen and unheard, still in his nightclothes and slippers. Patrice and his men turned and faced him expectantly.

"I heard you talking," Alphonse said. "What's going on?"

"How is Olivier?" Patrice asked quickly.

"Sleeping for now. He has been so delirious, seeing things, talking past us." Alphonse sighed, hunched over, almost defeated. "It is so upsetting for Marthe."

"I suppose rest will be good for him," Patrice said softly.

"You are not thinking of turning Jean-Marc over to the Germans, are you?" Alphonse said, taking a step into the room, holding one unsteady hand out in front of him, pleading.

Everyone turned to look at Patrice.

333

"Have you read this?" Patrice retorted sharply, holding out the notice.

"Of course."

"You would let *les Boches* destroy something of such irreplaceable value to Saint-Émilion, to France?"

"They will never do that."

"You can be so sure?" Patrice said.

"Jean-Marc is not guilty of any crime, remember that. He has had his wife and children taken from him by the Germans, his wine farm expropriated and vandalised by the Germans. He has done no more than any of you," Alphonse said, pointing at each one in turn. "You cannot make him the sacrificial lamb, he does not deserve that."

"So what do you suggest we do, Alphonse?" Patrice said.

Alphonse held out his hands, shrugged and made a throaty sound. "You are all Frenchmen, you are all Maquis fighting for France, with honour. You will think of a plan."

Patrice looked down at the floor and wrung his hands in his lap. He could understand the old man's loyalty to his neighbour, but in truth he did not know what he was talking about. Jean-Marc had put them all in danger, allowing himself to be swept up in an affair with a hot-headed person like Monique. Yes, Monique – it was actually her fault; she had corroded the unit's solidarity, brought Jean-Marc in and undermined his control over his men. Patrice breathed hard.

"We are not all Frenchmen," Patrice said softly, waiting a moment before looking up.

"Jean-Marc may be a Jew, but he is as French as you and me," Alphonse replied with conviction warbling his voice.

"Monique is British."

"What?" Alphonse said.

"You don't know this for sure, Patrice," Nicolas protested.

"I believe she is a British agent," Patrice continued, his confidence building.

334

"I don't believe it," Alphonse said. "She's from Normandy, I know her village."

Patrice rubbed his forehead and shook his head in disbelief. "You don't think she would come well-prepared?"

Nicolas leapt up and swayed on his weak leg. "And so what if she is? She has helped us, all of us. You're just pissed off because she loves Jean-Marc."

"Shut up!" Patrice spat.

"She makes a damn good Maquis," Anton said. "I wouldn't care if she was Jewish, I'd still follow her."

"Oh, you talk such shit, Anton. You're all just taken in by her good looks," Patrice said.

"And you're not?" Nicolas said.

"Please, please," Alphonse said with his arms outstretched. "Not here, not now." He glanced over his shoulder, up the stairs, his brows dipping in the centre.

Patrice felt instant remorse and simmered down. "I'm sorry. We are disrespectful to you, Alphonse, and to your family who have been so good to us." He looked around at his comrades, whose heads hung low in apology. "If there is nothing we can do to help, then we should leave."

Alphonse said nothing.

"Were you searched by *les Boches*?" Patrice asked.

Alphonse nodded sadly.

"Where are Federico, and Angelica?"

Alphonse's lip quivered and he met Patrice's gaze with watery eyes, bruised by so much suffering. "I don't know – they are gone. They must be in such danger at their age, and I think they did it to protect us."

What an audacious and selfless sacrifice, Patrice thought. Would sacrifice save the cathedral? Would it save them? Patrice fumed inside, incensed by the cascade of consequences that had been unleashed by Monique's impulsivity and which had now affected everyone at Château Millandes.

QUENTIN SMITH

"If there is blood spilled it will be on Monique's hands,"
Patrice said quietly. "She is British and she has interfered, she
does not understand how things work here, how we do
things." He looked up slowly and found Alphonse staring at
him.

Chapter Sixty One

Jean-Marc savoured a mouthful of silky smooth Château Batailley as he watched the sun set over the River Dordogne below the quayside at Le Chai. It had been another satisfying mission: a German freight train of some twenty wagons diverted at Coutras towards Périgueux and then ambushed in a tight valley, thousands of cases of wine destined for Berlin repatriated, as he liked to think of it.

"Penny for your thoughts," Monique said as she slipped in beside him.

"What?"

"It's an old English expression."

Jean-Marc swirled another mouthful of the wine in his mouth, both enjoying and simultaneously analysing the flavours and sensations. "I would like to be able to make wine like this," he said, enviously admiring the glass of garnet-coloured wine in his hand.

Monique hooked her arm through his. "I'm sure you do."

Jean-Marc looked into her eyes. "Even Alphonse's wine – not even *Grand Cru* yet – is regarded as better than mine and sells for fifty per cent more."

She rested her head against his shoulder. "I am so happy. I know it sounds… strange, us being at war and all that, but I really am."

Jean-Marc felt his heart miss a beat. "I am technically still a married man, but I am in love with you, Monique." He paused and turned to face her. "Does that make me a bad man?"

They stood in silence as the muted colours of a sinking sun reflected on the river's calmly flowing waters, silhouetting a pair of swans swimming together, never far apart.

"There will be a BBC broadcast on Radio Londres tonight from the Free French," Monique said.

"How do you know?"

"I heard the coded messages this afternoon."

"Coded message?" Jean-Marc teased. "*This is the BCRA calling all agents...*" he mimicked.

"No!" Monique said, punching his chest playfully. "*Jean has a long moustache*, and it has nothing to do with the BCRA."

"*Jean has a long moustache?*"

"When they are planning an airdrop of weapons and supplies it's *Saint Lignoui founded Naples.*"

Jean-Marc burst out laughing.

"There are thousands of different messages to groups all over France, but only very few are meaningful to us here in Bordeaux. It's designed to confuse the Germans," Monique said.

"I'm sure it does," Jean-Marc said, still chuckling.

"Monique, it's on!" Barjonet called from the enormous warehouse door.

They rushed inside and Barjonet pulled the heavy door closed and bolted it, plunging them into instantaneous darkness. As his eyes grew accustomed to the low light, Jean-Marc could make out the stacks of wooden wine cases they had recovered. They followed the square figure of Barjonet as he weaved his way between towering walls of recovered wine towards a back room, gouged into the limestone hillside on which Castillon met the River Dordogne.

338

"The British have landed in North Africa, and they have invaded Morocco and Algeria," he whispered.

"When?" Monique asked.

"I'm not sure, a few days ago I think. We'll hear on the radio."

Once locked inside the stone room, in the smoky yellow light of a single candle, Barjonet increased the volume on his Bakelite radio concealed within a wine barrel. The voices of the broadcasting Free French were crackly and tinny and all three leaned in to hear more distinctly. Barjonet smiled, his nicotine and tannin-stained crooked teeth visible beneath a druid-like moustache.

"*Ici Londres! Les Français parlent aux Français. British and American Allied forces have successfully landed in French Morocco and Algeria. A western force occupied the coast between Safi and Casablanca and as far north as Mehdia. An eastern force has taken Tangiers and a central force is at Oran in Algeria,*" said the jubilant voice on the radio.

"That's good, they will begin to drive the Germans out," Monique said.

Barjonet pulled a face. "We'll see."

"*Intercepted communications indicate that as a consequence the Germans intend to extend their occupation of France to include the Mediterranean coast in order to protect their flank.*"

"*Merde!*" Jean-Marc said loudly, straightening.

"Ssshhh!" Barjonet said.

"*Everyone in the zone libre east of the demarcation line should prepare for and expect German military rule any day now. This will bring to an end the Vichy regime of Marshal Pétain.*"

"Small mercies," Jean-Marc muttered.

"Amen." Barjonet nodded.

"Be careful what you wish for," Monique said.

"I only wish for the end of this occupation and the return to normal business," Barjonet said, leaning forward and lighting a cigarette in the candle. "Anyone?" he asked, holding forth the crumpled packet.

"There will be nowhere to hide," Jean-Marc said.

"This is what I fear, my friends – you are too exposed here in Castillon. You should return to Château Millandes and the safety of those cave tunnels," Barjonet said from within a cloud of grey smoke.

Jean-Marc looked into Monique's face and recognised her disappointment. Like him, she had been revelling in the opportunity to strike back effectively against the German war machine in relative freedom. Once they were back at Château Millandes they would once again become prisoners in those dark and lonely limestone excavations. It would become a long and tiresome war for them, watching daylight through a crack in the door and passing the days by treading grapes for Alphonse.

"I really should go back and see how Olivier is, anyway," Jean-Marc said. "I was there when he was born, you know."

Monique smiled at him. "OK. I can use the opportunity to brief my contact in Bordeaux about developments at the same time."

Silence.

"When will you leave?" Barjonet asked.

Jean-Marc looked at Monique and breathed deeply. He imagined that he could see his reflection shimmering in her steady, confident eyes.

"Tonight," Monique said, "before German troops begin heading east."

"OK, the boss has spoken," Jean-Marc said and slapped the table with the flattened palms of his hands.

"Be careful. It's getting very dangerous to move around," Barjonet said with unusual seriousness on his face.

"Look after the wine, Gilles, and don't drink it all!" Jean-Marc replied.

"Thank you for everything, Gilles, we'll see you soon," Monique said and kissed him lightly on each cheek.

Chapter Sixty-Two

"Where is Monique?" Jean-Marc shouted. He was rushing across the gravelled courtyard at Château Millandes, scattering the chickens in a flurry of feathers.

"Lost your girlfriend?" Patrice taunted, lifting his head out of the rear of the gasogene in the barn.

"Keep your voice down, you idiot, I've seen *les Boches* moving about outside your house," Nicolas said to Jean-Marc, gesticulating towards Château Cardinale.

"Where is she?" Jean-Marc repeated, standing inches from Patrice's unshaven face.

"Perhaps you shouldn't have slept so long," Patrice said.

Jean-Marc was rapidly losing patience with Patrice, whose mocking smile was goading him into physical retaliation. The anger he felt must have been evident on his face because Nicolas, standing behind Patrice and packing wooden logs into the gasogene's boot, broke the silence.

"She's gone into Bordeaux."

"When?" Jean-Marc said.

"She woke early, spoke to Alphonse, heard about the Monolithic Cathedral, and left in a hurry," Nicolas said.

Jean-Marc took a step back. "What are you talking about?"

"Haven't you heard?" Patrice said, resting both forearms on the top of the car's door.

Jean-Marc glared at him.

"*Les Boches* have threatened to destroy the Monolithic Cathedral in Saint-Émilion unless we are handed in to them," Nicolas said.

Jean-Marc stared at Nicolas in disbelief, his eyes flitting briefly across Patrice's derisive expression. "We?" he said.

"The insurgents behind the train sabotage. Have you not seen the leaflets?" Patrice said, nodding his head towards the main house. "Alphonse has one."

Jean-Marc couldn't think straight. This was surely a bluff, a ruse. His eyes were still gritty from the short night's sleep and a lack of morning coffee. What on earth was Patrice talking about? A German threat to destroy a national monument, a church of God, for a handful of Maquis: surely not.

"The British and Americans are in North Africa already," Jean-Marc said. "*Les Boches* are about to occupy the *zone libre* to protect the Mediterranean coastline. They'll probably leave here any day now."

Patrice took a menacing step around the car door towards Jean-Marc. "Occupy the *zone libre*?"

"We heard it on Radio Londres last night – from the Free French."

"The Free French," Patrice said dismissively, spitting on the dirt and making twirling movements above his head with one hand. "Your head is full of dreams and rubbish."

"It's all about to change. There will be no more demarcation line, all of France will be occupied," Jean-Marc said.

Patrice stepped towards Jean-Marc. "Your girlfriend is a British agent, isn't she?" His voice was accusing.

Jean-Marc felt anger rising within him as his breathing deepened. "Where has she gone to?"

Patrice shrugged and pulled a face. "Probably to meet her British contact. What do I care? We're going back to Bergerac, it's safer there."

Jean-Marc rounded on him. *"What do you care?"*

"She has got us all into this mess with her grand schemes to hijack trains. I warned you – both of you – several times. Now every German soldier in Bordeaux is looking for us. Don't you see?"

"Who went with her?" Jean-Marc said.

"Isn't that your job, lover boy?" Patrice retorted.

Jean-Marc rushed forward and grabbed Patrice's shirt, pushing him against the gasogene. "Is she alone?"

Patrice smiled back at him.

"Yes, she went alone," Nicolas said quietly.

"You idiots!" Jean-Marc shouted. "How could you let her?"

Patrice shook himself free and turned away abruptly, continuing to pack in the back of the gasogene.

"Where is the rendezvous?" Jean-Marc asked urgently.

Patrice ignored him and Nicolas shuffled, as if embarrassed, in the background.

"Where has she gone?" Jean-Marc was rapidly becoming desperate. Suddenly he leapt forward and pinned a shocked Patrice against the dusty gasogene, his elbow pressed into Patrice's throat. "Tell me where she is." He tightened his grip, snarling.

"If you want to risk your neck as well, go ahead, you're as foolish as she is," Patrice said. "The Cimetière de la Chartreuse."

"On Rue Georges Bonnac?"

"Uh-huh, we usually meet contacts deep inside, at a round temple with columns, the de Malescas family tomb."

Jean-Marc bared his teeth. "You fucking bastard, Patrice. If anything happens to Monique, I swear…"

Chapter Sixty-Three

Emboldened by gnawing concern for Monique's safety, and a dreadful feeling that he should have been by her side all the way, Jean-Marc managed to get right into Bordeaux without encountering any German roadblocks or checkpoints. Moving quickly but carefully, and with a confidence borne out of desperation to reach Monique, he alighted the bus one stop before Gare Saint-Jean and then walked the rest of the way: side streets, back roads, until he reached Rue François de Sourdis, which eventually intersected with Rue Georges Bonnac at the cemetery.

Pulling his beige coat collar up around his neck and lowering his head, he entered through the imposing stone archway and quickly disappeared down one of the side lanes that bisected Chartreuse's geometrical grid layout. Inside, the muted chirp of birdsong from the green canopies of interspersed avenues of trees shattered the eerie silence. A few people moved about, some alone and others in small huddles, bent in sombre meditation and carrying bunches of wild flowers.

Jean-Marc was dwarfed by the sheer scale of most of the monuments: towering crosses on plinths; columns with sculpted adornments; temples and mausoleums at every turn; macabre and frightening statues of winged skeletons carrying off the deceased; even the Grim Reaper was represented in bold, larger-than-life sandstone. The deeper he penetrated into the vast cemetery, the quieter it got, and the further away his access to the only escape route. Glancing over his shoulder furtively he measured the distance back to the arched entrance. If he should encounter Germans now he would have to run for it, and he didn't fancy his chances.

Beyond the sixth avenue of trees he caught sight of a domed monopteral temple surrounded by fluted Doric columns. It was both striking and imposing, and he was certain it was the one Patrice had described. For a brief moment he wondered whether he could trust Patrice; after all, his behaviour that morning had been elusive and vague, verging on gloating at Monique's predicament.

He looked around cautiously: just mourners moving dolefully between the countless rows of gravestones and memorials. He inched closer to the domed temple until he could read the etched words *de Malescas* above the encircling columns. Then he saw Monique in casual conversation with a man in a trench coat, both of them holding flowers, hers yellow and his of mixed colours. They appeared to be discussing the engravings on the temple.

His heart leapt with relief and he was unable to suppress a smile. Thank God, she was safe and exactly where Patrice said she would be. He began to move closer, not wishing to intrude on their privacy but hoping that perhaps she would catch sight of him and know that he was there, guarding and supporting her.

Suddenly, out of nowhere, four uniformed Wehrmacht soldiers rounded on the temple, followed quickly by an officer. Their rifles were held out menacingly and before Jean-Marc could utter even a muted gasp Monique and her contact were surrounded. Yellow, white and violet flowers fell to the ground and mingled on the dry gravel where they were trampled by the soldiers. The officer stepped forward and slapped Monique across the cheek with the black leather gloves he held in his hand. Her contact was struck by the butt of a rifle in his loin, and crumpled sideways, his hat falling off his head. Jean-Marc shrank back behind a ghoulish sculpture of a skeleton cradling a man in its arms, his heart threatening to leap out of his chest as his fingers closed around the Welrod in his coat pocket. But he knew that to draw the pistol now and begin firing would most certainly bring about not only his own death, but probably Monique's as well. They could never fight their way out of the heart of German-occupied Bordeaux.

Gripped by the inertia of nausea and helplessness, he looked down at the dry dirt. When he lifted his eyes again Monique and her contact were being frogmarched down the central lane of the cemetery towards the archway. There was nothing he could do expect pray, and he sank down against the warm stone and let his head drop forward onto his chest. He closed his eyes and clenched his fists, feeling utterly bereft.

Chapter Sixty-Four

The summer of 1945 in Bordeaux was celebrated. The Germans had been driven out, peace and sovereignty restored to France, and the warm, almost drought-like conditions had ripened the berries on the vines to levels of concentration that no one even dared to dream of during the dark years of occupation. The harvest was not abundant, but it was good.

Reunited with his beloved Château Cardinale, Jean-Marc rescued a reasonable harvest of ripe fruit from his surviving, if somewhat neglected and overgrown vineyards. It should have reinvigorated and filled him with enthusiasm and a hunger for the process of vinification that lay ahead: 1945 – the first noteworthy vintage following five long years of German occupation, and a mediocre to poor decade preceding that. But for the first time in his life the new harvest did nothing to excite Jean-Marc. In his humble château he pieced together the remnants of a once proud and warm family home, pillaged by the drunken antics of enemy soldiers. His grand piano, at least, even though wine-stained and abused, was still playable. His cellar was empty, stripped of every vintage stored in it, right back to those harvested and lovingly tended by his father, his grandfather, and his father's grandfather before that.

It was not just the cellar that was empty. Isabelle and their children, Odette and Claude, did not return in the months after victory was won. Many of those who had disappeared during the occupation of Bordeaux did not reclaim their homes, their vineyards, nor their former lives. They were simply gone. Even worse for Jean-Marc was that he could no longer bear to play, or hear, Debussy's *Clair de Lune*. He managed the rest of the *Suite Bergamasque*: the *Prelude*, the *Menuet* and sometimes even the *Passepied*, albeit with leaden, moribund fingers, but never *Clair de Lune*. It reminded him too painfully of Monique, whom he missed more than anything and anyone else.

Some days, as he emerged into the bright October sunshine, stained maroon from the waist down after an afternoon's *pigeage* in the fermentation tanks, he would experience anxiety at the prospect of seeing Isabelle walking across the vineyards towards their home. Would he still love her as he used to, as much as he had Monique? Could he tell her of his affair and share with her the affection he had developed for the feisty English girl during his sense of emptiness and loss in the war years? Would she ever be able to understand how deeply he still mourned Monique? Of course he could not expect this of his wife, and so it was with relief that he would stare at the empty rows of vines stretching away from his house, draped in glowing autumnal yellows and browns. No Isabelle meant no guilt, no tears, just regret and a yearning for revenge.

Even Alphonse managed to muster enthusiasm for his own harvest at Château Millandes, in the face of the devastating loss of Olivier before the war had ended. Olivier had finally succumbed to his wounds just three agonising months before the Germans abandoned Bordeaux. Jean-Marc felt that it was wrong to attempt winemaking with anything less than unequivocal passion and commitment. Despite the promise of the vintage and the incredible quality of the fruit, especially considering the years of neglect that had preceded it, Jean-Marc's heart was simply not in the winemaking, something that had always been his life, his God, his raison d'être. It was never something to do half-heartedly, constantly casting an eye over his shoulder into his past.

One warm Sunday afternoon he walked over to Château Millandes and gave full control of all the must in his fermentation tanks to a bemused Alphonse.

"And where are you going?" Alphonse said.

"Make it something really special, Alphonse, my fruit is exceptional, possibly the best I've seen – Brix of nearly twenty-five."

"But why... where?" Alphonse stammered.

"Goodbye, my friend. I'm not sure if I will see you again."

"I don't understand, Jean-Marc."

"Do it for me – no, do it for Monique," Jean-Marc said, patting Alphonse on the shoulder before walking off in the direction of Saint-Émilion. He did not even lock the front door to Château Cardinale.

The bus to Bordeaux rumbled on for two hours along pitted, dusty roads amidst a seizure of vineyard activity as far as the eye could see, in every direction. The journey terminated at Gare Saint-Jean, which evoked far too many memories for Jean-Marc. Walking away swiftly, he found Rue Delphin Loche and was both surprised and pleased to see the Cinema Fauvette open for business once again. Standing on the pavement amidst the bustle of effusive shoppers and occasional waves of diesel traffic fumes, he saw the current film advertised in black letters above the curved entrance: *La Grande Illusion* starring Jean Gabin. He smiled. Behind the glass window of the small ticket booth sat an angry, square block of a woman knitting something in green, her brown hair tied up in a bun resembling another ball of wool.

Jean-Marc had no sooner stopped in front of the glass than she tapped on the counter beside a folded *SOLD OUT* card without even looking up.

"No tickets today," she announced gruffly.

"I am looking for Juliette," Jean-Marc said.

The woman looked up. "Madame Felgines?"

"Juliette Felgines."

The square woman looked him up and down, raised her eyebrows and finally gesticulated with her head. "In the office off the foyer."

Juliette had cut her hair even shorter than he could remember and appeared lean, strangely muscular, and tanned beneath a charcoal trouser suit. They embraced like old friends, comrades in war. She left her hands on his shoulders as she withdrew to arms' length, staring into his eyes intently.

"I heard about Monique. I am so sorry," she said.

Jean-Marc felt the pain in his soul receive a fresh stab and a rubbing of salt, and looked away.

"What can I do for you?" Juliette said, turning into her office and pulling him with her. "Coffee? Real coffee?" She looked at him teasingly.

"I have come for a job. I thought, with your newly opened, that you might... you know..."

She sat on the edge of her desk, dangling one pinstripe-trousered leg that swung at the knee. "What about your vineyards?"

Jean-Marc shrugged and hung his head. "I need time away."

"Do you know cinema work?"

"No."

"Can you work a projector?"

"No."

Juliette smiled, her eyes wandering over Jean-Marc's figure. "Well, I can show you." She walked to the door and called into the foyer. "Gaston, get me two coffees please."

Jean-Marc and Juliette became lovers quickly, an urgent and deep need fermenting in both of them, selfishly demanding

351

satisfaction. He got the distinct impression that she too was lonely, perhaps in mourning, though neither ever spoke of their losses and emptiness, their ghosts from the war. It was not about love, and they both knew this. Their liaison served merely to fill a void, an aching abyss that had opened in their lives, functioning like a salve applied to a festering wound that refused to heal.

Juliette taught him to use the two carbon arc 35mm Cinemeccanica projectors, lacing them, reading the first and second cues and managing the changeover smoothly, while he welcomed the quiet, uninterrupted hours when he could sit in the darkened projection booth and smoke. Soothed by the repetitive staccato ticking of the projectors, his mind tried to make sense of the past six years while his hands were kept busy splicing films together. In return for all this Jean-Marc provided company for the single cinema owner, helped her run the establishment, and tended to her insatiable needs.

The reappearance of American films, no longer banned by the Germans, and the freedom of choice created a surge of interest among cinema audiences and Juliette decided to diversify into *cinema plein air* events over the summer months.

"You mean open-air cinema?" Jean-Marc said.

"Of course. You never been to one?" Juliette said, playing with his chest hairs as they lay in bed.

"No."

"Not even as a child?"

He shook his head.

"People come and picnic, drink wine and smoke, laugh, families gather, old friends meet up..." She seemed lost for a moment. "The film is shown in the market square against a giant screen on one side. It's wonderful," Juliette said.

"Where do you hold them?"

"Around Saint-Émilion and Bergerac, all those villages too small to have a cinema of their own."

352

Jean-Marc volunteered for it in a heartbeat. In a moment of unfettered clarity, achieved while sitting quietly in the projection booth during a matinee one afternoon, he had formulated the perfect plan. Being the projectionist for Cinema Fauvette *plein air* in small villages under the mauve darkness of clear summer skies would be perfect.

Finally, Monique, he thought to himself, *you will get your justice, and I will get my revenge.*

Chapter Sixty-Five

The first act of revenge was the easiest, partly because Nicolas – with his progressively deteriorating limp – was a defenceless target, and partly because Jean-Marc's hunger for justice had been brewing for too long. Jean-Marc was touring the villages around Bergerac with *Quasimodo* starring Charles Laughton, drawing huge audiences on Friday and Saturday nights, showing the horror film to delighted audiences that filled market squares wherever he went. He was welcomed and fêted like a prodigal son, plied with wine and cheese and local delights, never wanting for anything. He was the man who brought a little joy to their post-war existences: the entertainer.

"It is so good to see you again, Jean-Marc," they would say. "When are you back again? What film is next?"

Juliette loved his easy approach with the village folk. He was one of them, a simple winemaker who understood the hardships and needs of working people who lived humbly off the land.

It was in Issigeac that he saw Nicolas, his limp somewhat of a giveaway, as was his proud Gallic profile. Jean-Marc had been patient, completing at least one tour of each village as a scouting expedition: whom did he encounter, where was the portable projector situated, what was the layout of the market square? He took care to formulate the perfect plan, to ensure his alibi.

He used an innocent young boy – who buzzed around hoping to collect a scrap of film with images of his screen heroes captured for eternity in celluloid frames – to deliver a simple anonymous note.

"Georges, my boy, that man over there, with the limp, you see him?" Jean-Marc said, holding the boy by the shoulders in the direction he wanted.

Georges looked and nodded.

"His aunt wants to get a message to him – here it is. Please hand it over and then run off. Come back when the show is finished and I will keep a piece of film for you."

During reel three of *Quasimodo*, the longest at almost a full twenty minutes, he met Nicolas behind the water pump and troughs used for the Saturday fish market. They still smelled strongly of unwashed piscatorial residues. Nicolas was staring at the scrap of paper with a frown on his face, which lit up when he saw Jean-Marc.

"Jean-Marc! Is this you?" Nicolas said, holding forth the paper jubilantly.

"Come with me, quickly," Jean-Marc hissed in a hushed tone.

Impatient with Nicolas' limp, he virtually pulled him around several corners until they were in an alleyway.

"What are you doing here?" Nicolas said. "This note is from Monique, where is she?"

Checking that they were alone and with the booming sounds of the film still audible from the marketplace, Jean-Marc pulled out the Welrod pistol from his jacket.

"What in God's name are you doing?" Nicolas said, his eyes widening as he tried to take an unsteady step back.

"This is for Monique, you piece of shit!"

Jean-Marc pushed the silenced barrel against Nicolas' chest and squeezed the trigger, feeling the helpless jerk of his quarry's body as first one and then a second bullet tore through his heart. The pistol efficiently muted the gunshots, the only evidence of which was a smell of cordite, and Nicolas' body slumped against a stone wall, twitching convulsively.

Jean-Marc walked away quickly and returned to the covered market building in which Juliette's GBN portable projector rested on a waist-height wooden table. He checked the rapidly spinning reel of film: seven minutes to changeover. Perfect. His alibi was secured.

He found Gregoire at a *cinema plein air* screening of the ever-popular *La Fille du Puisatier* in Villefranche. Jean-Marc had no regrets over Gregoire, the snake, the traitor, though killing him had been marginally more difficult than Nicolas. Jean-Marc was unable to look Gregoire in the eye, not until his surprised face was drained of all colour and life, and in the aftermath he was haunted by a twinge of remorse for his old friend Alphonse, for he and Marthe had now lost both their sons.

Several months later he encountered Louis in Monpazier and then Anton in Monbazillac. Their deaths were reported in the local newspapers but the police had no clues, no suspects, nothing to link the victims. Not until somebody – perhaps it was Patrice – told the police that they were all Maquis during the occupation, and then the police were galvanised into action. But still, little progress was made. Jean-Marc knew there was just one more, the man he was struggling to locate having never seen him at any *cinema plein air* events – Patrice – and then he could disappear, for good.

If anyone deserved to suffer, to be denied the mercy of a pistol bullet to the heart, it was Patrice. How could a man who himself had loved Monique, have sent her to her death so callously? No such man deserved to live and enjoy the fruits of a free France that she had fought and given her life to secure.

All that Jean-Marc could remember was that Patrice lived around Bergerac, close to Monbazillac. He dared not enquire about his whereabouts for fear of leaving a trail that could be traced back to him. He did not even fully trust Juliette, or make use of her extensive network of wartime contacts. Alphonse and Brutinel might well have known, but Jean-Marc was neither callous nor foolish enough to approach either of them. He was operating alone, for Monique, and as the end approached he was no longer certain what it was that he hoped to gain from the final kill.

He began to fear that revenge would not be the emotional panacea he hoped it might be. He certainly knew that it would not bring Monique back. Nevertheless, he was well past the point of no return with four deaths already accomplished. Even if it cost him his freedom, or his life, Patrice had to die.

Finally, it was *Casablanca* that flushed Patrice out and brought him to Monpazier on a warm Saturday in 1948.

Chapter Sixty-Six

Having arrived in good time for the screening of *Casablanca* – certain to draw a large crowd – Jean-Marc set up the projector under the covered market stall in the centre of Monpazier's 13th century Place des Cornières, before occupying a strategically well-placed table outside the *Tabac*. Settling down with a pack of Gauloises and a bottle of Bergerac rouge, he leaned back in the warm sunshine as people milled about casually and breathed in the smells of the small, vibrant market town: cheeses, flowers, *saucisson* and powerfully aromatic pipe tobacco.

Trying to appear relaxed with his beret pulled down, he studied the ebb and flow of people passing the *Tabac* as his fingers twiddled his large moustache. He had been to Monpazier with the *cinema plein air* several times before, and had studied the layout of the beautifully preserved market square contained on all four sides by medieval, classical and bourgeois houses built above a surrounding Gothic-arched arcade. The screen would be erected by the *Mairie* workers later, somewhere between the church and Maison du Chapitre.

Jean-Marc knew that Patrice lived near Monbazillac and was certain that on occasion he would surely frequent Monpazier for its famed market. What if Patrice was married with children by his side? Would that matter, would it change his resolve? Would he still recognise Patrice; could he have changed in appearance? Of course he would recognise him: he could never forget that face, those cold eyes, that taunting grin, not for as long as he lived.

Jean-Marc was briefly distracted by a slender woman with very short black hair and a camel trench coat sitting down at the table beside him. Their eyes met briefly and she smiled in a businesslike manner before looking down at the *carte*.

"Excuse me, *monsieur*, I am not from the area – could you recommend a local wine for me?" she said in an assured voice.

Jean-Marc felt a touch of annoyance to be disturbed as he tried to concentrate on the faces of each and every person who walked by. "Yes, of course. Do you prefer red, white, rosé, sweet, fortified, full-bodied, light?"

The woman's eyes widened and the corners of her mouth lifted slightly. "Are you a vigneron, by any chance?"

Jean-Marc exhaled smoke. "Well, yes, I used to be. Sorry."

She chuckled. "Not at all. It is such a beautiful day, I would like something sweet, like a Sauternes, or Banyuls or even a sherry."

Jean-Marc nodded. "Try the Château Monbazillac, it is grown just a few kilometres away and it is magnificent."

"Thank you."

"Ask for the '29, or the '24 if they have it."

She ordered from the waiter and lit a cigarette, running her fingers through her short hair. In a strange way she reminded Jean-Marc of Juliette.

"Are you alone?" she said to him.

Reluctantly, Jean-Marc nodded.

"Do you mind if I join you?"

"No, please," Jean-Marc felt obliged to say.

She sat down opposite him, partially obscuring his carefully chosen view of people entering the market square. "If you are no longer a vigneron, what do you do?"

359

Jean-Marc stubbed his cigarette into the clay ashtray. "I am with the *cinema plein air*." He gesticulated towards the market stalls with his thumb.

She smiled broadly and nodded as the waiter placed a frosted glass of deeply golden-hued wine in front of her. "Sounds very interesting." Her eyes seemed to be examining him. "You must get around?"

"In the summer I travel to all the villages around here, showing the latest films."

The woman nodded and sipped her wine, beads of moisture running down the glass. "Very good recommendation."

Jean-Marc was not feeling conversational, and simply smiled. He wished he could extricate himself from her company, and did not wish to initiate any conversation that might deepen his involvement with her.

"Why did you stop being a vigneron?" she asked him, her eyes narrowing. "What a wonderful life that must be."

Jean-Marc sighed. "The war, the occupation, it changed everything for me." He shrugged and gulped at his wine, which in his assessment was insubstantial; fruity but unremarkable. "I needed a change, I needed to get away."

"Did you lose someone in the war?"

"Didn't we all?"

"Where did you live, if you don't mind my asking?"

"Saint-Émilion, Château Cardinale."

Her eyebrows lifted slightly.

"Have you heard of it?" Jean-Marc asked with a slight flutter of self-satisfaction.

"No, can't say I have, *monsieur*, but I was thinking that you must have left quite a lot behind."

He was unnerved by the steadiness of her gaze through the cloud of cigarette smoke that she generated. She was distant, measured, yet most certainly focused and intense.

"Do you like what you do now?"

360

"It serves a purpose." He hesitated. "I like getting around, you know, a different village every week."

Jean-Marc suddenly stiffened and felt the blood drain from his face. Walking towards him was Patrice, beret on his head, cigarette hanging from the corner of his mouth, leather sack with a protruding baguette slung over his shoulder. Jean-Marc lowered his face and buried it in his wine glass, turning away. His heart was pounding. At last he had caught up with Patrice. Tonight, he would confront him. Finally, he would be able to rest and so, he hoped, could Monique's soul. Patrice ambled past, seemingly oblivious to Jean-Marc's presence.

"Are you alright?" the woman asked perceptively.

"Yes, yes, of course. I must go, I have to set up the projector for this evening."

"Ah, well perhaps I will see you later."

"Perhaps. Are you staying for the film?"

"What is it?"

"*Casablanca.*"

"I saw it a few years ago," she said.

"It hasn't been long released down here," Jean-Marc said, a little confused. He stood up and downed his wine.

"I live in Paris," she added, extending her hand. "It was nice to meet you, Monsieur…?"

Jean-Marc shook her hand. "Valadie. My pleasure, Mademoiselle…?"

"*Madame* Balletty. *À bientôt.*"

Chapter Sixty-Seven

Three hours later Jean-Marc found himself in a fatally compromised situation. He had kept his eyes on Patrice, who was sitting with a group of friends, perhaps his wife and family, laughing, smoking and drinking wine. Soon after starting the second reel of the main feature, Jean-Marc saw his chance. Patrice stood up and walked off to buy a baguette from a *boulanger*'s wagon. His journey took him away from the crowd, along the darkened and abandoned areas beneath the vaulted arcade where Jean-Marc planned to confront him. Despite his vigilance and planning, however, Jean-Marc did not know that he had been followed as he pressed Patrice against the cool stone in the dimly lit shadows. He could smell the crisp minerality of the ancient limestone despite Patrice's sweaty gasps, heavy with garlic and alcohol.

"What the hell are you doing?" Patrice cried out. A baguette fell out of his hand and rolled on the paving, leaving a spray of crumbs.

Jean-Marc thrust the pistol harder into his victim's back, feeling the silencer slide off a rib as Patrice flinched and inhaled sharply. "I have been looking for you for years, you traitor," Jean-Marc hissed into the unwashed locks of Patrice's black hair, reeking of Gauloises smoke.

"What do you want?" Patrice said.

Jean-Marc tensed his body and leaned into his victim. "Revenge, you bastard. This is for Monique."

At the sound of a click from the pistol Patrice's eyes widened suddenly and his mouth fell open slackly. "I didn't do anything to Monique," he protested, raising his hands helplessly against the limestone wall, dirty fingernails splayed.

"The hell you didn't, you killed her – all of you – killed her!" Jean-Marc felt himself grimace, baring his teeth like a predator preparing for the kill.

"I didn't kill her, I swear!"

"But you got the Germans to do it for you, didn't you?" hissed Jean-Marc.

"No!"

"Goodbye, Patrice," Jean-Marc whispered icily.

"No, wait!"

As Jean-Marc's finger tightened against the scored surface of the trigger he felt something hard press into his spine.

"You are under arrest, Monsieur Valadie. Give me your weapon," said an assured, husky female voice.

Jean-Marc froze and turned his head, pressing his pistol ever more firmly into Patrice to discourage any attempts at escape. "You?" Jean-Marc gasped, surprise rippling through his body as he recognised the intruder. "Who the hell *are* you?"

Patrice breathed in rapid, shallow gasps, sweat beading on his skin, his eyes wide and frightened.

"I am Inspecteur Balletty from the Sûreté in Paris. I have been on your trail for months, *monsieur*, and I am placing you under arrest, Jean-Marc Valadie, on suspicion of the murders of Anton Caumont, Nicolas Renard, Gregoire Sabron and Louis Lafargue, not to mention the attempted murder of this gentleman, whose name I do not know."

Patrice emitted an anguished wheeze. "It was *you* who killed all of them?" he said. "In God's name, why, Jean-Marc?"

Jean-Marc laughed derisively. "Revenge, my old comrade, for what you all did to Monique."

"No! You have got it wrong," Patrice said, his voice rising in desperation.

"Monique was executed, that's what I know, and it was you and all of them, my so-called friends, who were responsible. You betrayed her to *les Boches*."

"Jean-Marc, listen…"

"How could you?" Jean-Marc hissed, grinding his teeth.

"Monsieur Valadie!" Balletty said firmly. "This is your last warning."

"Enough!" Jean-Marc shouted. "It ends, now."

He felt Balletty's barrel press into his back even harder. "*Monsieur*, give me your gun and I will not have to shoot you," she said in a calm but firm voice, leaving Jean-Marc in no doubt about her conviction. "The *epuration legale* is a matter for the police, not vigilantes."

Behind them the screen blazed brilliant white as the film reel ended abruptly. People stood up and began to whistle, turning their heads left and right as they called out.

"The reel has ended, I have to change it," Jean-Marc urged, craning his neck to meet Balletty's eyes.

"Give me your gun, *monsieur*."

Jean-Marc breathed hard and swallowed ineffectually, his mouth dry and sticky. "This is absurd," he protested, briefly lifting his left arm off Patrice in a frustrated gesture.

"Not from where I am standing, *monsieur*. Now, very slowly, give me your—"

A loud explosion burst in Jean-Marc's ears, echoing around the Place des Cornières. Jean-Marc's finger was still pressed tightly against the rough surface of the trigger, his ears ringing and his nose stinging from the acrid smell of cordite. He stumbled, confused. It was he who had pulled the trigger, so why did he feel as if a horse had kicked him in the back?

Patrice groaned under the pressure of Jean-Marc's Welrod pistol and sagged against the wall, the tension in his body suddenly gone. A deft movement from behind Jean-Marc's head twisted the Welrod out of his failing grasp, after which he was pushed down onto his knees, one arm pulled sharply behind his back, producing a stab of heat in his shoulder. Angry calls from the market square reverberated around the darkened Place des Cornières as the frustrated audience demanded the next reel of *Casablanca*.

"Where is the film? Where is the projectionist?"

"You idiot!" Patrice moaned as he crumpled down the limestone wall, his fingernails trying in vain to keep himself upright.

"*Attention*! This is an emergency! We need a *docteur*," Balletty called out, maintaining her firm grip on Jean-Marc's shoulder. "*Rapidement!*"

"You shot me!" Jean-Marc said in muted surprise, lifting a bloodstained hand to his face.

"I warned you, *monsieur*," Balletty said without pity. "Now you had better hope this man does not die."

"And what of me?" Jean-Marc said.

"I aimed carefully."

"He deserves to die," Jean-Marc said, spitting in Patrice's direction. "He betrayed Monique," he added, suddenly overcome with a pang of emotion. "What did she ever do to you?"

"It was not me," Patrice said, his breath coming in short gasps. "But if I had betrayed anyone it would have been you. It should have been you that they shot."

Jean-Marc tried to clear his head as pain began to localise around his shoulder, numbing his arm and paralysing his grasp in waves of throbbing discomfort. Bustling activity in the market square beyond the stone arches heralded the arrival of a doctor.

365

"Over here!" Balletty shouted.

"What about the rest of the film?" a gruff voice complained from the gathered crowd.

"Yes, do we get our money back?" called another.

The doctor burst through the tangle of inquisitive bodies, glowing cigarette hanging from his moustached mouth, and leaned over Jean-Marc.

"Not this one, he's OK," Balletty said sharply.

"They were all innocent," Patrice said softly, the energy slipping from his protestations, "and you killed them in cold blood."

"You're lying," Jean-Marc said, and then winced as he felt the pain intensifying in his shoulder. "Monique was the one killed in cold blood."

The doctor kneeled beside Patrice, who was now prostrate on the cool flagstones, one knee bent at thirty degrees, arms helpless by his sides. Balletty pulled Jean-Marc onto his feet and he felt cold steel clamp around each wrist, drawing breath sharply as she twisted his wounded arm.

"Tell me the truth now before you go to Hell!" Jean-Marc hissed.

"It was Alphonse," Patrice whispered, his heavy eyes finding Jean-Marc's before drifting away.

Cold horror rippled through Jean-Marc's body. This could not be true. Patrice was merely desperate and lying. "Never! You're a liar and a traitor," Jean-Marc shouted. "Alphonse would never..."

"He was protective of you to the end, the stupid bastard, and Monique... well, she was..."

"She was what? She did nothing to Alphonse," Jean-Marc spat.

"She was English, wasn't she?" Patrice barely managed to say between gasps, his eyes closed now.

Jean-Marc gasped too, but said nothing.

366

"She was, wasn't she?" Patrice said feebly.

"You told Alphonse?"

"Something had to be done to save Saint-Émilion," Patrice said barely audibly. "I'm only sorry it couldn't have been you."

"No! No, it cannot be!" Jean-Marc argued with no one in particular. "It's not true! Alphonse would never... it was you!"

"Come, *monsieur*, you are under arrest. Leave the *docteur* to save you from a fifth count of murder," Balletty said, pulling him away roughly.

"Let me go, I want to kill him, the bastard. Monique... he sent my Monique... he..." Jean-Marc began to sob between great gulps of air, the awful howl of a mortally tormented and wounded beast. The pain in his shoulder was now superseded by an enormous slice through his heart.

He turned around and saw the doctor pumping Patrice's chest, blood frothing out of his victim's mouth, and he wished that he too were lying on the flagstones, breathing his last. Could it be true that Alphonse had betrayed Monique to the Germans, to his friend Bömers, in exchange for the Monolithic Cathedral? Anguish twisted within Jean-Marc, hurling his conscience from one extreme to another; pangs of guilt alternated with the satisfied smack of requital. It looked as though he had got his man, but who was right? Who was wrong?

They had won the war of occupation ultimately, and yet it felt as though they had all lost. He had certainly lost everything. But so had Alphonse, and so too had their gang of Maquis.

"I heard you were a brave man, *monsieur*. Fought with the Maquis against the German occupation, saved a great deal of our precious French wine from their clutches." Balletty was making small talk as they walked slowly away from the dissipating crowd. She looked at him, her eyes searching for

367

something. "You were a hero, what happened? Why did you do all this?"

Jean-Marc's eyes felt puffy and his shoulder was really hurting. It was all over now and he realised that he would never see Château Cardinale again, never walk its vineyards or prune its vines, nor taste its wine. He thought of everyone and everything he had lost, physically, morally and spiritually, despite only the best of intentions.

"You wouldn't understand," Jean-Marc said.

"Try me."

Jean-Marc sighed. He was tired. "I used to play the piano, you know. I particularly loved playing Debussy's *Suite Bergamasque*, my favourite piece... *our* favourite piece." He paused, fighting back tears. "But now it is too painful, evokes too many memories." He stumbled on in a daze, his feet somehow striking the stones evenly and in line, despite the apparent disconnection of his brain. "I cannot even make wine anymore. The light has gone out."

"Monique?" Balletty ventured.

Jean-Marc nodded. "Her name was Monica."

Epilogue

Heinz Bömers, formerly head of Reidemeister & Ulrichs, Germany's largest wine importing firm, was sent to Bordeaux as its "weinführer" during the German occupation of France. Known in Germany as Beauftragters für den Weinimport Frankreich, he was one of three: Otto Klaebisch was sent to Champagne and Adolph Segnitz to Burgundy.

The Bömers family used to own Chateau Smith-Haut-Lafite but it was confiscated by the French after World War I. Bömers' father was a civil servant in Saxony and once snubbed Göring, a man he despised. Göring never forgot this insult and when war broke out he used his power to force Bömers to join the Nazi Party or lose the family wine importing business.

Hauptsturmführer (Captain) Ernst Kühnemann was the Commander of the port of Bordeaux for the duration of the war and Generalleutnant (General) Moritz von Faber du Faur was the senior officer in Bordeaux.

The war years in Bordeaux were a time of labour shortages, pesticide shortages, raw material shortages, requisitioned chateaux and unkind weather. They immediately followed the worst wine decade of the century in Bordeaux - the 1930s - and the Great Depression, the Russian Revolution and Prohibition in the United States. Many Bordelais were on their knees.

Not everyone in Bordeaux struggled during the occupation, though, and some vignerons managed to sell many of their wines, both good and bad, through Bömers to the Germans. Bömers had his preferred clients and tried very hard to mediate between Göring's outrageous demands and the vignerons he had come to know over the years.

Bömers, Kühnemann and von Faber are depicted as characters bearing their real names, but only as I imagine they might have been. For the rest, though set against historically researched events in Bordeaux during the war years, the actions of the maquis, the consequences of German occupation and the struggle of the wine makers, this novel is entirely fictional, a work of the author's imagination. Some liberties have been taken with the chronology of events in Bordeaux to suit the narrative.

Bordeaux Vintage Reports 1924-1945

1924

The year began with a wet spring and the summer was hardly any better. However, due to a perfect September with abundant sunshine, fruit quality was good with very little damage. Beautiful wines were produced, especially in Pomerol and Margaux.

1925

Described as a year without sunshine. Wines produced were weak and aqueous and always destined for early consumption. Following the glorious 1924, it was a year that the wine trade cast aside entirely.

1926

After a cold winter and spring a long, hot summer produced mature, concentrated berries full of tannins. Though a small crop the wines were strong, rich and endowed with ageing potential, particularly on the right bank.

1927

Following such a successful vintage in 1926, the weather turned on the Bordelais once again. Storms and rain throughout the summer and the autumn made harvesting conditions extremely challenging. The resultant wines were predictably terrible. Only the white wines of Sauternes and Barsac fared better.

1928

A very hot, dry summer resulted in tough skins on the berries, especially the cabernet sauvignon, compounding an already very tannic vintage. Harvesting commenced on 18th September. Merlot-rich right bank wines, being lower in tannins, were softer and more approachable. Most wines required decades of ageing to soften the tannins.

1929

Harvesting began on 26th September under warm, sunny conditions. Despite a very hot, dry growing season – the hottest on record since 1893 and the driest of the century to date – rains fell in September and salvaged the vines. Resultant wines were rich, ripe and luscious, and have aged beyond expectations.

1930

The weather was unfavourable at every crucial stage of growth, including the bloom and maturation. The quality of the resultant wine was poor and the vintage described as a catastrophe, just one year after The Wall Street Crash.

1931

The sun did not shine at all through the growing season and though marginally better than the year before, the resultant wines were very poor indeed.

1932

Very bad weather overshadowed the growing season. Even though the harvest was very late it was not enough to save the wines which were a catastrophe again, three years running.

1933

Violent winds at the time of the bloom affected the resultant crop producing a small harvest, marginally better than the preceding three years. Wines were light and pleasant.

1934

Harvesting started on 14th September under perfect, warm conditions. It was a very hot, dry year and following a two month drought much needed rain finally fell in September. A huge crop, the biggest harvest yet seen in Bordeaux, produced the wines of the decade: rich and attractive.

1935

A warm and dry summer yielded to a very wet September and the resultant wines were average and did not gather favour. As wine cellars were still bursting with the sumptuous and abundant wines of the previous year, the 1935 vintage was quickly forgotten.

1936

This was almost the complete reverse of the year before, with a wet summer and a poor September. Thin, weak wines of moderate quality resulted. Another forgettable vintage from this disastrous decade.

1937

Although the summer was mainly dry, it was cool. September was good but nevertheless the wines ended up being both tannic and acidic. Despite deep colour extraction they were undrinkable for decades with a hard edge described by some as 'green'. Most were only finally bottled at the end of the war.

1938

A stormy, chilly and damp summer delayed harvesting until late autumn. Mediocre wines of low ageing potential resulted, almost all of which were bottled

1939

The summer was late and interrupted constantly by stormy, wet and cold weather. The harvest was very late indeed and the wines were inferior, slightly perfumed but unremarkable

1940

Following a run of poor vintages in the 1930s, this was a classic year after a long and hot summer. Harvesting took place under the challenging conditions of occupation and labour shortages, and the consequent inattentiveness and inconsistency resulted in very variable quality. Some wines are described as well-rounded and have aged well.

1941

A poor year for Bordeaux despite a good summer. Conditions under the occupation significantly impaired wine making: lack of manpower to tend the vines and harvest, plus inadequate supplies of pesticides to control mildew. The wines reflected the conditions.

1942

A cold winter yielded to a beautiful summer that ended in a lacklustre September. Yields and production were down to half of pre-war levels, suffering under the difficulties of occupation and wartime restrictions. The resultant wines were best described as average.

1943

A good bloom yielded to a warm and dry summer producing the best wines of the wartime years: rich, fruity and even excellent in some cases. But disease in the vineyards and ongoing shortages of supplies and labour reduced yields to such an extent that wines were in very short supply indeed.

1944

A wet and rainy summer impaired growth and ripening of the grapes, and it rained again towards the end of September. Though the harvest was substantial it was uneven due to the inclement weather. Amidst all the other challenges the resultant wines were light and thin, lacking ageing potential.

1945

A very cold winter was followed by an early spring, though frosts in May ensured that yields were reduced. The growing season was warm and mostly sunny and dry, with these conditions persisting through to October bringing record temperatures every month. Harvesting commenced very early on 13th September under drought-like conditions. Berries were intensely ripe and concentrated with thick skins. The resultant tannins helped the wines to age beautifully for decades.

Bordeaux Wine Tasting Notes 1924-1945

Chateau Pavie 1924
Exhibiting a pale red tea colour, a bouquet of earth and tobacco, cherry and floral strawberry notes. The fruit is light, silky and earthy, with sweet and sour cherries, minerality and spice.

Chateau Brane-Cantenac 1926
A complex nose of smoke: cigar box and tobacco; truffles and earth; cherry pipe tobacco. On the palate a medium bodied sweetness, fresh red fruits and soft, elegantly refined textures.

Chateau Margaux 1928
The wine has a red-brown hue. Stewed fruit, leather, soy and earthy scents dominate the perfume. The palate reveals a deeply concentrated, very powerful wine with layers of sweet, ripe cherry and strawberry.

Chateau Latour Grand Vin 1929
A bouquet of dried orange peel, spices, minerals, cedar and walnuts. In the mouth gorgeous rich, ripe, sweet fruit is perfectly balanced as deep, multiple layers of syrupy, ripe fruit glide over the palate.

Chateau Lafite Rothschild 1934

A heady and pleasurable nose of cigars, truffles, spice and tar mingles with earthy black fruit and hints of orange. In the mouth the wine expresses the patina of age with soft, black fruit and spice. A long elegant and silky finish lingers with notes of plums and dark berries.

Chateau Pontet-Canet 1945

The bouquet is a medley of coconut, smoke, caramel, coffee and tobacco, intensely concentrated as though still young. On the palate a gentle swathe of fresh strawberry, cassis and ripe black cherry eventually finishes with a lingering sweet, syrupy texture.

Recommended Further Reading

Life in occupied France, 1940-1944: an overview of attitudes, experiences and choices. Professor Rod Kedward, University of Sussex. Occupied France; Wiley-Blackwell, 1991

Wine and War; by Don and Petie Kladstrup. Hodder & Stoughton, 2001.

Acknowledgements

I am extremely grateful to Sebastian Payne MW for reading an early draft and commenting on the historical aspects of wine making in Bordeaux during the period 1930-1945. His contribution added considerably to the historical accuracy of the text.

My thanks also to Gordon Pfetscher, who patiently took me through the German dialogue, and to my editor who has such a sharp eye and a faultless instinct.

I would also like to thank Dianne for her enthusiasm on this project from an early stage. Your support and patience, as always, is invaluable.

About the Author

In addition to being an anaesthetist, Quentin Smith has a long-standing passion for writing. He has published articles and papers in The British Journal of Anaesthesia, Anaesthesia News, Anaesthesia and Critical Care, Hospital Medicine, Today's Anaesthetist, Spark, and Insight.

Following a five year term as editor of Today's Anaesthetist, he undertook creative writing study through The Writing School, New College Durham, The London School of Journalism including a coveted place on the Curtis Brown Creative fiction course in 2014.

He is the author of three previously published novels: The Secret Anatomy of Candles (Matador 2012); Huber's Tattoo (Matador 2014); 16mm of Innocence (Matador 2015). Huber's Tattoo was runner-up in The People's Book Prize 2015 and 16mm of Innocence was a finalist in The People's Book Prize 2016. His recent novels reveal his interest in European history and the Second World War in particular.

BY THE SAME AUTHOR...

FROM THE RUNNER UP OF
THE PEOPLE'S BOOK PRIZE 2015

QUENTIN
SMITH

16mm
OF INNOCENCE

RARELY, IF EVER, DO CHILDREN
FORGIVE THEIR PARENTS

FROM THE AUTHOR OF
'THE SECRET ANATOMY OF CANDLES'

HUBER'S
TATTOO

QUENTIN
SMITH

WAS THE NAZI AMBITION TO BREED
A SUPER RACE ACTUALLY REALISED...?

QUENTIN SMITH

The
SECRET
ANATOMY
of
CANDLES

Justice is temporary…

Lightning Source UK Ltd.
Milton Keynes UK
UKHW021217131019
351525UK00017B/546/P